HIGH PRAISE FOR AMANDA HARTE!

RAINBOWS AT MIDNIGHT

"*Rainbows at Midnight* is a page-turner; a well-written love story with impeccably crafted descriptions of life in Alaska. . . . A fine tale that will never disappoint."

—*Romance Reviews Today*

"Amanda Harte knows how to reel her readers in with her cast of compelling characters. . . . This is a great read. . . . Don't miss it!""

—*The Belles and Beaux of Romance*

MIDNIGHT SUN

"*Midnight Sun* is a beautifully written story. . . . Amanda Harte breathes such life into her settings and characters!"

—*Romance Communications*

"A terrific read by Ms. Harte. . . . This is a fresh setting, a can't-put-down novel."

—*The Belles & Beaux of Romance*

"If you're looking for a well-done historical with intricate conflicts, *Midnight Sun* is a must read."

—*CompuServe Romance Reviews*

NORTH STAR

"*North Star* is thought provoking, poignant, and a very satisfying read. Don't miss it."

—*The Belles & Beaux of Romance*

"*North Star* is a well-written and intelligent read, with depth and richness that is extremely satisfying."

—*Romance Communications*

A MAGIC MOMENT

When Sam spoke again, his voice was harsh with barely suppressed pain. "The only time I saw my father cry was the day they buried my mother. I remember being as frightened by that as by the fact that my mother was in a coffin. That night when I couldn't sleep, Papa held me in his arms. He tried to comfort me by saying that Mama would always be near us, even though we couldn't see her. And then he said he hoped one day I would find a woman I could love as much as he had loved my mother. I remember him sobbing when he said that he had lost his midnight rainbow." Sam stroked his mustache, and Laura wondered if it was to hide his emotion. One thing was certain: He was no longer meeting her gaze.

"I always remembered that," Sam continued, "and I kept looking for a rainbow at midnight. I thought that if I could find one, my mother would come back, and we'd be happy again."

"Are there really rainbows at midnight?" To Laura's dismay, her own voice quavered. Sam's story and his obvious pain had touched chords deep within her.

"I haven't seen one, but I'm told they exist." Sam's voice was once again as calm as it had been when they had discussed the students' woodworking. "It's logical that you'd see one in June. The midnight sun can create midnight rainbows."

Laura, the woman who never cried, found herself fighting tears. "It's a beautiful image." For her, rainbows were the symbol of hope, the beauty that came after rain. And a rainbow at midnight—how better to describe the magic of Alaska?

Other *Leisure* books by Amanda Harte:
NORTH STAR
MIDNIGHT SUN

AMANDA HARTE

Rainbows at MIDNIGHT

LEISURE BOOKS  NEW YORK CITY

For my sister, Judith Bailey Stumpf,
who shares my love of Alaska.

A LEISURE BOOK®

January 2002

Published by

Dorchester Publishing Co., Inc.
276 Fifth Avenue
New York, NY 10001

ISBN 0-8439-4953-8

Printed in the United States of America.

Visit us on the web at www.dorchesterpub.com.

Rainbows at MIDNIGHT

Chapter One

Late August 1911

"I need a bride."

Silence greeted Sam Baranov's announcement. The other two men seated at the table, the cards and chips from their poker game strewn carelessly in front of them, stared at each other for a long moment, neither raising his gaze to meet Sam's eyes. This was worse than he had expected. Sam had known Alex would be of no help. That was why he had waited until Alex had left before telling the others of his dilemma. Surely these two would have a suggestion. Surely they would say *something*. At length, the doctor laughed.

Sam glared. This was not a laughing matter. Far from it. He turned to the man whose house was the site of tonight's game. William Gunning was never at a loss for ideas, and most of the time they were mighty fine ones. Sam raised one eyebrow, hoping the gesture would encourage William. While his host's lips twitched, he at least managed to keep a sober mien as he said, "So that's why you played such poor poker tonight. I wondered. It's not like you to lose every hand." Though William had yet to meet Sam's gaze, he hadn't laughed the way Dr. Ben had. That was a good sign. "So, who's the lucky lady?" William asked.

"I don't know."

This time William could not disguise his emotions. Color drained from his face as his eyes moved to meet Sam's. "You're joking."

If only that were true! Sam gripped the coffee mug so tightly that he expected to see his fingerprints etched into the tin.

"I reckon Sam's been drinking," Ben said with an assessing look.

Sam took a deep breath. "Look, fellas, you haven't been listening to me." He spoke slowly and distinctly, as if that would force them to hear what he was saying. "I told you I *needed* a bride," he repeated, "not that I *wanted* one."

Now that the wind had subsided, the loudest sound was the ticking of the grandfather clock that stood in the hallway. William leaned back in his chair and closed his eyes for a moment, as if trying to believe what he'd heard. "Does this have anything to do with the letter you got from Seward?" he asked.

Clenching his fist to keep his annoyance from showing, Sam groused, "Are there any secrets in this town?"

"Not many," William agreed. "Gold Landing's not much different from any other town in the territory. You were born in Alaska, Sam. You shouldn't be surprised by the way news travels."

Sam wasn't surprised. What he was was frustrated that his friends were of so little assistance. He rose and began to pace the length of the spacious kitchen. The sound of his boots on the wooden planks was oddly comforting. Sam had never understood why Ben paced. Now he knew. The motion and the sound seemed to help him marshal his thoughts.

As he turned, Sam saw Ben lean his arms on the table and

peer over the rims of his spectacles. "What was in the letter?" Ben's brown eyes sparkled with interest.

"What was in the letter?" A short brittle laugh emerged from Sam's throat. "The fact that I need a bride."

Opening his eyes, William reached for his mug, as if he needed sustenance to continue the discussion. "All right. I'll ask the obvious question. Why do you need a bride?"

Sam stopped his pacing and stood next to the table, glaring down at the other men. "You two have got to swear you won't tell anyone." They nodded. "Not even your wives."

Ben groaned. "Ella worms everything out of me."

"Not this." Though they were his closest friends, Sam wouldn't have confided in Ben and William if he hadn't been desperate. He was.

Slowly Ben nodded.

Sam swallowed deeply and resumed his pacing. When he reached the window, he thrust the curtains aside. Night had fallen, and clouds obscured the stars. Sam swallowed again. "It seems my father left me an inheritance." Odd. His voice sounded perfectly normal, as if he were used to pronouncing those words, when the truth was, he had never thought he would say them.

"Your father? I didn't know you had one." It appeared Ben was in a joking mood tonight.

"Look, Ben, I reckon Sam had a good reason for not talking about his pa before this."

Sam spun around and flashed William a smile of gratitude. "My father owned a shipping company in Seward," he told his friends. "When he died, my stepmother said he'd left it all to her." Sam turned back to stare out the window, though there was little to see on a moonless night. He couldn't let the others guess how much—how damnably much—it had hurt to believe that his father hadn't loved him enough to leave him at least a part of the company. There were some things a man didn't tell even his closest friends.

"But he *didn't* leave it to her," Ben ventured.

"He left it to her *in trust* for me." Sam stared into the

distance, looking for the glimmer of light that would reveal the river. But it was hidden, just as his father's will had been. Sam knew that Hilda had deliberately neglected to reveal that particular clause of the will, the way she had done so many other deliberately cruel things in the years she had been Nicholas Baranov's second wife. Sam turned and faced his friends. "I'll inherit the company on my twenty-fifth birthday."

"And where does the bride fit into this?" William reached for the coffeepot, pouring them all another round as Sam took his seat again.

The bride. She was the wild card in the hand his father had dealt him. She was the reason he was here tonight, with worry threatening to outweigh the sheer joy that the letter had brought. Papa had not disowned him! No matter what Hilda had said or done, Papa had left his only child the enterprise that had been so important to him. If Sam met all the conditions.

"I inherit only if I'm married."

A low whistle was Ben's sole response.

"Now you see my problem." Sam leaned forward, hoping to impress them with the gravity of his situation. Behind him he heard the wind begin to blow again, an audible reminder that fall's changeable weather was approaching. After autumn came winter and Sam's birthday.

"I've got just over six months to find a bride, and—in case you hadn't noticed, gentlemen—Gold Landing isn't exactly filled with unattached females." Though Alaska was the land of opportunity for many men, one opportunity that was sorely lacking was marriage. Men vastly outnumbered women, and unwed women were as rare as bears in December.

"You could advertise," Ben suggested.

As a gust of wind rattled the windowpanes, Sam shook his head. Others might advertise for a wife the way Dr. Ben had for an assistant, but Sam was not going the mail-order-bride route. "I heard Pete was gonna do that," Sam said. The owner of the roadhouse had made the announcement last month, even soliciting Sam's advice on the proper wording of his advertisement. "I don't think there's enough time for me. Besides, I want to get to know the woman before we're married." The thought of wedding a stranger filled Sam with dread. What if his bride turned out to be like Hilda?

He knew better than to expect love. If it truly existed and wasn't simply a poet's invention, it didn't seem to find its way to Baranovs, despite what his father had said the day they buried Sam's mother. Happiness didn't appear to run in the family either. But surely Sam could find a bride who wouldn't despise him, maybe even one who could be a friend. As desperately as he wanted his inheritance, Sam knew he could never again live in a household filled with hatred.

"You've got a point about getting to know each other." William flashed a grin at Ben. "Remember the day I first met Amelia? Love takes time."

Sam plunked his cup on the table, sloshing hot liquid over the rim. "Didn't you listen? I don't have time!" To his annoyance, Ben simply smirked, while William looked pointedly at the spilled coffee. With an exasperated sigh, Sam pulled out his handkerchief and mopped the table. Things sure had changed since William's marriage. He never would have cared about—hell, he never would have noticed—a little spill like that before Amelia moved in. It was enough to make a man reconsider the whole notion. Sam couldn't do that. The inheritance was too important to him. It would be worth the rules a wife would impose and the inevitable nagging he'd endure to have his father's legacy.

Sam glared at his friends. "You two sure didn't win any prizes for quick marriages."

"But we're happy." A fatuous grin seemed to confirm Ben's words. It was true that both of their marriages appeared happy. That, however, wasn't the issue. Finding a bride for Sam was.

"Do you have any suggestions?" he demanded. Seeing Ben's mischievous expression, Sam added, "About a possible wife, that is."

Ben peered over his spectacles, apparently serious once more. "What about the new schoolteacher? Ella says she sounds like a fine lady." Ben took a long swallow of coffee, then nodded solemnly. "You could do worse, Sam. She's a widow with two children, so she knows all about marriage and babies."

The howling of the wind underscored the ferocity of Sam's thoughts. If he didn't find an answer soon, he'd be like a wolf baying at the moon. Sam clenched his teeth. "Absolutely not." Ben had no way of knowing that he had touched a still-raw nerve. "I don't want to be saddled with someone else's children." His own, for surely he and his bride would have babies, would never suffer the agony of half brothers or half sisters.

William stroked the crescent-shaped scar that marred his left cheek as he appeared to consider the limited supply of unmarried women. "What about Vera Kane?" he suggested. "She was disappointed when Ben married."

Ben snorted. Sam shook his head. "No widows. I want a fresh start." Marriage was going to be difficult enough without adding complications.

"You know, my friend, for a man with a problem, you're being mighty particular." Ben pushed his glasses back onto his nose and looked pensive. "Let's see." He closed his eyes for a second, then blinked them open. "What about Charlotte Langdon? *She* was disappointed when William married."

"Touché!" William laughed.

Ignoring his friends' bantering, Sam pictured the woman in question. "She's not bad-looking." He pushed a poker chip to the side. "Never married." Another chip. "Comes from a good family." A third chip. "Charlotte's a fine idea, Ben."

When Ben extended his hand, as if for payment, William frowned. "If you ask me, it sounds like you're contemplating a business deal." His voice held the slightest chiding.

"That's exactly what it is."

A round of laughter greeted Sam's declaration. "Do you

want some advice on how to court Miss Langdon?" Ben asked when he'd wiped the smirk from his face.

"From you two?" Sam raised both eyebrows. "You didn't have an easy time. Why would I emulate you?"

William laughed again. "Fine. Make your own mistakes."

It was not a mistake. Laura Weaver Templeton repeated the words to herself as she had a hundred times since she had first answered the newspaper advertisement. She had made many mistakes in her life—some of them enormous—but this was not one of them.

"No, Matt," she said, pulling her son back from the railing for the twentieth time in as many minutes. What was it about water that so fascinated him that he wanted to jump overboard, while his sister clung fearfully to Laura's hand and refused to approach the side of the boat? Could it be that Matt, as the firstborn, had inherited his father's daring, leaving Meg saddled with Laura's caution? While the twins shared physical characteristics, even from the first week, it had been apparent to Laura that they had two very different personalities.

Keeping a tight grip on her son's hand, Laura let her gaze roam over the countryside. Alaska was so beautiful! Though she had seen pictures, they had not prepared her for the grandeur of this land that was soon to become her home. It was dressed now in autumn finery, the underbrush a blaze of red and brown, the sky still a vivid blue, which made it difficult to believe that snow was only days away. Each bend of the river brought a new vista, and with each mile, Laura realized that she had left more than Seattle behind. She had also left behind her old life and the Laura she had been for twenty-three years.

"Yes, Meg, we're almost there." She stroked the little girl's blond curls and smiled at her. This land of almost incredible beauty, this vast wilderness where moose and bears outnumbered humans manyfold, was their chance to begin again.

It was not a mistake.

"Right around the next bend, Mrs. Templeton." The ship's captain, continuing the string of small kindnesses he had showered on them during the journey upriver, pointed toward the right bank of the river. To Laura's untutored eye, it looked like every other bend on the Tanana's meandering course.

As the boat turned slowly and headed toward the shore, Laura gasped. In the distance she saw log cabins, frame houses, and a church steeple. She had seen that before. What made her gasp was the sight of more people than she had seen gathered anywhere in the territory. "Who are all those people?" A crowd of at least a hundred stood near the landing, apparently waiting for the boat to dock.

The captain smiled, his eyes twinkling with amusement at her surprise. "The arrival of a boat's a big event in Gold Landing, same as it is for most towns in Alaska," he explained. "I'm bringing supplies and newspapers and what folks value even more: mail. Besides, there's you. It's been years since this town got a new schoolmarm. I reckon everyone wants to be the first to greet you."

Suddenly as shy as Meg, Laura ducked her head. Then, realizing how much depended on her making a good impression, she fixed a smile on her face and drew herself up to her full five feet two inches. She had learned years ago that a regal manner helped to compensate for her lack of stature. If she pretended to be confident, no one would learn of the doubts that were her constant companions. She had left the past behind as surely as if she had buried it. This was her future.

As the boat maneuvered into position and cheers rose from the shore, Meg buried her head in Laura's skirts. "It's all right, honey." Laura knelt between her children and wrapped an arm around each of them. "We're almost home." She pressed a quick kiss on each of the children's cheeks, then rose and took their hands. "Hold tight to Mama."

Her head held high, she descended the gangplank. It was not a mistake.

The crowd parted as Laura and the twins reached the ground. She had a quick impression of smiling women, their hair neatly coifed, their clothing dark and serviceable, and children whose shy expressions reflected their curiosity about the new schoolteacher. Suddenly Meg refused to take another step and began to wail, hiding her face once more in Laura's skirts. Timid Meg had never seen so many people. Laura gathered her into her arms.

A dark-haired woman who stood only an inch taller than Laura herself stepped forward to take Matt's hand. "Welcome to Gold Landing. I'm Ella."

Even without the introduction, Laura would have known this was the schoolteacher she was to replace, for Ella had the commanding yet soothing air Laura had observed in successful teachers. Matt trusted her instinctively, and even Meg peered at her through teary eyes.

"My husband stayed with our buggy." Ella gestured toward the street where a row of carriages stood.

Though it appeared that every woman and child in town had come to meet the boat and nod a greeting to the new schoolteacher, there were few men. Unlike the women, those few remained silently on the periphery. No wonder Dr. Ben had not joined his wife. It appeared that the men preferred not to display their curiosity as openly as the women.

"You must be weary from all the traveling," Ella said as she led the way through the crowd. "I can't imagine how difficult it must have been with the children." She glanced at her stomach, then blushed.

"You'll know soon enough," said Laura. Ella's pregnancy was the reason she had resigned her position as Gold Landing's schoolteacher, hiring Laura to take her place. Ella, who was already caring for an infant during the day, had volunteered to watch Meg and Matt while Laura was at school. Though Laura had had qualms about leaving her children with anyone, Ella's letters had allayed many fears, and now—having met the woman—she was confident that she had not made a mistake in this either.

As a team of dogs raced by, dragging a sled and barking and yipping more loudly than any dogs Laura had ever heard, Meg tugged on Laura's ear in a plea to be set down. "No, honey, you can't pet the dogs," she told her. Though her daughter feared many things, dogs were not among them. Laura gathered Meg more tightly into her arms and smiled when Ella picked up Matt. "Thank you," she said softly.

Afterwards, Laura couldn't have said what had attracted her attention, but for some reason she found herself scanning the crowd. It wasn't as if she could expect to see a familiar face. She knew no one in all of Alaska. That was one of the reasons why Ella's advertisement had seemed like the answer to her prayers. No one would know her here. Her past would not follow her. But as she looked at the townspeople, returning smiles, nodding in response to mouthed greetings, her eyes met a frown.

The man was tall, at least six feet, with a shock of hair so dark it could have been black. His eyes were brown, a shade that Laura knew could be warm and friendly, for Ella's eyes were the same brown, and they radiated as much warmth as the summer sun. The man's were colder than the snowcapped mountains in the distance. Though a luxuriant mustache hid his upper lip, the stern lines of his face told Laura he was frowning. And judging from the glare he directed at her when their gazes met, for some reason he was frowning at her. It made no sense. She had never seen him before. She had no idea who he was. He couldn't possibly know. . . . Of course not. There was absolutely no reason why he should be so disapproving of her.

"My buggy's this way." As Ella spoke, Laura turned toward her, grateful for the distraction. "Ben wouldn't come into the crowd, but he'll take us home," Ella continued. "William's having your trunks delivered to your house."

Since those words made sense, Laura focused on them. The strange man's behavior was of no account. He was probably one of those people with a naturally bad disposition. The fact that he was so handsome meant nothing. After all, Laura had good cause to know that a handsome face could hide a rotten interior.

Holding Meg a little tighter than necessary, Laura followed Ella as she continued to make her way through the crowd. Her legs felt unexpectedly weak, and for a second Laura was afraid they would buckle. It must be that she had grown accustomed to the ship's motion. Surely this fatigue—for that was what it must be—was not caused by the stranger's glare.

"Yes, school will start next week," Ella told an anxious mother. "Mrs. Templeton will have a meeting of the mothers the first day."

Laura nodded her agreement. That was the schedule she and Ella had established. As they passed through the crowd, it began to disperse. Laura noticed that her legs were steadier now. She had obviously regained her land bearing.

They had almost reached the street when the sounds of shouting disturbed the relative quiet. "Stop! I tell you, stop!" Laura turned and saw two figures running toward them, one obviously pursuing the other. "Stop!" The older man's voice was firm and commanding, but the young man continued to run, his boots pounding on the hard-packed dirt. Laura saw his head move quickly from side to side, as if he sought an exit route, and she felt a twinge of sympathy for the young man. *Stop it!* she admonished herself, remembering the last time she had befriended an underdog and the pain her tender heart had caused her.

All conversation ceased as the townspeople watched the new drama unfolding in their midst.

"Stop!" Though the fugitive was swift, the other man was faster. A moment later, he tackled his quarry, bringing him to the ground almost in front of Laura and Ella. Matt stared wide-eyed, while Meg buried her face in Laura's neck. "Now, give it to me," the older man ordered.

"I don't got it." Laura heard defiance and something else, perhaps fear, in the young man's voice. Looking at him, she realized he was younger than she had thought, probably in his late teens, a tall, scrawny youth whose clothing was dirty and poorly patched. A smudge of dirt marred a face that might have been handsome, had it not been sullen, while light brown hair in sore need of washing hung lankly over his forehead. Laura's heart turned over, despite her admonition to ignore him. She hated thieves, truly hated them, she reminded herself.

"You know you took it." A woman joined the fray. Unlike the alleged thief, her clothing was immaculate, and her face bore a smile when she turned to the older man. "Make him give it back."

"I don't got it."

The woman frowned. "Don't lie, young man. I saw you lurking outside my window."

The lad straightened his shoulders. "It's a free country," he declared. "Alls I was doing was walking down the street."

"C'mon, son." The older man tightened his grip. "Give Mrs. Kane her nugget."

"I didn't take no gold." As the young man reiterated his innocence, Ella touched Laura's hand. "Let's get out of here." She led the way to her buggy, introducing the driver, a middle-aged man with spectacles perched on the bridge of his nose, as her husband Ben. Ben helped Ella and Laura into the back of the buggy, then handed the children to the women. Though the stern woman and the older man continued to flank the purported thief, the remaining onlookers began to leave.

"I'm sorry you had to hear that," Ella said as the horses began to move forward. "That wasn't the kind of welcome Gold Landing usually provides."

"What happened?" Ben turned his head toward them. "I heard the commotion."

"Later, Ben," Ella said with a soft smile for her husband. "I want to help Laura get her bearings." She gestured toward the road in front of them. "This is River Street," she said. A single set of deep ruts scored the center, causing the carriage to lurch slightly as it passed over them. "The first building on the left will be the mine office," Ella continued. "Then you'll see the sawmill."

Laura inhaled deeply. When she had disembarked, she had been aware of the scents of pine trees and dirt mingled with something she could not readily identify. It was, she realized, sawdust.

"So, what happened?" Ben repeated.

"Vera Kane accused Jason Blake of stealing some gold," Ella said, her sigh telling Laura the impromptu tour had been a delaying tactic as she had tried to deflect her husband's questions. "The mayor had to intervene."

"Typical." Ben snorted. "Vera wanted attention again."

As if he understood the man's words and sought attention himself, Matt tugged on Meg's braids. "Now, Ben," Ella chided gently while Laura separated the twins, shifting Matt to the outside. "Don't give Laura the wrong impression of our town." Turning toward Laura, Ella said, "Vera Kane's a widow, and she's lonely. Everyone in Gold Landing knows she's looking for a husband. Why, she set her sights on Ben a couple years ago."

Ben's chuckle turned into a full-fledged laugh. "The number of house calls I made were good for business." Ben, Ella had told Laura, was Gold Landing's first doctor.

"Be sure to turn on Second," Ella directed her husband. "I want to show Laura her house." When Ben nodded, Ella continued the story. "Now that we're married, Vera has turned her attention toward the mayor. That was him, Glen McBride."

Laura was puzzled. "Why was the mayor chasing the thief?"

Ben slowed the buggy as they turned right onto a narrow street. The ruts were less prominent here. "That's your house." Ella pointed to the second building on the right. It was a small log cabin, not much different from the one next to it. Compared to the house where Laura had been raised, it was hardly worth noticing. And yet she could not stop her heart from racing or her lips from curving into a wide smile.

She hugged Matt so tightly that he squealed. The house was hers! She and the twins would be safe here.

"Gold Landing's not as big as Seattle, so Glen serves as sheriff as well as mayor," Ben explained when Laura had finished admiring her new home. "We don't even have a jail. So far there hasn't been a need, although Sam Baranov's ready to build one."

"Sam owns the lumber mill you saw back on River Street," Ella said. "He's also the best builder in town. Of course, you probably won't be needing any building done on your house, at least not for a while."

Ben shook his head, his next words confirming Laura's impression that Dr. Ben wasn't easily distracted by his wife's attempts to steer the conversation away from the young thief. "It's a pity. Seems like every time there's trouble, Jason Blake's in the middle of it. That boy needs something to do with his time."

Ella leaned forward and touched her husband's shoulder. "Ben, you can't reform all of Gold Landing. Now, let's let Laura settle in. We don't want her to get the wrong impression of our town." The smile she flashed Laura transformed her face from ordinary into pretty.

Ella pointed out the general store and church on Main Street, and smiled again when Ben turned onto First Street. "Almost home." Ella smiled at Meg, who had overcome her initial shyness and was fingering the soutache braid on Ella's cloak. "I thought you could leave your children at my house while you supervised the unpacking at yours." Ella's smile broadened when Ben stopped the buggy in front of a two-story white frame house.

As she walked up the short path to the front door, a child clinging to each hand, Laura assessed the house. Though smaller than some of its neighbors, it was freshly painted, with neatly turned flower beds lining the path and carefully clipped bushes growing next to the porch. Laura suppressed a smile. The house was so like Ella! Her letters had revealed a woman with impeccable penmanship and faultless grammar, leading Laura to surmise that she was a perfectionist. What would the pupils and the parents of Gold Landing think when they met Laura? She was not the perfect teacher Ella had been.

The inside of the house was as neat as Laura expected, with nary a speck of dust visible. Still, the sight of a pipe and a neatly folded newspaper on one table told Laura that Ella's husband had made his presence felt. What changes would their baby bring?

Laura settled the twins in a corner of the kitchen and gratefully accepted the cup of coffee Ella offered her. She had taken only one sip when Ella said, "I've invited a couple of friends to join us for supper tonight. It's not a party, of course. That wouldn't be appropriate, since you're still in mourning."

Laura nodded. This was the Ella she had come to know through her letters, a little prim and proper, very concerned about socially correct behavior. "Tonight is just a friendly dinner," Ella continued. "In another month or so, we'll start introducing Laura to the men."

Laura felt the blood drain from her face. *No! Not that!* Ella had good intentions, but she couldn't indulge in matchmaking. Not in a month. Not ever. To hide her confusion, Laura turned quickly, as if she were making certain Meg and Matt were still playing quietly. "There's no need for that," she said when she had regained her composure. "I'm sure you mean well, but I won't ever remarry."

Ella gave her a knowing smile and continued to rock. It was clear she didn't believe Laura's protests were genuine. "I never thought I'd marry at all, but look at me now." She patted her stomach with a self-conscious smile.

Laura stared at Ella. She was willing to trust her with her children. This was much less important, and yet she couldn't voice the words. There was no reason that she should tell Ella why she would never marry again. "I'm not ready," Laura said. That much was true. The rest . . .

"Of course." Ella nodded as she reached down to hand Matt a wooden block that had tumbled under the table.

A few minutes later, the front door opened again. "Good morning," the visitor said. "You must be Mrs. Templeton. I'm Charlotte Langdon." The young woman appeared to be in her late teens. With her light brown hair, pale blue eyes, and fair complexion, Charlotte was not a woman who would attract attention; yet when she smiled, Laura realized that she could be considered pretty.

"I hope you don't mind if Charlotte helps you settle into your house," Ella said when she had offered a cup of coffee. "She has volunteered to be your assistant at the school, and I thought this would give you an opportunity to get acquainted."

Laura smiled at the young woman. "What a generous offer." Assistants, Laura knew, were not paid for their services, and few teachers were fortunate enough to have one. Laura was certain she would welcome help with what Ella had told her was the largest class in Gold Landing's brief history.

The sun was directly overhead as Charlotte led the way back to Laura's house, and Laura reveled in the warmth. At this time of the year, Gold Landing was warmer than Seattle. Since that difference would last only another few weeks until the Alaskan winter began, she resolved to keep the twins outdoors as much as possible.

"The school is the other direction on Main Street at the very end of town," Charlotte said. "We can go there once we get you settled."

Unlike Ella's house, the one that would be Laura's home was not well cared for. Though the interior had once been white, the paint was faded and peeling in spots, and one of the shutters sagged. Still, Laura felt the same bubble of excitement that had risen when Ella had first shown it to her. It was hers; it was a cabin, and that was a vast improvement over the boardinghouse where she had expected to live.

"This will be perfect," Laura said as Charlotte showed her the large room that served as kitchen and parlor. Furnished with a simple table and four wooden chairs in the kitchen section, a rocking chair and a shabby sofa on the parlor side, it certainly couldn't compare to her parents' mansion. It was, however, larger and more elegant than the last home she had had. The peeling paint could be replaced; the sofa could be recovered. It took little imagination to picture her home looking as inviting as Ella's.

"You're fortunate this was available," Charlotte said. "It's too late in the season to build now, and I shouldn't think you'd want your children in a boardinghouse."

Laura nodded, wondering what Charlotte would think if she knew the places where Laura and the twins had lived. "When I first took the position, Ella told me there were no single homes available," Laura said. "Do you know what happened?" It was almost a rhetorical question. In Gold Landing there would be few if any secrets.

It was Charlotte's turn to nod. "A man lived here with his mother. He died, and she went back to the States. San Francisco, I think."

Laura shuddered, thinking of the pain the unknown woman must have endured when her son died. Once children passed those dangerous first few years, a mother expected them to outlive her. What would she do if she lost Meg or Matt? Laura shuddered again. She wouldn't borrow trouble; she had more than enough already.

Apparently unaware of Laura's distress, Charlotte opened one of the two doors that led to the back of the house. "There are two bedrooms," she announced. "This is the smaller one."

Though tiny, the room held a double bed and a chest of drawers. "This will be the children's room," Laura said, smiling at the thought of her twins in a room of their own. What luxury it would be, not sharing her bed with them!

A wistful smile softened Charlotte's face. "Your twins are beautiful. You're so lucky to have them."

"Yes, I am," Laura agreed. "They're the most wonderful thing in my life."

No matter what had happened, Matt and Meg were not a mistake. And maybe, just maybe, coming to Gold Landing wasn't either.

Chapter Two

It was absurd. Sam Baranov shook his head as he stared at the pile of papers spread out on his desk, waiting for him to make sense of them. He had had a dozen more important things to do than meet the boat. Every man in Gold Landing knew that meeting the boat was women's work. Oh, a few men would just happen to be in the general vicinity when one arrived. It was pure coincidence, of course, not any silly desire to see the newcomers disembark. Once a man was nearby, it would be downright rude to leave, especially if a new resident was expected. A man wouldn't want the other townsfolk to get the wrong idea. After all, Gold Landing's citizens were friendly people. Manners mattered.

Sam glared at the papers, wishing he had an assistant to help him keep track of orders and inventory. He would much rather be in the mill doing real work than sitting here staring at pieces of paper and counting the days until his birthday.

He crumpled a sheet and hurled it at the wall. His bride. That was why he had gone to the landing. It wasn't as if he had wanted to catch a glimpse of the new schoolmarm. No, sirree. He had no interest in her. It didn't matter what Ben and William said; a widow woman with children had no place in his life. On the other hand, Miss Charlotte Langdon most certainly could have a place in his life. In fact, if Fate shone on him, she would have a very important place in his life. And Charlotte, Ben had mentioned, was going to be the new teacher's assistant. As such, it made sense that she'd have gone to meet the boat.

Sam had it all figured out. He would pretend that he was just walking by. He'd look around, as casually as he could. Maybe he would pretend that he was looking for Ella, that Ben had given him a message for his wife. And then when he saw Charlotte, he would just happen to walk in her direction. Once he was close to her, good manners would require that he greeted her, wouldn't they? Sam wasn't sure what he would say to Charlotte, but he could always ask her what she thought about the weather. That was a safe topic. It might not be a brilliant conversational gambit, but it was a start. And a start was what Sam needed.

The clock was ticking. The sand was running out. It didn't matter which metaphor you used. The simple fact was, Sam could not afford to waste any time if he was going to be lawfully wedded before his birthday.

A second piece of paper joined the first one. Damn it all! He had wasted a whole morning. He had gone to meet the blasted boat; he had stood there with all those women who cooed more than a cote full of doves, and what had he accomplished? He had seen the schoolmarm.

Sam knew what schoolteachers looked like. After all, he had had his share of them, and he knew Ella Taylor. This woman had not been like any of the teachers he had ever seen. She was even shorter than Ella, and though the heavy cloak enveloped her, something about the way she walked had made Sam think that she was more generously proportioned than Ella. Sam liked women with meat on their bones, particularly when the meat was distributed in the right places. That was one of the few faults he could find with

Charlotte. She was thin. Ben claimed she was slender, but to Sam's mind she was skinny. Still, a skinny bride was better than none at all.

The schoolteacher had been dressed all in black. Naturally. She was a widow. A black widow, just like the spider. But her hair was a silver blond that reminded Sam of moonlight reflecting on the newly fallen snow, and when she had glanced in his direction, he saw that her eyes were a bright blue-green. No one in Gold Landing had eyes like that. They were even more brilliant than the ocean on a sunny day. And her face. Sam caught his breath, just remembering what she had looked like. Her face was the most beautiful one he had ever seen, with delicate features and lips that begged a man to taste them.

No! He rose from his chair so swiftly that he knocked it over. He was not going to taste the schoolmarm's lips or anything else on that beautiful body. She might look like a princess, and she might start his blood to boiling, but she was not the woman for him.

Sam clenched his fists, then reached for his coat. He had to get out of here, away from those treacherous thoughts. Paperwork be damned! He'd go into the mill and plane a few boards. Timber wasn't deceptive the way women were. If a piece of wood was beautiful on the surface, it was beautiful all the way through.

Hilda had been beautiful, but only on the surface. That was how she had snared his father. She had worked her widow's wiles on him, bewitching Nicholas Baranov so much that he forgot all about his son and the wife he had just buried. That wasn't going to happen to Sam.

Sam stormed into the mill. Ignoring his men's friendly greetings, he reached for a saw. This was honest work, much better than remembering that scene at the landing. He wouldn't think about the way the schoolmarm had knelt and gathered her children close. He wouldn't think about the smile she had given them, a smile so full of love that Sam's stomach had begun to churn. Had Hilda ever smiled like that? Sam knew she had never given him that kind of affection. Every ounce of love she had had been reserved for her precious George.

Sam eyed the length of the board, deciding which side to smooth first. He wasn't going to make the kind of mistake his father had. No, sirree. The Widow Templeton was not the woman for him. Charlotte Langdon was.

"What do you think?" Charlotte stretched her arms in both directions, gesturing at the large room. Her blue eyes shone with such enthusiasm that Laura knew that even if she hated the school, she would not admit it and risk dashing Charlotte's pleasure. Happiness, Laura knew all too well, could be fleeting. She would do nothing to destroy it.

"This is the most beautiful school I've ever seen," Laura said truthfully. Though it was a simple log cabin and lacked the well-stocked bookshelves and finely carved cabinets she had had in others, those deficiencies were more than compensated for by the fact that this schoolroom was in Alaska, in a town where everyone, with one possible exception, seemed to welcome her. Matt and Meg could grow up here. They could be happy here in lives where they need never be ashamed. In Gold Landing, her children would never have to know what had happened before. That was beautiful.

Charlotte raised one pale eyebrow. "But you're from Seattle," she said, her voice reflecting her skepticism. It was clear that although she loved the school, she had not expected Laura to share her enthusiasm. "I thought everything was nicer there."

"Not everything." Laura shook her head as she looked at the whitewashed walls and the heavily starched blue gingham curtains hanging over the one window. They were simple but clean and serviceable. "I've taught in fancier schools," she admitted, "but that doesn't mean that they were better." As a child, she had heard that money couldn't buy love. At the time, she hadn't understood what it meant. She'd had money; she had thought she had love. It was only later that she had learned just how true the adage was. Now she had neither money nor love.

As Charlotte dusted the shelves, Laura opened the trunk of books that she had brought with her. At Ella's suggestion, she had chosen books for older children, since some had outgrown the school's existing selection. "We can put these on the top shelf," she told Charlotte. "The little ones won't be reading them, anyway." *Ivanhoe* and *Nicholas Nickleby* were designed for students in their teens. Laura had not brought any of Jack London's tales, wrongly assuming that the school would have copies. Perhaps the general store had some. If not, she would order them from Seattle. The older students needed to read the stories that had made their home so famous in the States.

"I've always wanted to be a teacher," Charlotte confessed as she studied the titles already on the shelves. Her wistful tone made Laura look up from the novels she was sorting. Since Charlotte faced the wall, Laura could not see her expression, but she sensed this was a long-standing desire.

"I know there are no normal schools in Alaska," Laura said, remembering what she had read about the Alaskan school system, "but you could go to Seattle. That's where I got my training."

Books thumped. Laura looked up, startled. Had Charlotte dropped them accidentally, or was she like Matt, who would release his anger by making loud noises? "It's not that simple." Though her voice was once more even, as Charlotte turned toward Laura, her face betrayed her pain. "My parents don't want me to leave home. I'm an only child," she said, as if that explained everything. "They want me to marry and stay here with them."

Laura made a quick decision. "Let's have a cup of tea and some of those cookies you brought." The smell of the freshly baked sweets had tantalized her from the moment Charlotte had opened the basket. Though she had planned to wait until they finished their work, the "accidentally" dropped books and Charlotte's obvious distress made Laura decide that now was the right time for tea, cookies, and conversation.

"I'm an only child, too," Laura told Charlotte as the young woman set water to boil. Laura's parents hadn't been excited about the thought of their daughter teaching school, but they had humored her wish, thinking it simply a passing fancy. Afterwards, Laura had been more than thankful that she had insisted. She wasn't sure how she and the twins would have survived if she had not had her teaching certificate. But she could not tell Charlotte that, not without revealing things that she had sworn no one in Alaska would ever learn.

"What about you?" Laura asked as calmly as she could. Thank goodness she had the excuse of pulling napkins from the basket as a reason for keeping her head averted. "Don't you want to get married?" From everything Laura had read and the comments she had heard on the journey north, single women were in short supply in Alaska. Now that she was marriageable age, Charlotte should have no difficulty in finding a husband. If that was what she wanted.

"Of course I do," the young woman agreed as she poured boiling water over the tea leaves. "But he has to be the right man." She handed Laura the plate of cookies.

Laura took a bite and smiled. Charlotte might not be a teacher yet, but one thing she would never need to learn was cooking. Her food was as delicious as Ella had claimed.

"You're still young," said Laura. Though she was only a few years older than Charlotte, she felt ancient. "You don't need to rush into marriage." *Don't make the same mistake I did*, she wanted to tell her assistant.

A dreamy expression crossed Charlotte's face. "What was your husband like?" She placed her cup on the desk they were using as a table and looked at Laura, her blue eyes intent.

Her husband. There were few topics Laura was less eager to discuss. Still, she knew that she had to answer, for silence would raise even more questions. "Roy was the most handsome man I had ever seen," she told Charlotte. That was the truth. "He literally swept me off my feet." That too was the truth.

"Really?" Charlotte's eyes widened, and Laura knew that the tale would soon be known throughout Gold Landing. Good. Excellent, in fact. If everyone believed her marriage had been perfect, they would think they understood why she had no desire to remarry, and they would ask fewer questions.

Laura nodded and took a sip of her tea. It was, not surprisingly, perfectly brewed. "I know it sounds silly, but Roy smiled at me, and I was so caught up in smiling back that I stepped into the street right in front of a carriage. Roy pulled me into his arms to save me."

As Laura had intended, Charlotte sighed with pleasure. "It sounds like a fairy tale."

And it had been. At the beginning.

A branch scraped against the window. "I didn't realize it was supposed to be windy today," Laura said, grateful for the distraction. It had been perfectly calm when she and Charlotte had walked to the schoolhouse. Perhaps a storm was brewing.

To her surprise, Charlotte flushed. "Oh, it must be getting late. I'd better go home. My parents will be waiting." She rose, hastily clearing the dishes, then gathered her cloak and gloves. "Good afternoon, Mrs. Templeton."

As Charlotte closed the door behind her, Laura raised one eyebrow. The normally calm Charlotte had been babbling. And, if Laura wasn't mistaken, she had turned left, not right. Wherever Charlotte was going, it wasn't home.

Sam tried not to stare at the man who sat opposite him. The Reverend Langdon was a tall, distinguished man, one of the original settlers of Gold Landing, and one of its most respected residents. All the dealings Sam had had with the minister had been pleasant. But all the other dealings had been professional. Either the Reverend had approached Sam, asking his help in building the church or the adjacent parish hall, or Sam had asked for spiritual guidance. Never before had Sam gone to him or any man to ask for his daughter's hand in marriage.

The parsonage parlor, where Sam had sat at least a dozen times, seemed oddly formal and unwelcoming today, and the Reverend's face, which Sam had seen every Sunday for as long as he had lived in Gold Landing, looked cold and forbidding. That couldn't be true, Sam told himself. He had surprised the minister with his request. That was all. He would agree. He had to! So much depended on his answer.

Though Sam longed to lean forward and demand a response, he sat quietly while Reverend Langdon studied him. It was only Sam's imagination that the man was trying to see into his very soul, to learn precisely why he had come to the Langdon household today. There was no way the minister could know that reasons besides Sam's affection—he would not lie and use the word "love"—for Charlotte had precipitated his visit.

"Of course, the choice is Charlotte's," the older man said at last. His smile held more than a hint of sadness, making Sam wonder whether he regretted the answer he was about to give or the fact that his daughter was old enough to marry. "Bertha and I would never force Charlotte into a marriage," he continued. "But yes, Sam. If you can win our daughter's love, we would be proud to have you as a son-in-law."

The tension he had been only vaguely aware of began to ebb from Sam's shoulders. He had cleared the first hurdle.

"Thank you, sir," he said, his voice fervent with emotion. "I'll take good care of Charlotte. Now, may I see her?"

Reverend Langdon rose and shook Sam's hand. "Charlotte's not at home this afternoon. I believe she's at the school with Mrs. Templeton."

A minute later, Sam was on his way to the school. There was no time to lose.

The day was once more calm, the breeze that had knocked a branch against the window apparently having subsided. Laura smiled as she breathed in the fresh scent of evergreen trees. The crisp late afternoon air reminded her that though it was not yet September, snow would soon cover the ground and blanket the trees' boughs. A bird warbled in the distance, its cry so plaintive that Laura wondered if it had lost its mate. That was silly, of course. The bird was probably searching for food. It was only Charlotte's questions about marriage that made her think of mates.

The man who approached was walking quickly, as if anxious to reach his destination. Laura raised one brow, wondering just what that destination might be. The only building on this side of town was the school, and she knew it was empty.

"Good afternoon, Mrs. Templeton." As he came within speaking distance, the man raised his hat in greeting.

It wasn't hard to guess how he had known her identity. Though her cloak was black, as befitted mourning, Ella had told her that the new slim style had not yet made its way to Gold Landing. That and Laura's less-than-large stature would make her immediately recognizable. The man, however, could be any one of the three hundred or so she had not met.

When he came closer, Laura's eyes widened as she realized that this was not a total stranger. Though she had never met him, she had seen him. He was the person who had glared at her as she disembarked from the boat, the one Laura had named "The Angry Man." With an effort, she kept a smile on her face. Perhaps yesterday was an aberration. Perhaps he was not always so hostile. She hoped not. Gold Landing was a small town; there was no need to make enemies unnecessarily. Still, Laura wondered why the man was heading toward the school. Surely he had nothing to say to her.

"Good afternoon, Mr. . . ." She let her voice trail off, waiting for him to introduce himself. He was taller than she remembered, perhaps an inch over six feet, and she had to tip her head up to meet his gaze. The man's hair and eyes were as dark as her memory of them, but today at least, his eyes radiated warmth, and a smile softened the planes of his face.

Though he was not handsome in the conventional way that Roy had been, his was a face a woman would not soon forget.

"Baranov. Sam Baranov." He inclined his head in a formal gesture, giving her a grin that was oddly engaging. Was this truly the same man who had glared at her only a day before? Today he seemed as welcoming as anyone she had met.

"Good afternoon, Mr. Baranov." Laura smiled her greeting and continued to walk toward town, trying to remember where she had heard that name before. Of course. Ella had referred to him as the owner of the sawmill. He was also the man who helped build houses.

Sam Baranov held out a hand, as if to slow her pace. "I wondered if you had seen Charlotte Langdon," he said in a voice that reminded Laura of hot chocolate, dark and sweet but with an underlying strength. *Stop it!* she told herself. *Don't let your imagination play these games. There's no reason to be so fanciful and every reason not to. You should have learned your lesson about handsome men.*

"I heard Charlotte was with you," he continued.

Laura managed a small smile as she reminded herself that this man was not Roy and she was no longer a naïve nineteen-year-old. "Charlotte was here," she told Sam, "but she left the school about half an hour ago." Laura would not divulge the fact that, although Charlotte had claimed to be going home, she had hurried in the opposite direction.

A cloud scudded overhead, momentarily blocking the sun at the same time that Sam's face darkened. "Oh." His voice was cooler now, his expression betraying disappointment. "Then I guess there's no point in my going to the school, is there? May I escort you into town?"

For a second Laura was unable to respond. She had not expected such good manners from a man who had glared at her with unmistakable hostility only yesterday. At the time, she had believed him to be an uncouth, uneducated man. Today she realized that that impression had been wrong. He was well-mannered, his voice cultured. Laura still had no idea what had angered him, but it no longer mattered. Perhaps this friendly overture was his attempt to apologize. Perhaps she had been mistaken, and he hadn't been glaring at her.

"Certainly," she agreed. It would be rude of her to refuse. Besides, hadn't she heard that there were bears in the forest? A woman couldn't be too careful here in Alaska.

They walked in silence for a few seconds. The sun had emerged from the clouds, and though the air was still cool, Laura felt cheered by the light. She had come too late in the season to experience the midnight sun, but next year she and the twins would enjoy the almost constant summer sunshine.

Sam broke the silence. "May I ask why you came to Alaska?" His voice was once more smooth and warm, setting her at ease.

"To see the midnight sun," she quipped.

Sam stopped and stared at her, as if trying to determine whether she was serious. "You're two months too late, you know."

"Or ten months early." When he chuckled, she continued. "I thought everyone in Gold Landing knew why I was here. I'm the town's new schoolteacher."

Sam's mustache quivered as his chuckle turned to laughter. "I know that. What I wondered was why you chose Alaska. Surely you could have found a school in the States."

"You're right, Mr. Baranov." His name rolled off her lips as smoothly as the hot chocolate that his voice conjured. "It wasn't just the allure of the midnight sun and the northern lights. The fact is, I wanted my children to grow up here." Though the words were part of her carefully crafted story, they were true. "I wanted them to know the independence and self-sufficiency of the frontier." That was also true. "After all, Alaska is our last real frontier." Everything Laura had said was true. It simply wasn't the whole truth.

Sam nodded. Perhaps it was just her imagination that his lips seemed to curve in amusement. It was difficult to tell behind that mustache. "All that you say is true," he agreed. "Then too, you have a good chance to find them a stepfather here."

Her step faltered as she reeled from the shock of his words. *Careful, Laura,* she admonished herself. *Don't let anyone see how vulnerable you are.* She schooled her voice to remain calm. "I assure you, Mr. Baranov," she said with a forced note of mirth, "that is the last thing on my mind. But if I might turn the tables, would you answer a question for me? Doesn't anyone in Gold Landing think of anything other than marriage? It seems to be not just the favorite but the only topic of conversation."

She had expected a denial. Instead, Sam's expression was pensive, and he remained silent for a long moment. "That's a good observation, Mrs. Templeton. I won't even try to deny that you're correct. The fact is," he said, echoing her phrase, "I just asked a young woman's father for permission to court her."

Charlotte. That was the reason Sam Baranov was heading toward the school. That was why he'd asked for her. Laura closed her eyes for a second, trying to picture Sam and Charlotte together. The image would not focus. She could see Charlotte. She could see Sam. But putting them together did not work.

"I wish you luck, Mr. Baranov," she said.

"Thank you, ma'am. Luck is something I'll surely need."

As she took another step forward, Laura tried not to frown. Why had he said that?

"You took such a risk!" Charlotte clasped her hands together, trying to stop their trembling. Though the day was not cold, she was shaking more than she had when she had caught a chill. How could he have been so foolish? "Mrs. Templeton almost saw you."

"But she didn't. You said she figured it was the wind." As Jason Blake grinned, Charlotte felt her heart skip a beat. How often had she dreamt of his smile, then wakened, certain she would never see it? Now here he was, smiling at her, and it was more wonderful than she had imagined. Charlotte nodded, unable to speak. People in Gold Landing might call Jason a bad boy, but she knew otherwise.

Jason ducked his head as they moved into the small stand of evergreens at the far end of the parade ground. Once the Fourth of July festivities were concluded, few of the townspeople came this direction, for there were no houses this far out of town. Charlotte and Jason were taking no chances. Even a casual passerby would not see them with the trees' curtain shielding them.

When they reached the center of the copse, Jason turned to face her. "I couldn't wait no more to see you," he said, his voice low but fervent, his gray eyes sparkling with something Charlotte could not identify. "It was a hell of a week."

Color rushed to her cheeks. "Shush," she said. "You know my parents don't approve of cursing." She lowered her eyes in confusion, then raised them slowly. She wanted to look at him. Oh, yes, she did. There was no reason to feel embarrassed. It was just that no boy had ever told her he wanted to see her. The thought that Jason did was exciting but scary at the same time.

Jason's lips thinned. "He—heck, Charlotte," he corrected himself, "I reckon they don't approve of much I do."

Charlotte blushed again. Her parents were the most forgiving people she knew, slow to condemn anyone. Though they weren't exactly disapproving, even they admitted they were worried about Jason. Charlotte didn't want to think about what they would say if they knew how often she met him. "They would like you if you gave them a chance to get to know you the way I do," she insisted, unsure whether she was convincing Jason or herself.

"Sure they would." Using the toe of his boot, Jason pushed fallen pine needles into a pile, leaving a small patch of ground bare. "They're like everyone else in Gold Landing. All's they gotta do is see me and they think the worst."

"That's not true!" Yes, Charlotte admitted, most people felt that way, but her parents wouldn't. Not if they knew the real Jason. She pulled at a branch, inhaling the spicy fragrance.

"Isn't it?" he demanded. "You're the only one who believes me. The others wanna run me out of town."

Releasing the branch, Charlotte put her hands on her hips and faced Jason. "I know you didn't steal Mrs. Kane's gold." Her voice was fierce, reflecting the anger she felt over others being so quick to blame Jason. She wished she had been at the landing. She would have told Mrs. Kane she was wrong, that Jason wouldn't have stolen anything.

Jason ran a hand through his hair, and a crooked smile lit his face. "Funny thing is, I think the mayor believed me, too. As soon as the widow left, he let me go. No lecture, nothin'."

A small ground squirrel scampered through the brush; another's antics stirred the tree boughs. Neither sound could compete with the pounding of Charlotte's heart or the rush of pleasure she felt because someone else believed in Jason. "I heard Mrs. Kane's sweet on the mayor," she said softly. Her mother might claim that it was wrong to gossip, but Charlotte didn't see any harm in telling Jason what she'd heard.

He scuffed the ground again, keeping his head lowered. "Like I'm sweet on you?" he asked, his voice so soft she barely heard the words.

As the meaning registered, blood drained from Charlotte's face, then rushed back. *Oh, dear me! What must Jason think? My face is probably redder than a geranium. Now he'll know how often I've dreamed of him, and Mother said that's something a girl is never supposed to admit.* Not daring to meet his gaze, she countered his question with one of her own. "Are you?"

The branches rustled again as Charlotte held her breath, waiting for his answer.

"You know I am."

"Oh!" This was what she had longed to hear, the words she had dreamt of. Charlotte couldn't count the number of times she had whispered them, pretending it was Jason's voice she was hearing.

They stood silently for a moment, neither looking at the other. It was odd. Charlotte had always been able to talk to Jason. He was the one person in Gold Landing she could count on to understand her. But now, now that he'd said those wonderful words, she found that her own supply of conversation had dried up. What could she say to him?

Jason cleared his throat. "Charlotte." He pronounced her name, then paused, as if waiting for her to reply. "Could I?" He scuffed the ground again, his head inclined as if he was studying his boots. "Would you?"

This time he raised his head. Charlotte lowered her eyes in confusion. What was she seeing reflected in Jason's eyes?

"Please . . ." There was something so plaintive in his plea that she forced herself to meet his gaze.

"What is it?" she asked. This was Jason, her friend, she reminded herself. She shouldn't feel awkward around him.

He shook his head. "No, I couldn't ask you. It's too much."

A feeling of warmth swept through Charlotte as she realized that Jason was as uncomfortable as she. "Tell me, Jason," she said, suddenly emboldened by his shyness.

He scuffed the ground again, then stood perfectly still for a long moment. Charlotte saw him swallow deeply, as if trying to muster the courage to speak.

"Please, Jason. What is it?"

He stared at her and swallowed again. "Could I hold your hand?" he blurted out at last.

He wanted to hold her hand! He had told her he was sweet on her, and now he wanted to hold her hand! Was there ever such a wonderful day? "Why, yes, of course." Though the words sounded embarrassingly like a croak, Charlotte extended her right hand toward him.

Jason stared at it, his face reddening. "Could I hold your hand?" he asked again, emphasizing the last word. "Not your glove?"

He wanted her to take off her glove! Charlotte felt the blood rush to her face. "Mother wouldn't approve." A lady didn't do such things. Especially not a lady who was the parson's daughter.

Jason's lips tightened. "I knew it," he muttered, and his eyes clouded.

Charlotte bit her lips as she made a decision. "Mother's not here," she said, peeling off her glove with fingers that, despite her best intentions, trembled. The air was cool against her bare flesh, and for the briefest of moments, Charlotte was certain she had made a grave error. Was this the temptation she was supposed to resist? She shook her head. Surely she couldn't go to Hell for a simple touch. Her hand dropped to her side as she tried to muster the courage to give it to Jason.

"Please, Charlotte." He reached for her hand, his face wreathed in a smile.

Charlotte managed a small smile of her own as she extended her hand. This was Jason, her friend. It couldn't be wrong.

And when his fingers touched hers, she knew that this could not possibly be a sin. Jason's hand felt nothing like hers. His fingertips were rough; hers were smooth. His palm was calloused; hers was soft. Separately, neither was special. But together they were magic. Pure magic.

Chapter Three

"You're so lucky." Ella poured a glass of buttermilk, handed it to Laura, and took her seat at the kitchen table. When Laura had returned from her day of preparation in the classroom, she had found Dr. Amelia sitting with her friend, apparently taking an unexpected break from her rounds, while Amelia's son Josh slept in his cradle and the twins built a wall of wooden blocks. Despite the presence of three children, the room was immaculate. Laura sighed, thinking of the chaos she had left in her own kitchen.

"Is there any special reason you think I'm lucky?" she asked. There was no doubt Laura considered herself fortunate. In the few days that she had been in Gold Landing, she had started to feel safe, and that feeling was more precious than the gold William Gunning and his miners took from the ground. This sense of security was why she had come to Alaska. But Ella had no way of knowing Laura's fears or the reason she felt so fortunate.

Ella smiled as she set her glass back on the table. "Let's start with the fact that those children of yours are perfect."

Laura couldn't help it. She started to laugh. "I can't quite believe that," she told Ella. "They're wonderful, and I love them dearly, but I would never, ever describe them as perfect."

On the other side of the table, Amelia raised her glass to her mouth, her expression making Laura wonder whether she was thirsty or simply wanted to hide her amusement. The sparkle in those sapphire eyes made Laura suspect the latter. The first time Laura had seen Amelia, she had been speared by envy. The young doctor was not just beautiful, she was tall and slender. Amelia was quite simply everything Laura admired most. Now that she knew her better, Laura's envy had disappeared, and she counted Amelia as her closest friend besides Ella. She and Amelia had even laughed over the fact that as a child Amelia had longed to be petite and blond.

Laura looked at her friends. "Didn't Matt spill his lunch?" she demanded.

Ella shrugged as if that were insignificant. "Part of it," she conceded.

"And once Matt spilled something, Meg turned her spoon into a catapult." Laura continued her recital of the normal mealtime scenario.

"Well . . . yes."

"And you call them perfect!" Laura hooted.

As the grandfather clock chimed the half hour, Meg scrambled to her feet, apparently wanting to find the source of the sound. "No, sweetie." Laura handed her daughter a block and set her back on the floor.

"Ella has babies on her mind," Amelia said when Laura rejoined her and Ella. This time she made no effort to conceal her mirth. "That's a common ailment in Gold Landing. Since I've been here, it seems like every woman of childbearing age has had at least one child."

"I love babies so much," Ella said with a fond glance at the twins, who now played quietly in the corner of the kitchen, their midday hijinks forgotten. "I still can't believe I'm having one of my own."

There were notes of both reverence and fear in Ella's voice. "You'll be a good mother," Laura reassured her.

"I hope so."

"I know so. I can tell by the way you care for Meg and Matt." The twins had not had a single tantrum since they had come to Gold Landing, a fact Laura attributed to Ella's calming influence.

Ella blushed, as if unaccustomed to praise. "Are you ready for tomorrow?" she asked, obviously wanting to change the subject. "I remember how nervous I used to be before the first day of school."

Laura knew exactly what Ella meant. "I'm as ready as I'll ever be." It was daunting, thinking of teaching a totally new group of pupils. She would calm her own nerves by reminding herself that the pupils were even more nervous than she. She might not be a perfect teacher like Ella, but she knew she was good. Still, she preferred not to dwell on what was going to happen tomorrow.

"I'm almost all unpacked," Laura said. "But I do need to buy some soap. Somehow, Matt managed to lose my last bar."

As if on cue, Matt giggled. Ella smiled, while Laura shrugged. Though she doubted Matt understood the whole story, she had no doubt that he had recognized and responded to his name.

"Herb Ashton will have soap at the store." Amelia opened her watch and frowned. "I'd offer to pick up some for you, but . . ."

"I want to visit the mercantile anyway." She would see whether they had any of Jack London's books in stock. Laura pleated her skirt between her fingers, counting the months until she would be able to wear a color other than black. Though Amelia's skirt was dark blue, almost black, it seemed infinitely more cheerful than Laura's. "I do have a favor to ask," she continued. "Does either of you have a small wagon I could borrow?"

"How small?" Amelia drained her glass, then rose to place it near the sink.

"Big enough for two not-so-perfect children to ride in. I thought we'd go exploring this afternoon."

Amelia nodded as she reached for her black bag. "William made a wagon for Josh, but it should be big enough for the twins. Of course you can borrow it."

"Where are you going?" Ella asked.

"I thought we'd cross the bridge. I want to see the rest of Gold Landing."

Ella's face paled, reflecting her horror. "Don't do that!" she cried. "It's not safe."

"Now, Ella, don't alarm Laura." Amelia laid a cautioning hand on Ella's shoulder, squeezing it gently.

But Ella would not be reassured. "I know you go there, Amelia, but no one else does." She stood and walked to the window, keeping her back to the other women. Her rigid spine and the set of her shoulders told Laura that while this was not a new discussion, it was one that caused Ella great distress.

"The other side of the river is the part of town most people want to ignore," Amelia explained. Her voice was low, her words carefully enunciated. "There are two settlements there, a group of out-of-work miners and the Athapaskan Indians. You wouldn't be in any danger if you went to either village." Amelia's sapphire eyes gleamed with what appeared to be moisture. "The only thing to fear is the sight of poverty."

Laura was no stranger to the sights, sounds, and smells of poverty. "Will any of those children be at school tomorrow?"

Ella spun around to face her. "No!" she said.

"I see." And Laura did. Though Alaska was a land of vast opportunity, it had its share of prejudice and distrust. She took a deep breath, exhaling slowly. Her instinct not to tell Ella, or anyone in Gold Landing, of her past had been a good one. Though they might be understanding, there was also the possibility they would not, that she would face the same revulsion as the poor people on the other side of the river.

There was the possibility that the people of Gold Landing would believe that children should pay for the sins of their fathers. That was a possibility Laura did not want to explore.

"Good afternoon, Mrs. Templeton." Sam entered the schoolroom, doffing his hat. The teacher sat behind her desk, her head bent over a pile of papers. At Sam's greeting, she rose, coming forward to welcome him. But it was not Mrs. Templeton Sam wanted to see. He let his eyes move around the room, trying to make his perusal seem casual. Yes, there was Charlotte, arranging books on one of the shelves.

"I thought you might need some assistance." He directed his words to the teacher. Then, as if he had just spotted her assistant, Sam bowed slightly. "Good afternoon, Miss Langdon. It's a pleasure to see you."

Today Charlotte was dressed in a light gray dress that leached the color from her pale face. When they were married, he would insist that she wear brighter colors. There was no reason for Sam's wife to look as if she was in partial mourning. It was bad enough that the schoolteacher was clad in unrelieved black. Of course, Sam had to admit, the black provided a nice foil for that silvery hair, and it only deepened her already vibrantly colored eyes. Sam's own eyes moved appraisingly from the top of Mrs. Templeton's head to her neatly shod feet. This was the first time he had seen her without her cloak, and he was pleased to note that his imagination had not failed him. He had thought she would have a well-rounded figure, and she did. Unlike Charlotte's angles, Mrs. Templeton was all soft curves. Her dress might be unadorned black, but it did not hide the fact that the body beneath it served as its own adornment. Why would a woman need ruffles and furbelows when she had hips and breasts like that?

"Thank you. We could use some help," the object of his thoughts said. "Would you mind putting this box on the top shelf?" She gestured toward a shelf that, while an easy reach for him, would have been a stretch for her. For, while the schoolteacher was all womanly curves, she was inches shorter than Charlotte.

When Sam had deposited the box in its designated spot, Mrs. Templeton gave him an appraising look, then glanced at Charlotte. Her eyes narrowed slightly, as if she was considering what to say next.

"Charlotte, would you show Mr. Baranov the woodpile?" she asked. "He'll be able to tell if we have enough." The twinkle in those blue-green eyes told Sam she remembered his comment about courting a woman and had surmised that the object of his affections was Charlotte. This was her way of helping him. He hadn't expected any assistance, but he sure as mosquitoes in June wouldn't refuse.

"Thank you, ma'am." He gave her an answering smile. Moments later, he and Charlotte stood near the woodpile. A cursory glance told him there was plenty of wood, and he suspected the schoolteacher knew that. Still, he was happy for the time alone with his chosen bride.

"You're looking very pretty today," he said. It wasn't a lie. Charlotte did look pretty if you didn't compare her to Mrs. Templeton. It wasn't her fault that the schoolteacher was the prettiest woman in Gold Landing.

Charlotte stared into the distance, her eyes searching for something. She stood motionless; then, as if she was suddenly aware of his presence, she turned and faced him. "I beg your pardon. Did you say something?"

Sam suppressed a sigh. "Nothing important." Perhaps she hadn't heard him; perhaps, though, she was uncomfortable with compliments. He would try a different tactic. "Do you enjoy working with Mrs. Templeton?" Surely that wasn't too personal a question.

Charlotte nodded. "Yes," she replied. Her gaze did not meet his, and she thrust her hands inside her cloak in a gesture that was almost furtive. It was surely his imagination. There was no reason Charlotte Langdon should feel that she had to hide her hands from him. It wasn't as if he had any intention of touching them today. A man couldn't move too quickly with this courting business.

"We'd better go back inside," Charlotte said. Suiting her actions to her words, she began to walk toward the steps. Sam followed, wondering what he had done to make her so skittish. When they were once more in the schoolhouse, Charlotte hurried toward the blackboard and began to wash it.

"May I help you?" he asked. Women, or so he had heard, didn't like to put their hands in cold water. Perhaps that was why Charlotte had concealed hers; perhaps they were chapped. He gave them a furtive glance. They looked all right to him.

"No, thank you, Mr. Baranov." Though her words were polite, Charlotte did not face him when she refused his offer.

Sam had seen pupils wash boards; he had seen an occasional teacher clean one. Never had he seen anyone apply such diligence to the simple task of cleaning a blackboard. Charlotte kept all her attention focused on the slate, scrubbing as if her very existence depended on removing the last stubborn streak.

"It was very nice of you to come here." The schoolteacher's melodic voice attracted Sam's attention. Though she did not raise it, Sam guessed that not one of her pupils would fail to heed her commands, for there was an underlying note of authority.

He gave her a quick glance, then looked around the room, searching for a reason to prolong his visit or—even better—to return. He had hoped he could help Charlotte with her daily chores, but if that tactic didn't work, he would find another. Sam put no stock in the adage that absence made the heart grow fonder. He planned to see Charlotte every day until she agreed to be his bride. Time was too precious to waste.

"Looks like you could use some more shelves." Sam gestured from the open trunk in one corner to the heavily laden bookcases. Though he addressed the schoolteacher, he stood where he could observe Charlotte.

"I'm afraid I brought too many books." Mrs. Templeton laughed. "I suspect that's an occupational hazard for teachers."

From the corner of his eye, Sam saw Charlotte move toward the window. She glanced outside, her head moving slightly as she appeared to be searching the horizon. She was, Sam noticed, looking in the same direction she had looked when they were standing near the the woodpile. A moment later, her shoulders slumping slightly, she returned to her post at the blackboard.

"I'd be happy to build some shelves for you." Sam continued his conversation with the teacher. He would have to measure the space several times, and then there would be final fittings. He might even want to stain the shelves here, to be certain they matched the others. Of course, Sam admitted, if he were making shelves for anyone else, a single measurement would suffice, and he would stain them at the mill. But this wasn't an ordinary set of shelves. No, sirree. These shelves were the means to an end. And the end was Charlotte Langdon's agreement to become Sam Baranov's bride.

"I don't want to impose." Mrs. Templeton looked down at the books, then glanced at Charlotte.

"It's no inconvenience at all." That was an understatement. Sam would welcome the opportunity to spend afternoons here with Charlotte, a fact he suspected the schoolteacher knew quite well. "Now that fall's arrived, the mill's not so busy."

Charlotte darted another glance at the window. What was it she sought? The school was far enough out of town that no one passed by. Most of Gold Landing never went beyond the school, except for the few men who claimed that hunting was best on this side of town, yet Charlotte kept looking out the window in the same direction.

"Was your father a sawyer?" Mrs. Templeton asked.

Sam shook his head. She was a nice lady, asking all these

questions so that Charlotte could learn about him. "No, ma'am. I started the business myself." And if he sometimes regretted being in the Alaskan interior rather than in a seaport, if he occasionally wished for the scent of salt air and the feel of waves beneath his feet, there were other compensations.

"So you didn't want to be a miner?" She continued the gentle inquisition.

Sam shook his head again, then remembering that Charlotte could not hear a gesture, he answered, "No."

"I suppose there's a lot to be said for steady work rather than the boom or bust of mining."

He didn't want to mislead her. Charlotte, that is. "The truth is, I don't much like being underground. Placer mining might have been okay, but the streams were pretty much played out by the time I got here." Though Mrs. Templeton looked at him with interest shining from those sea-blue eyes, as far as Sam could tell, Charlotte considered the blackboard far more engrossing than anything he was saying. "William's found a couple good lodes, but it means spending the day in a shaft. That's not for me."

"I can understand that," Mrs. Templeton agreed. She had a pretty smile. Oh, it wasn't as warm as the one she had given her children, but it didn't chill a man the way Charlotte's back did. "I enjoy looking outside."

As if on cue, Charlotte returned to the window and gazed outside. This time she shook her head slightly and her lips curled downwards, as if she were distressed by what she saw . . . or didn't see.

"Ella and Amelia told me that you're a skilled carpenter and builder," the teacher continued. Charlotte cleaned another imaginary speck from the blackboard.

Sam shrugged. "It helps sell lumber and gives me something to do during the winter. Besides," he admitted, "I enjoy working with wood."

A gust of wind rattled the panes. As Mrs. Templeton shuddered, Sam was reminded that she was from Seattle. How would she fare during an Alaskan winter? She was so tiny that Sam doubted she could manage a dogsled. That meant she'd have to travel by snowshoe, and that could be mighty tiring.

"Is there anything you especially enjoy making?" The woman was wonderful! Who else would have continued talking to him, asking all these questions, helping Charlotte to get to know him?

"Rocking chairs are my favorite," he answered. Mrs. Templeton nodded, encouraging him to continue. Charlotte scrutinized one corner of the blackboard. Why couldn't she show at least a modicum of the interest the schoolteacher displayed? "They're more difficult to make than ordinary chairs, but most people enjoy rocking."

"I know I do." Mrs. Templeton's skirts rustled slightly as she returned to her chair behind the desk. She smelled nice, like some sort of dried flower. "Did you by any chance make the rocker that's in my cabin?"

Sam shook his head. "Frank's ma brought that with her. To hear Frank talk, it didn't rock too well."

She laughed. "He didn't exaggerate. The chair lurches more than it rocks."

"Let me see what I can do about that." He had a chair almost finished that he could give her. It would be a nice way to welcome her to Gold Landing, and Charlotte would be sure to hear about his generosity. Then too, he could make a chair for Charlotte. Weren't brides supposed to have a hope chest or something like that? He could give Charlotte a special chair the day she agreed to marry him. Sam grinned.

Charlotte turned her head toward the window. This time she did not walk the extra three paces to stare outside.

"What don't you enjoy making?" It was Mrs. Templeton who spoke. Charlotte appeared tongue-tied today. Hadn't William complained about that the year he had bought her July Fourth picnic basket? Some men claimed it was restful being around a quiet woman. For his part, Sam preferred one who wasn't afraid to voice her thoughts. At least that way you knew where you stood.

What didn't Sam like to build? There was no question about that. "Coffins."

The schoolteacher nodded, a stray lock of hair bouncing gently on her cheek. Sam wondered if it felt as silky as it looked. "I can understand that."

She didn't understand, of course. No one could. It had been horrible, without a doubt the worst day of his life. Sam would never forget the darkness, the cramped space, that terrifying certainty that he would never escape, that no one would miss him, that he would indeed die there. No one who hadn't experienced it could understand just how frightening being locked inside a coffin had been for a six-year-old boy. Sam blinked, trying to force the bitter memories away. He would not think about George. Never, ever again.

"It's time for me to go home." For the first time, Charlotte spoke. Though her words were ordinary, Sam thought he heard a note of distress in them, and she kept her head carefully averted from the window. What had she been searching for outside the school?

"May I walk you home?" He wouldn't ask her about the window, of course. But the walk would give him a chance to ask her a little about herself. Surely now that she had learned so much about him, she would be willing to talk.

Charlotte's pale face grew even whiter, and for a moment he thought she might swoon. Then she nodded. "Yes."

It was the last word she said until they reached the parsonage, though Sam tried his best to engage her in conversation. The pines and fallen needles made more noise than Charlotte Langdon.

"Good-bye, Mr. Baranov."

It was a simple farewell. Surely it was only his imagination that made it sound like a dismissal.

Snow was coming. She could feel it in the air. It was hard to believe that early September could bring major snow to

Gold Landing. In Seattle, September was one of the warmest, driest months, a time that made a mockery of the damp winters. Here, though, the seasons were different. Though glorious, an Alaskan summer was brief, and winter held reign for most of the year.

Today might be her last chance. Meg and Matt were napping, and Charlotte had agreed to stay with them, giving Laura time to explore on her own. This time, though, she had not told anyone her destination. She would not face the censure she knew would come if she admitted that she was going to cross the bridge.

As she left her house, Laura headed down Second Street. The whine of saws told her that the mill was working, albeit at reduced capacity. "The only bad thing about your house," Ella had said that first day, "is that you're too close to the sawmill." So far, the noise had not bothered Laura. With her windows closed, though she was aware of the sound, it was not unpleasant. In fact, it reminded Laura of the drone of insects. By the time summer came and Sam Baranov ran multiple shifts, she hoped she'd be so accustomed to the sound that she would hardly hear it.

"Good afternoon, Mrs. Templeton." Sam Baranov stepped into the street and doffed his hat. Laura wondered if her thoughts had somehow conjured him. Though he came to the school each afternoon, always with an imaginative excuse, this was the first time she had seen him near his mill.

"Please call me Laura," she said with a warm smile. The man had such perfect manners that she knew he would never presume to call her by her first name without an invitation. Still, if they were going to see each other regularly, and she suspected that was the case, since he was clearly courting Charlotte, they might as well become friends.

"I'd be honored. And I'm Sam." He replaced his hat, then gazed at her with a wry smile. "Dare I ask where you're going? The only establishment on this part of Second isn't one I would expect you to frequent."

Laura matched his smile. It was hard not to smile when

Sam Baranov looked at you that way, as if you were the most fascinating creature on the face of the earth. Laura suspected that he was practicing today, trying to hone his skill, because for some reason Charlotte seemed immune to his charm. If Laura's pulse beat a little faster than normal and she found herself wishing she had worn her other, more flattering, hat, it was nothing more than any red-blooded woman would expect when such a handsome man tried to charm her, no matter what his motive was.

"I've been warned about Gloria's," Laura said in response to Sam's question. Though Ella had referred to it by euphemisms, Amelia had been blunt in explaining that it was a whorehouse. "I assure you, that's not my destination." Although, when he learned where she was going, Sam would probably be as disapproving as if she were going to visit the house of ill repute. "I wanted to see the other side of the river."

A raised eyebrow was his only sign of concern. "Will you forgive my asking why?"

The day was cold and damp. A moment earlier Laura had been shivering. Now she started to relax. At least Sam hadn't berated her for her decision. "In one word: curiosity. I want to learn as much as I can about my new home, and the Indians are part of it."

Sam fingered his mustache in the gesture she had noticed he employed when he wanted to ponder. "It's not a place where many go," he cautioned.

"Amelia does."

"That's different. She's a doctor."

"And I'm a teacher. If I'm going to be a good one, I need to keep learning."

There was a second of silence, when the only sound Laura heard was the whine of the saws and a distant dog's howl. Then Sam's brown eyes crinkled with amusement. Laura wondered what he found so entertaining. Was it her assertion of the need to learn or the fact that she wanted to be a good teacher?

"If I can't dissuade you, may I accompany you?" His voice was warm and smooth, devoid of the mirth she had seen on his face. "Perhaps," he added with a self-deprecating smile, "I can learn something too."

Laura nodded. In Seattle she would never have agreed to go walking with a man. Even here, though her status as a widow granted her more latitude, she would have refused every other unmarried man in Gold Landing simply to avoid the speculation that she was looking for a husband or—as Sam had phrased it—a stepfather for the twins. Sam was different. She had no need to fear him, for he had no interest in her. Sam was courting Charlotte.

As he crooked his elbow, Laura placed her hand on his arm. How long had it been since she had walked with a man? Surely it had been a lifetime since she and Roy . . . Laura forced the bitter thoughts aside. This was Gold Landing, not Seattle, and Sam was most definitely not Roy.

They spoke of inconsequential things as they walked down Second Street. Laura pretended not to notice the men who strode purposefully toward Gloria's house. Who was she to condemn them? They at least were honest in their intentions, whereas she had become the queen of false pretenses.

As they crossed the bridge, Laura turned to look back at Gold Landing. From this bank, the primary landmarks were William Gunning's mine, Sam's sawmill, and Gloria's establishment. The large houses that lined Main and the smaller ones on the numbered streets were hardly visible, dwarfed by the forested hill and the snowcapped mountains in the distance. Alaska, Laura realized, had a way of putting everything in perspective.

Sam gestured toward the left. "The Indian village is this way," he said. They walked for a few minutes, speaking of ordinary things like the advent of winter and Laura's need for snowshoes. As they approached the village, Sam's steps slowed. "Let's stay on the outside," he suggested.

Laura nodded, recognizing the merit in Sam's recommendation. They were conspicuous enough, walking on this bank of the river. If they strolled down the middle of the village, the Athapaskans would know that they had come out of curiosity. Treating them like an exhibit in a zoo was not what Laura wanted.

Even though she had been warned, the conditions shocked Laura. The Indians lived in worse poverty than she had ever seen. Their wickiups were made of tattered hides, the holes so large that she wondered how they could endure an Alaskan winter. And the children! While her twins were chubby, their cheeks rosy and clear, these children were uniformly thin, almost emaciated, and she saw an unhealthy pallor beneath their light brown skin.

As she walked at Sam's side, Laura's hands began to tremble. To think she had once believed she had lived in poverty! What she had endured was nothing, nothing at all, compared to these people's lives. She started to turn, then forced herself to continue walking. She had wanted to see the village. She would see it. All of it. Only when she had reached the last teepee would she turn around.

They were at the second-to-last wickiup when the woman emerged, tears streaming down her face, a still form held in her outstretched arms. Though the form was completely wrapped, Laura knew what the animal hide contained, and she felt as though a steel band was slowly tightening around her heart. The poor woman! How could she bear it? No other children clung to her legs; there were no sounds from inside the teepee. Was the woman burying her last child?

"Oh, Sam!" The words came out with a sob. Involuntarily, Laura's fingers clutched at his arm. "I had no idea it was like this."

He placed his hand on top of hers, squeezing it slightly. Though it was nothing more than a polite gesture, Sam's touch reassured her. His hand was warm and firm and alive, telling her without words that life was not all tragic. Sam turned and walked quickly away, his long stride forcing Laura to take two steps to every one of his. Yet she did not complain, for the rapid pace meant that they were putting distance between them and that poor woman who had lost her child.

When they reached the bridge, Laura started to cross it. "Let's continue," Sam said. "There's something I want to show you."

Though she felt an almost overpowering need to return home, to hold her children in her arms, Laura knew that she was still distraught. The twins would sense her mood, and they'd become distressed. Sam was right. She should not go home until she was calmer.

They walked for a few minutes longer, turning away from the river. The sky was leaden, as gray as her mood, and Laura found herself wishing for snow. The clean white flakes would help obliterate the most obvious signs of poverty and suffering. Gradually the underbrush disappeared, replaced by a vast open area. To Laura's surprise, it was neither green nor brown, the two colors she would have expected. Instead, the ground was carpeted in bronze.

"It's the tundra," Sam said. "Isn't it beautiful?"

"Magnificent." Laura dropped to her knees and stared at the vegetation that formed the Alaskan tundra. Though she had read about the variety of miniature plants and the beautiful but almost invisible flowers they bore each summer, the reality of their autumnal foliage was more glorious than she had expected, and it sent a surge of hope through her. Nothing could erase the memory of the Athapaskan woman's sorrow, but the tiny plants reaffirmed the beautiful side of life.

"William says that Amelia comes here because it reminds her that life continues," Sam explained.

Laura touched one of the plants, marveling that it was smaller than her littlest fingernail. "What a beautiful display," she said. It was not difficult to understand why Amelia found this sight so reassuring. Though confronted with the almost incredible ferocity of an Alaskan winter, these tiny plants continued to live and grow, year after year. If they could withstand hardship, so could she.

When Laura rose, she was once more calm. "I'm ready,"

she told Sam with a nod in the direction of Gold Landing.

He placed her hand on his arm again, covering it briefly with his own. "We all learn to deal with our fears in different ways."

Laura stopped and stared at Sam. What had made him say that? Though his brown eyes were somber, they gave no indication of his thoughts. Laura's shiver had nothing to do with the damp day. She hadn't spoken of fears, so why had Sam? Most men would have assumed that what she felt was simply sorrow for the Athapaskan mother. Had Sam somehow guessed that the sight of the Indian woman with her child's body had made Laura fear that she would lose her own children either to death or to something worse? There was nothing on earth that Laura could imagine being more painful than the loss of a child.

She started walking, once more anxious to hold Meg and Matt. "How do you deal with your fears?" she asked Sam as they retraced their steps through the brush.

Sam's face was solemn, and he fingered his mustache. "I told you that I don't like dark confined spaces. If you walk by my house, you'll see that I have more windows than anyone else in Gold Landing. The townspeople told me I was crazy and that I'd have to cut every tree in Alaska to heat it, but I need to see the sky. The windows help."

Laura shuddered, her mind once again picturing the Indian woman. She wasn't sure that anything would allay her fears or keep her nightmares from recurring. "I wish I could overcome my fears that easily."

Sam shook his head slowly. "I didn't say that I had overcome them—just that the windows help." Laura nodded. Sam had confirmed her thoughts.

"Do you want to talk about it?" Sam asked as he helped her cross a small stream. Some of the stones were rough and cut into her feet. Laura almost welcomed the pain, for it forced her to think of something other than her fears.

She shook her head. "I can't." Not today, not ever.

Chapter Four

Laura glanced at the clock. Six-thirty. Roy should be here by now. She eased herself into one of the kitchen chairs. There; that felt better. At least now the pressure on her feet wasn't so great. She would unbutton and remove her shoes as soon as they had eaten, but—even though her feet ached from the unusually long day at school—she would not risk Roy's anger by serving dinner in her slippers. While they might no longer have their rightful position in society, he had told her on numerous occasions, there was no reason to lower their standards. And so, each night when she returned from teaching, she would spend a few precious moments playing with the twins before she fed them and bundled them into bed, hoping that they would not cry and annoy their father. Once the children were settled, she would cook Roy's supper, then change into one of the fancy dinner gowns that she had worn a lifetime ago, pretending the scarred table and chipped plates were nothing more than temporary inconveniences.

Laura leaned forward and touched the geranium that served as a centerpiece. It was a far cry from the lush floral arrangements that had graced her mother's table, just as the stew that still sim-

mered on the stove was far different from the succulent roasts her parents' chef had prepared. So much had changed in a year! Twelve months ago, Laura had been the seemingly pampered daughter of one of Seattle's finest families, living in a mansion high on First Hill. Now she was a wife and mother of twins, living in a two-room flat that, try though she might, never lost the smell of cooked cabbage and onions.

Rising, she stirred the stew, then checked the clock for the fifth time in as many minutes. Where was Roy? Her heart began to pound as it always did at the thought of her husband. How could she regret the changes in her life when they had brought her Roy and the children? Roy, the almost incredibly handsome man who had swept her into his arms and his life, wooing her with words of love and the promise of happily ever after. Roy, who had called her his princess, insisting that he was a frog who needed her to free him from an evil spell. Roy, whose lightest touch had set her pulse to racing.

Laura settled back in the chair. He would be here soon. Perhaps he had found a job, and they wanted him to start working today. That must be it. That was the reason he was late. He would be here soon, and then they would have another of their magical evenings. It would be like the first few months, when Roy had refused to believe that the rift with her parents was permanent. "They'll come to their senses," he had promised, making light of Laura's attempts to cook and the inevitably burned meals. But Chet and Myra Weaver had not relented, not even when Laura had told them they were to be grandparents. They no longer had a daughter, they insisted, so how could they have a grandchild?

It hurt. Oh, yes, it hurt to realize that her parents cared so little for her that they could dismiss her from their life as easily as they did a clumsy servant, telling her that she had failed to live up to their expectations. Though Laura had dreamed of a reconciliation, as the months passed and her parents rebuffed every attempt she made to see them and completely ignored the announcement of the twins' birth, she had finally accepted the reality that her parents had indeed disowned her. Now her life was Roy and Matt and Meg.

Where was Roy?

When she heard the front door open, Laura jumped to her feet, a smile lighting her face. Though she no longer felt like a princess, Roy was still her Prince Charming. He was the one who made her life worthwhile.

"This place looks like a pigsty!" Roy snarled as he moved toward the back of the flat, kicking aside a book that had fallen from its shelf. Roy must not have found a job if he was in such a foul mood. Mentally, she calculated how long they would be able to live on the meager wages she earned as a teacher.

"I'm sorry, darling." Laura raised her face for Roy's kiss, and tried not to be hurt when he walked past her and sank onto a chair. "At least dinner's ready."

A scowl marred his handsome face. "What kind of slop do you expect me to eat tonight?" he demanded.

Laura closed her eyes. It wasn't the first time Roy had criticized her cooking. The days when he had pretended to enjoy dinner had ended about the time she had discovered she was pregnant; still, he wasn't normally so cruel.

"It's beef stew," she said quietly. Of the few dishes she had managed to master, stew was Roy's favorite.

He glared at her, his blue eyes blazing with anger. "You useless bitch! You're the biggest mistake I ever made."

Laura felt the blood drain from her face. What had happened to Roy? Where was the man who had courted her so tenderly, the man who had whispered words of love when he brought her little tokens of his affection, promising her that when their fortunes changed the purloined dandelion would be an orchid and the tiny bottle of toilet water would be a crystal atomizer filled with French perfume?

"It'll be easier once you're working." She ladled stew onto his plate, then sliced the loaf of freshly baked bread. At least it had risen properly today.

Roy broke off a piece of bread and stuffed it into his mouth. "That's where you're wrong," he said when he had swallowed. "Haven't you figured it out yet? I'm not going to work. I'm not cut out for it."

Laying down her fork, Laura faced her husband. "But Roy . . ." She knew that he didn't relish the thought of being an employee. Still, he had never before refused to discuss the possibility. He knew that the money Laura had gotten when she had pawned her watch and her grandmother's pearls would soon be depleted, and that her pay would not cover rent and food for the four of them.

"Don't you 'but Roy' me," he said with another snarl. "Why the hell do you think I married you?"

That was easy. He had told her the reason so many times. "Because you love me," she said.

"Wrong!" Roy pushed the plate aside. "You're even more stupid than I thought. Love is just a word; it's not real. Only you would be dumb enough to believe it."

Though Laura heard the words, for a second they did not register. When they did, she recoiled as if he had slapped her. "But Roy, you told me . . ."

He laughed, a sound that sent shivers of dread along Laura's spine. This was not a temporary bad mood. "I told you what you wanted to hear, Laura. The truth is, I married you for your money. I needed an heiress, and when I heard how much you were worth, you looked like the right one." He snarled. "Who would have guessed your parents would be so stubborn?"

If she hadn't been sitting, Laura feared she would have collapsed. Her legs felt weak and rubbery, and the room had begun to spin. She closed her eyes and took a deep breath. "Papa was right." She forced the words out as she opened her eyes and stared at the man she had married. "You are a fortune hunter."

Roy shrugged, as if the epithet had no power to hurt him. "That's right," he agreed. "I hunt fortunes. Since you no longer have one, it's time for me to go hunting again." He laughed, the cruel sound making Laura cringe. "One thing's for certain, I'm not going to stay with a useless, unlovable bitch like you any longer!"

Laura woke with a shudder, then reached for the matches. Though it had been weeks since she had last had the nightmare, she knew that the only way to dispel the trembling that was its normal aftermath was to bathe the room in light and force herself to walk. No matter how cold the room might be, the simple action of moving her arms and legs seemed to help her cope with the pain that Roy's words still caused.

That night in Seattle had been the last time she had seen him. True to his promise, he had gathered his belongings and left both Laura and the city. At first it seemed as if he had disappeared, but when several months had passed, Laura had heard rumors that he had been seen with a wealthy widow in Portland. Apparently the widow had been wiser than Laura and had not surrendered her fortune to the charming Roy Templeton, for the next news had been that Roy was in prison, arrested after a bungled attempt to rob a bank.

Laura's slippers slapped rhythmically against the wooden floor as she walked from the door to the window and back again. Roy might be serving his sentence, but Laura felt that she was the true prisoner. In one evening, he had destroyed her innocence, for until that moment, she had believed that—no matter what her parents had said or done—she was still a lovable woman. Roy had shown her how foolish that belief had been. Silly Laura, to think that anyone could ever love her! She would not make that mistake again. Words of love, no matter how sincerely they were uttered, were nothing more than empty shells. She would put no stock in them, and she most definitely would not build her life on such a feeble foundation.

When her breathing had returned to normal, Laura walked to the twins' room, pushing the door open so that she could assure herself they were still sleeping. Matt lay on his back, a smile on his face, while Meg had burrowed under the covers, only a small bump revealing her presence. Even in sleep they revealed their personalities: Matt outgoing and confident, Meg sweet but shy. They were so precious, these children of hers!

Laura gripped the door frame. No matter what happened,

what sacrifices she had to make, one thing was certain. She would keep them safe. Her children would never suffer the same fate she had. They would never learn of their father's shame, and they would never, ever doubt how much she loved them.

"What's the finest candy you've got?" Sam looked around him. Though he had been in Herb Ashton's store hundreds of times since Herb had first opened it, scandalizing the citizens of Gold Landing with the striped awning at the same time that he delighted them with the variety of goods he stocked, Sam had never had a reason to purchase candy.

Herb grinned and stroked his beard. "So it's true. You're courting Charlotte Langdon." Herb's naturally loud voice was in great demand when the town needed an auctioneer or someone to call out dance steps. Today Sam wished the man were suffering from laryngitis.

Glancing around to make sure that his own words were not overheard, Sam groused, "There are no secrets here, are there."

Two women entered the store, heading straight for the dry goods. Sam wasn't deceived. He knew they'd listen and that within hours the story of his confectionery purchase would have spread through Gold Landing.

With a shrug, Herb pointed toward a small display of chocolates and fancy hard candies. "I reckon there's only one reason a man buys candy, and that's a woman. Either he's courting her or patching up an argument. Besides," he added with another grin, "I heard tell you've been spending most every afternoon at the schoolhouse. I figured you wouldn't be courting the teacher, being as she's still in mourning. That left the preacher's young'un."

Sam couldn't fault Herb's logic. The truth was, he was courting Charlotte. As for arguments, there wasn't much chance of that. Both parties had to talk to start an argument, and Sam had never met a woman with as little to say as Charlotte. Weren't women supposed to be like birds, chattering constantly from dawn to dusk? Not Charlotte. She was as silent as a fish.

Half an hour later, a gaily wrapped package stuffed in his pocket, Sam headed toward the school. He had deliberately left the sawmill earlier than normal today because he wanted to spend more time with Charlotte. Surely, once he had given her the candy, she would want to talk. Sam wanted—no, he needed—to learn more about the woman who was going to be his bride. At the rate they had been going, he was afraid he would know little about her other than her name by the time he proposed, and that just wasn't enough. He didn't want to marry a stranger. Though he had no reason to believe Charlotte was like Hilda, a man could not be too careful, not when his whole life was at stake.

Sam whistled softly as he approached the school. Candy was a good idea. He had heard that the best gifts for a lady were candy, books, and flowers. This time of the year, flowers were scarce in Gold Landing, and Charlotte had more books than any one person could hope to read. That left candy. Sam grinned. She'd like it. Of course she would.

He heard a loud rustling in the small copse just beyond the school.

Reaching for his gun, Sam moved as silently as he could toward the trees. It was probably nothing more than a deer, but if a bear had come this close to the school, Sam would have to scare it away. He couldn't have an animal as dangerous as a bear that close to the teacher and her assistant.

The rustling grew louder. Sam cocked the gun and sniffed. With the wind blowing toward him, a man could normally smell a bear. Sam smelled nothing other than pine trees and a faint, almost sweet scent. No bear he had ever encountered smelled that way.

A branch snapped, and Sam saw a dark form silhouetted against the trees. It was most definitely not a bear. As the figure emerged from the trees, Sam grinned and slid his gun back into its holster. He certainly wasn't going to shoot Charlotte. He was going to marry her.

Sam started to greet Charlotte, then closed his mouth as she turned and stared back into the forest. Odd. There wasn't anything interesting in this part of Gold Landing. No cabins or fields, not even a good view of the mountains. Still, Sam couldn't argue with the fact that whatever Charlotte had seen in the trees had put a soft smile and a most becoming flush onto her face. This afternoon, for whatever the reason, Charlotte was downright pretty.

"Good afternoon." He called the greeting, then took another step toward her.

Charlotte's head jerked as if she was startled, and Sam watched the color drain from her face. "Good day, Mr. Baranov," she said in the quiet tones he had heard so often. Her face had lost its pretty glow, becoming as colorless as her voice.

"I hope you'll call me Sam." He had waited until she was next to him before he spoke. A man didn't want to shout things like that, even though there wasn't anybody close enough to hear.

Overhead the sky was blue and cloudless, the kind of late summer day Sam enjoyed. There was no wind, no sign of a storm, no reason for the birds to be squawking warnings. Sam looked back at the trees, wondering what was disturbing the animals.

"Please call me Sam," he repeated.

"I couldn't do that." Charlotte shook her head violently. It was the greatest display of emotion Sam had seen from her. "That wouldn't be proper."

He tried to bite back his disappointment, telling himself that it wasn't important. Some couples spent their whole lives calling each other "Mister" and "Missus." That wasn't the kind of marriage Sam wanted, but there was time for Charlotte to change, to unbend a little, once they married. In the meantime, he would concentrate on what was important: wooing her.

"I brought you something," Sam said, reaching into his pocket. When he proffered the box of candy, Charlotte put her hands behind her back in a gesture that reminded him of a reluctant child. But Charlotte was no longer a child. She was old enough to be a bride. His bride.

"I cannot accept gifts from a man," she said primly. He should have realized that the minister's daughter would have deeply instilled ideas of right and wrong.

Sam shook his head slowly. Though he thought Reverend Langdon would have told his daughter of their conversation, it appeared he had not. "Your parents have given me permission to court you," he told her. This sure as winter snow wasn't the way he had thought the afternoon would proceed. He had envisioned smiles and gratitude, not a sullen silence.

The remaining color drained from Charlotte's face. "Oh," she said, apparently unable to think of any other reply. It was hardly the response he had expected.

The birds' chattering had subsided, as if whatever had threatened them had disappeared. Though Charlotte's gaze continued to flit back to the trees, Sam saw no motion in the copse. He extended his hand, offering her the candy a second time. This time she took it. "Thank you," she said with none of the passion he had heard when she refused to use his first name. With a final glance at the trees, she led the way into the schoolhouse.

Inside, the schoolteacher sat at her desk, her head bent over a small pile of papers. When she raised her face to greet them, Sam noticed that she had dark circles under her eyes, as though she had spent a sleepless night. He wondered whether one of her children had been ill.

"Would you like a piece of candy, Mrs. Templeton?" Charlotte opened the box. Sam noted that she did not take a piece for herself. Was she one of those silly women who refused to eat sweets lest they spoil their girlish figures? If so, she was wrong. Sam reckoned Charlotte could use a bit more meat on her bones.

The schoolteacher appeared to have no such compunctions, for she took a piece of chocolate. "It's delicious," she said, obviously savoring the sweet. Sam watched the tip of her tongue dart out to lick a speck of chocolate from the corner of her mouth. It was a simple gesture. There was no reason it should make him wonder whether her mouth tasted as sweet as the candy. "This is better than any candy I had in Seattle," she added.

Though Sam kept his eyes focused on Laura, he hoped Charlotte was listening. She had moved to the blackboard and was once again washing it. Sam had never seen a woman so obsessed with the cleanliness of a blackboard. "I can't take any credit for the chocolate," he admitted. "Herb Ashton recommended it."

Laura smiled that sweet smile that made her blue-green eyes sparkle, and motioned to Sam to sit. "Herb knows his stock the way you know woodworking," she said. "The rocking chair you made is wonderful." Sam had delivered the chair two days earlier. Unlike Charlotte's less-than-enthusiastic reaction to the candy, Laura had been visibly pleased by the gift. She had insisted that Sam bring the chair into the cabin and see how nice it looked in the parlor half of the main room. They had, of course, left the front door open for propriety's sake.

"The chair is beautiful to look at, and it rocks so smoothly." Laura's voice was warm and enthusiastic, far different from Charlotte's bland expression of thanks.

Sam darted a glance at the woman he planned to marry. If she heard Laura's praise for his handiwork, she gave no sign. "I'm glad you're enjoying it," he said.

Charlotte dipped her rag in the pail, then wiped another section of the board. Today, at least, she was not staring out the window.

"Oh, I am enjoying it," Laura said. "And so are my children. Fortunately, they both fit in it at the same time, so we haven't had any arguments about who gets to rock." A wry smile turned the corners of her mouth upward. "I'm afraid to think about what will happen next year when they've grown a couple inches."

Sam tried not to frown. Laura's children were one thing

he didn't want to think about today, tomorrow, or next year. She wasn't like Hilda. He told himself that. If Laura had married a widower with children, she wouldn't have treated her stepchildren the way Hilda had him. After all, look at the love Laura lavished on her pupils. They were no relation at all to her, and she treated them far better than Hilda had her husband's son. But though he knew it was absurd, that there was no reason to be bothered by the thought of Laura's children, Sam couldn't deny the fact that when his mind wandered and he pictured Laura with the twins, he got a sinking feeling in the pit of his stomach, worse even than the time he had eaten green apple pie. The solution was simple. He wouldn't think about them.

He turned to Charlotte. She was the reason he was here. She was the one whose image should occupy his thoughts, all of them. "May I walk you home?" he asked.

She hesitated for a moment, casting a glance at the window. Then she nodded. And, as she had every other time he had walked with her, she remained silent until they reached the parsonage.

"Good-bye, Mr. . . . er . . . Sam."

At least that was an improvement.

Laura leaned back in the chair, her foot maintaining the slow, easy rocking that she preferred, her arms resting on the chair's smooth arms. The twins had finally fallen asleep, exhausted by their after-supper playtime. Now Laura could relax for a few minutes in her new chair. It was beautiful. She hadn't exaggerated when she had told Sam that it was the finest piece of furniture she had ever owned. Oh, some of the antiques in her mother's home might have been more valuable, but none had possessed the combination of simple yet graceful lines and exquisite workmanship that Sam's rocker did. She closed her eyes, smiling as she thought about how greatly her life had changed since she had come to Gold Landing. For the first time since that awful night when Roy had left, she felt safe.

She rocked, thinking about her pupils and the challenges that each day in the schoolroom brought. Like any town, Gold Landing had its share of mischievous children, ready to disrupt the others' studies, and at those times, Laura was doubly glad that she had Charlotte to help her. Keeping Johnny Keller separated from Mary Ashton seemed like a full-time endeavor, and when Mabel and Martha Mackensie decided to play tricks . . .

A brisk knocking on the front door interrupted Laura's reverie. Her eyes flew open, and her heart began to pound at the unexpected sound. People in Gold Landing did not normally pay social calls after dark.

Laura raced to the front door. "Sam!" Why on earth was Sam Baranov standing at her front door, a decidedly uneasy expression on his face? "What's wrong?" she asked, her anxiety doubling at the sight of Sam's discomfort. Had the school burned down? Had something horrible happened to one of her pupils? Whatever it was had to be important, or Sam would have waited until tomorrow afternoon and his normal visit to the schoolhouse.

He shook his head slightly, and a shadow of a smile crooked his mouth. "There's no disaster," he said. "I feel badly about bothering you tonight, but I need some advice, and I don't reckon there's anyone else who can help me." He gestured toward the street. "I wondered if we could take a walk."

It was Laura's turn to shake her head. "I can't leave Meg and Matt alone. I'd invite you inside, but . . ."

The light spilling from her house showed concern in Sam's brown eyes, along with disappointment. "I understand. A lady can't be too careful of her reputation."

If only he knew! But Laura merely said, "It's even worse for a schoolteacher." They were expected to be paragons, second only to ministers' wives and children in their exemplary behavior. She thought quickly, unwilling to turn away the man who had been so kind to her. "Let me get my coat. If we stay on the porch, I'll be able to hear the twins."

A moment later, she and Sam stood on the small stoop in front of Laura's house. As was normal for this time of the evening, there were no other people outside. A block further down Second, miners would gather when the shifts changed, and men would pay their calls on Gloria's establishment, but this portion of the street was usually quiet after dark.

Sam stroked his mustache, then thrust his hands into his pockets. "What is it?" she asked, disturbed by this further evidence of his nervousness.

Sam's brown eyes met hers, and she saw both worry and something else—could it be vulnerability?—reflected in them. "I reckon you know that I'm courting Charlotte," he said. Though he kept his hands in his coat pockets, Laura could see that they were fisted. Surely that wasn't the normal reaction of a man in love.

"I surmised as much," she said quietly. A wolf bayed in the distance, his cry setting several dogs to barking.

Sam frowned. "I don't appear to be making much progress. You've seen Charlotte. She's polite to me, but it's like I'm a stranger." There was no mistaking the frustration in Sam's voice. Laura was surprised. She would have thought Sam to be a patient man. Surely anyone who would carve intricate designs in the back of a rocker must possess an almost infinite amount of that virtue. But tonight he seemed distinctly impatient.

"Charlotte rebuffs every attempt I make to get to know her." Sam sighed. "I don't think she likes me."

Laura knew she was not an expert on love—far from it—but Sam sounded more like a man having trouble with a business partner than one who was disappointed in love. Still, she could not dispute his allegation, for she had indeed observed Charlotte's cool reaction to Sam's visits. Though it might be dislike, Laura believed there was another explanation. "Perhaps Charlotte is shy around men." She certainly wasn't reticent in the schoolroom, so Laura knew that her shyness didn't extend to all portions of her life. However, since Sam was the only man she had seen with Charlotte,

Laura wasn't sure whether this was the way she responded to every man or only to him.

"I don't know whether it's shyness or not, Laura." She noticed that Sam appeared to be clenching and unclenching his fist, and her heart went out to him. No matter the cause, he was unhappy, and Laura had never been able to resist trying to make people happy. That was part of what had drawn her to Roy. *Stop it! This is Sam, not Roy.* There was no reason to think about Roy and the way he had wooed her with lies.

Sam shook his head in what appeared to be bewilderment. "I swear, Charlotte hasn't said more than a dozen words to me in the fortnight I've been walking her home."

That was not the Charlotte Laura knew. "It must be shyness. She's quite talkative—I might even call her loquacious—with me and the pupils."

Sam leaned back against the railing, crossing his arms in front of him, and Laura saw the lines of frustration between his eyes. "So, what should I do?"

Laura almost smiled at the irony of someone asking her, a woman no one could love, for advice in matters of the heart. She wished she had an easy solution for Sam. Unfortunately, there wasn't much he could do. "All I can suggest is that you give her time. Maybe the idea of love and marriage is new to her."

Laura knew that Charlotte cherished the dream of teaching. Perhaps that was why she was resisting Sam's courtship. Perhaps she feared that if she married, she would move from her parents' home to her husband's and would never have the opportunity to turn her dream into reality. Perhaps once she had taught for a year or two, Charlotte would be ready for marriage.

Sam slammed a fist into his other hand, the sound startling Laura as much as the act itself. "Time is what I don't have!"

His voice was so fierce, the anger and frustration etched so deeply on his face, that Laura recoiled until she felt the opposite railing against her back. "I don't understand," she said. They were talking about love and marriage, not a race. Why did Sam have such a sense of urgency?

Sam stared into the distance for a moment before he answered, as if he were trying to decide what to tell her. Two men, their loud voices and slurred words leaving little doubt that they had imbibed heavily at Gloria's, stumbled past the cabin. Though they appeared oblivious to Sam and Laura's presence, he waited until they were out of earshot before he spoke.

"I need to marry Charlotte before February."

This made no sense. "I'm sorry, Sam. I still don't understand. What happens in February?"

When his eyes met hers, Laura saw frustration and something else, something she might have called hope if it weren't so improbable, reflected in them.

"My twenty-fifth birthday is in February," he said, as if that explained everything.

Laura was reminded of a small child trying to keep a secret but bursting to confide in someone. Sam seemed to have the same mixed emotions. She sensed a reluctance to reveal whatever it was that made this birthday so significant, along with a need to tell someone.

"What is special about your birthday?" she prompted him.

Sam frowned. "Can I trust you not to tell anyone?" he asked. "I wouldn't want Charlotte to be hurt."

His words sounded ominous, his tone even more so. Whatever it was that linked Charlotte and Sam's birthday was causing him great anguish.

"I know how to keep a secret," she said. That was one area where Laura had had all too much practice.

Sam clenched and unclenched his fists again, then forced his hands to rest at his sides. He swallowed deeply, then blurted out, "I need Charlotte to marry me so I can inherit my father's company."

Dear God, no! Laura gripped the porch post to keep from falling. *Sam was just like Roy.*

Chapter Five

"That's despicable." Had he ever thought Laura's blue-green eyes were warm and friendly? In no more time than it had taken for him to explain his dilemma, they had changed from compassionate to condemning. Though he knew it to be an impossibility, the temperature of the night air seemed to have dropped ten degrees, chilled by Laura Templeton's cold anger. "How could you even contemplate such a thing?" she demanded.

Something certainly had riled Laura. Although his friends William and Ben had laughed when he'd told them he was going to find a bride, Laura was not laughing. Far from it. She stood on the other side of the small porch, her hands clenched as if she was forcing herself not to hit him.

"What is it you're questioning?" Sam asked, trying to guess why Laura's mood had changed so rapidly. When he had come to her house, he had expected that she would be able to help him, to give him some of the guidance that she provided to her pupils each day. He could have asked Ben or William, but he had figured that Laura would be of more help. After all, she was a woman. If anyone could understand the workings of Charlotte's mind, it would be another woman—especially one as sensible as Laura. Or so he had thought.

"What is the problem?" he asked. "The fact that I want to claim the inheritance my father left me or the fact that I'm planning to marry Charlotte?"

Laura raised her head in a regal gesture. If she were taller, Sam had no doubt she would have looked down her nose at him. "The marriage, of course." She acted as if that should have been apparent, as if only an ignorant schoolboy would not have realized that. Laura unclenched her fist and jabbed a finger at him. "How can you even consider marrying a woman you don't love?" Another jab. "How could you do that to yourself and Charlotte?"

Her vehemence surprised Sam as much as her anger had. This was not the cool, calm Laura he had seen in the schoolroom each afternoon. In that woman's place he saw fury personified. "Don't be naïve, Laura," he said, trying to keep his own voice even rather than succumb to the temptation to shout his frustration. "It happens every day. People marry for many reasons other than love—money, security, to join property or combine businesses. Surely you know that."

The sparks in those lovely eyes and the way she tossed her head told Sam Laura hadn't liked his explanation any more than she had his initial declaration. "Of course I know that," she said, the cold, steely tone leaving no doubt in Sam's mind that this was the voice she used when she dealt with a particularly difficult child. "The difference is, in those situations, both parties understand the arrangement." She spoke as if she were delivering a lecture to her students. "What you're proposing is different." A light breeze teased a lock of Laura's hair loose. It danced against her cheek, looking as soft as silk. It was, Sam suspected, the only soft part of Laura tonight. She stood opposite him, as rigid as a soldier on guard duty. "You're deceiving Charlotte."

He stared at Laura. She couldn't believe that. Not really.

"I am not deceiving Charlotte," he countered. "I never told her I loved her." Sam swallowed deeply, surprised at the pain Laura's words had inflicted. He hadn't realized how anxious he had been for her advice and approval. Though he shouldn't care, it hurt to realize that Laura didn't understand that he had a sense of decency. Surely she should have known that he was an honorable man. It wasn't as though he liked the situation. It wasn't as though he had chosen to be forced into marriage. But distasteful as the idea of this marriage was, he had done his best to make sure that he was fair. He had been careful not to use the word "love" when he spoke with Reverend Langdon, and he had never misled Charlotte with false declarations.

Laura's hand sliced the air in a gesture of dismissal. "You ought to be a lawyer, the way you're excusing yourself on a technicality." The hair bounced against her cheek again. "Just because you didn't lie directly doesn't mean you aren't wrong, Sam. All it is is a different sin—omission, rather than commission." Sam flinched at both the word "sin" and the cold fury that he saw in Laura's eyes. Though she might be a small woman, there was nothing small about her anger. She was like the volcano he had once seen, spewing lava and ashes, destroying everything in its path. Sam wondered what could have triggered Laura's eruption. Surely her reaction was out of proportion to the cause.

Laura jabbed her finger at him again in an accusing gesture. "You've neglected to tell Charlotte the truth, and in my book, that's as bad as telling her you loved her. In any case, you've let her think you care for her."

"But I do." Sam ran a hand through his hair in pure frustration. He wasn't sure why he was defending himself. Surely he had learned during the years he had lived in Hilda's household that there was no point in doing that. He had always been condemned and sentenced without a hearing. Tonight, it appeared, was no different. And he had thought Laura was different from Hilda!

A wagon lumbered by on River Street. Sam glanced at it,

wondering who was headed toward the landing at this hour. Not that it mattered. What mattered was setting the record straight. He had obviously made a serious mistake in confiding in Laura. But now that he had, it was important that she understand that he wasn't a monster.

"I care about Charlotte," he said. And he did. If Charlotte aroused no passion, perhaps that wasn't so bad. A placid life with Charlotte was bound to be easier than living with a woman like Laura. Not that he had ever considered that. From the beginning, he had known that Laura was not the woman for him. Tonight only proved that.

"I care about Charlotte," he repeated. "And I know she'll be a good wife and mother." Though Laura's eyes widened, she said nothing. "I've heard she's a good cook and knows how to keep house."

Laura's eyes widened even further. Sam watched as she bit her lower lip in an apparent effort not to speak. It failed, for she blurted out, "Now I understand." Instead of jabbing her finger at him, she fisted both hands and held them rigidly at her sides. Though her voice was cold, there was no mistaking her fury. "You get what you want: a housekeeper and a woman to bear your children, in addition to gaining your inheritance. Fine." The look she shot at Sam said she believed it to be anything but fine. "Now tell me, what does Charlotte get in return?"

If Laura thought he hadn't considered Charlotte, she was wrong. Sam had thought long and hard about what he had to offer a woman. "She'll have a husband who's a good provider and who'll treat her with respect."

Another curl tumbled from Laura's crown, bounding against her cheek. She brushed it back impatiently. "Respect." Laura spat the word as if it were a curse. "Is that what you think she wants?"

Of course it was. Everyone wanted respect.

When Sam nodded, Laura continued. "You're cheating her, Sam. Charlotte deserves more than respect."

The wagon returned, a little slower this time. That was

odd. Sam would have expected it to move more quickly if the driver had unloaded cargo at the landing. Sam shook his head. Why was he thinking about a wagon when he was faced with the angriest woman he'd ever met?

"What do you think Charlotte deserves that I'm not giving her?"

When Laura raised one eyebrow in a gesture that was imperious rather than inquisitive, he had the feeling that he was seven years old and back in school, trying to explain to the teacher why he hadn't finished his homework.

"Love," she said succinctly.

They were back to that. He couldn't believe that Laura, a worldly, educated woman, put stock in a concept that had obviously been invented by poets. "Do you honestly think love exists?" he asked her. Sam knew beyond the shadow of a doubt that it did not. He had lived almost twenty-five years and—despite what his father had once said—he had seen no evidence that love was any more real than goblins, fairies, and other children's fantasies.

Laura took a step forward, and for the first time since he'd told her his reason for marrying, Sam saw something other than anger on her face. Though he had no idea why, Laura looked sad. She took a deep breath, then exhaled slowly, as if she were considering her answer.

"Yes, I do believe in love." Her voice was firm with conviction.

For a second Sam stared at Laura. There was no mistaking the sincerity on her face. For some reason, sensible Laura put stock in a fantasy. "Then," he said slowly, "I was wrong about you. You're not naïve; you're a fool."

Laura looked as if he had slapped her. "And you," she said, not bothering to disguise the scorn in her voice, "are a miserable excuse for a man."

The twins were still asleep when Laura began to dress for school the next morning. She had lain awake, too fueled by anger to sleep for the first few hours. Then, gradually, as she paced the floor the way she did after a nightmare, the anger began to subside, replaced by a combination of disappointment and disillusionment. Now, though she wanted nothing more than to bury her head under the covers and remain in bed, she had to get ready for school.

She shook the wrinkles from the petticoat with more force than normal. How could Sam even consider marrying Charlotte? Laura had thought he was different from other men. He certainly had seemed to be. Sam was polite and thoughtful, and she enjoyed his company. No matter what topic she raised, he had an opinion that he wasn't afraid to voice. Listening to him, Laura had learned about subjects as diverse as Alaskan history, timber grades, and salmon fishing.

Even though she had known he was spending time with her because Charlotte was her assistant and he wanted to be near Charlotte, Laura hadn't minded. She would serve as chaperone every day of the week if it meant that she could spend time with Sam. He was such good company!

For the first time in her life, Laura had a man as a friend, and she liked it. Now that friendship was ended, destroyed by the knowledge that Sam was no different from Roy.

Laura stared into the mirror as she arranged her hair in a pompadour. What a fool she was, thinking Sam and Roy shared nothing other than gender. Would she never learn? Sam had been using her, just as he was using Charlotte, and Laura could no longer be a party to his courtship. She would have to forbid him to meet Charlotte at the school, for she did not want her assistant to be hurt.

In the few weeks that she had been in Gold Landing, Laura had come to care deeply for Charlotte, and she wanted to spare her the pain that Roy had dealt her. Oh, there were differences. If Roy's cruelty was black, Sam's was only dark gray. At least Sam was trying to preserve his own inheritance rather than stealing his wife's. And unlike Roy, Sam hadn't lied to Charlotte, deluding her with claims of love. But he was still wrong. So very wrong.

Laura shuddered. Maybe Sam was right. Maybe she was a fool.

"Are you going to the church social, Mrs. Templeton?"

Laura glanced up from the fire that she was stoking. Surely it was only her imagination that Charlotte was looking out the window, as if searching for someone, while she asked the question.

Laura shook her head. Though she had heard the minister announce the date, asking for volunteers to help his wife, and even though Ella had assured her it was the main event of Gold Landing's fall season, Laura knew she would not attend.

"I'm still in mourning," she said. "It wouldn't be proper."

Charlotte returned to the blackboard and began copying today's lessons onto it. "Everyone goes," she told Laura. "You wouldn't have to dance if you didn't want to, but it would give you a good chance to meet all the parents."

Ella had used the same arguments, adding that if Laura wanted to be fully accepted by the town, she should participate in its quarterly social events: the Christmas pageant, Easter breakfast, fall social, and—the biggest gathering of all—the Independence Day celebration. Though Ella had not mentioned it again since Laura had protested her plans to be a matchmaker, Laura knew that the social was considered a good opportunity for unmarried men and women to meet. People who didn't always get into town for church services made a special effort to come to the socials.

Laura closed the stove door and brushed her hands. Today the thought of courtship was more abhorrent than normal. Today it wasn't just her own situation that pained her, but also the thought of Sam and Charlotte's nuptials. Laura wanted to warn her assistant not to be as gullible as she had been; she wanted to protect her, but she could not. For no matter how much she hated what she had heard Sam say, she had promised that she would not tell Charlotte of their conversation. While she might question Sam's sense of honor, she would not renege on a promise. That would be a betrayal of her conscience.

"I'll think about the social," Laura said, although she had no intention of doing so. To change the subject, she picked up her lesson book and handed it to Charlotte. "Would you like to drill the fourth-graders on their multiplication tables?" she asked.

Charlotte's pale blue eyes widened. "Could I?"

Laura smiled. "Of course you can. You've seen me do it enough times that I'm sure you know how. If you want to . . ." If Laura had had any doubts, they were extinguished by the enthusiasm she saw reflected on Charlotte's face. Her eyes sparkled, and her smile transformed her normally plain face into one that was almost beautiful.

It was odd, Laura reflected as she watched Charlotte take her place in front of the classroom an hour later, her face radiant. Never once had Laura seen the younger woman display such pleasure when she spoke to Sam. Perhaps Charlotte was wiser than Laura had been. Perhaps she didn't need Laura's warnings. Perhaps she recognized Sam's insincerity and hadn't been fooled by his smiles and soft words. How Laura hoped that was true!

Other than Charlotte's lesson, the day passed like every other one, falling into the normal pattern. Only one part of the pattern had altered. For the past three days, ever since the night Sam had told her about his reasons for marrying, he had not come into the schoolhouse after the students left. Instead, he would come half an hour later than before, late enough that he would meet Charlotte as she was leaving the school.

Laura bit her bottom lip. It was obvious that Sam was no more anxious to see her than she was to see him. He knew that their meeting would be awkward, and so he was avoiding her. How thoughtful of him. She was glad he no longer came to the schoolhouse. She was glad she had not had to forbid him to meet Charlotte here. She was glad she didn't have to try to make polite conversation with him anymore. Of course she was.

What an infuriating woman! Sam stalked through the mill, trying to vent his anger in the way he knew best, by working. He ran his hand along the side of the freshly cut wood, checking that the saws had been properly sharpened and had left no splinters.

She had a voice like a harpy. When the main saw whined, its pitch rising as one of the workers fed a log through it, Sam shook his head. That wasn't true. Her voice wasn't shrill and ugly like a harpy's. It was clear and sweet. It was only Laura's words that were hateful. Sam nodded his approval of the cleanly split timber. It took skill to slice a tree without binding the saw, particularly when the tree had as many knots as this one.

Laura was wrong. He wasn't cheating Charlotte; he hadn't given her any false expectations or made any promises he didn't intend to keep. If he hadn't been one-hundred-percent honest with her, well . . . that wasn't a crime, no matter what that prim and proper schoolteacher said.

Sam clapped the sawyer on the shoulder. The man was good at his job, just as Sam was. They both liked to do a full day's work and see the results. That was what made this business with Charlotte so frustrating. Though he'd been working at it for weeks—working hard, too—he had yet to see any results. That was going to change today. Today he would take the next step. Yes, indeed. He would talk to Miss Charlotte this afternoon. But he sure as the midnight sun wasn't going to talk to *her*. It would be a hot day in December before he talked to Laura again.

"Have you read the book I gave you?" Sam asked Charlotte as they walked back into Gold Landing. So far, everything had gone according to plan. The weather had cooperated. Though dark clouds still scudded overhead, threatening rain or even snow, the day remained dry. Sam had arrived at the schoolhouse just as Charlotte was leaving, and he'd slowed his pace. Being polite, she hadn't hurried ahead but had matched her steps to his. Normally Sam didn't like to dally, but this way they would have more time to talk. "Did you read the book?" Sam repeated his question.

"Yes." That was good. Sam knew that Charlotte hadn't eaten any of the candy he had given her, and had changed his tactics, giving her a book of poetry that the town's lawyer had recommended. The attorney had told Sam he was mistaken, that a person could never have too many books.

"Did you like it?"

Charlotte continued walking, her eyes fixed on the path in front of them. "Yes," she said. Sam felt a bubble of frustration begin to rise at her curt reply.

"Was there any poem that you liked especially well?" Surely she would take the opportunity he had offered her and discuss the poetry.

"No." Charlotte's boots crunching fallen leaves were louder than her voice.

The bubble of frustration grew. Was the woman incapable of more than a single-word response? Surely she wasn't so taciturn in the schoolroom! Sam tried not to clench his fists. He couldn't let Charlotte see his dismay. That was not the way to woo her. Still, he couldn't help wishing she were more communicative. Laura might have a waspish tongue when she was displeased, but at least she had opinions and wasn't afraid to express them. At least Laura spoke!

As they approached the parsonage, Sam slowed his pace even further. He couldn't let the day end without taking the next step in his courtship. No matter what Laura said or thought, he had to marry Charlotte before February. "I wondered if you would grant me the privilege of escorting you to the church social." The formal words sounded stilted, but Sam had learned etiquette at an early age, and he knew what was expected.

Charlotte let out a small gasp. Surely she was only surprised, not dismayed by his invitation. Her head swiveled, and Sam realized that she was trying to look behind them. She stared for a moment, then returned to staring straight ahead. Not once, to Sam's knowledge, had she looked directly at him since they had left the school.

"I don't know." Her words came out so softly that Sam had to strain to hear them.

The clouds darkened with imminent rain. Sam tried not to groan. If it started to rain, Charlotte would rush indoors without answering him. "Are you going with someone else?" That was the only reason he could imagine for her ambivalence.

Charlotte twisted her hands, and he saw twin spots of color rise to her cheeks. "Er . . . um . . . no," she said at last.

At least he didn't have to surmount that obstacle. Sam knew enough about women to know that most preferred to have a companion for an event like the church social. Charlotte, it appeared, merely needed a little more persuasion.

"It would give me great pleasure to escort you," he said, falling back on the formal speech patterns Hilda had drummed into him. The fact that she had taught him how to conduct himself in society was the only good thing he could say about the woman.

For the first time, Charlotte looked at Sam, her light blue eyes appearing to question his sincerity. She stared at him for a long moment, then said softly, "All right."

Sam suspected martyrs on the way to their deaths showed more enthusiasm.

It was all her fault. Roy Templeton kicked the wall. Nothing had gone right from the day he had met Laura Weaver. She was supposed to have been the answer to his prayers; instead, she had turned into his worst nightmare. Roy winced as his toe connected with the wall. Who would have guessed that those hoity-toity parents of hers would cut her off? The bitch claimed it was because they didn't approve of the marriage, but Roy figured she must have done something to rile them.

Still, what kind of people were they that they wouldn't

relent after he'd done his duty and presented them with grandchildren—two at one time? You'd think they would have appreciated the fact that not many men could have done that. You'd think they would have come to their senses then.

"Pipe down, Templeton," the man in the next cell shouted as Roy let loose a string of curses. Let the old fool complain. Roy sure as hell would remember that when he figured out who he was gonna take with him. He was getting out of here, just the way he got out of Seattle. A man didn't have to wait for an engraved invitation, not if he was smart like Roy. No, sirree. A man like Roy saw the writing on the wall and got out when he could.

It was only bad luck that that rich widow hadn't been willing to part with her money. To this day, Roy didn't understand how the old bag could have been so dumb. He had offered her everything a good-looking, virile man like him had to offer, and she'd turned him down. But she'd let slip how her late husband's bank had payroll deposits delivered regular like clockwork. That was the answer. Roy knew it was. Why waste his time flattering a wrinkled old prune, trying to get a few thousand dollars, when he could collect tens of thousands simply by being in the right place at the right time? Roy kicked the wall again. It was just bad luck that he'd gotten caught. Who could have predicted that they would double their guards that week?

Roy sure didn't like life in prison. Lousy food, lousy clothes, no women, and those mean sons of bitches for guards. Twenty years, the judge had declared before he banged the gavel. Roy knew better. He was leaving. Soon. Real soon.

"Everything's going wrong." Charlotte thrust her hands into her pockets. Though she couldn't forget how good it had felt to have Jason hold her hand, she couldn't let herself be distracted today. Not when she had so much to tell him. They were inside the forest, standing by what she had come to call "their" tree. Though a light rain had begun to fall, the trees would keep them dry for a few minutes. Today, thank goodness, Jason had been waiting when she had left the school, and she'd managed to get away before Mr. Baranov arrived.

"What do you mean?" Jason's gray eyes darkened. "I ain't been in no trouble. I didn't steal no wagon, even if ole Pete said I did." Jason slammed his fist into the tree. "He—heck, Charlotte. The only problem I got is that I can't git a job."

Charlotte pushed her own worries aside. How could she forget, even for a minute, that Jason's lot was worse than hers? "I'll ask my father," she said quickly. "You know he talks to all his parishioners. Maybe he knows of someone who needs a helper."

Though Charlotte saw the quick flare of hope on his face, Jason shook his head. His hair was cleaner today, as if he'd visited the bathhouse. That was a good sign. Surely someone in Gold Landing would hire a young man who was trying to improve himself.

"Your pa ain't gonna help me," Jason said. "He don't like me."

Charlotte pulled her right hand from her pocket and grabbed one of the branches to steady herself. "It's me he doesn't like." And that was only part of the problem.

"What do you mean? Everyone in town knows your pa dotes on you." Jason took a step closer and held out his hand. Though Charlotte wanted nothing more than to give Jason her hand, she didn't dare. What would he say when he heard her news? He might not want to see her ever again, and then what would she do?

The raindrops were falling steadily now. In just a few minutes, she and Jason would have to leave. Charlotte bit her lip, trying to find the right words. There was no easy way to tell him, so she blurted out, "Papa told Mr. Baranov that he could court me." There, it was out in the open.

Charlotte watched as Jason started to curse, then bit back the epithet. He was trying so hard to be someone her parents could like. This just wasn't fair.

Jason's eyes narrowed as he pursed his lips. "You gonna marry him?" he demanded.

Charlotte shook her head and brushed the raindrops away. "I don't want to." Jason's lips started to curve into a grin. "I don't want to marry anyone for a long time," she told him. To her surprise, Jason's grin turned into a frown and he kicked the tree again. Charlotte hated to make Jason unhappy, but he had to know the truth. "You know I want to be a teacher. The only way I can do that is to get trained."

He looked dubious. "You sure you can't do that here? Can't Mrs. Templeton teach you?"

Though the rain continued to fall, Charlotte felt a flicker of warmth deep inside her as she realized that Jason didn't want her to leave Gold Landing. This was almost as wonderful as the first day he had held her hand.

"Maybe," she admitted. "She let me teach one of the classes yesterday, and—oh, Jason—I loved it."

"See?" he said, reaching for her hand a second time. "Not everything's bad. You can figure out a way to teach right here in Gold Landing, and you won't have to marry old Mr. Baranov."

Charlotte managed a little smile. "He does seem old, doesn't he?" She held her hand out to Jason, her smile broadening when he clasped it in his. "But it's not just me who has problems. I'm worried about Mrs. Templeton. She doesn't seem happy anymore, and I don't know why."

Jason squeezed her hand. It felt so good, even through her glove. "Ask her," he suggested.

"I couldn't." Charlotte shook her head for emphasis. "I couldn't pry into her life that way."

"Why not?" Jason began to peel her glove from her hand, his hands fumbling with the buttons. "I asked you what was wrong, didn't I?"

"That was different." With a little cry of impatience, Charlotte pulled off the glove. "You're my friend," she told Jason as she slipped her hand back into his, reveling in the warmth and the sensation of being where she belonged. To Charlotte's surprise, he frowned and muttered something so softly that she couldn't distinguish anything other than the word "more."

He was a fine figure of a man, George Baranov reflected as he stared at himself in the mirror. He parted his hair in the middle, then frowned when he saw a lighter color strand. It wasn't gray. Of course it wasn't gray. It was only the sun bleaching his hair. Just to be safe, he yanked the strand out. Now no one would guess that he was thirty-one, four years younger than the poor bastard he was going to see in less than an hour.

"Ready, precious?" George winced at the sound of his mother's voice. She knew he hated it when she called him that. It reminded him of his childhood, when Hilda had made sure everyone knew who was the preferred Baranov boy. "Why, Nicholas couldn't love him more if he was his own son," Hilda would tell anyone who'd listen. "Precious is much more of a man than Samuel."

"Precious!" Her voice rose. "Are you ready?"

"Yes, Mother," George said, returning the favor.

Hilda Schultz Baranov strode into his room, her heels clicking on the polished floor. "Now, George, I've told you not to call me that," she announced as she brushed a hair from his shoulder. "It makes me sound so old."

The old biddy was ancient, but George wasn't going to be the one to tell her that. Especially not today. "Yes, Hilda," he said, emphasizing her name, "I'm ready to go." He crooked his elbow, placing his mother's hand on his forearm as they descended the front steps. Although the Baranov residence might not be a mansion, it was one of the nicest homes in Seward. George blinked at the bright sunshine. It sure didn't seem right to be going to a funeral on a day like this. "Poor Henry," he muttered as he helped his mother into the buggy. "Who would have guessed that he'd do himself in?"

"Shush." Hilda reached over and laid her fingers on his

lips, the way she had when he was a child. "No one's supposed to talk about that."

George flicked the reins, taking a small measure of pleasure when the abrupt start sent his mother back against the seat. "You're right, of course," he said smoothly. "No one talks about Henry any more than they talk about the suspicious circumstances under which my dear lamented stepfather departed this earth."

George snuck a look at Hilda. As he had expected, her face had paled. "Why, George! What a dreadful thing to say!"

"You didn't think I knew, did you?" His mother had always underestimated him. She hadn't realized just how much a boy could learn by listening at keyholes and poking around in desks. "I reckon old Nicholas must have had his suspicions too. Why else would he have put that clause in his will?" At the time of his stepfather's death, George had been as outraged as his mother at the fact that Nicholas had left the shipping company to Sam. But as the years had passed and he'd grown from adolescence to adulthood, George had developed a grudging respect for the old man. Nicholas had been wily. What the old man hadn't realized was, George was even wilier.

Hilda laid her hand on George's arm again. "In five months, it will all be ours . . . forever and ever."

George turned and faced his mother. "In five months and twelve days," he corrected her, "it will be mine. All mine." And if she thought he would tolerate her interference one hour beyond that, she was mistaken.

Hilda's laugh was not a pretty one. "Unless, of course, dear darling Sam decides to marry."

"He won't."

Chapter Six

It was probably weak of her, Laura reflected as she stepped into her long black skirt. She should have continued to refuse, but the simple truth was, she wanted to attend the church social. She could lie to herself and say that the reason she was going was because the twins would enjoy the evening. They would, but so would she, and it was more for her pleasure than theirs that she had finally acceded to Charlotte's pleas.

Laura fastened the small cameo brooch to her collar, smiling at her reflection in the mirror as she remembered the past week. The children at school had been so excited about the idea of ice cream that she had had difficulty controlling her classes. Henry and Jeremy had engaged in a spirited debate about the flavors that would be offered, despite Charlotte's insistence that there would be nothing more than vanilla. Vanilla, strawberry, or chocolate—the children didn't seem to care. They were looking forward to the treat.

Laura was looking forward to a treat of a different kind—adult companionship. Since Sam had ceased his afternoon visits to the school, she had found herself craving conversation. It was silly, of course. She didn't care that Sam no longer visited. After all, the only reason he had ever come was to court Charlotte. The only reason he had talked to Laura was to avoid silence. It wasn't as though he had enjoyed their bantering any more than she had. And yet . . .

Laura patted her hair, then turned toward the door. Meg and Matt would be waking from their naps in a few minutes, and she needed to finish her preparations before those whirling dervishes rejoined her. When Charlotte had told Laura that Gold Landing's women baked cookies and cakes to accompany the ice cream, Laura had experienced a moment of panic. She could manage to cook a simple dinner, but her prowess as a baker was nonexistent. While Charlotte's concoctions were delectable, Laura's were at best edible. The people of Gold Landing were not in for a treat if she baked.

Under other circumstances, she might not have minded, but Laura hated the thought that her first public event would show her in a less than favorable light. It was too much to hope that no one would sample her offering. Since she was a newcomer, the other residents would consider it common courtesy to try the schoolteacher's food. And then they would know that, no matter what her skills as a teacher might be, she would never win a baking prize at a county fair.

It had been Ella who had provided the answer. "Do you know how to make punch?" she asked one day. Ella's normally neat hair had escaped from the pins, and curls framed her face. The heightened color in her cheeks told Laura she had either been chasing the twins or was distressed about something. Since the twins were asleep and a cookbook lay open on the table, Laura guessed that Ella was concerned about some culinary problem. Surely it couldn't be anything as simple as punch.

Laura nodded in response to Ella's question. Her parents' parties had been famous for their delicious refreshments. While Laura had never been permitted to assist the pastry chef, the cook had allowed her to help mix the punch. She had quickly learned how to add a few spices that turned simple ingredients into a memorable beverage. "It's easy."

Ella shook her head as she frowned at the cookbook. "You'll never convince me of that. Why did I volunteer to make punch this year?"

It took no effort at all to convince Ella that Laura would be pleased—no, delighted—to provide the punch for the social in lieu of baked goods. She had prepared the base earlier today. All that remained was to add the fruit juices at the church hall. Being responsible for the punch solved two problems. Not only did Laura not have to bake, but she was also given a ready-made activity. Rather than mingling with the other guests, she would stand behind the table, ladling punch. That would give her the opportunity to converse with Gold Landing's residents without putting her in the awkward position of having to explain a hundred times why she wasn't dancing. It was the perfect solution.

"Ooooh!" Meg cooed as they entered the hall. Built as an addition to the church, the hall served as one of the town's two primary gathering places. While the church itself was used for town meetings as well as regular services, the adjacent hall was the site of informal gatherings, wedding receptions, and the annual social. Tonight, in keeping with the autumn theme, garlands of brightly colored leaves draped the walls, while the refreshment tables that lined two walls were decorated with dried gourds.

Though Laura had planned to arrive early, Matt had lost his teddy bear and refused to leave the house without it. It had taken Laura half an hour to find the toy, wedged behind the wood box, only a little worse for wear. Judging from the smirk she had seen on Meg's face, Laura suspected her daughter was paying her brother back for having torn her doll's skirt that morning. Children!

Laura looked around the room, surprised by how crowded it was half an hour before the social would officially begin.

The pegs that served as coat hooks in the vestibule were filled, and the sounds of dozens of conversations drowned out the noise of the musicians setting up their stands.

"No, sweetie," Laura said as Meg tried to grab a gourd from one of the tables. "You and Matt are going to play with the other children." Ella had explained that one corner of the room would be reserved for the children and that the mothers who were not serving food would take turns supervising their offspring. Laura bit back a smile at the sight of the short picket fence that marked the children's area. Matt would climb it in a minute, if for no other reason than to challenge the mother in charge.

Laura placed both children in the corral and walked toward the beverage table. It was, she noted with approval, located on the opposite side of the room from the youngsters.

"This is wonderful," Laura said to Amelia Gunning as she joined her and Ella at the beverage table. Ella had agreed to pour coffee for the first hour, and Amelia was helping arrange the silver tea service that her sister had brought from Philadelphia. Both women were dressed in brightly colored gowns, making Laura regret the necessity of wearing black.

It was foolish to wish she had no need for mourning and could don one of the pretty dresses that had once constituted her wardrobe. The only way that would have been possible would be if she had not married Roy. Though she might dream of what her life would be like if he had been different, Laura could not wish she had never met Roy, for without him she would never have had the twins. Mischievous as they sometimes were, Laura would not have traded them for anything on earth.

She gestured toward the children's corral. "Matt and Meg are so excited. They've never seen this many children." Laura added a quart of grape juice to the punch. "The truth is, I don't think I've ever seen so many in one place." She dipped a spoon into the huge bowl and tasted her concoction. This was the first time she had mixed cranberry with the other juices, but in the short time she had lived in Gold Landing, she had become fond of the native cranberries. They added a welcome tartness to the syrup base.

Laura handed Ella another spoonful to taste. When she had nodded her approval, Ella looked down at the table and moved the sugar bowl half an inch to the right.

Laura tried not to smile at Ella's typical behavior. Amelia had no such compunctions. Flashing Laura a conspiratorial smile, as if she had deliberately misaligned the bowl so that Ella would have a reason to straighten it, the young doctor said, "It's wonderful for me, seeing all the children. It seems like only a couple of months since I delivered most of those babies, and now they're walking."

Walking? Laura grinned. Matt was running, and he had half a dozen boys following his example. The poor mother who had drawn the first hour would have her hands full.

The noise level in the room increased as still more people entered the hall, making the center so crowded that Laura wondered how they would ever dance.

"Babies are miracles," Ella said as she moved back behind the table and reached for the coffeepot. "Coffee, Amelia?" she offered.

Amelia shook her head. "I'm waiting for that husband of mine. He promised me the first dance." She looked around. "The real miracle is that we've gotten so many people to come tonight."

The scents of women's perfume and men's tobacco mingled with the sweet smells of cookies and cakes. It could have been an unpleasant mixture, but Laura found it appealing. It smelled real, which was how she thought of Gold Landing. Life here was real. People were genuine. There was no pretense . . . except hers.

"It looks like the whole town is here." Laura's eyes scanned the room. She was only helping Amelia look for William. She wasn't looking for anyone else, most definitely not a tall, dark-haired man with brown eyes, a mustache, and a bad temper. No, she most definitely did not want to see Sam Baranov.

"I don't see Mrs. Kane." Ella poured a cup of coffee for one of the men, while Laura ladled punch for his wife.

As the musicians began to tune their instruments, Amelia frowned, obviously perturbed by William's absence. "Is Vera Kane the woman who reported a theft the day I arrived?" Laura asked. She didn't particularly care about the woman, but she wanted to take Amelia's mind off the fact that she was going to miss the first dance.

"Yes." Ella thrust a cup of coffee into her friend's hand. As Amelia began to sip it, Ella said, "Oh, there she is. Vera's next to the mayor."

The sound Amelia made might have been a sniff of amusement. The musicians' tuning stopped, and they launched the first dance of the evening.

"What about the boy she accused?" Laura asked.

As couples began to whirl around the center of the room, Amelia raised one eyebrow. "Jason Blake?" she asked. "I doubt he'd come tonight." A frown crossed her lovely face, and Laura knew it was caused by more than William's absence. "It's such a sad case," she said. "There are so many children in that family that they leave Jason on his own. It's no wonder he turns to mischief. William and I've speculated that he needs something to occupy his time."

Laura's eyes moved from her friends to the dancers. She recognized many of the couples. Reverend and Mrs. Langdon, the mayor and Mrs. Kane, Sam and Charlotte. As her heart lurched, Laura turned her attention back to Amelia. She wouldn't think about what it might feel like, dancing with a man again. She absolutely would not think about dancing with Sam. Or looking up into his eyes. Or laughing when he said something funny.

"What about school?" Laura forced her thoughts back to Jason Blake. Though she didn't remember the young thief clearly, she thought he was of school age.

Ella shook her head. "I tried to convince him to come, but he refused. I think he'd be self-conscious, being older than most of the other students."

The dance floor was as crowded as Laura had feared. She saw couples bump into each other, and one woman wince when a man's foot landed on hers. Still, judging from the smiles she saw, no one seemed to mind.

The song was half over when Amelia's face began to glow. "William," she said as her husband approached the refreshment tables. "I missed you." She laid her half-filled cup on the table and extended her hand.

William took his wife's hand in his and smiled at her, his face as radiant as Amelia's. For a second, Laura was consumed with an unfamiliar emotion. It couldn't be jealousy. Surely she didn't begrudge Amelia and William their happiness. Of course she didn't. They were her friends, two wonderful people who deserved every minute of the joy they had discovered together. Still, Laura wished that once—just once—someone would look at her that way, as if she were the most beautiful, most precious object on earth.

"I'm sorry I was late," William said. Though he had smiled at Ella and her, Laura knew that only good manners had produced those polite smiles. William's attention was clearly focused on his wife. "Ben needed some help," he continued. "Is your dance card filled, or may I have the next one?"

Amelia nodded. "Of course. Now, go talk to the mayor or whoever it is Ben wants you to charm. I'll be here waiting for you."

William raised one brow. "How did you know?"

Amelia's smile included Laura and Ella. "We women have our ways." When William had moved into the crowd, Amelia said, "William likes to champion causes."

Though she had not meant to introduce the topic tonight, the opening was too good to miss. Laura looked from Amelia to Ella. "I have a cause of my own. I've been thinking about holding special classes in the evening," she confided to her friends. Since the music was winding down, Laura spoke quickly. "They would be designed for people who can't come during the day—adults one night, maybe the Athapaskan children another."

There was no disguising the dismay that crossed Ella's face. "Don't do that, Laura. Not the Indians." She touched her stomach in the protective gesture Laura had noticed she used when she was distressed.

Amelia laid her hand on Laura's arm. "You know I love this town," she said, her sapphire eyes serious, "but I can't advise you to use the school for classes like that. It's too risky. You'd be stirring up emotions that are best left alone." Amelia's words did not surprise Laura. She had heard of the resistance Amelia had faced when she had started treating Indian patients and the way someone had burned her clinic to the ground. Still, the thought of the children she had seen on the other side of the river going without schooling of any kind disturbed Laura. It was bad enough that they lived in poverty. She might not be able to change that, but she could offer them the opportunity to learn.

"It's important," she said.

"I know." Amelia squeezed Laura's arm. "Believe me, I know. I'm not disputing the need for education, only the use of the school." From the brief expression of pain that she saw on Amelia's face, Laura guessed that she was thinking about her clinic. "Have you considered teaching in their village? The children would be more comfortable there."

Laura nodded. That had been one of the first options she had evaluated. "The problem is, there's no suitable place. There aren't any empty wickiups."

"Good evening, ladies. Dancing surely gives a man a thirst."

Laura started so violently that she knocked her hand against the punch bowl, setting the liquid to sloshing. Though she had been vaguely aware that the music had ended, she had not heard Sam approach. She stared at him, then dropped her eyes in confusion. It was odd how her memory had deceived her. He was taller than she remembered, his face more finely chiseled than her recollection. What she had not forgotten was the warmth of his smile, a smile that was now directed at Ella.

"No, thank you, ma'am," he said with another smile when Ella reached for a coffee cup. "Miss Charlotte and I would prefer punch." He accepted the two cups from Laura with a polite acknowledgment, then made his way back onto the dance floor. Laura clenched the ladle. Not once had Sam's eyes met hers. It didn't matter. Of course it didn't matter. What mattered was a place to teach the Athapaskan children.

"What about an addition to my house?" Laura suggested. From the corner of her eye, she saw William moving toward the beverage table. "Would anyone object to that?"

Amelia shook her head. "I don't think so." As the musicians reached for their instruments, Amelia winked at her husband. His pace increased, and Laura wondered how many feet he was trampling on his way to Amelia. "Sam would be the man to build the addition," Amelia said. "The only problem is, it's too late now. You'll need to wait until next summer."

As couples gathered in the middle of the floor, Laura looked around, noting who was partnered with whom. On the other side of the room, Charlotte stood close to Sam, her face intent on something he was saying. Laura's gaze moved quickly to the next couple.

"It looks like Sam is courting Charlotte," Ella said.

Though Amelia's eyes were focused on William, she was obviously listening to the conversation. "So that's why he goes to the schoolhouse every afternoon. Half a dozen patients have asked me about it."

Laura was surprised. Though she knew how quickly word spread in a small town, she hadn't realized that Sam's visits were the subject of gossip.

"Of course that's why he comes," she said. "What other reason would there be?"

Amelia slid an arm through her husband's crooked elbow. "It could be you he's courting," she said, and glided onto the dance floor without so much as a backward glance.

"That's absurd!" Laura felt the blood rush to her face at

the mere thought of her name being linked with Sam's.

"Why?" Ella took a sip of coffee. "Why wouldn't Sam be interested? You're young, you're attractive, and you need a husband."

The color drained from Laura's face. "A husband is one thing I don't need!" she declared. *I already have one.*

"You're looking very pretty tonight," Sam told Charlotte as they whirled across the floor. She was looking prettier than usual, a slight flush coloring those normally pale cheeks. Her dress was some sort of soft fabric that swished as they danced, the light pink a pleasant change from her sober daytime clothes. His bride-to-be was pretty, all right. If she wasn't as pretty as Laura, well . . . a man ought not be thinking about Laura Templeton anyway. He ought not to be looking in that direction, and he most certainly ought not be thinking about how that black dress made her hair look like moonlight and how those eyes sparkled more than the sea.

"Thank you." As Charlotte flushed slightly at his compliment, Sam resolved to give her more of them. It appeared that, whatever else the Langdons had done while raising her, they had not lavished compliments on their daughter.

The steps of the dance took them toward the perimeter of the room. Sam nodded a greeting to several acquaintances, watching the speculative glint in the women's eyes when they saw him with Charlotte. It was time the people of Gold Landing realized that he was courting her. They would all be invited to the wedding, so they might as well get used to the idea.

As they passed the room's sole window, Sam thought he saw a face peering through it. Nonsense. It must have been a reflection. The majority of Gold Landing's residents were already inside the hall, and those who hadn't come would have no reason to stand outside.

"It's a pleasure dancing with you," Sam said, acting on his resolution to praise Charlotte more often. The truth was, he wasn't overly fond of dancing, especially when the room was this crowded, but he knew ladies liked to dance.

Charlotte made a moue. "Please don't insult me," she said. "I know I don't dance well."

It was, Sam realized, not just the truth. It was also the longest sentence she had ever spoken to him. Perhaps this complimenting business was working. Maybe that, and not books or candy, was the way to reach Charlotte.

"Would you prefer to sit?" he asked. A row of chairs lined one side of the room. Sam hadn't thought anyone would choose to sit there, but if there was one thing he knew, it was that you couldn't predict what Charlotte would like.

"No." She shook her head and gave him a little smile. "My mother expects me to dance," she explained.

A woman bumped Charlotte, then apologized profusely. Sam was thankful when she moved away, because her perfume reminded him of a particularly nasty medicine Hilda had once forced down his throat.

"Do you always do what your mother expects?" If anyone had asked him, he would have said that Charlotte Langdon was a dutiful daughter.

She shook her head again, and this time the smile broadened. "Not always. That's why it's important for me to do something Mother wants."

Sam matched her smile. She was talking! Charlotte was really talking to him. Maybe this was the beginning of a new phase of his courtship. Maybe Charlotte liked him. And maybe, just maybe, one of the things she would do to please her mother was to marry him. It looked as if the fates had started shining on Sam Baranov.

A man tapped his shoulder. "May I cut in?"

Sam frowned. Not now. Not when Charlotte had finally started talking to him. But the man was William, and Sam knew better than to deny a friend.

"Only if I may dance with your wife." Amelia stood next to her husband. She was beautiful, almost as beautiful as Laura. Sam tried not to frown at the directions his thoughts had taken. Charlotte was the woman he wanted to marry.

She was the only woman he should be thinking about.

As Amelia moved into Sam's arms, William led Charlotte in the opposite direction. "This is a real pleasure," Sam said a minute later. No doubt about it, Amelia Gunning was a far better dancer than Charlotte.

As if she could read his thoughts, Amelia said, "Charlotte will learn. She's probably like Ella and didn't have much practice as a child." Ella, who had abandoned her position at the beverage table, was dancing with her husband. No one watching them would have thought that two years earlier, she had refused to set foot on a dance floor.

"What changed Ella?" Sam asked.

"The love of a good man."

Love! Why did people keep bringing up that word? Did every woman in Gold Landing think that that mythical state actually existed?

Sam managed a short laugh. "I thought you would have said she took dancing lessons."

"She did." Amelia smiled. "From Ben. But I don't want to talk about Ella's dancing. I asked William to cut in so I could dance with you."

Sam didn't bother to mask his surprise. He had thought that William, for some reason, wanted to partner Charlotte. "Really? I'm flattered. I hadn't realized I was reputed to be such a good dancer."

Amelia tapped her fingers on his shoulder and laughed. "You're not. I'm thankful you're not crushing my toes. The truth is, Sam, I need your advice."

Sam twirled them closer to the wall so that fewer people would overhear her question. Whatever it was Amelia wanted to know didn't need to be broadcast through Gold Landing. When she spoke, her question surprised him. "Is it possible to add another room to Laura's cabin before next summer?"

"Laura Templeton? Why does she need another room?" A sinking feeling filled his stomach, making Sam regret the punch he had drunk. Was Laura marrying again? Was that why she wanted an extra room? It didn't matter. Laura Templeton could do anything she wanted. He didn't care. Not one whit. And he would not, absolutely would not picture her in another man's arms.

"She's looking for a second schoolroom." As the words registered, Sam began to relax. She wasn't marrying. He almost missed the rest of Amelia's explanation. "Laura wants to teach adults at night and possibly the Indian children. So, Sam, can you do it?"

He took a deep breath before he replied. "You know I like earning an extra buck as much as the next man, but it's not a good idea."

"Building now or the school itself?"

Knowing what had happened to Amelia's clinic, Sam understood her question. "The timing," he said. He was back on firm ground now that he knew why Laura wanted the extra space. "I can provide the lumber, but I don't have all the other materials I would need. Besides, it's awfully cold to get men to work now."

As the song reached its final refrain, Amelia admitted, "I was afraid you'd say that. Still, it was worth asking. You can't blame me for trying."

Sam nodded. He knew all about trying. He had spent his childhood trying to please his father, to not displease Hilda, and to stay out of George's way. Now he was trying to woo Charlotte at the same time that he was trying his best not to miss his conversations with Laura. And as he drew Charlotte back into his arms for another dance, he tried not to think how it would feel to hold Laura.

She was scared. Charlotte could feel the blood pound as she slid her arms into her coat sleeves. Her fingers fumbled when she tried to fasten the buttons, and her mouth was dry with apprehension. She was seventeen years old, and she had never ever done anything like this. It was wicked and wrong and she shouldn't have even considered it. But there was no way she could have refused.

She snuck out the back door, moving carefully, lest the sound of her boots reveal the fact that she was leaving the parsonage in the middle of the night. Her parents would be angry. More than that, they would be disappointed. But if she didn't go, Jason would be hurt.

She moved stealthily, keeping inside the shadows. It was only when she had reached the edge of town that she began to run. No one would hear her here.

"You came!" Jason's voice was filled with wonder. He stood on the perimeter of the forest that bordered this side of Gold Landing.

"What's wrong?" Charlotte pressed her hand on her breast, trying to slow the pounding of her heart. She wasn't sure what had caused it to race most—running or Jason's message. "I was so scared when I got your message." Somehow, he had managed to slip a piece of paper inside her coat pocket while she was at the church social. The crudely printed words had alarmed her more than the thought of her parents' anger if they discovered she was gone. "What happened?"

Jason reached for her hand. As he gripped it between both of his, holding it so tightly that she winced, he said, "I had to see you. I couldn't wait until Monday."

"What's wrong?" Charlotte couldn't imagine why Jason was so upset.

"I saw you dancing with Sam Baranov."

For a second, Charlotte wondered how Jason had seen them. Then she remembered dancing near the window and thinking that she had seen a face peering inside. It had disappeared so quickly that she had dismissed the image as nothing more than her imagination.

"I had to dance with him. You know that."

"That doesn't mean I have to like it." Jason's voice was low, but so fierce that Charlotte almost recoiled. This wasn't the Jason she knew. That Jason was her friend. This Jason was a stranger.

"You could have come to the social, too," she told him.

"Sure!" In the moonlight, she could see his upper lip curl

in disgust. "I wouldn't have been welcome. You know that."

Charlotte heard the pain in Jason's voice, and she felt an echoing pain in her heart. Her parents weren't perfect, but at least she knew they loved her. All of Gold Landing knew that Jason's parents rarely acknowledged his existence. Whatever love they had was given to their younger children. "I would have welcomed you," she said. "I would have danced with you."

"Sure you would have. And what would your parents have said?"

Squeezing Jason's hand, Charlotte said steadily, "It doesn't matter. You're my friend, Jason."

He was silent for a moment, as if trying to decide whether to believe her. Then he stared at her for a moment longer. "If you're my friend, will you dance with me?"

Charlotte looked around. "Here?"

"Why not?"

There was plenty of room. Even if they stayed within the forest, they would have more room than she and Sam had had when they were surrounded by other dancers. Still . . . no one Charlotte knew had ever danced in a forest. Her parents would be scandalized if they learned of it.

"There's no music," she said.

"I can hum a tune," he countered. "Please, Charlotte." He released her hand and took a step backward, waiting for her answer.

This was Jason, her friend. So what if it was unconventional?

"Please, Charlotte." She heard the plea in his voice and knew that he was asking for more than a dance. Jason sought the approval he lacked at home.

"Yes." She nodded and moved into his arms.

Their coats were bulky, their boots ill designed for dancing. The forest floor was covered with pine needles; tree roots threatened to trip them. Neither one of them had taken dancing lessons, and so their movements were awkward. And yet, as they moved together, Charlotte knew that there had never been such a wonderful dance. Jason's arm circled her waist, making her feel protected. Her hand rested on his shoulder, the other was clasped in his. If they stumbled occasionally, if their steps were less than perfect, she didn't care. What mattered was that they were together.

If only the dance would never end!

Chapter Seven

If luck was a lady, she sure as the northern lights was a fickle one. Sam leaned forward, studying the cards in his hand. Not a single face card all night. At least none that he remembered. It wasn't his night. Hell, it wasn't his month. The little progress he had thought he had made with Charlotte the night of the church social had evaporated, and she had reverted to her monosyllabic replies to his questions. She was a very cold woman.

Sam tried not to think what it would be like, sharing a house with her, facing that mildly disapproving look across the breakfast table every morning. As for sharing a bed with a woman who plainly held him in no high regard . . . there were things a man shouldn't consider too closely, especially when the alternative was so much worse. Sam frowned and tossed a card onto the table.

"We lost him again." Ben pushed his glasses back onto his nose, frowning. The poker game was at his house tonight. Sam had almost laughed at the way Ben bustled around the kitchen, making sure they scraped the mud off their boots and serving nothing stronger than coffee. Marriage sure had changed Ben Taylor. It was almost enough to make Sam reconsider. Almost.

On the other side of the table, William shrugged. "If I didn't know better," he told his friend, "I'd say he was lovestruck. But we both know that's impossible. Sam's courtship is a business arrangement."

Idly, Ben picked up a stack of chips and began shuffling them. The loud clinking of ivory was one of the more annoying sounds Sam had heard.

"Maybe that's it," Ben said when he had plunked the chips back onto the table. "Maybe Sam doesn't like his business arrangement." He laughed. "Serves him right for not listening to us. We told him we'd help."

Sam gritted his teeth. "Would you two stop acting like I'm deaf!" For Pete's sake, they were supposed to be his friends. They had no call to be treating him that way.

"Sure we will," William said, his voice so calm that Sam had to force himself not to smash his fist into William's face. "We'd do that, if you were really here. I tell you, Sam, I've never known you to play so badly."

"It's like it's the first time you played poker." Ben continued the explanation. "We might as well have been playing with one of your logs."

Sam looked across the table at Alex Fielding, daring him to concur with the others. Alex wisely said nothing, but kept his eyes fixed on the table.

"I guess I've been a little preoccupied," Sam admitted. These were his friends, after all. There were some things he could tell them.

"A little!" William scoffed. "At times I swear you just disappear. Your body's sitting there, but it's an empty shell."

That was odd. The last word Sam would have used to describe himself was empty. That would have been infinitely better than what he had felt for the past month. He had not felt empty, not at all. Instead, he had been filled with a regret so deep it was almost physical.

"So, what's wrong?" Ben asked.

"Nothing." The more Sam thought about it, the worse the idea of telling them anything seemed. They'd either laugh or—worse yet—offer him advice he didn't want.

"C'mon, Sam, we know you." William leaned back in his chair, as if he thought the extra distance would relax Sam. These days, nothing was going to relax him. Nothing short of a minor miracle. "What's wrong?"

"I already told you. Nothing." Other than the fact that his days had seemed pointless ever since he had stopped going into the schoolhouse and his nights had been filled with agonizing dreams of lost treasures. It was ridiculous, missing his conversations with Laura. He was a grown man, the owner of a successful business. His days were filled with important activities. There was no reason to feel that something was missing. Besides, Laura wasn't what was bothering him. Laura wasn't the reason he would wake in the middle of the night. She wasn't the treasure he kept losing. It was Charlotte who haunted his thoughts. Charlotte was the faceless woman he pursued in his dreams. All that mattered was making Charlotte his wife. That was all.

"What's wrong?" he said. "Everything!"

It was a beautiful October morning. Though the sun was late to rise, reminding her that the long Alaskan winter had begun, the newly fallen snow squeaked beneath her feet, and the sky above was clear. It was the kind of day Laura had always loved, when the world felt fresh and new and everything was possible. It was the kind of day when she should be singing, or at least humming a happy tune as she walked to school. There was absolutely no reason she should feel like crying.

Laura hadn't cried in years, not since the day Roy had left and her dreams had died. She wasn't going to cry now. There was no reason for it. She loved Alaska. She loved teaching. She had two beautiful children and an enthusiastic teacher's aide. She had many friends in Gold Landing, and if she had one fewer than she'd had a month ago, that was hardly cause for tears. Her life was under control. Everything was fine.

An hour later, when a student had spilled a bottle of ink and another had swallowed a piece of chalk, Laura had to force herself not to cringe. Mishaps like these were common occurrences. There was no reason to assign them any undue importance. "Would you like to teach the fourth class arithmetic?" she asked Charlotte. A bright smile told Laura how much her assistant enjoyed teaching.

Laura took a seat in the back of the schoolroom, watching Charlotte's normally pale face flush with pleasure as she began the lesson. The young woman was a born teacher. As Laura looked at the pupils' rapt attention to Charlotte, she wondered whether she should speak to Reverend and Mrs. Langdon, adding her recommendation to Charlotte's pleas that she attend normal school. *No*, Laura told herself. She would not meddle in others' lives. She had enough trouble with her own.

As the image of a tall man with dark brown hair and a mustache that looked as soft as silk flashed before her, Laura clenched her fists. The man was despicable. Only a foolish woman would entertain thoughts of him, and Laura Templeton was not a foolish woman. She would banish every thought of Sam Baranov from her mind.

A second later she jumped to her feet. "Stop it this instant!" she shouted as Jeremy began to tug Mary's pigtails. "Jeremy Caldwell, take your slate and sit in the corner." Drawing herself up to her full five feet two inches, Laura pointed to the corner that her students dreaded, the one where their every movement could be seen and scrutinized by the entire class. "I want you to write a hundred times, 'A gentleman does not pull a lady's hair.' "

"But she's just a girl," Jeremy protested.

"Jeremy!" Laura's tone brooked no further disagreement. "You will now write it a hundred fifty times."

As Jeremy slunk to the corner, the classroom was silent, the only sound Charlotte's gasp. Laura gave her assistant a quelling look. How dare she criticize her actions. As Charlotte continued drilling the students in their multiplication tables, Laura noticed that several pupils darted glances in her direction but did not meet her gaze? A few wore perplexed expressions. Laura ignored them all. *She* was the teacher.

When the pupils had been dismissed for recess, Charlotte moved to Laura's side. "Is something wrong?" she asked quietly as she took the seat next to Laura.

Though the white-hot anger that had erupted deep within Laura had begun to subside, embers remained. "Of course something is wrong." She managed a smile to soften her words. "Jeremy knows better than to pull Mary's hair."

For a moment the only sound was the crackling of the stove. Then Charlotte shook her head slowly. "I've never heard you shout at the children before, and we both know Jeremy pulls someone's hair almost every day."

It was foolish to deny the obvious. "You're right. I must be more tired than I realized." The mirror had confirmed the deep circles under Laura's eyes.

A look of sympathy crossed Charlotte's face. "Were the twins awake last night?"

It would be easy to blame her mood on the children, but Laura wouldn't lie. At least not about that. "No," she admitted. "I just didn't sleep well." And not just last night. For a month she had lain awake, thinking about the new schoolroom, about Sam Baranov's expression the day they had argued, about the adults she wanted to teach, about the way Sam had held Charlotte while they danced, about the Indians she hoped to encourage to attend school, about how empty her afternoons seemed now that Sam no longer filled them with his laughter, about how his smile had warmed her more than a roaring fire, about how infuriating he could be. But of course, Laura said none of that to Charlotte. "It must have been something I ate," she lied.

Charlotte seemed to accept the explanation. She nodded, then turned toward the window. When she turned back, Laura saw the same pained expression that had been on

Charlotte's face so often in the past few weeks. "What about you, Charlotte? Is anything wrong?"

The strand of hair that had escaped Charlotte's pompadour bounced against her cheek as she shook her head. "No. Nothing."

She was lying, but Laura was hardly the one to challenge her. Not today.

No one had ever called him a coward. Still, Sam had to admit that coming here today was more difficult than he would have guessed. Though he forced his feet to keep moving, his pace had slackened. This was ridiculous! What was the worst she could do? She wouldn't berate him or lock him in a coffin. The absolute worst was that she would refuse his offer. And if she did, he would be no worse off than he was now. With a firm step that belied his inner turmoil, Sam walked up her front walk and knocked on the door.

"Good evening." Though her voice was low and polite, she did not manage to hide her surprise. It was no more than Sam had expected. She was probably remembering the last time he had come here. He knew he was.

"Good evening, Laura." She hadn't slammed the door in his face. That was a good sign. "I heard you have a problem."

She flushed as if he had touched a sensitive spot. "I am perfectly capable of taking care of the children," she declared.

"Of course you're capable," he told her. Sam wondered why she was so defensive. Had one of the parents questioned her abilities as a teacher? With an effort, Sam kept his hand from fisting. If he knew who had insulted her, he'd rearrange his face. "I'd like to talk to you for a minute. Why don't you get your coat?" The night was too cold for her to stand in an open doorway, and Sam wouldn't flout propriety by asking to enter her house.

For a second he thought she would refuse. Then she nodded. A minute later she emerged, a heavy woolen cloak covering her black dress, a scarf hiding most of her bright hair. Nothing could hide the rigid set of her shoulders. Laura, Sam saw, was as ill at ease as he. She was wrong, of course, in condemning his reasons for marriage, but tonight that didn't matter. That was Sam's problem. He would deal with it. What mattered now was solving Laura's dilemma.

"I heard you had a problem with the location."

"The location?" She looked as if his words needed translation.

Sam leaned against the front porch pillar. Maybe if he made a conscious effort to relax, some of the tension that she was unable to hide would dissipate. It wasn't as if he harbored any special feelings for her. He would have done the same for any of his business associates. That's all that Laura was, or what she would be if she agreed to his plan.

He took a deep breath, exhaling slowly to relieve his own tension. "Amelia said you wanted to build an addition to your cabin. Something about teaching at night."

Laura nodded, and in the moonlight, he could see the sadness in those lovely turquoise eyes. Sam felt a wrenching pain deep inside him. How he wished he could banish her sadness! He swallowed, startled by the thought. It wasn't personal, of course. He would have felt that way about anyone. "I understand that it's too late," she said.

"That's true. I wouldn't want to build this late in the year. That's why I'm here." She looked at him, curiosity beginning to replace the regret. The cold lump that had settled in Sam's stomach on the walk to Laura's cabin began to shrink. "I figured you wouldn't want to lose a whole season of teaching."

At this time of the night, the street was silent. A few lazy snowflakes drifted to the ground, and an occasional cloud obscured the moon. It was a tranquil night, or it would be if Laura agreed to his proposal.

She nodded. Perhaps it was only his imagination that she seemed less tense than when he'd first arrived. "I'd hate to wait until next year," she said. "Some people learn quickly. They would be able to catch up, but not everyone can do that." When she clasped her hands in front of her, Sam wasn't sure whether she was cold or whether it was an unconscious gesture of supplication. "I wish I could use the schoolhouse."

"But you can't. At least not for the Indians. That's why I came." Sam wasn't going to admit how many sleepless hours he had spent pacing his bedroom floor, trying to find the right answer, or how many logs he had planed while he mulled over options. He wasn't doing it for her, of course. He was doing it for the children.

Though he had lived in Gold Landing for years, Sam had never thought about the number of boys who had gone to work in the mine rather than attending school, or the fact that not a single one of the Indian children had had a day's formal education. The problems weren't new. It was only Laura Templeton who had made him see them. And once she had done that, there was no turning back.

He thought about those children and what it must be like, not knowing how to read. George had always taunted Sam because he enjoyed reading. Books were for girls, George had declared. But Sam knew differently. Books were for everyone, and he couldn't imagine a world without them. What George and Hilda never knew was that those books they had disdained so vocally had helped Sam escape from the reality of life in the Baranov household to worlds where people were happy and justice prevailed.

"What are you suggesting?" Laura asked. This time there was no mistaking the interest and warmth in her voice.

Sam moved forward a pace. When she did not move backward, the lump in Sam's stomach shrank a bit more. Surely this was a good sign. "It's a slow time at the mill, and my office is good-sized," he told her. Though he had searched for other solutions, he kept returning to this one. "I could turn half of the office into a classroom for you. I could even build a wall, so you'd have a separate room."

Those lovely eyes that had haunted more dreams than he would ever admit widened with surprise. "You'd do that for me, even after—"

"I'm doing it for the children and the others," Sam said, interrupting her before she could flay his hide again. They had both said a lot of things that night that he had no desire to relive. This had nothing to do with that night. She had to understand that. "Learning is important," he said firmly.

This time it was Laura who took a step forward, helping to bridge the distance between them. The remainder of the lump in Sam's stomach vanished as she smiled that sweet smile that made her face even more beautiful than normal. Sam caught his breath, fighting the urge to touch her lips, to see if they were as soft as they looked.

"That's very generous of you," she said with another smile.

Sam looked down. He didn't want her to get the wrong idea. It wasn't as if he was doing this so that he'd have a reason to see her every day. It wasn't as if he was looking forward to hearing her voice, or as if he planned to make the wall thin enough that he could listen without appearing to. This was all for the children.

"I'd like to think that it'll be good business," he said. "Folks will hear about how I'm helping others, and maybe that'll get them thinking about the sawmill and how they could use a new room or a shed or something else." Sam had heard his father talk about community relations. That was what this was, not an effort to help Laura Templeton.

She was silent for a moment, emotions flitting across her face. Sam saw pleasure, anticipation, and then something else, something darker.

"I haven't changed my mind about your courtship of Charlotte," she said at last.

So that was what was bothering her. "I didn't expect you to. This is separate. Like I said, learning is important."

Laura's blue eyes met his, and he could feel her gaze boring into his, as if she was trying to assure herself of his sincerity. When she spoke, her voice was warm. "Thank you, Sam." She extended her hand to him.

There was a spring in Sam's step as he headed home, and

his heart felt lighter than it had in weeks. Perhaps his luck had just changed.

"I hope you don't mind that I brought the twins with me." Sam looked up, surprised to see the children gripping Laura's hands. The boy stared at Sam, his eyes wide with curiosity, while the girl buried her head in Laura's skirt. Sam tried not to cringe at the thought of the mess two young children would make in his office. Why had Laura brought them? He and Laura had arranged that she would come to the mill this afternoon to see the office and decide where she wanted the chairs and tables placed. Surely she didn't think she needed the twins as chaperones.

"Ella was indisposed," Laura explained, "and Charlotte wasn't available."

Sam nodded, oddly pleased that she hadn't been anxious to bring her children. "I'm afraid I don't have any toys here," he said.

Laura patted the cloth sack that hung over her arm. "I brought some books. Matt and Meg will sit quietly with them for a few minutes. That should give us enough time to work out the arrangements." She looked around the office, and Sam wondered what she was thinking. Was she expecting something more elaborate? For Pete's sake, it was an office, not a parlor. It was functional; that was what an office was supposed to be. He had a desk, a file cabinet, and two chairs for visitors. What more could she want? Sam sure as summer sun wasn't going to fill the corners with potted plants and doodads.

"This is very nice." Laura's smile appeared genuine. "Come here, Matt." The boy was fingering the beading on the edge of the desktop. Ben had told Sam it was unnecessary trim and that he shouldn't have wasted his time. Seeing Matt's pleasure, Sam was glad he'd added the finishing touch.

Laura settled her children in one corner, handing each a book. "I expect you to stay here until I come back." Two faces regarded her somberly, then nodded. As they bent their heads over the books, Sam saw them grin at each other, and wondered how long they would remain in the corner. He might not have children of his own, but Sam knew a mischievous look when he saw it.

"Aren't they too young to read?" he asked.

Laura nodded. "There are some pictures in the books, and they pretend to read the words. They see me reading so often that they want to do it."

The twins were turning pages so rapidly that Sam doubted they were even looking at the pictures. "Is that the teacher or the mother in you, setting an example?" he asked.

She shrugged. "Both, probably. Did your mother read to you?"

Sam guided Laura toward the other side of the room. "I don't know." He had a vague memory of sitting on her lap. Though he could no longer conjure her face, he remembered that she smelled nice and spoke softly. Had she been reading to him? Sam wasn't sure. "She died when I was five," he said.

Sam heard Laura's sharp intake of breath. "I don't know what to say, Sam. 'Sorry' seems inadequate."

It was odd how her words touched parts of his heart he hadn't known existed. Sam hadn't been looking for sympathy when he'd told Laura of his mother's death. It was a fact, part of his life, just like the fact that he now owned a sawmill. But hearing the concern in Laura's voice had lit a tiny flame. "That was a long time ago," Sam said, surprised at how gruff his voice sounded. Clearing his throat, lest she guess how she had affected him, he changed the subject. "Now, here's where I thought I'd put the wall."

For a few minutes, Sam and Laura conferred about the number of chairs and tables—for they both agreed that older students would prefer chairs and tables rather than desks—and the placement of the blackboard. Then he heard a soft rustling.

Laura spun around, biting back what Sam guessed was an instinctive smile and forcing a firm expression onto her face. "No, sweetie," she said as she picked up her son, who had been creeping toward his mother. "You need to stay with Meg and read your books." She deposited him back in the corner, pressed a kiss on his blond head, then bestowed another on her daughter's. "Just a few minutes more."

Sam watched in amazement. She was unlike any mother he had ever known. If love existed—and it would take more than this to convince him that it did—Laura loved the twins. He had never seen a woman act that way with her children. It was for certain Hilda had never treated him like that. Sam had been the recipient of curses and slaps, while George had been given kisses and hugs. Even so, Sam reflected, Hilda had never looked at George with the expression he had seen on Laura's face.

The flame inside Sam grew. Laura was different. He hadn't realized that when he had first met her, but now he knew that she would never treat a child—anyone's child—the way Hilda had treated him.

Clearing his throat again, he turned to Laura. "How many chairs would you like?"

"I'm worried." Charlotte curled her toes inside her boots, trying to warm them. Her parents would be furious if they learned how much time she spent in the forest each afternoon. It was foolish, they would say. How could she be so silly as to stay outside when the snow was falling? But how could she not meet Jason? The moments that they stole to be together were the happiest, the most exciting part of her days.

"What's wrong?" Jason's gray eyes met hers, and she saw worry reflected in them. "Didn't your parents listen when you said you didn't want to marry Sam Baranov?"

As Charlotte felt the color begin to rise in her cheeks, she dropped her gaze. "I didn't tell them," she mumbled.

Jason's boots crunched on the snow as he took a step toward her. "Why not?" he demanded.

Charlotte hung her head. She had promised she would talk to her parents. One night, she had even started to introduce the subject at dinner, but then she had stopped. "I couldn't," she told Jason. "I can't disappoint them."

She hated hurting people. The problem was, someone was going to be disappointed, and that made her miserable. If she didn't marry Sam, her parents would be hurt. If she did, Jason . . . Though he had never said it in so many words, Charlotte thought Jason would be sorry if she married Sam. She hoped he cared enough for her that it mattered that she might marry another.

Charlotte stared at a tree branch as she tried to find the words to make Jason understand.

"Look at me, Charlotte."

She did. His expression was angrier than she had ever seen it. Charlotte swallowed. This was worse than she had dreamed. He didn't care; he was simply angry.

Jason reached for her hand and squeezed it so tightly that she winced. "You can't marry Sam," he declared, his voice fierce. Charlotte's heart skipped a beat. Jason's anger wasn't directed at her after all. She hadn't been mistaken. He did care. "I won't let you marry Sam."

"I won't." Charlotte felt as if a huge weight had been lifted. Jason cared about her. He did! He didn't want her to marry Sam. Now that Jason had said the words she wanted to hear, Charlotte's course was clear. She wouldn't marry Sam, no matter what her parents said. She wasn't sure what she would say or do, but she would find a way to avoid the marriage.

Maybe Mrs. Templeton could help her. But that brought Charlotte full circle. "I'm worried about Mrs. Templeton," she told Jason. "She's been so short-tempered lately. Something's wrong, and I don't know what it is."

A hank of hair fell over Jason's temple as he shook his head. For a second, Charlotte wondered what it would feel like to brush his hair back. She tugged her hand from Jason's and raised it toward his head. Then, embarrassed by her action, she let her arm drop to her side. Of course she couldn't touch his hair. A lady didn't do things like that.

"I don't care about Mrs. Templeton," Jason announced. "You're the only one I care about."

Charlotte felt the blood rush to her face, and for a second she felt so light-headed that she grabbed a tree trunk for support. What a wonderful day this was! Jason cared! He had done more than imply it; he had actually spoken the words.

As the snowflakes continued to fall and daylight began to fade, Charlotte stared at Jason, unable to speak. At length he broke the silence. "C'mon, Charlotte. Let's dance."

She moved into his arms as he began to hum. Ever since the night of the church social, each time they had met in the forest, they had danced. Charlotte refused to think what her parents would say if they knew. This was worse—far worse—than just meeting Jason and talking to him, worse even than letting him hold her hand. But it felt so wonderful, being held in his arms, that she knew even her parents' censure wouldn't stop her.

She and Jason twirled, moving more easily than they had the first time. Now they knew the steps and each other's movements so well that even though their heavy clothing hampered them, they moved almost as lightly as a couple on a dance floor. Charlotte laughed with sheer pleasure and smiled up at Jason. He stared back, then stopped humming. A second later, his feet stopped moving, though he did not release her. As he stared at her mouth for a long moment, Charlotte could feel the color rise in her cheeks. What was he thinking? Was he wondering the same thing she was, how his lips would feel on hers? Oh, she couldn't think that! It was wicked.

Slowly, Jason tipped his head toward hers. Slowly, she raised her face toward his. They wouldn't. They couldn't. But her lips refused to obey her thoughts, and they puckered as Jason inched ever closer. She could feel his breath, warm and sweet as he closed the tiny distance between them. Though it was the softest of touches, a mere brushing of lips, Charlotte was certain nothing on earth had ever felt as good as her first kiss.

* * *

"So, what do you think?" To Laura's surprise, Sam sounded tentative, as if he weren't certain of her response. How could he not be, when he had done so much? Four tables were arranged in a U-shape with two chairs at each, just as they had agreed. But what Laura hadn't expected was that the chairs would be brand-new. Sam must have spent the majority of his time making furniture for her students.

"I don't know what to say. I didn't expect all this," she said, gesturing toward the new classroom, running her hand over the smooth surface of one of the tables. Was Sam somehow clairvoyant that he guessed how much she sometimes missed the warm mahogany furniture from her parents' house? Was that why he had stained the pine such a dark tone?

"It was my pleasure," he said, his voice as warm as the wood. Laura watched, bemused, as Sam pulled out one of the chairs and installed her behind the table with a courtly gesture. Not for the first time she wondered which was the real Sam Baranov. Was he the coldly calculating man who planned to marry for the basest of reasons, or was the real Sam this generous man who gave so freely of his time and talent?

"I'm glad to see your dreams coming true," he said.

For a second Laura wasn't sure what he meant. Which dreams? She already knew that her childhood dreams of happily ever after would never come true. The school. Of course that was what he meant. Laura nodded. "The adult class has six enrolled in it, but I'm not sure how many of the Athapaskans will come." She had gone to the village several times with Amelia, telling the mothers of her plan and inviting them to bring their children. So far, none had agreed, although Amelia had told Laura not to give up hope.

Sam, who had taken a chair at an adjoining table, stroked his mustache. "You'll start with a couple," he predicted. "When the others hear how much those children are learning, you'll have almost more than you can handle. At least that's what happened with Dr. Amelia's practice."

"I'm also hoping to reach some of the older children right here in town, the ones who dropped out early or never went to school."

He nodded, and his eyes were warm with what appeared to be approval. "You'll succeed."

Laura wished she could be as confident as Sam. Until the classes began and students actually attended, this dream would be unfulfilled. "You sound so sure, Sam."

Sam stared out one of the oversized windows. Laura had been surprised when she had seen that his need for open spaces had extended not just to his house but also to the mill office. Even though the room had been divided, this portion had windows on two sides.

A shadow crossed Sam's face. "I wish I were that confident of my own success," he admitted.

"Are you having trouble persuading Charlotte?" Laura hated thinking that he was like Roy, a mercenary who cared nothing for the people he hurt as he tried to reach his own goals. It was so hard to reconcile that side of Sam with the kind man now sitting only a few feet from her.

"I'm afraid so. At the rate we're going, my birthday will have passed, and she still won't have agreed to marry me."

Laura was silent for a long moment, trying to decide what to say. The marriage was so very wrong, and yet . . . "Does the money mean that much?" she asked at last.

Sam shook his head. "It's not the money that I care about; it's the fact that my father's company is at stake." He leaned across the table, his expression earnest. "Papa was the first of his family to come to Alaska. Like many immigrants, he brought little more than his wife and a determination to succeed." Laura smiled at the realization that Sam had inherited at least one characteristic from his father. He was the most determined man Laura had ever met.

"They settled in Seward," Sam continued, "and through sheer hard work, he built up a successful shipping company. I can remember how proud he was of it and how he used to say that the Baranov Shipping Company would be his legacy to me." Sam clenched his fist. "I want that legacy, Laura. I want it more than I've wanted anything in my life."

There was no disguising the passion in Sam's voice. Though Laura might not agree with his plans for marrying Charlotte, she now understood his motive, and she was filled with relief. Sam wasn't mercenary like Roy; he was a man whose family mattered more to him than anything else. Laura felt a flicker of envy. Her own parents had never spoken of legacies to her—not even before she married Roy. She had never felt the connection, the intense loyalty to her family, that Sam's father had obviously engendered.

One thing puzzled her. If the company was so important to him, why had Sam been living in Gold Landing while his father was on the coast? "It must have been difficult, losing your father and having to marry so quickly."

Sam shook his head. "My father died almost fifteen years ago."

Laura's eyes widened in surprise. "I don't understand. Why didn't you inherit the company then?" Though he would have been a young man, it wasn't unheard of for a boy to inherit and have a guardian handle the business until he was of age. Laura's face must have reflected her confusion, for she saw a hint of amusement on Sam's. That was quickly replaced by pain. Perhaps to prevent her from seeing his expression, Sam rose and stood facing the window.

"It's complicated," he told her. "You know that my mother died when I was only five. Papa remarried a few months later—a widow with a child of her own. When Papa died, Hilda told me he had left the company to her and George, her son."

Laura gasped. Knowing what she now did about how close Sam had once been to his father, she realized how horrible it must have been for him, feeling that he had been rejected in favor of a stepson. Though the pain of Laura's own parents' rejection had begun to diminish with time, she knew Sam's had been worse. Laura had been able to argue with her parents, and though she knew it unlikely, she could still dream of a reconciliation. But death was so final. It had robbed Sam of the ability to ask his father "Why?"

"What changed?" she asked. For something had changed, to make Sam believe he would inherit if only he married.

Sam turned, his lips curled in what could only be contempt. "Hilda lied to me. Papa left the company to her in trust for me until I was twenty-five. I learned the true terms of the will two months ago. The attorney said he'd been told I was dead. In that case, the estate would go to George." This time Sam's smile was rueful. "It was sheer luck that the lawyer learned I was alive. One of his other clients had traveled through Gold Landing on his way to Fairbanks and happened to mention that he'd seen my name on the sawmill. He wondered if I was any relation to the Seward Baranovs."

Seward. Laura blanched as she considered one of the consequences of Sam's inheritance. "Are you willing to live in Seward?" She couldn't imagine Sam hiring someone else to run the shipping company, not after he had explained what it meant to him.

Sam nodded. "I've been happy here, and I'm proud of the sawmill. Probably," he admitted with another wry smile, "as proud as Papa was of his shipping company. But I can't turn this down. Baranov Shipping is my father's legacy to me. It's the only thing I'll have of his."

Laura clasped her hands in her lap in an attempt to keep them from trembling. Nothing, it appeared, was as clear as she had once believed. Sam's problem wasn't black and white or even dark gray. Perhaps it was wrong for him not to tell Charlotte why he was anxious to marry her, and yet how could Laura condemn him for wanting something that had been so important to his father?

Family was important. Wasn't that why she had brought the twins to Gold Landing? She wanted them to be a family living a normal life. Sam wasn't wrong about that. Perhaps he wasn't even wrong about courting Charlotte. Laura wasn't sure about that. The one thing she was sure about was that she didn't like the prospect of Gold Landing without Sam.

Chapter Eight

"How are you finding your first Alaskan autumn?" Sam asked as he walked into the classroom. It was odd, Laura reflected as she rose to greet him, that while he no longer entered the official schoolhouse, saying that he preferred to meet Charlotte outside, he never failed to join Laura when the last of her students had left what she called the lumber room. Perhaps he felt more comfortable here since it was, after all, part of his office. Perhaps, though, he was only seeking an excuse to delay his paperwork. Sam had groused on numerous occasions that he wasn't meant to keep accounts. That must be why he was here, not that he was anxious for her company.

Laura tilted her head from side to side, trying to ease the crick that had plagued her for the last hour. There was no reason she should have been so tense. Tonight's class was the adults, and they—unlike the Indian children—never misbehaved. There was no reason she should have worried that they were too noisy, that they were disturbing Sam, that he would order them to leave.

She pulled a chair near the stove and motioned to Sam to bring another. "It's hard to believe it's fall and not winter," she told Sam with a glance at the window. Though the sun had set hours before, the full moon reflected on the snow. Laura shivered. "Between the snow and the short days, this is very different from autumn in Seattle." When Sam looked a little disconcerted, Laura realized he might have misunderstood her meaning and thought she was criticizing his home. "Don't think I'm complaining, though. I love it here. Alaska's very, very beautiful, and my twins are ecstatic."

Even if she hated Gold Landing, which she did not, Laura would have been happy that she had come north, if only because of the joy that the children had found in their new life. They had adjusted to Alaska far more quickly than Laura had expected, and seemed to thrive on the frontier. As for herself, she had made more friends here than she had in all the time she had lived in Seattle. There were Ella and Amelia and Charlotte and Sam. Especially Sam. Laura lowered her gaze to the floor, lest Sam read the confusion in her eyes.

"My little pioneers want me to get a dogsled." The children were a safe topic. "Matt likes the idea of the sled itself, while Meg just loves dogs. She'd be happy if we had a whole team living in our cabin."

Sam chuckled at the picture. "I don't have a team, but William does. I imagine he'd let me take the twins for a ride."

The tension that had cramped Laura's neck began to subside. It must be the full moon that was affecting her mood and making her worry about Sam. He was once again her friend. Though they might not agree on everything—especially Sam's marriage—they were friends. "That would be wonderful, but I don't want to impose on you. You know Matt and Meg can be a handful."

Sam laughed, and she wondered if he was remembering the afternoon the twins had somehow managed to topple every one of the chairs onto their sides. At the time, he had declared that he should harness their energy to break up logjams on the river. "It'll give me a chance to practice," Sam said. "You can call it a lesson for when I have children of my own."

Sam's children. Of course he and Charlotte would have children. Laura tried not to frown. Hadn't Charlotte told her how much she loved babies? And with the way Sam felt about his father's legacy, Laura was certain he would want a child who could inherit the shipping company someday.

If everything went according to Sam's plan, by this time next year, Amelia might have delivered his first baby. If it was a boy, perhaps he and Charlotte would name him after Sam's father. Though Laura struggled to picture Charlotte holding a small version of Sam, the image refused to focus. "You're right," she said at last, trying to ignore the empty feeling that the thought of Sam's babies had somehow wrought, "it would be good practice."

The idea was obviously more pleasing to Sam than to Laura, for his face was wreathed with a grin. "So you've settled into Gold Landing."

She nodded, glad for the change of topic, and leaned back in her chair. Though she had worn no watch since she had been forced to sell hers, Laura knew it was growing late and she would soon have to leave. Even so, she was in no hurry to end her time with Sam. These moments that they shared were so pleasant. It was, of course, only that she enjoyed adult conversation, not that Sam was special.

"I'm still a *cheechako*," Laura said, using the term Alaskans applied to newcomers during their first year in the territory, "but I'm so thankful I came." Here there were no reminders of the past. Here she had begun a new life, one where she and her children were safe. Was it any wonder she felt happier than ever before?

Laura rose and laid a hand on the smoothly finished bookcase that Sam had brought into the classroom earlier that day. "I can't thank you enough for this room." She smiled as she looked at the small room that was now as familiar to her as the official school. "Two of the adults told me that they would not have gone to the schoolhouse. Although they didn't give any reasons, I imagine they would have been embarrassed to go to a children's school."

Sam nodded his understanding. He too had risen, and was now standing on the other side of the bookcase, so close that Laura could smell the scents of sawdust and fresh air that clung to him. "How are your Indian students progressing?" he asked.

Laura couldn't help smiling. "One of the four, a boy named Adam, is especially bright. Oh, Sam, I wish you could have seen his mother's face when he read a book to her." Laura had been walking through the Indian village when Adam insisted she go into his wickiup with him. Though she'd been appalled anew at the conditions in the small teepee, she would never forget his mother's joy. "I thought Spring Flower was going to cry from sheer happiness."

Sam leaned forward at the same time that Laura did. It was purely accidental that their fingers touched. The contact lasted only a second before they both retreated, but Laura felt as though her fingers had been singed. Who would have thought that such a fleeting touch could send ripples up her arms and down her body?

"That must make you feel good."

It did. Oh, how it did! Laura blinked, not sure how to answer Sam. Then she realized he was speaking of Spring Flower. "It's probably the way you feel when you've built a room or finished a chair," she said, pleased that her voice was so steady. It was ridiculous, of course, to have reacted so strongly to a casual brush against her fingertips. The full moon's effect was obviously greater than she had realized.

Sam shook his head. Judging from his perfectly calm expression, he accorded the incident the importance it deserved: none. It was only Laura who was being so silly. "It's not the same," he said. "You're molding people, not wood."

He pulled out a chair and quirked an eyebrow, as if asking Laura to stay a while longer. She nodded. Though she really ought to go home, she was reluctant to see the evening end.

She sat, then shook her head at Sam, contradicting his

assertion. "An accomplishment is an accomplishment. Who's to say one is better than another?" One of the lessons she had learned from her parents was how important it was to value people for what they could do rather than berate them for what they could not. Not that her parents had known they were teaching that lesson.

"I'm envious of you, being able to make something like this," Laura said as she ran her hand over the back of a chair.

Sam shrugged and looked out the window. Though few sounds carried inside this building, Laura heard the distant baying of a wolf.

"Now that you've got your special school started, what's next?" Sam turned back to face her.

Laura raised an eyebrow. "What makes you think there's something else?"

"Just a hunch. I figured you for a woman who always needed to have a challenge in front of her."

He was right, of course. Laura chuckled, amused that in the space of a few short months Sam could know her so well, better even than her own parents had after a lifetime together. "The Christmas pageant comes next. Ella told me how important it is to the whole community." After seeing the turnout for the ice cream social, Laura didn't doubt that the townspeople considered the pageant a key event, and she was more than a little daunted by the prospect of being responsible for it. "Fortunately, Ella saved all of last year's costumes." Ella, it appeared, was as good a seamstress as Charlotte was a cook. Laura was thankful that the residents of Gold Landing were not depending on her to make costumes. Though she could direct a play and teach the children to sing Christmas carols, she was not deft with a needle.

"The costumes are good," Sam agreed with a look that made Laura wonder if he realized what an inadequate seamstress she was, "but if you want to impress the town, you need better sets."

Laura did want to impress the town. There was no point in denying that. "What do you mean?"

"You need a good stable and manger to go with those nice costumes."

"Ella told me they use a wooden crate for a manger." At the time, it had sounded like a creative approach.

Sam shook his head in mock disgust. "We can do better."

We? "What are you suggesting?" Surely he wasn't expecting her to help build a manger. She had never used a hammer in her life.

"I thought your older pupils might want to learn basic woodworking. They could start by making some props," Sam said.

It was a wonderfully generous offer, and one that Laura had no intention of refusing. She had noticed that some of the older boys were bored, and she worried that they might drop out. Sam's special class could be the inducement she needed to keep them in school. "They'll be thrilled to learn something different," she agreed, "especially since you won't be giving them any tests."

Sam grabbed a pencil and a piece of paper. Leaning over the table, he began to sketch. "Here's what I thought."

Two days later, when Laura came to the mill office for her class, she found Sam slumped in his desk chair, resting his head on the wall behind him. "How do you do it?" he demanded, barely rising to greet her. "I spent two hours with those boys, and I'm more tired than after a whole day at the mill."

She tried not to smile at the thought of Sam coping with her most active pupils. Laura sank into one of his visitors' chairs so Sam would not have to remain standing. "You'll get used to it. Their enthusiasm is infectious."

Sam's mustache quivered as he frowned. "Laura, the word is 'exhausting.' You're a teacher. You ought to know that."

This time she did smile. "It is exhausting at first," she admitted. "I used to come home, soak my feet in hot water, and dream of excuses so that I wouldn't have to go back the next morning. But think of it this way, Sam. It's more of your preparation for parenthood."

"If that's a sample, I might reconsider."

"Coward."

"You've got the wrong word again, Laura. It's called wisdom. I'm a wise man."

"And I'm a wise woman who says that tomorrow morning you'll be counting the hours until the boys return."

Sam chuckled. Then his face sobered as he said, "Your parents must have set a good example for you."

Laura's breath escaped with a whoosh. Her parents? What had given Sam that idea? Her first instinct was to pick up her bag and hurry into the school side of Sam's office. But that would be the act of a coward, and one thing Laura was not was a coward. "Why would you say that?" she asked as calmly as she could.

"I thought that was obvious. You're such a good mother yourself, firm but loving at the same time, that you must have learned it at an early age."

The easy answer would be to nod, to pretend that Sam was right. That was what she would have done if Ella or Amelia had made the comment. But Sam was different. Sam had opened his heart to her, telling her about his father and stepmother. How could she be less than honest with him?

Laura shook her head slowly. "It's odd," she said, clasping her hands in her lap. "I thought my parents loved me. After all, don't all parents love their children?" The quirk of Sam's eyebrows made Laura think he was remembering his stepmother, who most definitely had not loved him. "Then I discovered that what they loved was the idea of a daughter. As long as I fit their image of what a daughter should be, everything was fine. But then . . ." Laura stopped abruptly, unwilling to admit her failure.

"I can't imagine you displeasing anyone."

"Oh, but I did." Laura forced herself to meet Sam's eyes. When she did, she saw both concern and understanding in them. "I married the wrong man, and they haven't spoken to me since."

"That's horrible!" Sam's face mirrored the shock and anger Laura heard in his voice.

Laura unclasped her hands and placed them on the edge of Sam's desk. Her fingertips were white from being pressed so tightly against her hands. "I won't deny that it hurt, because it did." Even now, though the pain had faded, there was an emptiness in her heart whenever she thought of her parents. "It wasn't all bad. For one thing, I've learned to depend on myself." Though Roy had helped with that lesson, Laura wasn't going to talk about Roy today . . . perhaps ever. There were some things she couldn't tell anyone, not even Sam.

"If you think I'm a good mother, it's probably because I vowed that I would never treat my children the way my parents did me. I wanted to be sure that Meg and Matt would always know that I loved them for themselves—not for some ideal I had of them."

As Sam nodded slowly, Laura felt herself relax. Sam had heard her story, and he had not turned away. Instead, he had acted as if he understood. What a wonderful friend Sam was proving to be!

They sat in silence for a few moments. Then Laura asked the question that had echoed in her mind from the day Sam had first told her of his inheritance. "What was your father like?" She had tried to picture the senior Mr. Baranov, but could conjure nothing other than an image of Sam with gray hair, and that did not ring true. The Sam she knew would never have left his son so vulnerable.

Sam stared out the side window for a long moment, though there was little to see in the darkness, and she knew he was trying to decide whether to answer her question. When he turned around, she saw that his eyes were clouded, though whether by pain or confusion, she wasn't sure.

"That's a hard question to answer," he said slowly, "because I resented my father for so long." Sam paused, then managed a small smile. "I have vague memories of him with my mother, and it seems to me that we were happy before she died. All I know is that everything changed then." He leaned back in his chair, and Laura sensed that he sought to distance himself from his memories.

When Sam spoke again, his voice was harsh with barely suppressed pain. "The only time I saw my father cry was the day they buried my mother. I remember being as frightened by that as by the fact that my mother was in a coffin. That night when I couldn't sleep, Papa held me in his arms. He tried to comfort me by saying that Mama would always be near us, even though we couldn't see her. And then he said he hoped one day I would find a woman I could love as much as he had loved my mother. I remember him sobbing when he said that he had lost his midnight rainbow." Sam stroked his mustache, and Laura wondered if it was to hide his emotion. One thing was certain: He was no longer meeting her gaze.

"I always remembered that," Sam continued, "and I kept looking for a rainbow at midnight. I thought that if I could find one, my mother would come back, and we'd be happy again."

"Are there really rainbows at midnight?" To Laura's dismay, her own voice quavered. Sam's story and his obvious pain had touched chords deep within her.

"I haven't seen one, but I'm told they exist." Sam's voice was once again as calm as it had been when they had discussed the students' woodworking. "It's logical that you'd see one in June. The midnight sun can create midnight rainbows."

Laura, the woman who never cried, found herself fighting tears. "It's a beautiful image." For her, rainbows were the symbol of hope, the beauty that came after rain. And a rainbow at midnight—how better to describe the magic of Alaska?

"That's all it was—an image." Sam's voice was harsh, dispelling the romantic picture Laura had conjured. "Papa said he loved Mama. I believed him that night, but when he married Hilda a few months later, I started hating him. How could he have done that? It seemed like a betrayal of Mama's memory. Even now, I don't understand why he remarried so soon."

Laura heard the pain in Sam's voice, and wished there was something she could say to comfort him. "Perhaps he was lonely," she said. Many men, especially ones with a small child, found they needed a woman in their lives for the most basic of reasons. Love didn't necessarily form part of the equation, while companionship, a clean house, hot meals, and care for a child did.

"I suppose that's possible." Sam sounded dubious. "Still, you didn't remarry as soon as your husband died."

Laura blinked, trying to think how to answer without lying. At last she said only, "No, I didn't."

"Good morning, Nelson." George wouldn't give the man the courtesy of calling him "Mr. Nelson." "I hope this will be quick. I have an important meeting in an hour." It was a lie. George had nothing scheduled for the rest of the day, but he had no intention of letting this useless lawyer think he was important. It was bad enough that the man had summoned him to a meeting rather than coming to George's office to discuss whatever it was he thought was so urgent. George wasn't going to concede anything else to the man.

He looked around the office. The back wall was lined with books, floor to ceiling. George wasn't sure why anyone would want so many books. It must be to impress stupid clients. That was the only reason he could imagine. Some folks might be dumb enough to think that Nelson had read all of them. George knew better. They were for show.

George didn't like lawyers in general. They were always trying to tell a man what to do and why, just because they had spent more time in school than most folks. George figured it was because they couldn't be successful any other way. That was lawyers in general. Then there was Nelson—the worst lawyer George had ever met. If he hadn't been forced to deal with him because of Nicholas Baranov's will, you could be sure he wouldn't be here.

"So, what is so important?" George propped his feet on the attorney's desk. Let the old fool say something. If he dared.

He didn't. Nelson just looked at him over those ridiculous half glasses. George hated those spectacles almost as much as he hated Nelson himself. "I wanted to inform you that I have received an epistle from Sam Baranov."

"Epistle." He probably thought George didn't know that that was just a fancy term for "letter." George wanted to tell the lawyer he was a fool, but now wasn't the time. He had to hear what Sam had said. Then he'd deal with Nelson.

It was all the lawyer's fault. He'd had no call to send Sam a letter in the first place. George didn't hold much with Nelson's claim that it was an ethical requirement that he notify Sam of his inheritance. Ethics be damned! Whether it was ethical or not, nothing and no one was going to get between George and his inheritance.

"What did he say?"

Nelson smiled. "Your brother plans to marry. He will meet the terms of his father's will." It wasn't George's imagination. The lawyer enjoyed telling him that. George clenched his fists. He'd get even with him. Oh, yes, indeed, he would.

George slammed his feet on the floor, then stalked to the door. "I see." What he saw was that it would be a shame if Sam met with an accident—a fatal accident—on his way to Seward. And then, when Sam was gone, it would be time to reward the lawyer for his part. George smiled at the thought.

The wind was howling, driving snow against the side of the schoolhouse, as Laura and Charlotte readied the room for the next morning's classes. This was the quiet time of the day, their chance to discuss the pupils' progress and their plans for the coming day.

"You're doing very well with arithmetic," Laura told Charlotte. Ever since she had seen how much her assistant enjoyed teaching, she had asked her to take one class a day. "You've got a natural talent for teaching."

Though Charlotte flushed at the praise, her face was solemn. "I only wish I could convince my parents to let me go to Seattle for normal school."

"Have you asked them?"

Charlotte nodded. "They didn't refuse, but they told me how much they would miss me."

Laura wondered what the Langdons would say if they knew that Sam planned to move to Seward as soon as he and Charlotte married. If they didn't want their daughter to leave Gold Landing for normal school, Laura doubted they would be pleased with the prospect of a permanent move.

"School is only for a year," she said to Charlotte.

"That's what I told them, but they acted as if it were forever." Charlotte moved toward the window, staring out at the blowing snow. Though Laura could see nothing other than white, Charlotte smiled. "I'd better get home," she said, and reached for her coat.

Laura waited until Charlotte had left before she walked toward the window. She hadn't been mistaken. There was a definite pattern to Charlotte's departures. Most afternoons she would wait until her regular time, but occasionally she would suddenly seem to be in a hurry and would race from the schoolroom. And always, the precipitous departures occurred after she had been standing at the window.

Laura stood by the side of the window, where she could see outside but would not be visible to anyone approaching the school from that direction. As she watched, Charlotte ran toward the small copse of trees. That was odd. The town was the opposite way.

Laura remembered that Charlotte had gone that direction last summer. At the time, she had thought Charlotte wanted to stroll, but surely no one would want to take a pleasure walk in this weather. The wind was fierce, and the snow felt like tiny shards of ice.

Charlotte continued, her gait eager, and Laura's puzzlement grew. Then a second later, a figure emerged from the trees, his hands outstretched. Charlotte was meeting someone! Laura wasn't sure what surprised her more, the fact that Charlotte was meeting someone or that the rendezvous was clandestine.

Who could he be? It certainly wasn't Sam. The man wasn't tall enough; his shoulders weren't as broad as Sam's, and he didn't hold himself with Sam's self-assurance. Laura looked more closely, trying to recognize the stranger. She knew she had seen him before, but she couldn't place him. Then a memory clicked into place. Jason. The young man Charlotte was meeting was Jason Blake, the boy who had been accused of stealing.

Laura stared, astonished by what she had seen. Unless her eyes deceived her, Jason and Charlotte were more than casual acquaintances. This was a planned assignation and, by the looks of it, a regular one. No wonder Charlotte was so cool toward Sam. If she viewed Jason as more than a friend, she would never marry Sam.

Laura gripped the windowsill. Poor Sam! What would he do now?

Chapter Nine

Secrets. How she hated them! Laura looked both ways before she crossed the street. Though at this time of the day there was rarely so much as a pedestrian, much less a wagon laden with timber, some habits were so ingrained that she doubted she would ever lose them. As for the secrets, she wished she could forget a few. Since she had come to Gold Landing, it seemed that she had been privy to far too many. Her own were enough of a burden. Now she knew both Sam's and Charlotte's, and those weighed as heavily as her own. Perhaps more heavily, for she could see no happy ending for two people who were among her dearest friends.

Sam needed a wife, and though he might deny it, he longed for a happy marriage. But since Charlotte's affections were, as Laura's mother might have said, otherwise engaged, it was unlikely that Sam would find the happiness he so desperately needed with her. Laura clenched her fists, then straightened her fingers, trying to work some of the tension from them. It didn't work. She doubted that Charlotte would even consider marrying Sam. That meant he would have to find another woman to be his wife. As for Charlotte, it was difficult to picture the Langdons approving of Jason.

Laura's boots squeaked on the freshly fallen snow while stars twinkled in the clear sky. It was an evening when everything seemed at peace. Everything except her thoughts. They continued to churn.

Who was Sam to marry when there were very few single women of marriageable age? Laura understood why Sam had chosen Charlotte, for she was the most logical choice. But Charlotte was unwilling, and Laura was unable to think of anyone else that Sam might consider. Oh, how she wished she were one of the mythical creatures from the stories she had read as a child, able to wave a magic wand to create happy endings. Unfortunately, she wasn't.

Laura forced a smile onto her face as she opened the door to the sawmill office. There was no reason to let Sam suffer from her doldrums.

He rose from his desk so quickly that a pile of papers tumbled to the floor. With a wry smile that told Laura he had been engaged in one of his least favorite activities, Sam gathered the papers and tossed them haphazardly on the desk.

"Good evening, Laura." He carried her book bag into the classroom while she divested herself of her coat.

"There's something I want to show you," Sam said, gesturing back toward the office portion of the building. With a gesture that was oddly flamboyant for him, he pointed toward a large irregularly shaped object in one corner before whipping the cloth from it.

"Oh, Sam!" Laura gasped with pleasure. "It's beautiful." She stared at the manger. Although it was designed as a utilitarian piece, Sam had somehow managed to turn it into a work of art with graceful lines and gleaming wood. Laura doubted that even the cradles William Gunning made for his friends' children were more beautiful.

"I can picture the baby in it," she said, reaching forward to stroke the manger. At the same moment, Sam stretched his hand out. It landed on top of hers, and for a second Laura was unable to move as a jolt of pure pleasure swept through her. This was the simplest of touches, the kind of unplanned encounter that happened dozens of times a day. Laura touched students; she touched Charlotte; she touched her friends. Yet nothing had ever felt the way this casual brush did. It was like the time Sam's fingertips had touched hers, and yet it wasn't. This was far more powerful, the difference between a flickering candle and a room lit with electricity.

Laura stared at Sam, wondering if he felt the same sparks, if his fingers seemed as if they were on fire. Did his arms tingle with pleasure and something else, something darker? Of course not! It was nothing more than her imagination.

Laura dropped her gaze. "I hear the children," she said, suddenly anxious to put a wall between her and Sam. He nodded, and she saw something in his eyes that had not been there before. Was he as disturbed as she by the flames that had been ignited when they had touched? Laura shook her head. She had to dismiss these fanciful thoughts. She was here to teach the Athapaskan children, nothing more.

A few minutes later, Laura's newfound worries were overshadowed by the fact that only three of her Indian students had come.

"Where is Adam?" she asked. The boy was normally the first to arrive. Tonight the other three swept into the room in a flurry of boyish chatter, then were abruptly silent when Laura asked about their absent companion.

"Adam very sick," the youngest of the boys said. Laura had noticed that although he was several years younger than the others, when Adam was not wirh them, he served as the spokesman. Tonight she wished he had happier news.

"Has his mother called Dr. Amelia?" Whatever ailed Adam had to be serious to keep the boy from class. Spring Flower's son was so anxious to learn that he had come to class one time when he could barely talk, and another when he had sneezed so often that Laura had been convinced he was going to infect the others.

The young boy nodded. "She there now."

Laura took a deep breath and opened her books as she prepared to teach. If Amelia was with Adam, he would be fine. Everyone in Gold Landing knew that Amelia was a talented physician. Still, though she tried to keep her attention focused on the class, Laura kept picturing Adam, wishing he was sitting in one of the newly carved chairs, shooting his hand into the air each time he knew an answer.

Though the class was only an hour long, to Laura it seemed to last forever. The other boys' enthusiasm was clearly flagging. Without Adam to goad them on, they seemed to have little desire to learn. As soon as the children left, Laura gathered her books. Tonight she would not stay to talk to Sam. Somehow, worrying about Adam had tired her more than a full day of teaching.

"What's wrong?" Sam asked. He leaned against the doorway between the schoolroom and his office. Though his posture seemed relaxed, Sam's brown eyes were alert and filled with concern.

Laura raised an eyebrow, surprised by his question. "Is it that obvious?"

"It is to me. You don't normally have that little line between your eyes. Want to tell me about it?"

Suddenly, rushing home no longer seemed like the right thing to do. She would stay for just a few minutes. Laura nodded, oddly relieved to have someone to whom she could confide her worries. It had been so long since she had been able to rely on anyone else. Not that she wanted to rely on Sam; it was simply that she wanted to share her concerns.

"I'm worried about Adam," she admitted as she reached for her coat. "He was too sick to come to school tonight."

Sam held the coat while she slipped her arms into it. "Children get sick," he said mildly. "It's normal."

"I know that." Laura's twins had had their share of childhood illnesses. "The problem is, Amelia told me that Adam had diphtheria a year or so ago. I'm afraid that's made him more susceptible to other illnesses." To Laura's dismay, her voice cracked.

Though Sam said nothing, she knew he had heard her distress. "Would you feel better if you saw him?"

Would she? Laura nodded. "It may be silly, but yes, I would."

Sam grabbed his parka. "We'll tell Charlotte that you'll be late tonight, and then we'll go." Charlotte cared for the twins while Laura taught her special classes.

"We?"

"It's dark, Laura. I'd worry if you went alone."

Laura stared at him for a moment. She could not remember the last time anyone had worried about her, and it felt good—oh, so good—to have someone care about her well-being. That was what friends did, wasn't it?

"So, the twins were asleep," Sam said as he and Laura crossed the bridge, moving smoothly on the snowshoes that had once seemed awkward to Laura. She tried to focus her thoughts on the twins, on the stars that hung in the dark sky, on anything other than Adam's illness. But with each step that took her closer to the Athapaskan village, Laura's uneasiness grew. She had visited the village numerous times. Why, then, did she remember only the first time she and Sam had come here, when she had seen a woman holding her child's body? Surely that wouldn't happen again.

"Adam will be all right," she said, more to convince herself than Sam. They were approaching the village, and her foreboding grew.

"Children are stronger than most of us think," Sam said. His voice sounded confident, and for a second, Laura felt herself relax.

"I hope so. I just can't seem to dismiss my fears."

Sam tilted his head to one side as he looked at the sky. "There's a new moon," he said. "George used to tell me that evil spirits had eaten the moon, and they were still hungry, so they were coming for me." When Laura started to laugh, Sam added, "I was six years old. I believed him."

Laura's laughter died. "George sounds like a monster. Who was he?"

"My stepbrother."

"How awful!" The fable had sounded amusing when Laura had thought that boys in their teens had shared it. But telling a young, impressionable child? That was something else. Only someone with a streak of cruelty would do that. Laura stared at Sam, wondering why he had told her that story tonight. Was he trying to distract her so that she wouldn't worry about Adam, or did he still harbor some of those childhood fears?

As they approached the wickiup where Adam lived with Spring Flower, Laura's footsteps slowed. There was no reason to be filled with such foreboding. Amelia was with Adam; he would be fine. But Laura's feet did not listen to her mind, and she found it difficult to place one in front of the other. As if he knew the reason for her hesitation, Sam slipped his arm around Laura's waist. It was merely to steady her, of course. He didn't mean anything else. But, oh, it felt so good to be able to lean on someone, to draw strength from him. Sam was such a good friend!

Together they walked to the flap that served as the door to the wickiup. Although she could hear a low sound coming from inside the teepee, Laura could not distinguish any words. "Amelia," she called. A moment later her friend opened the door and peered out.

"Laura, Sam. Why are you here?"

Though only a pale light spilled from the wickiup, Laura could see the lines of fatigue on Amelia's face. "I was worried about Adam," she said, her fear intensifying at the sight of the doctor's grave expression. "Sam and I came to see him."

Amelia's beautiful blue eyes darkened. Even before she spoke, Laura knew what Amelia would say. "You're too late." They were three simple words, but filled with such sadness that Laura reached forward to clasp Amelia's hands, wishing she could give her some measure of comfort. "Adam died a few minutes ago." The low sound Laura had heard was a woman's keening.

Though Laura's eyes were dry, her heart was heavy as she walked toward the tall, gaunt woman who crouched over a pallet at the other side of the wickiup. "Your son was very special," she said softly.

At first Laura thought Spring Flower had not heard her, for she did not acknowledge Laura's words. Then Spring Flower turned from her child's bed and faced Laura. Her normally stern face was contorted with grief and something else, an emotion Laura had never seen on the young woman's visage. "Your books killed him!" she cried, her voice filled with fury. "Words made his head too full."

For a moment Laura stood speechless. Dimly she was aware of a large animal, perhaps a moose, lumbering by outside the wickiup, a reminder that Alaska was an untamed land, a place where animals roamed, but surely not a place where children died. Laura stared at the Athapaskan woman. What was she saying? Surely Spring Flower didn't truly blame Adam's schooling for his death.

"That's not possible," Laura said as calmly as she could.

Amelia came to Laura's side and laid a cautioning hand on her arm. "Adam had a high fever," she said softly. "I don't know what caused it."

Though Amelia spoke only a few decibels over a whisper, Spring Flower heard her. "Books!" She spat the word as if it were an epithet. "Books bad." She gave Laura a long, malevolent look. "You bad."

Laura recoiled in shock. Never before had she been faced with such virulent hatred. Roy might have used her for his own purposes, and her parents might not have loved her, but no one had ever hated her. She gasped.

"Come with me," Sam said, moving from his position at the door. Taking Laura's arm in a firm grip, he drew her away from Spring Flower.

Amelia nodded. "Spring Flower needs to grieve alone."

When they were outside the teepee, Laura turned to Sam.

"My books didn't kill Adam," she said fiercely. How could Spring Flower believe that? It was horrible that Adam had died. The knowledge that she would never again see the boy's pleasure when he learned a new word, or hear him blurt out an answer to a problem, filled Laura's heart with sorrow. She ached for Spring Flower and the pain she was enduring, for there was nothing Laura could imagine that was worse than losing a child. But she would not—could not—believe that her school had played any part in the young boy's illness. "Books didn't kill him," she repeated.

"Of course they didn't." Sam helped Laura strap on her snowshoes. "People say things they don't mean when they're grieving."

Though the thin leather walls, Laura could hear Spring Flower's angry voice and Amelia's conciliatory tones. "It's such a waste! Adam was the brightest of my students. Why did he have to die?"

As they glided away from the village, Sam shook his head slowly. "I don't know, any more than I know why my mother or your husband had to die when they did. Only God has those answers."

When she returned to her cabin, Laura stood next to the bed and watched her sleeping children. "I love you so much," she told the silent figures. "I don't know what I'd do without you."

"Mrs. Templeton is very upset." Charlotte sat stiffly in the tall wing chair, her feet placed so precisely in front of her that Sam wondered if she'd measured the distance between them. When their walks and the small gifts had not thawed her coolness, he had decided to pay a formal call on her. So far, it was no more successful than his previous attempts to woo his future bride. Charlotte rebuffed his every attempt to get to know her, responding to his questions with her normal monosyllabic replies. It was only when Sam asked about the school that Charlotte displayed any enthusiasm.

"She's taking Adam's death harder than I expected," he

agreed. Sam had known that Laura cared about her pupils, and some sorrow was normal, but she acted as if one of her own children had died.

"She's such a loving woman," Charlotte told him, her cheeks coloring as she stared at Sam, almost as if defying him to dispute her statement. "It must be hard for her to face death again when she lost her husband so recently."

Sam was silent for a second. Since Laura never spoke of her husband, he had no idea how long it had been since he died. The black clothes she wore could mean that she was in traditional mourning, and her husband had died within the last year, but it was also possible that Laura was like some of the widows he had seen in Seward, who wore black for the rest of their lives.

"I wish I could help her." To Sam's surprise, Charlotte was still speaking.

He flashed her a brief smile. "You do," he said, "just by being her friend."

As an answering smile illuminated Charlotte's face, Sam was struck by the change that the smile made. Though he would never describe her as beautiful, when she smiled, Charlotte Langdon was more than pretty. She was striking.

"I hope you're right," she said fervently.

Half an hour later as Sam walked home, he was still pensive. It was obvious that Charlotte was capable of deep emotions. When she spoke of Laura, she was not the cool, passionless woman he normally saw. Why was it that he was unable to tap those emotions? What was he doing wrong?

"Okay, Hazleton. You know what we gotta do." Roy spoke carefully out of the side of his mouth so that the guards on the other side of this stinking room wouldn't notice him. It was bad enough that they watched his every move when he was in his cell. He wasn't going to let them wreck today.

"You sure it's gonna work?" Hazleton mumbled the words, keeping his head lowered as they lined up for the slop this place called food. The man was dumb, but at least he could follow directions. That was the only reason Roy had picked him. That and the fact that they were the same size. If Hazleton could get through a tight space, so could Roy. He was counting on that.

"It's foolproof," Roy declared, "just so long as you follow the plan." Thank God Hazleton was too stupid to try any variations. The man had blond hair and blue eyes like Roy's, but he sure didn't have any brains under that blond hair, and the eyes didn't exactly shine.

"How come I gotta be the one to shout 'Fire'?" Hazleton's mumbling took on a whining tone.

"Cuz you got a good voice," Roy said, watching the man preen with pleasure. "That's why." That and the fact that the guards wouldn't suspect Hazleton of plotting anything. The man was dumber than a chamber pot.

"You sure this is gonna work?"

Roy didn't bother trying to mask his impatience. "Look, if you ain't got the guts to go through with it, I'll find myself another partner. I thought you wanted to get outta here."

Hazleton bobbed his head. "I do."

"Then shut your mouth and do what I told you to do." And when it was all over, Roy would take care of him. Oh, yes, he would.

It was a foolproof plan; Roy knew that. He and Hazleton were going to break out of this hellhole of a prison tonight. Roy had picked supper time for the escape. There was always a lot of confusion then; the guards were at the end of their shifts and tired, and it was dark outside. What better time could there be?

"Fire!" Hazleton shouted. "Fire!"

As Roy had known, that single word created panic and confusion. Inmates and guards alike began to run, no one seeming to know where to go, everyone wanting to go *somewhere*. Roy gave Hazleton the second signal, and the man knocked over the guard at the door. Good old Hazleton might be dumb, but he packed a mighty wallop.

While his partner kicked the guard out of the way, Roy

forced the door open and ran outside. Freedom was so close he could smell it. Three strides and he'd be across the yard. The wall was only a small barrier; Roy had practiced scaling walls during a misspent childhood. And if Hazleton couldn't get over it, well . . . that would make one part of the escape easier.

"Stop! Stop them!" Damn it all! The guards had moved faster than he'd expected. They were so close, he could practically hear their breathing. Roy jumped, grabbing the iron spike on top of the wall. Success! With a movement so swift the guards had no way of catching him, he swung himself on top of the wall. A grunt told him Hazleton was right behind him.

"Stop!"

But Roy had no intention of stopping. He crouched, ready to jump to the other side and freedom. A shot rang out, and then there was only darkness.

"Looks like you're ready." As he opened the door for Sam, the boy grinned and pulled his hood closer around his face. Though Laura had told Sam she would have the children ready for the sled ride he had promised, he hadn't expected them to be completely dressed in their outdoor togs.

Laura smiled and placed a hand on Matt's head. "He's so excited I could hardly get him to eat breakfast. Meg was almost as bad." The little girl hid behind her mother's skirts, only one blond braid betraying her presence. Meg's timidity surprised Sam almost as much as Matt's eagerness. He thought she had gotten over her shyness, at least with him.

"Want to help me get the sled ready?" he asked Matt. When the boy responded with an emphatic nod, followed by a questioning look at his mother, Sam turned to Meg. "I've got a special treat for the dogs if you want to help feed them a little later." The girl's eyes glowed with enthusiasm.

Laura's gaze moved from her children to Sam, and he saw amusement in those beautiful blue-green eyes. "You certainly figured out the way to their hearts," she said as she helped Meg button her coat.

What about yours? Sam was so startled that he stepped back a pace and almost bumped into the door. Where had that thought come from? He swallowed deeply, then asked only, "Are you ready?"

As Laura reached for a bulging sack, Sam took the children outside. The weather could hardly have been better for a sled ride. An inch of fresh snow had fallen overnight, there was no wind, and the sky was a faultless blue. The dogs, who had been resting quietly while he was inside Laura's house, began to leap and bark with excitement. For a second Meg hesitated. Then she ran toward them.

"Wait a minute." Sam snagged the back of her coat. "Those dogs are ready to run, not play." Though he doubted they would deliberately hurt Meg, they were powerful animals that were bred for one purpose: to pull a sled.

Laura scooped her daughter into her arms while Sam showed Matt how to load cargo onto the sled. Moments later, Matt and Meg were installed on the sled, while Sam and Laura stood behind it. They drove through the town, Sam keeping the pace slow so that the children wouldn't be frightened. Nugget, the lead dog, turned to glare at Sam several times, as if reminding him that the team was anxious to run, and Sam glared right back. William had stressed the importance of letting the dogs know who was in charge . . . and that it wasn't Nugget.

"I thought we'd go out by the school, then turn around and go to the other end of town," Sam told Laura. She nodded her agreement, not seeming to mind that the pace that Nugget and the other dogs considered so sedate required her to practically run. Her cheeks were rosy, and her lips curved into such a sweet smile that Sam found himself wondering if they tasted as sweet as they looked. *Don't be ridiculous*, he admonished himself. *Laura is a friend. A good friend, but only a friend. It's Charlotte's lips that should tempt you.*

As they approached the school, the twins swiveled around

to smile at their mother. "Yes, sweeties, that's where Mama teaches."

Sam was so engrossed in watching Laura's smile that he barely saw the figure slip into the trees. Though it moved quickly, there was something familiar about it.

"Did you see someone?" he asked Laura. "I thought it looked like Charlotte."

Laura glanced into the trees. "You must have been mistaken," she said in a voice that somehow didn't sound convincing. "There's no school today, so Charlotte would have no reason to be out here." But though she denied anyone was in the forest, Sam noticed that Laura's gaze stayed on the trees until they turned around and headed back into town.

When they reached the other end of the Gold Landing, Sam led the dog team up a small bluff. "This is where Amelia's clinic used to be," he said, gesturing toward the cleared area. He halted the team and helped the children off the sled. Their eyes gleamed almost as brightly as their mother's, and they chattered rapidly, interrupting each other in their eagerness to tell Laura how much they had liked the sled ride.

Sam felt a flicker of warmth deep inside him at the children's simple pleasure and the knowledge that he had helped create it. When Laura's eyes met his, he saw amusement and something else, something he could not identify, in them. The warmth became a conflagration, threatening to consume him. He looked away.

"Would you like to give the dogs their treats?" he asked Meg.

Meg nodded and started toward the dogs. When Laura touched her shoulder, the little girl said primly, "Yes, sir. Thank you." But it was clear that Meg's attention was focused on the canine members of the party. She knelt next to Nugget, giggling when the husky licked a piece of suet from her hand.

"What about me?" Matt stood beside the sled, clearly bored with his sister's feeding of the dogs.

"I thought you might want to drive the team," Sam said. He had had no difficulty knowing what Meg would like. Matt was more of a challenge, so Sam had tried to remember what it was like to be a small boy. "We'd leave your mother and Meg here for a few minutes and go off by ourselves. That is, if you want to."

The way Matt's eyes gleamed with anticipation told Sam he had read the boy's interests correctly. "Can I?" Matt asked his mother.

She looked more dubious than her son. "If Mr. Baranov wants to take you." Her expression told Sam that she didn't expect him to do this.

"It would be my pleasure."

"All right then." She laid a cautioning hand on Matt's shoulder. "You do whatever Mr. Baranov says. And"—she turned her attention to Sam—"just a couple of minutes."

Sam settled Matt on the runners in front of him and threaded the reins through his fingers, giving the boy the illusion that he was controlling the sled. When they returned to the bluff ten minutes later, he asked Matt, "Well, son, what did you think?"

"Fun!"

Laura, who had spread a blanket on the snow and was obviously playing some sort of game with her daughter, flashed Sam a smile. His heart skipped a beat. It must be the exertion, not the fact that this woman who reached only to his shoulder had given him a smile as big as Alaska.

Meg pouted. "Would you like to go on a special ride all by yourself?" Sam asked her.

Meg gave her mother a quick glance, then nodded. As Sam sat Meg on the sled, piling blankets on either side so that she would not fall out, he said, "You know only big girls can ride alone."

Nodding solemnly, she said, "Not scared."

Laura's smile told Sam how amused she was by her normally shy and cautious daughter's declaration of fearlessness. "Hold on tight," she admonished.

"Mr. Sam keep me safe."

As Meg said the words, Sam felt a glow of pleasure begin to spread through his body. It was odd how that little gesture of trust made a man feel good. "You can count on that," he told Meg's mother, and was rewarded by another one of her brilliant smiles.

When Sam and Meg returned to the bluff, they found Laura opening the sack she had brought with her. "Does anyone want hot cocoa?" she asked.

Two shouts of glee were her answer. The children raced to Laura's side, then sat quietly while she poured the steaming liquid. When they had taken their first sips and were settled on the blanket, she handed a cup to Sam.

The chocolate smelled delicious, but what tantalized Sam's senses was Laura's own scent. It was sweet and spicy and unlike any perfume he had ever smelled, just as Laura was unlike any woman he'd ever met.

"This is delicious," he said truthfully when he'd tasted the cocoa. "It's almost as good as the punch you made for the church social."

Laura shrugged her shoulders. "I'm not much of a cook, but there are some things I can do."

Her apparent diffidence surprised Sam. He had thought of Laura as a self-confident woman with no vulnerabilities.

"You're a wonderful mother," he said, "and that's a priceless talent."

Laura flushed with pleasure, as if compliments were not common occurrences.

That night as he walked back to his house, Sam found himself remembering Matt's shouts of joy when they let the dogs race and Meg's shy smile while she fed the team. He hadn't expected to enjoy the day. When he had suggested the ride, it had been because he remembered what it was like being a child, and he had wanted to give Meg and Matt a happy memory. Sam hadn't expected to create happy memories for himself. But he had.

It was more than the images of the children's smiling faces. Today, for the first time in a very long while, he had felt as if he was part of a family. The children had filled an empty spot deep within him. As for Laura . . .

Stop it! Sam shook his head in disgust. Charlotte was the woman he planned to marry. She was the one who should occupy his thoughts. There was absolutely no reason to keep thinking about Laura and the way she had smiled, the pleasure he had seen on her face when he had told her she was a good mother, the way her lips had curved around the cocoa mug.

There was no reason to wonder how those lips would feel beneath his, or whether she would make small whimpers of pleasure if he kissed her. No reason at all.

Chapter Ten

Laura shivered as she crossed the street. Though it was only a short distance from the sawmill to her cabin, the air was so cold that it seemed to penetrate her cloak. Charlotte was right. While the calendar said that winter would not arrive for another five weeks, there was no doubt that it already reigned in Alaska. The days had grown progressively shorter, with the sun now rising for only a few hours. It seemed odd, walking to school in the dark and watching the sun set before she dismissed her students, and yet Laura found the changing seasons exhilarating. If anything, the snow and darkness only enhanced Gold Landing's beauty. There was a majesty to the landscape that reminded Laura that Alaska was, as she had once told Sam, America's last frontier.

She was smiling as she opened the door to her cabin. Truly, she was a fortunate woman. She had two wonderful children who appeared to be thriving in their new life. They had a home that, while it might not be a mansion, was warm, clean, and comfortable. She was doing work that she enjoyed and that was making a difference. Laura was pleased with the progress of her daytime students, and though the number of adults and Indian children she taught was small, they brought her a special satisfaction.

And then there were her friends. Ah, yes, her friends. She was so lucky to have them. Especially Sam, whose conversation she enjoyed so much and who added a much-needed masculine influence to her children's lives. Laura shivered, remembering those weeks when she and Sam had been estranged. Thank goodness they were ended! Her life might not be perfect now, but it was awfully close.

As Laura shed her coat, Charlotte put a cautionary finger to her lips. "The twins just fell asleep," she whispered, and started to rise from the rocking chair, offering it to Laura. Laura shook her head, amused by the fact that, while Charlotte seemed immune to Sam's charm, she obviously enjoyed the chair that he'd made.

Laura sniffed as she pulled out one of the kitchen chairs for herself. She and Charlotte normally shared a cup of tea or a glass of warm milk when Laura returned from her evening classes. Tonight, though, an unfamiliar aroma greeted her. "What smells so delicious?" she asked.

Charlotte's smile was self-deprecating. "I tried to make mulled cider," she said, pointing to a small saucepan. Her hands gripped the chair arms, as if she was nervous about something. Surely it couldn't be the cider, yet it seemed that something was bothering Charlotte.

Laura lifted the lid and sniffed appreciatively. Her own cider, although good, had never smelled like this. As she poured the steaming beverage into two mugs, Laura asked about her children. "Did they give you any trouble getting to sleep?" Perhaps Charlotte had had problems with them, and that was why she appeared disturbed.

Charlotte shook her head. "We read a long story tonight." She wrapped both hands around the mug. "You're so lucky to have Meg and Matt."

"They're the best part of my life," Laura agreed. Settling into her chair, she looked at Charlotte. Unless Laura was mistaken, those were tears in Charlotte's eyes. "What's wrong?" she asked softly.

For a moment the only sounds were the hiss of the gas burner and the clock's loud ticking. Charlotte blinked furiously. "Oh, Mrs. Templeton, I'm so confused."

Laura inclined her head slightly to encourage Charlotte. It was a positive sign that she was speaking rather than keeping whatever bothered her bottled up inside. "Do you want to talk about it? I'm a good listener."

Charlotte took a sip of the cider, and Laura guessed she was trying to decide how much to tell her. "I don't know what to do," Charlotte said at last, her eyes still swimming with tears. "I don't want to disappoint them."

Rather than pressure her assistant, Laura nodded and tasted the cider. Like all of Charlotte's culinary efforts, it was excellent. "Delicious," she said, and watched a faint blush of pleasure color Charlotte's cheeks. "Why don't you start at the beginning?"

For a second, Laura thought she would refuse. Then Charlotte said, "I love my parents. I want to make them happy, but . . ." Her voice trailed off, and Laura knew she was reluctant to say anything more.

"But what?"

Charlotte placed the mug on the floor and began to rock. "I just can't," she said, her eyes fixed on the far wall as if the crack next to the window held the answers to life's mysteries.

"Can't what?" Laura prompted her.

Charlotte's feet increased their pace, and she was rocking so quickly that Laura guessed she was trying to diffuse her frustration with physical activity. It was a ploy Laura knew all too well, although she usually resorted to pacing the floor. At last Charlotte stopped the chair's rhythmic motion and fixed her gaze on Laura. "My parents want me to marry Mr. Baranov."

Laura nodded. She had suspected that Charlotte's distress was related either to Sam or to Charlotte's desire to attend normal school in Seattle. "Sam's a good man," Laura said in as neutral a tone as she could manage. Sam was her friend, her very good friend, but even though there were few things Laura wanted more than for him to receive his father's legacy, she didn't want to influence Charlotte, particularly if what she suspected about Charlotte and Jason was true.

Charlotte began to rock again, more slowly this time. "You may be right, but I don't love Sam. I . . ." Once again she refused to complete a sentence.

"Do you love someone else?" Laura had seen Charlotte meet Jason on several occasions, and the eagerness that her assistant displayed when she hurried from the schoolhouse to the forest seemed to confirm Laura's suspicion that Charlotte regarded Jason as more than a friend.

Color flooded Charlotte's face, and she dropped her head, staring at the floor. "Yes," she said, so softly that Laura had to strain to hear her. "That is, I think I do." Charlotte raised her eyes and looked at Laura. "Tell me, Mrs. Templeton, how do I know if I'm in love?"

How indeed? Laura closed her eyes for a second, wishing she had the answer. She could quote poets, citing verses from Ovid to Browning, but that wouldn't answer Charlotte's question. It wouldn't help the young woman any more than it had helped Laura when Roy had come into her life, literally sweeping her off her feet.

"How do you feel when you're with him?" she asked, careful not to mention Jason's name. If Charlotte wanted her to know the identity of her love, she would tell Laura.

Though Laura swirled the cider in her mug, keeping the spices in suspension, she watched Charlotte from the corner of her eye. The young woman's face took on a dreamy expression. "I feel hot and cold and scared and excited all at the same time."

Laura hoped her face did not betray her surprise. Though she had believed herself to be in love with Roy, she would never have described her feelings that way. Roy had never made her feel either hot or cold. "Warm" was the most she could say. As for "scared and excited," perhaps at times she had felt apprehension, but it had centered on her parents' reaction to Roy, not on Roy himself. And even in their most intimate moments, she had felt only mild pleasure, not the grand passion the poets promised.

Charlotte rocked for a moment, then stopped, clasping her hands in her lap and leaning forward. Her blue eyes met Laura's, and she smiled shyly. "He makes me feel beautiful," she said, her faintly bewildered expression confirming what Laura had suspected, that no one had ever told Charlotte she was beautiful. Laura herself had heard the compliment so often that when Roy had praised her beauty, she had not reacted the way Charlotte did. For Laura, it had been nothing special, while for Charlotte the feeling would be both unexpected and, oh, so special.

"How do you feel about him?" Laura asked. It was odd. Though Charlotte was asking her advice, it was Laura who was learning about love. While others might disagree, she had little doubt that what Charlotte felt for the unnamed young man was love. The infatuation Laura had felt for Roy in the early days of their marriage was nothing like the feelings Charlotte was describing. Those sounded like the poets' paeans.

The clock chimed the hour. Though normally Charlotte would have left before this, she made no move to rise. Instead, she picked up her mug and took a sip of cider. "I want to make Jason happy," she told Laura with another shy smile.

Laura leaned back in her chair, feigning nonchalance and hoping that Charlotte didn't realize she had just divulged her love's name.

"I want to protect him from all the people who don't understand him," Charlotte continued.

Laura nodded. Love had a protective component. That was part of what she felt for her children. Oddly, though, she had never felt protective of Roy. "And you don't feel that way about Sam." It was a statement, not a question. Laura had seen Charlotte with Sam too many times to think that she harbored any affection for the sawmill owner. Though, for

Sam's sake, Laura might wish it were different, she knew that love could not be mandated.

"No." Charlotte shook her head emphatically. "When I'm with Sam, I feel awkward and ugly."

This time Laura could not camouflage her surprise. "That doesn't sound like Sam. He's always so polite that I can't imagine him saying anything cruel to you."

Charlotte sipped her cider, the line between her eyes telling Laura she was considering the statement carefully. "It isn't anything he says," she admitted. "It's just the way I feel when I'm with him." Charlotte frowned. "You probably think I'm silly." Her frown deepened. "I know it's not rational, but it's the way I feel."

Laura shook her head. "You're not silly, Charlotte. Love isn't rational. You can't analyze it, and you can't decide to fall in love with someone." *Although I tried to do exactly that,* she admitted to herself. *Roy came at a time when I needed someone, so I convinced myself that I loved him.*

"Then what do I do?"

That was easy. "Follow your heart." Laura smiled her encouragement. "Don't settle for anything less than love." *Don't make the same mistakes I did.*

The house smelled wonderful, redolent with the aromas of roasting game birds, winter squash, and succulent dressing, confirming Ella's reputation as a good cook. Though she had wanted to host a party in Laura's honor before her pregnancy was too advanced, Ella had respected Laura's wishes and had agreed to wait until she was out of mourning. But even though Laura had protested, Ella had insisted that Thanksgiving dinner with a few close friends was not a party and was a perfectly acceptable social event for a recent widow.

Now that she was in the neat white house at the far end of First Street, Laura was glad she had come. The twins, who had been fed an hour earlier, were playing happily in one corner, occasionally peering into the crib that held Amelia and William's son, while the adults gathered around the table. It was a larger group than Laura had anticipated, and yet she could not complain, for they were all her friends. Though she had known that Ella and Ben would invite Amelia and William, Laura hadn't expected Reverend and Mrs. Langdon and Charlotte and Sam to be among the guests.

Laura tried not to smile when she saw the seating arrangement. Though Ella had deliberately separated husbands from their wives, she had placed Sam next to Charlotte. It was surely only coincidence that Laura was on Sam's other side, next to Ben. Undoubtedly, Ella expected her to converse with Ben, leaving Sam free to talk to the woman all of Gold Landing knew he was courting.

"Ben and I want to start a new tradition," Ella said when Reverend Langdon had completed his blessing and the guests had started serving themselves from the heaping platters. "We thought each of us could mention one reason we're especially thankful today." A low murmur of assent greeted her suggestion. "I'll start," Ella volunteered. She smiled at Laura. "Although I have many things to be thankful for," she said with an involuntary glance at her thickening waistline, "I'm especially grateful for my new friend, Laura."

Laura caught her breath in surprise. Though she counted Ella as her dearest friend—except perhaps for Sam—she hadn't realized that Ella felt the same way. Laura waited until her blush had subsided before she said, "I'm appreciative of the welcome you've all given me. I feel at home here." And home was something Laura would never again take for granted.

The Langdons each spoke, then turned toward their host. Ben peered over his spectacles, then flashed his partner a smile. "I thank God every day that I have Amelia here to deliver Ella's baby."

"I second that," William said. "Amelia's been the answer to all my prayers."

Though Amelia's cheeks turned a rosy hue, she said calmly, "I'm most thankful for William, who loves me despite my imperfections."

As Laura watched the obvious love that flowed between the two, she thought of her conversation with Charlotte and wondered what Charlotte and Sam would say. Since Laura knew Charlotte would not mention her love for Jason, she suspected she would thank her parents. As for Sam, who knows what he would be grateful for?

Charlotte laid her butter knife on the delicately patterned plate and smiled at Laura. "I'm thankful that Mrs. Templeton has given me the opportunity to teach." Laura watched the elder Langdons exchange startled glances. Hadn't Charlotte told them she was teaching a lesson every day?

Only Sam was left. His gaze moved around the table, pausing at each person, and Laura wondered what he was thinking. Was he, like her, a little uncomfortable with the conversation? When a mischievous grin crossed his face, Laura knew two things. He had made a decision, and whatever he would say would be designed to amuse them.

"I'm thankful for the two people who've reminded me of the beauty of simple pleasures." To complete his sentence, Sam gestured toward Matt and Meg, playing in the corner. As if on cue, Matt snatched a wooden block from his sister's hand and banged it on the floor. Meg began to wail.

Everyone laughed as Sam's words diffused the gravity of the conversation. "Simple pleasures like fighting," Laura said, excusing herself from the table. When she returned from settling the children into their naps, she found the adults engrossed in what appeared to be a serious discussion.

"It may not be as bad as you fear," Ben was saying. He was stirring his coffee with a ferocity that seemed at odds with his calming words.

"What did I miss?" Laura asked as she took her seat again and accepted the piece of pumpkin pie that Ella offered her. Judging from the few crumbs left on the others' plates, it was as delicious as the rest of the meal.

"I'm afraid we may be facing an epidemic of pneumonia," Amelia said, her expression grim. She took a sip of coffee, then looked directly at Laura. "There have been a few iso-

lated cases, but I'm afraid that with the holiday gatherings, it may spread." Amelia shuddered. "Pneumonia is one disease that I fear."

When Amelia's blue eyes filled with pain as she looked at her husband, Laura was reminded that William had almost died from pneumonia.

Laura felt her appetite disappear. If there was an epidemic, it would likely be more severe in the Indian village, where—despite Amelia's efforts—medical care was less prevalent than in Gold Landing itself. And disease, Laura knew, was most dangerous for the young and the elderly. Her students would be at risk. Suddenly aware that her hand was trembling so badly that the coffee threatened to slosh onto Ella's linen tablecloth, Laura set her cup on the saucer.

Perhaps Ben was right. Perhaps there would be no epidemic. Perhaps no babies would die. With every fiber of her being, Laura hoped that was true. She couldn't bear the thought of another mother suffering the way Spring Flower had when Adam died.

As if she sensed Laura's distress, Ella said, "Please. Can we talk about happier topics?"

"How about the pageant?" Charlotte suggested. Though Ben had kept Laura engaged in conversation through most of the meal, Charlotte had said very little, barely responding to Sam's questions. Now that the discussion was more general, she appeared to have lost her inhibitions. "It's still a month away, but the children are so excited that it's hard to keep their attention on their lessons."

Ella chuckled. "How well I remember that problem." She poured another cup of coffee for Charlotte's father. "Maybe I shouldn't tell you that it's only going to get worse. Of course," Ella added, "I think the parents are just as anxious."

Amelia passed the sugar bowl to Reverend Langdon. "Last year the discussion was all about who had which role," she said. "This year my patients keep asking me about the new scenery." Amelia raised her glass in a toast to Laura and Sam. "You two know how to build anticipation. No one seems to know what the scenery looks like, so it's all they can talk about."

Sam laid down his coffee cup and wiped his mouth. "You mean the boys haven't told anyone what we're making?"

It was, Laura knew, remarkable that anything remained a secret in a town as small as Gold Landing. Sam had suggested to the boys that they not tell anyone, but neither she nor Sam had expected half-a-dozen boys in their teens to be able to avoid confiding in someone. And once one person knew, the rest of the town would not be far behind.

William shook his head. "I've even heard some of my miners speculating, so I'd say your secret is safe."

As the conversation flowed, Laura watched Sam and Charlotte. Though they were seated next to each other and spoke occasionally, there were obviously no sparks between them. It was, she reflected, a shame. Love couldn't be forced, and the last thing Laura wanted was for Charlotte to marry someone she didn't love. But . . . still . . .

Laura wished there were some way she could help Sam claim his inheritance. He was such a good man! Look at the way he had given his time so selflessly to make a classroom for her special students. Look at the way he had volunteered to make scenery for the Christmas pageant. Look at the way he fostered camaraderie among the boys at the same time that he taught them a useful skill.

Laura wanted Sam to be happy. Everyone deserved happiness, Sam more than most. Laura tried to keep smiling, though it wrenched her heart to think that Sam would not receive his inheritance when it meant so much to him. Dear, wonderful Sam! Laura felt the blood drain from her face as she realized how deeply she cared about him. It was only friendship, of course. Nothing more. She would feel that way about any of her friends. But, oh, how she wished she could help him.

When the dishes were cleared and the conversation began to drag, Amelia turned to Laura. "Are you sure you don't mind?"

She shook her head. "Of course not. I'll be happy to take dinner to Shantytown and the Indian village." Ella had told Laura how William always ensured that the less fortunate people on the other side of the river shared in the town's celebrations.

"I'd go," Amelia explained, "but I have some patients I still need to see this afternoon." Though she did not elaborate, Laura guessed that these were the people whose pneumonia so worried the doctor. "Naturally, William will go with you."

Sam, who had been moving toward the door, stopped. "There's no need for that. You know I can mush the sled."

William looked relieved. "I'd appreciate it." He nodded toward his son, who was fussing in his mother's arms. "It looks like Josh wants his own bed."

Within minutes, Sam had loaded the containers of food onto the sled, and he and Laura were crossing the bridge. Though it was still mid-afternoon, the sun had just set, streaking the sky with rosy fingers. It was a magical time of the day, one that Laura loved, but today she barely noticed the natural beauty, for her thoughts continued to stray to the man who walked next to her. Sam was such a special friend. There had to be a way she could help him!

As they unloaded the first set of parcels in Shantytown, several of the unemployed miners joked with Sam, while their wives flashed Laura smiles of gratitude. Laura had heard from Amelia about the men who, when their own gold stakes played out, were too proud to work in William's mine, valuing their independence so much that they would rather eke out an existence than work for another man. These men's lives were not easy, and some families barely survived.

Though he had no obligation to them, William always found ways to deliver food without hurting their pride. Sam, it appeared, had developed that same easy camaraderie with the men, instinctively knowing what to say to keep the food from looking like charity.

"We've got a little problem," he told a group of men, "and

I sure as snow don't know how to solve it." When the men gathered closer, Laura heard Sam say, "I reckon you've heard about the Christmas pageant the new schoolteacher is planning." There was a murmur of assent, and Laura could almost feel the curious looks that came her way. "The schoolmarm's got her heart set on having camels, although Lord knows where she thinks we're gonna find a camel in Alaska." The men laughed, obviously amused by the *cheechako*'s ignorance. Laura tried to keep her surprise from showing. Since she and Sam had never discussed animals of any kind, there had to be a reason he was telling this tale.

"You fellas got any idea what we could use?"

Several men spoke, but their words were so low that Laura couldn't distinguish them. She handed another basket to one of the women. The men's discussion continued, apparently with no resolution. Then one man said, "What about a moose? I reckon those wise men could ride a moose."

From the corner of her eye, Laura saw Sam appear to consider the suggestion. "You could be right. Only one problem I see, and that's how to make a bull moose do what we want. We all know better than to mess with a cow." The men laughed.

More discussion ensued. At length, one of the men suggested that they hunt a moose, tan it, and stuff its hide.

"You know, that just might work," Sam said. "I'll bet Mrs. Templeton would be mighty grateful if you'd help her that way. That would be a mighty neighborly thing to do."

As they headed the dogsled toward the Indian village, Laura turned to Sam. "A camel, huh?"

He shrugged. "The men like to hunt. Their families can use the meat. And this way they've provided a service to the town." It was, Laura realized, a way to bring the two sides of the river together and to keep the dinner they had just delivered from looking like charity.

"You know, Sam, I was thinking." Laura flashed him a quick smile. "The pageant really does need a camel."

They were still laughing when they reached the center of

the Athapaskan village. As the sound of the dogs' yipping alerted the town to their arrival, two of Laura's students emerged from their wickiups, followed by several of the adults. Laura smiled at her students, and tried not to let her distress show. Even the covering of snow could not disguise the poverty or the squalor. Though Shantytown was miserable, its shacks seemed palatial compared to the Athapaskans' wickiups. Laura noticed that some of the teepees had no plumes of smoke emerging from their tops, and she wondered how the families were surviving without heat, since the leather walls would not retain warmth.

"Today is Thanksgiving," she told her students in a voice that she struggled to keep steady. "You remember that we talked about the traditional celebration and how we share with those who've helped us. I'm thankful for what I've learned from you." The students' eyes widened as they considered that they might have taught the teacher. "In return," Laura continued, "Mr. Baranov and I would like to share our celebration with you." She gestured toward the parcels on the sled.

One of the students spoke rapidly, obviously explaining the significance of Thanksgiving to his parents and the other adults. The Athapaskans looked dubious at first, but the child continued, his arms moving rapidly as he used signs to punctuate his words. At length, one of the older men smiled. The boy's cry of glee told Laura the town elder had approved of the gift.

"Thank you," the boy said.

But a tall, gaunt woman emerged from her wickiup. "No reason for thanks," Spring Flower announced with a baleful look at Laura. "Books kill my son."

Chapter Eleven

Tonight was the night. Sam tried not to frown as he shaved for the second time in a day. Though something about tonight didn't feel right, time was running short. He could delay no longer, and so he had made his plans. He winced as the razor scraped sensitive skin. It was probably foolish. She wouldn't notice whether or not he had shaved. She might not even care that he had put on a fresh shirt and collar. But Sam knew there were conventions to be observed. That was why he had spent so much effort planning this event.

The hotel's dining room was fancier. That was where Sam would have liked to have gone. But Sam couldn't picture Charlotte Langdon agreeing to spend the evening with him in a hotel, even if it was only in its dining room. That was about as likely as flowers in December. Though Pete's Roadhouse might not be as elegant a setting, there was no reason Charlotte or her parents could object to their spending an hour or so there. With its bright lights and the constant flow of patrons, they would be adequately chaperoned. They would share a good dinner there, and then . . . Sam frowned again and grabbed his coat. It was time to go.

"Good evening, Reverend," he said as Charlotte's father opened the parsonage door. "Is Charlotte ready?"

"Just about." Surely it was only Sam's imagination that Reverend Langdon's smile was sympathetic. He couldn't have guessed what Sam intended to do tonight, could he? Sam had told no one that tonight was the night. No one at all. Not even Laura.

"You're looking very pretty tonight," Sam said when Charlotte joined him in the parlor. In truth, she looked much the same as she did every day. That gray dress made her look like a little mouse, and her face was so pale that he wondered whether she was ill. But Sam knew what was expected, and compliments were on the list of "must do's."

Though Sam had considered taking his buggy to the roadhouse, he decided it would be better to walk. Charlotte appeared to enjoy walking, and he had found a secluded spot between the saloon and the roadhouse that would be perfect for his plans. It had a view of the river, and rivers—or so Sam had heard—were considered romantic settings. Even the weather had cooperated. The night was ideal: the sky clear, with only a few lazy snowflakes drifting, the evergreens still cloaked in the snow that had fallen yesterday.

Sam knew he should be filled with anticipation, the blood singing through his veins at the thought of what was to come. He was out walking with the woman who soon would be his bride. If she was quieter than he might have liked, answering his questions with no more than her customary monosyllabic replies, surely he shouldn't have been disappointed. And there was no reason that, as he walked toward the roadhouse, he should remember the day he had driven a sled with Laura and her children along this same street. It wasn't fair to compare Laura's children's exuberant reaction to Charlotte's passivity, and it most definitely wasn't fair to compare Laura's vibrant smiles and the stimulating conversations they had with Charlotte's quiet responses. Charlotte was the woman he was going to marry. Tonight would make that official.

When Pete had seated them at one of the long wooden tables and had taken their orders, Sam turned to his bride-to-be. Charlotte was looking around the roadhouse with such obvious interest that he surmised this was her first visit. Though she appeared to like the casual eating establishment, Sam noticed that she kept edging away from him on the bench, as if she were afraid she might inadvertently brush against him. That was not a good sign. If they married—*when* they married, he corrected himself—he certainly intended to touch more than Charlotte's fingertips.

Sam tried not to frown as he thought of the times he had touched Laura. Though she had drawn away, obviously distressed by the contact, Sam couldn't forget the jolt of excitement that had raced up his arm. Her skin was soft and smooth, like the silk of her best dress, but unlike silk, Laura's hands were warm and tender.

As he looked around the roadhouse, Sam wondered whether Laura had eaten Pete's moose or bear stew. Though children rarely accompanied their parents, he could picture Matt and Meg's expressions as they watched the heavily laden travelers deposit their packs in the corner, then settle onto a bench and begin speaking with their table companions. At Pete's, no one was a stranger for long. Would Meg enjoy the boisterous atmosphere? Sam was sure Matt would. As for Laura . . .

Stop it! Sam admonished himself. He was here with Charlotte; he should be thinking of no one but her. Charlotte was the woman he was going to marry. Charlotte was the woman who would share his life, his dinner table, his bed.

"So you enjoy teaching," Sam said when Pete had placed bowls of stew and a plate of the flaky biscuits that were his specialty in front of them. Though it wasn't a brilliant conversational gambit, Sam hoped that he could elicit more than a single word from her.

"Yes." Charlotte's smile was radiant as she broke a biscuit and buttered it. For a moment Sam tried to tell himself that the smile was for him, that she was enjoying their evening together. But her next words dashed his hopes. "Teaching is what I want to do more than anything else."

The mouthful of stew that had seemed delicious a second before lost its flavor. Sam swallowed and laid his spoon on the table. Though he knew he should be grateful that Charlotte had spoken a whole sentence, he wished she would show some of that enthusiasm for him. It was going to be difficult having a bride who wanted to be doing something besides being his wife. Perhaps if he directed her thoughts to some of the advantages of marriage, she would look more favorably on the institution.

"Laura says you care for her children the evenings that she's teaching. Do you enjoy them?"

Once again Charlotte's eyes lit with pleasure, and her face looked almost pretty. Not as pretty as Laura's, of course. *Stop it!* "Oh, yes," Charlotte said. "I hope my own children are as good as Mrs. Templeton's."

That was the first good sign Sam had seen tonight. If Charlotte wanted children, she surely realized that she needed a husband to assist in that particular project. Perhaps she would favor his suit after all. Sam decided to probe a little more deeply. He took another bite of stew, then said as casually as he could, "It looks like we have something in common. You want children. So do I."

The door opened, admitting two men who stomped the snow from their boots and announced to anyone who would listen that Pete's biscuits were the best in the territory. Charlotte frowned. It must be that she didn't like the fact that the men took seats across from them. Surely it wasn't the thought of Sam's having children that was so distasteful to her. "I do want children," she admitted, a blush coloring her face. "Someday." She paused and spread some of Pete's apple preserves on her biscuit. "I want to teach for a few years before the children are born," she explained.

Sam tried not to sigh. He didn't have a few years. He had only a few months, a very few months. "Is there a rule against married teachers?" he asked, thankful that their table companions were strangers. At least they wouldn't carry tales of this conversation back to town.

"No, but it's hard if you have babies." Charlotte took a bite of the biscuit, then said, "These are very good biscuits." She included the strangers in her announcement.

This time Sam did sigh. Charlotte hadn't been particularly subtle about changing the subject. It was obvious she was reluctant to discuss marriage, and that did not bode well for his plans. Still, maybe the romantic atmosphere near the river would change her mood. Women were, after all, changeable creatures. Sam knew that. Just because Laura wasn't flighty didn't mean that others weren't.

"I imagine you've been busy helping Laura with the pageant," he said. That at least was a neutral subject. Though Sam knew more than almost anyone about the status of the pageant and had no desire to discuss it, it was better than sitting here in silence, realizing that by tomorrow morning everyone in Gold Landing would know that he had brought Charlotte to Pete's and that they had spent most of the time eating rather than talking. Speculation would be rife, and he'd take more than a normal share of ribbing over his courtship. Of course, if the evening ended the way he had planned, he'd be able to answer the smug smiles with an announcement that would provide new grist for the rumor mill.

For the rest of the meal, Sam tried to engage Charlotte in conversation. Though she would answer his questions, even smiling occasionally, there was no denying the fact that she provided no more than desultory replies. It didn't matter, Sam told himself. He needed a bride, not a brilliant conversationalist. Good marriages had been based on less than that. But as he watched Charlotte sip her tea and butter a biscuit, he tried to picture her sitting on the opposite side of the dinner table from him every night. Sam had a vivid imagination. That was part of what had made his day in the coffin so horrible. He could conjure pictures of almost anything.

Why, then, couldn't he imagine spending the rest of his life with Charlotte?

He had to. There were no alternatives. He needed a wife, and Charlotte was his best—his only—chance. It wasn't as if he wanted to marry Laura. Widows with children were not for him. No, sirree.

At last the meal was over. Sam helped Charlotte don her coat. Though he might have let his hands linger on her shoulders, Sam was careful not to touch her. There was no point in frightening her, not tonight of all nights. He opened the door. The air was so cold that he winced as he took a gulp of it. He should have known better. A man didn't breathe Alaskan air the way he drank beer.

Sam took Charlotte's elbow and led her toward the road, noting that the evening was as nice as it had been before. That had to be a good sign. The spot he had chosen was only a few hundred yards away. Charlotte would not be chilled by the time they reached it. Surely she would not refuse to stop. Surely she would not refuse. . . . Sam opened his mouth, then closed it without uttering a word. There was no need to try to engage Charlotte in conversation now, for soon he would ask her the most important question he had asked anyone.

Sam looked at the woman who walked beside him. It was odd. When he walked with Laura, he didn't mind the silences, because they were punctuated with lively discussions. But Charlotte never seemed to have an opinion, no matter what topic he raised. The only subject he had found that interested her was teaching.

It didn't matter.

As they approached the location Sam had chosen, he began to smile. It was just as he had expected—quiet and peaceful, with a view of the moon shining on the river. Surely this was the perfect spot to ask a woman to marry him.

Sam slowed his steps and placed one hand on Charlotte's arm to stop her. He touched her gently, then moved so that he was facing her. This was the part where he was supposed to kneel in front of her and take her hand in his. He would do it. Of course he would. But his knees refused to move, and his throat was so dry that he was forced to clear it.

"Charlotte," he said when he could speak again, "there's something I want to ask you."

"Yes?" Her face betrayed no emotion, not even curiosity.

He would do it. Of course he would.

But when Sam opened his mouth, all he said was, "Did you like the bear stew?"

Mary Peterson tried not to shudder as the wind buffeted the small farmhouse. Though storms were not uncommon in this part of Washington, tonight's seemed particularly fierce. It was silly to worry about John. Even though the snow was blinding in its intensity, he could find his way back from the barn. Hadn't they planted trees along the path for just that purpose?

The door banged open, and Mary let out the breath she had been holding. "John!" she cried. "I was worried."

He laughed as he shook snow from his coat and cap. "You worry too much, Mother. The animals will be fine. I left extra water for the cows and a double ration of hay for the horse."

As if she cared about the livestock! "Oh, John, you know I wasn't worried about the animals. It was you."

He laughed again and sniffed appreciatively. "Somethin' sure smells good."

"Chicken and dumplings," Mary said, and began to ladle food onto their plates. "I do hope Junior and Linda are all right."

Her husband slid his arm around her waist and squeezed her. "Stop worrying, Mother. You raised a good boy."

"It's a mother's right to worry," she said with a quick smile as she pulled out her chair and settled at the table. They bowed their heads, and John began to pray. A loud banging on the door interrupted John's blessing.

"Who on earth . . . ?" Mary felt her heart begin to pound.

In a storm like this, the only reason people went out was for an emergency. Junior! Something had happened to Junior!

John flung the door open. A tall man covered with snow stood outside. Though the wind buffeted him, he pulled off his hat in an oddly formal gesture. The stranger, Mary saw, was no older than her own Junior, but while Junior was dark-haired, this man was blond, and there was nothing in his expression that made her think he was bearing bad tidings. Her heart began to slow. Maybe Junior was all right.

"Come in, come in," John said. "Ain't no night to be outdoors."

The man smiled, and Mary realized he was a fine-looking young man. "Thank you kindly," he said. "It 'pears I lost my way." Mary took a deep breath when she heard the man's explanation. Her son was safe.

The stranger looked at the table, and Mary thought she saw him swallow deeply. It appeared he was hungry as well as lost.

"Would you like to join us for supper?" she asked. Mary hoped that if Junior was ever lost in a snowstorm, some other woman would take him into her home and feed him supper.

The man smiled. "Thank you, ma'am. Something smells mighty good."

Though the stranger was obviously famished, he displayed the best table manners Mary had ever seen on a man. His mama had surely raised him well.

"How far is it to town?" he asked when he had finished his second helping of her apple cobbler, declaring it far superior to any he had ever eaten.

John met Mary's gaze. She nodded in response to his silent question. "Son," John said in his raspy voice, "it's too far to go tonight. The storm 'pears to be worsening."

As the young man's face fell, Mary wondered what he had planned to do in town. She would have heard if anyone had been expecting a visitor. "I wouldn't want to impose," he said in that same polite voice, "but I would surely appreciate it if I could sleep in your barn tonight."

"Nonsense." Mary didn't wait for her husband's response. "We've got a perfectly good bedroom that's not being used. You can stay with us."

"That's mighty generous, ma'am, but I couldn't impose like that."

"It's our pleasure," Mary said, again picturing a faceless woman offering Junior shelter from a storm.

The stranger yawned as politely as he did everything else. "No need to rush in the morning," John said as their guest made his way to his room. "But I will tell you that Mary's flapjacks are a real treat."

"He's such a nice boy," Mary whispered to her husband.

When they wakened the next morning, the stranger was gone, and so was the money Mary had hidden in her cookie jar.

There was no doubt about it. Something was wrong. Laura could feel the tension begin to build in her neck, tensing her muscles and making her head throb. She had tried to tell herself that it was nothing more than a minor illness, that he'd be better the next day, but she could delude herself no longer. Matt was sick. Her normally active son was listless and burning with fever. No doubt about it. He needed a doctor.

Laura frowned, wondering what she should do. She didn't want to leave Matt alone while she looked for Amelia. Though he was sleeping now, Laura knew that he could wake at any moment, and in his current condition, he would be frightened to find himself alonc. Laura pushed aside the crisp muslin curtains and stared outside, looking for a solution. It appeared a minute later.

"Sam!" Laura cupped her hands around her mouth and shouted from her front step. "I need you!"

The morning was overcast, threatening more snow. It had fallen throughout the long night while Laura had watched over her son, willing him to be well. Fresh snow covered the road, obliterating the traces of yesterday's traffic, the only tracks those of a lone moose who had ventured into town to browse, and now Sam's. He sprinted across the street. "What's wrong?"

Though nothing had changed, Laura felt a bit of her panic subside. Sam was here. He would help. She motioned him into the house and closed the door behind them. Meg looked up from the corner where she had been playing house with her doll and gave Sam a smile. "That's right, honey," Laura told her daughter. "Just stay there." As she explained her worries to Sam, he nodded, his face solemn. "I'll get Amelia," he promised.

Ten minutes later, he returned with the doctor. Though Amelia kept a bright smile on her face and spoke reassuringly to Matt, Laura saw concern reflected in her friend's eyes. "Be good for Dr. Amelia," Laura told her son. The admonition was unnecessary, for it was a measure of Matt's illness that he did not protest when Amelia peered inside his throat and tapped on his back.

When she finished, Amelia took Laura's arm and led her into her bedroom. Closing the door firmly behind them, the doctor said, "I'm afraid Matt has pneumonia."

And Laura, who remembered the discussion over Thanksgiving dinner, blanched. "How serious?"

"I won't lie to you, Laura." Amelia rubbed the back of her neck, the gesture betraying her worry as much as her clouded eyes did. "It could be very serious. We won't know for several days, but in the meantime, Matt will need constant nursing. Do you want to bring him to my office?" Laura had seen the small infirmary that Amelia had set up in one room of the medical office. Though not as large as the clinic she had once had, it was a cheerful place and well equipped to treat infectious diseases. For many patients, it was ideal. But not for Matt.

Laura shook her head. Matt was so young that she didn't want to leave him. Surely she could be his nurse. "If you tell me what to do, I'll do it." No one, not even Amelia, could give Matt the loving care that she could.

Outside the cabin, the wind began to blow. The chill of fear that ran down Laura's spine owed more to Amelia's diagnosis than the frigid Alaskan winter. "What about Meg?" Laura asked. "Will she catch it too?" Matt had been the stronger of the twins. If he was so sick, what would happen to his sister? Laura shuddered again. It couldn't happen. Surely if God was the loving Being Reverend Langdon claimed, he wouldn't let both of her children be stricken.

Amelia's blue eyes were serious. "Meg shouldn't be exposed to the germs any longer." It was what Laura had feared. She would have to put Matt in the infirmary or else send Meg away. In either case, she would be forced to be parted from one of her children. An intense need to hold her daughter filled Laura, and she rushed into the kitchen.

"How is he?" Laura started at the sound of Sam's voice. In her worry over Matt, she had forgotten that Sam was still in the kitchen. He was sitting cross-legged on the floor, playing with Meg. Laura couldn't help smiling at the picture of her normally shy daughter offering a cup of make-believe tea to the man who had once seemed so forbidding. But her smile faded as she explained the situation to him.

"Could Ella care for her?" she asked.

Laura turned to Amelia, who had followed her into the kitchen. The doctor shook her head. "I don't think that's wise in Ella's condition."

Laura bit her lip and tried to think. Though she knew that almost any of the women in Gold Landing would care for her daughter, she was afraid that timid Meg would be terribly frightened by the combination of being away from her mother and being in a strange home.

"Charlotte could do it," Sam suggested. "Meg knows her."

It was an answer, but . . . "Meg can be a handful." There were days when Charlotte was definitely frazzled by caring for the twins.

Sam shrugged. "It doesn't seem that you have a lot of choices. I'll ask Charlotte." He reached for his coat.

*   *   *

It was, it appeared, Sam's morning to summon women to the Templeton cabin. When Charlotte arrived, seemingly eager to care for Meg, Laura packed a bag of clothing and toys. "Just ask if you need anything else," she told Charlotte, then gave Meg a big hug. "Be good for Charlotte, sweetie."

Laura watched from the front porch until they had disappeared from view, then came back inside and stared sightlessly out the parlor window. Nothing was right today. Matt was sick, and Meg was gone. Laura swallowed hard. This would be the first night since they were born that she had been separated from one of her children.

"Where's Amelia?"

For the second time that day, Sam's voice startled Laura. This time he was seated on one of the kitchen chairs in the far corner. Why was it, she wondered, that she hadn't noticed him today? Normally, she was very conscious of his presence. When she was teaching her special students, even though a wall separated them, she was always aware of Sam in his office. It could be that she was so preoccupied today with her children that she wasn't thinking of anything else, but Laura doubted that. Was it, perhaps, that Sam seemed so comfortable here that she didn't feel as if there was a stranger in her home? Somehow, Sam seemed to belong.

"Amelia had other patients," Laura told him. "She'll be back tomorrow. In the meantime, she explained what I had to do." And if the most daunting part of the regimen became waiting, somehow Laura would manage that too.

Sam rose and reached for his coat. "I'd better go," he said.

Laura could feel a flush color her face and neck. It was most unseemly for Sam to be here with her. She knew that, and yet she was oddly reluctant for him to leave. It had felt so good to have him here, helping her. He had been the one who had suggested Charlotte; he'd been the one who had kept Meg entertained. Without Laura's asking, he had seemed to know what she needed.

When they had gone to the Indian village the night Adam had died, Sam had let her lean on him. That day he had provided physical comfort. Laura had vague memories of being a child and running to her mother when she was hurt. Today she had leaned on Sam in a different way. This time she'd sought—and received—emotional support. Though she could remember her mother providing comfort when she had skinned her knees, Laura could not remember anyone giving her emotional support. It was a new experience, being able to rely on someone else, and Laura found that she liked it.

"I don't know how to thank you for everything you've done," she said as she walked to the door with Sam.

His brown eyes shone with warmth. "I'm glad to help you. That's what friends do."

Friends. Of course that's what they were. There was no reason the thought should leave her feeling empty inside.

"Oh, Jason, she's so sweet." Charlotte tugged off her glove and savored the warmth of having her hand clasped between both of Jason's. It was probably foolish, exposing her skin to the cold, but Charlotte wasn't going to deprive herself of a pleasant experience. They were standing in the small copse that Charlotte now considered their special place.

"Who's sweet?" Jason asked. "Besides you." He brought her hand to his lips and licked one fingertip. "Sweet," he murmured.

Snow had started to fall, and the wind was rising. It was more than foolish, it was foolhardy to have removed her glove. Charlotte didn't care. "Oh, Jason!" she sighed. How could her parents and the other adults in Gold Landing think that Jason was a bad boy? He was good and kind and gentle, not the ruffian many believed him to be.

"So who's sweet?" he asked again as he prepared to lick a second fingertip.

Charlotte smiled, remembering the little girl who had turned her bedroom topsy-turvy, who had spilled half her food on the floor, and who had wrenched Charlotte's heart when she had laid her head on Charlotte's shoulder and fallen asleep.

"Mrs. Templeton's daughter," she said. "The boy is sick. Dr. Amelia thinks it's pneumonia, so Mr. Baranov asked me to take care of Meg."

Jason's smile turned into a scowl, and he kicked the closest tree. "Sam Baranov. Who does he think he is, asking you to do something like that?"

Charlotte's eyes widened at Jason's apparent anger. Was it possible that that was jealousy she heard in his voice? How silly! She had told him that she wouldn't marry Sam. But for some reason, Jason had never liked the older man.

Charlotte decided to ignore Jason's question. "The baby is more work than I thought," she admitted. "It's different from just watching her for a couple hours. She misses her mother and brother, and so she cries a lot. But Jason, when she smiles at me, there's nothing nicer." Though Charlotte knew she was babbling, she couldn't help herself. It had been wonderful, caring for Meg Templeton these last three days, even better than teaching.

"I can think of something that would be even nicer than that," Jason said with a crooked smile.

A gust of wind set the snow to whirling. When Charlotte shivered, Jason helped her put her gloves back on, though he refused to release her hands. He was so handsome standing there, blocking the wind for her.

"What could be better than a baby's smile?" Charlotte hadn't expected to be so enchanted by her young charge, but now that she had had the experience of mothering Meg, she couldn't imagine anything she would enjoy more.

"How about watching your own baby smile?" Jason asked with a smile of his own. He gave Charlotte a long look, then mumbled something that sounded like "our baby."

Their baby. Charlotte's heart leapt with joy.

Chapter Twelve

"He's worse, Amelia. I know he is." Laura could hear her voice quavering, and there was no point in trying to disguise the trembling in her hands as she stood next to her son's bed, waiting for the doctor's verdict. Though the morning sun streamed through the window and the world outside the cabin seemed bright and clean, Laura felt as if she was living inside a dark tunnel with no end. Day and night had blurred into what seemed like an endless nightmare.

Though in her more lucid moments she knew it was irrational, Laura was certain she would never be able to chase the smell of illness from the room or the taste of fear from her mouth. Who would have dreamt that fear could be so pervasive, so paralyzing? She wouldn't even try to deny its effect, for she was more frightened than she had ever been.

In the week since Matt had been stricken with pneumonia, the disease had followed what Amelia had told her was its normal path. He had developed a chill that caused his small body to shake, despite the fact that his forehead seemed to burn with fever. Perhaps it was normal, but Laura couldn't help but be frightened by the delirium that accompanied his fever and the cough that hurt him so much that he cried.

Her baby was sick—dangerously so—and there was nothing she could do to help him. That scared Laura almost as much as the illness itself. Always in the past she had been able to soothe an ache or a scrape. But when Matt stared at her with eyes that did not recognize her, a feeling of helplessness threatened to overwhelm her.

Laura stood silently by Matt's bed, watching as Amelia examined him. Though the doctor was careful to mask her expression, she was unsmiling when she faced Laura. Laura closed her eyes for a second, dreading Amelia's diagnosis. If only this were a bad dream. If only she could wake and find Matt playing with his sister. But Laura knew it was not a dream. Matt was ill, and Meg had spent the last week with Charlotte.

"His lungs are congested, and his fever is higher," Amelia confirmed, the solemnity of her voice telling Laura how serious Matt's condition was. Amelia picked up Matt's hand and studied the fingernails. Surely it wasn't Laura's imagination that they were turning blue. She didn't need a medical degree to know that was not a positive sign.

"He's going to die, isn't he?" Laura hadn't wanted to even think it, but—try though she might—when she watched Matt struggle against the disease that so wracked his lungs, visions of Spring Flower standing over Adam's bier and the image of that other Athapaskan woman carrying her child's body seemed to be indelibly etched on Laura's memory. Though the thought that her son might die had haunted her from the beginning of his illness, it was only today, when Matt seemed so much worse, that she voiced the words.

Amelia's head jerked up, and she turned to face Laura, her voice fierce as she said, "Not if I can help it." Laura blinked, startled by her friend's ferocity. Amelia reached into her black medical bag for a bottle. "Let's see if we can get Matt to drink some more quinine. Then we'll bathe him with cool water."

The two women battled the Grim Reaper throughout the day, alternately coaxing Matt to swallow the bitter medicine, then sighing when a fit of coughing forced him to spit out the liquid. Laura lost count of the number of times she refilled the bucket with snow, using the frigid meltwater to bathe Matt's forehead, or how often she would take his hand in hers, willing him to recognize her. As the sun reached its zenith, then began to set, the women worked almost silently. Amelia fought with every weapon in her medical arsenal, while Laura murmured silent prayers that a mother's love would be strong enough to save her child. But as the clock chimed five, Matt took one final shallow breath.

For a moment Laura stared, unable to believe that Matt was so silent, so still, so pale. Then Amelia bent down and gently closed his eyes.

"No!" The word came out in an anguished cry as Laura fell to her knees and laid her head on Matt's chest. But the small heart that had once beat so steadily was stilled.

"No!" Laura pounded her fists on the mattress. Matt couldn't be gone. This was some cruel joke. The empty shell on the bed was not her son.

"No! Dear God, no!" But as Amelia laid her hand on Laura's shoulder and tried to draw her to her feet, Laura knew that her deepest fear had come true. She had lost a child. She pressed a kiss on Matt's cheek, and as she did, the tears began to fall. Laura, the woman who had not cried in years, began to sob uncontrollably.

"Oh, Laura!" Amelia wrapped her arms around her. Though the doctor's arms were warm and strong, all Laura could remember was how cold and fragile Matt looked. She closed her eyes, trying to block out the sight, then forced them open again. This was Matt, her Matt. Amelia murmured words that were meant to comfort her, but Laura barely heard them. Instead, her mind replayed Matt's tortured breathing and then that dreadful silence.

"I'm sorry," Amelia said. "I wish there was something I

could do to comfort you." Nothing would comfort her. Not ever again.

Laura pulled away from Amelia and walked to the window. There was no moon tonight, and a thin layer of clouds hid the stars. She gripped the windowsill as she shuddered. How was she going to live without Matt? It wasn't fair! Laura dug her fingernails into the wood. How could God—if there was a God—take her son from her? Wasn't it enough that neither her parents nor her husband had loved her? How could He take away one of the only two people on earth who did love her?

"Do you want me to give you something to help you sleep?"

Laura swung around and stared at Amelia. "No!" she shouted. "I don't want to sleep." Dimly Laura knew that she was wrong to lash out at the doctor. Amelia had done what she could. She had no way of knowing that Laura's worst nightmare had come true.

At length, Amelia cleaned her instruments and left Laura alone in the cabin. Gradually Laura's sobs subsided, but she refused to move from the room where Matt lay, so still and white. She couldn't leave him, and so she knelt by his side, alternately praying that God would restore him and cursing the fate that had taken Matt from her. And through it all, she tried to convince herself that it was a mistake. Maybe this was another one of her nightmares. Maybe she would awake in a minute and hear Matt laughing with his sister.

But Matt did not move, and the only sounds Laura heard were a firm knocking on the front door followed by the scrape of boots on the floor.

"Laura." It was Sam. She knew she ought to answer, just as she should have said something when Amelia tried to comfort her. Laura opened her mouth, but no words came out. A moment later, Sam strode into the bedroom. He was big, so much bigger than Matt. He smelled of sawdust and fresh air, not quinine and death. Laura could hear his even breathing, and he seemed to fill the room with his sheer size and life. She stared at him, suddenly filled with rage that she and Sam were alive when Matt was not.

"Amelia told me," he said. Laura's anger disappeared, replaced by the same empty sense of helplessness that had plagued her since Matt had been stricken. She couldn't be angry with Sam, not when she heard the anguish in his voice. If Laura had been able to speak, she thought her voice might sound like Sam's, so filled with pain that it almost hurt to hear it. "I wish there were something I could do or say to take the pain away."

Laura shook her head. "It won't ever go away." Her throat ached from weeping, and her words came out like a hoarse croak. She didn't want the pain to end, for if it did, that would mean she no longer cared that her son was gone.

Sam came closer, and Laura saw that the anguish she heard in his voice was reflected in his eyes. Tonight there was none of the customary warmth in them, only a cold despair. "The pain won't disappear," he told her, "but you'll learn to live with it. You're strong, Laura."

She shook her head again. "Then why do I feel so weak?" Just speaking seemed to exhaust her. How would she ever walk, when her legs felt as if they would collapse under her weight?

As if he could read her thoughts, Sam stretched his hands toward her. "It's okay to lean on someone. That's what friends are for." He took her hands in his and drew her to her feet, then pulled her close to him, wrapping his arms around her. For a long moment, neither of them said anything. Laura leaned her head on Sam's chest, listening to the even breathing that was so different from Matt's tortured inspirations. Matt! Her baby! She slid her arms around Sam's waist as tears began to flow again. "It's okay to cry," Sam said, and drew her closer. "Go ahead." And though she had thought she had cried until there were no more tears, Laura wept.

When her sobs subsided, Sam stroked her back gently. "Mrs. Langdon will be here soon to help you with Matt." As

Laura stiffened, his hand moved to the back of her neck, kneading the tight muscles. "It has to be done. You know that." Gradually she began to relax. Then Sam said, "Charlotte will keep Meg tonight."

"No!" Laura jerked away from him. "I want my baby here!" She had lost one child. How could she bear to be parted from the other?

The room was silent save for their breathing—Sam's deep and even, Laura's shallow and ragged. She clenched her fists as she stared at Sam. Though his eyes were still bleak, his voice was soft as he gestured toward the bed and said, "I know you want to hold Meg, but do you want her to see her brother that way?"

With a long look at the still figure, Laura shuddered. "No." Sam was right. Matt, her precious little boy, no longer looked like himself. Meg would not understand the change. Better that she remembered her brother as the mischievous child who was both her playmate and her tormentor.

The next few hours were a blur to Laura. With Mrs. Langdon's help, she bathed Matt and dressed him in his best clothes, then agreed to the hymns the minister's wife suggested for the funeral. Vaguely Laura remembered Mrs. Langdon insisting that she drink a cup of tea and eat some of the sweet biscuits she had brought. She had a distant memory of other women coming to the cabin, bringing dishes of food that the minister's wife placed in the kitchen. But mostly Laura was conscious of an emptiness deep inside her that she was certain would never be filled.

Her apathy was roused only when Sam reappeared with a tiny, beautifully made coffin. "No!" she cried. How could she put her Matt into a box? But with Mrs. Langdon's assistance, they laid him in his final bed.

"My husband will be back to pray with you," Mrs. Langdon said. The other women had left, and the cabin was once more unnaturally quiet. Laura hadn't realized how many sounds her children made, even when they slept. But now, deprived of both of them, the small rooms seemed cavernous and far too silent.

Laura shook her head, refusing the offer. "Later, maybe." Her emotions were still too raw, her anger too deep to listen to the minister. The older woman nodded as if she understood, and slipped her arms into her coat. As Sam prepared to follow her, Laura whispered, "Come back. I need you."

And so, when Mrs. Langdon was out of sight, Sam retraced his steps. Wordlessly, he closed the door to Matt's room and led Laura to the parlor side of her main room.

At first, neither of them spoke; then Sam said softly, "I'll always remember the day Matt drove the dogsled." For the first time since he had learned of Matt's death, there was a twinkle in Sam's eyes. "He was so proud of not falling off the runners."

Laura managed a small smile as she too remembered that day and her son's joyful grin when he and Sam returned. For days afterward, Matt had recounted his adventure to Meg, and timid Meg's eyes had widened in admiration of her brother's courage.

"What I remember most is the trip from Seattle," Laura said. "Matt almost drove me crazy with his constant questions. Each day I would swear that he was the most curious child ever born and wonder why I had been cursed with him." Tears filled her eyes and threatened to spill down her cheeks as she realized that Matt would never again demand the answer to an unanswerable question. "Oh, Sam, why did he have to die?"

Sam reached for her hand, clasping it between both of his. Though the stove still burned, it seemed to Laura that the only warm object in the room was Sam's hand.

"I don't know why Matt died," Sam told her. "I never thought death was fair. How could I, when I lost first my mother, then my father?" As Sam tightened the grip on her hand, Laura wasn't certain whether he sought to give or take comfort. All she knew was that Sam's hand was a lifeline, her sole connection to the world that had once seemed such a wonderful place.

Sam leaned forward, his expression earnest. "I thought I hated my father for marrying Hilda. There were times when I was sure I didn't care whether he lived or died. I even told myself that he meant nothing more to me than a stranger would, but when he died, I realized that I had this huge hole in my life."

Laura nodded. Sam understood. Amelia and the other women had murmured condolences, but no one else had said the words that told her they knew the anguish she was suffering. Sam did. He knew how she felt tonight, as if a big chunk of her heart had been wrenched away.

Though Sam continued to hold her hand, his right hand moved to his mustache in a gesture that Laura knew meant he was distressed. She squeezed his hand, trying to tell him without words that he didn't have to say anything more. But Sam continued. "Even though I resented the fact that Papa didn't spend much time with me after he married Hilda, now I realize that he was there when I most needed him." Sam stroked his mustache again. "He helped me through the worst night of my life."

There was so much pain in Sam's voice that Laura wanted to tell him to stop. Yet she couldn't, for it appeared that Sam needed to talk, just as she had needed to cry. "Why was it so bad?" she asked.

Sam stared at her for a long moment, as if debating what to say. Then he blurted out, "I was shut in a coffin."

A coffin! Laura's gaze flew to the door to Matt's room. Her son was lying in a coffin, cold and silent. That was horrible. But Sam had been alive. That was worse. The image stunned Laura so much that she blinked. "Oh, Sam!" Anyone would have been frightened, but Sam must have been a young child. He would have been terrified. "What a horrible accident! How did it happen?" Though Laura couldn't imagine why a child would be playing near a coffin, children had odd ideas of appropriate playgrounds. Her own Matt had found the outhouse a fascinating place for hide and seek.

Sam released her hand, then threaded her fingers through his. "It was no accident," he said baldly. "To this day I don't know where he got it, but somehow George found a coffin."

Laura shuddered. From what Sam had said in the past, she knew that he had no love for his stepbrother. This was undoubtedly part of the reason.

"I should have been suspicious when George wanted to play with me," Sam continued. "He had never done that before. But I was so happy to have his attention that I didn't protest when he told me to hide in the box. It was only when I heard the nails that I knew something was wrong."

Laura shuddered again. "George must be a monster."

Sam managed a wry smile. "I can't disagree with you." Though he tried to make light of it, Laura saw that the smile did not extend to his eyes. They were still filled with pain and sorrow.

Laura raised their clasped hands to her face and brushed her lips against the back of Sam's hand. "How long were you in there?"

He shook his head slightly. "I don't know. It felt like forever. All I know is that I was never so scared either before or after that day." Sam swallowed deeply. "I was sure I was going to die in that box." Laura remembered his comment that he didn't like confined spaces and that that was why he had not wanted to work in an underground mine. No wonder. No wonder he had oversized windows in both his house and office. After such a traumatic experience, Laura doubted the fear of darkness and small spaces would ever completely disappear.

"How did you escape?"

Sam released her hand and rose, striding to the other end of the room, then beginning to pace. She had never before seen him so agitated, but there had never been a day like this. He reached for one of the oil lamps and lit it, then moved to the next. Only when he had lit them all did he turn back to Laura.

"My father rescued me," he said in a voice that held a hint of wonder. "When I didn't come to dinner, he knew something was wrong. I don't know what he said, but somehow he found out what George had done. Papa was shouting when he found me and cursing in ways I'd never heard before." Sam opened the stove to check the fire. "He didn't get angry very often, but when he did, I had learned to run the other way. That night, though, I wasn't scared as he ripped the top off that coffin, because I knew his anger wasn't directed at me."

Sam stared at the stove for a long moment. Then he turned and his gaze returned to Laura. This time she saw a new warmth in his eyes. "We sat in the parlor that night with every lamp lit." Just as they were tonight. "Papa held me in his arms until I stopped shaking. Then he spent the rest of the night talking about my mother."

The tears that were never far from the surface threatened to spill out of Laura's eyes again, but this time they were tears of happiness that Sam's father had been so loving. "He must have been a very kind man," she said.

Sam's face was sober as he admitted, "I didn't always believe that, but now I know it's true." He fingered his mustache and frowned. "Do you know what I wish most, Laura? I wish I could see him once more to tell him how much I loved him."

Laura knew the feeling. Oh, how she knew the feeling. She would give almost anything to hold Matt in her arms again and whisper words of love to him. But Sam should not worry about his father. "He knew," she said firmly.

Sam looked unconvinced. "Why do you think that?"

She stood and faced him, looking up into those brown eyes that held so much doubt. "Because I'm a parent, Sam. Parents know when their children love them. I can see it in my children's eyes, and I know your father saw it in yours. No matter how angry Matt and Meg get with me, there's no mistaking the fact that they love me." Her voice cracked as she realized she would never again see that love on Matt's face. "I just hope Matt always knew how much I loved him."

"He did." Sam sounded as firm as she had a minute earlier.

"Why do you say that?" Though she wanted desperately to believe that her son had lived with the assurance of her love, tonight she was certain of very little save the fact that her precious boy was now lying in the wooden box that would be his final bed.

Sam took a step toward her, his smile gentle as he said, "Because I saw you with him. Laura, there's no mistaking your love for your children. It surrounds them like a warm blanket."

Oh, how she wanted to believe that! Laura stared at Sam for a long moment. Afterwards, she wasn't certain who moved first. All she knew was that Sam opened his arms, and she moved into them. They were warm, comforting, sheltering, and for the first time since Amelia had closed Matt's eyes, Laura felt a tiny flame ignite deep inside her. Nothing would fill the emptiness. She knew that. But maybe, just maybe, if she stayed here, some of that dreadful cold would dissipate. Nothing would bring her baby back, but somehow being with a man who had known a grief as deep as hers made the thought of the future less frightening.

"Oh, Sam!" she said. His gaze was as warm as his arms, and the tiny flame began to grow. Her own gaze fixed on his lips. They were moving closer, ever closer. She tipped her head up toward his, her lips parting as she sought the warmth that was now only inches away.

At the last instant Sam drew back, and she saw a question in his eyes. "Yes," she whispered. It was wrong. She knew that. Sam was courting another, and she was married. But tonight the normal rules did not apply. Tonight they were two friends who sought to comfort each other.

His lips were firm, yet gentle, teasing hers with the lightest of kisses before they settled on her mouth. He gave her warmth and sweetness, and for a moment nothing mattered but being held in his arms. For a moment there was nothing in the world beyond the circle of Sam's embrace. For a moment she cared for nothing but the pressure of his lips on hers and the wondrous way their breaths mingled. When at last they broke apart and reality returned, the pain was ever so slightly less.

Somehow Laura got through the funeral. When she arrived at the church, expecting to see only Amelia and Ella and a few other close friends, she was stunned. The church was filled. It appeared that everyone in Gold Landing, with the exception of Charlotte, who was still caring for Meg, had come to pay their respects to Laura and her son. Laura stared, amazed. This was a gesture of friendship beyond any she had ever dreamt. A lump lodged in her throat, and she could not speak. Instead, she nodded, blinking back her tears. When she had left the cabin, she had told herself she would cry no more. Tears would not bring Matt back, and they would only alarm Meg. But the tears she shed in the church were tears of wonder, not sorrow.

After the service, Laura understood why the women had brought her so much food, for the townspeople came to her cabin. They came in small groups, probably so as not to overwhelm her, and they stayed only half an hour or so, long enough to express their condolences, pressing her hand, touching her shoulder, or in a few instances, hugging her. Then they would drink some of the seemingly endless pots of coffee that Ella brewed, and sample some of the food that Amelia had arranged on the kitchen table.

It was all, Ella had assured her, customary. But Ella had no way of knowing that for Laura this was not ordinary. Never in her life had she felt so blessed. Never had she been surrounded by so many caring people. Never had she felt so loved.

Love. The thought brought a new flood of tears to her eyes. For so long, Laura had felt that no one could love her. Her parents had told her—in so many ways other than mere words—that she was unlovable, and Roy had reinforced that belief. But today, the citizens of Gold Landing had rallied for her. In words and deed, they had shown her that they cared, that they shared her sorrow, that they loved her.

The last of the guests had left, and the cabin was once more silent as Laura walked from room to room, trying to marshal her thoughts before she went to the parsonage to bring Meg home. Was it possible? Reverend Langdon had told her that there was a reason for everything and that somehow, someday she would see that something good had come from Matt's death. Laura had barely listened to him. There was *nothing* good about her son's dying. And yet, though today had been horrible, it had not been as devastating as she had feared, because she had not been alone.

Could it be that her parents had been wrong? Perhaps the problem had been them. Perhaps it was not that she was deficient, but that they had been incapable of loving her. Though she had many memories of her childhood, Laura could never remember being held in warm, comforting arms. She could not remember her mother drying her tears or her father helping to banish nightmares. She had none of the loving memories that Sam did, and she had never once felt protected and cherished the way she had in his arms.

It was not good that Matt had died. Laura would never believe that, and yet she could not deny that today felt a little less bleak than she had feared. With a lighter step than she would have dreamed possible, Laura set out for the parsonage.

"Come here, sweetheart." She knelt and stretched her arms to Meg. Wrapping her arms around her daughter, she vowed that nothing—nothing on earth—would hurt this precious child.

"Will you go back to school tomorrow?" Charlotte asked as she held out the small bag that held Meg's toys and clothing.

Laura shook her head. It was too soon. Her sorrow was still too close to the surface to be with other children when one of her own was lying in the cold, cold earth. Laura knew it would disturb the children to see her weep, but tears were one thing she could not control. Not yet.

As the days passed, though Ella and Amelia urged her to return to her normal life, Laura remained in the cabin. Laura told the women that Meg needed her, that she was lonely without her brother. That wasn't a lie. Meg didn't understand where Matt had gone and why he would not return. But the real reason Laura did not resume her teaching was that she could not bear the thought of letting Meg out of her sight. Perhaps it was a foolish superstition, but she feared that if she left Meg with someone else, she too would contract pneumonia. No, it was better to keep her at home where she would not be exposed to such dangers.

"Mr. Sam!" Meg's face lit with a smile when he knocked on the front door. Though Sam no longer came into the house, mindful of the gossip that might result from his unchaperoned presence, he came to the cabin each afternoon and spent a few minutes on the front stoop with Laura and Meg.

As Sam swung her daughter into his arms, Laura found herself wishing she were the one being held in those arms. As Sam pressed a quick kiss on Meg's head, Laura remembered how his lips had felt on hers. It was senseless, remembering things that could never be repeated. Sam knew that, and so did she.

"Are you going back to school tomorrow?" he asked.

She shook her head. "I'm not ready yet."

A look of concern crossed his face. "It's time, Laura. You can't stay locked up in your cabin forever."

She shrugged. "I'm not locked in the cabin now."

But he would not let her dismiss him so easily. "You know what I mean. The only way to stop the pain is to fight it."

Laura knew he was right, and yet she could not force herself to return to the school. She and Meg were safe here. That was what mattered.

Afterwards, Laura wasn't certain how long she would have

remained at home, nursing her sorrow, had she not had an unexpected visitor.

"Spring Flower!" Laura could not mask her surprise when she opened the door and saw the Indian woman standing on her front stoop. Involuntarily she took a step backward, remembering the fury that Spring Flower had unleashed the last time she had seen Laura. Why was she here? As far as Laura knew, the Athapaskan mother rarely came into town.

The woman was as tall and gaunt as Laura remembered. Her expression was as grim as before, but today Laura saw only sadness on Spring Flower's face, not anger. "Come in," Laura said, gathering Meg into her arms. If Spring Flower lashed out again, Laura needed to be able to protect her daughter.

Spring Flower betrayed no curiosity over the cabin, but kept her eyes focused on Laura's face. "Heard boy dead," she said when Laura had closed the door behind them.

Laura nodded, squeezing Meg so tightly that the little girl squirmed.

Spring Flower's expression was grave as she said, "Only mother know how big pain. Am sorry."

Laura swallowed deeply. Spring Flower had come in sympathy, not hatred. Laura reached forward and touched the Athapaskan's hand. "Thank you, Spring Flower. I grieve for both of our sons."

The woman remained only a few minutes longer, but when she left, Laura felt oddly comforted. Perhaps Reverend Langdon had been right. Perhaps something good had come of Matt's death, for it seemed that shared sorrow had healed Spring Flower's anger. Though she had not said the words, Laura knew that the Indian mother no longer blamed her for her son's death.

Laura set Meg on the floor and strode to her room. Pulling her bag from underneath the bed, she began to fill it with her teaching supplies. It was time to return to her daily life. Sam was right. She was accomplishing nothing remaining here, but as a teacher, she could help others. That was important, helping everyone she could.

Laura reached for a small pile of children's stories, trying not to wince when she realized that the last time she had read them had been to Matt.

How selfish she had been! The image of Adam's excitement when he had mastered a new word flashed before her, and Laura felt a pang of remorse. Charlotte had taken over the classroom, but while Laura had remained at home, no one had taught the adults and the Indian children. That would change, starting today. If there was anything Laura had learned, it was that life was too short to waste a single minute. Nothing she could do would bring Matt back, but she could help others make their lives as happy and fulfilling as possible.

As she bundled Meg into her coat and hat, Laura frowned. She could help her students. That was easy. She knew their needs, and she had the means to satisfy those needs. But Sam . . . Sam was not so easily helped. Laura knew what he needed. After hearing the story of his relationship with his father, she realized that Sam needed his inheritance not for its monetary value, but as a symbol of his father's love. He had to inherit. He just had to, and to do that he needed a wife. Unfortunately, it didn't seem that Charlotte was going to fill that role.

Laura frowned again, wishing she had the means to help Sam. He was her friend, the kindest man she had ever met. She would do anything in her power to help him. Sadly, there was nothing she could do.

If only she weren't still married!

Chapter Thirteen

He would do it today. The time for excuses, for procrastination was gone. He had already spent more than half the available time on preliminaries. Now, with only two months left before his birthday, he had to take the next step. He had to know that his inheritance would be safe. And she would need time to plan the wedding.

While Sam might have once thought that getting married was no more involved than asking the minister to perform the ceremony, both William and Ben had disabused him of that notion. Weddings were big productions, bigger even than the children's Christmas pageant, and brides-to-be did not take it kindly if they weren't given enough time to plan those productions properly. Sam was taking no chances. He would give her enough time.

He thrust his hands deep into his pockets, lengthening his stride as he walked down Main Street toward the parsonage. December was not his favorite month. Not only were the days the shortest of the year, but the wind seemed to howl louder than at any other time, its force penetrating even the many layers of clothing he wore. His breath came out in small white clouds, the moisture freezing in miniature icicles on his mustache.

Sam turned the corner and approached Charlotte's house. If his heart did not race with anticipation, it was surely only because he was walking into the wind, and concentrating on taking shallow breaths was taking more effort than he had expected. There would be time enough to celebrate when Charlotte had accepted his proposal. Then his pulse would race and his heart would fill with happiness.

Tonight, Sam had decided, would be far different from the evening he had taken her to Pete's Roadhouse. This time he would not ply her with dinner and a romantic walk along the river. Instead he would take the traditional approach to courting a lady. He would speak to Charlotte in her parents' parlor, sinking to his knees in the way he had heard ladies preferred. And tonight his lips would do his brain's bidding. There would be no faltering. This time he would pronounce the words that women throughout the ages had longed to hear.

But as the parsonage came into view, Sam's steps slowed. This was absurd! He wanted to visit Charlotte. Of course he did. Sam forced himself to keep walking. There was no reason on earth why, when he thought about parlors, he should remember the night he had sat in Laura Templeton's front room. There was no reason why, when he thought about holding a woman in his arms, he should remember just how good Laura had felt in his, the way her soft curves had molded to the hard planes of his body. And there most definitely was no reason why, when he thought about kissing his bride, he should remember how sweet Laura's lips had felt beneath his.

For Pete's sake, the woman was a widow who had just lost her child. First her husband, then her son, all within a short space of time. She was twice bereaved, in double mourning. She wouldn't be ready to think about marriage for a long time, even if Sam were interested in discussing matrimonial affairs with her. Which, thank goodness, he was not. Of course he wasn't. It was Charlotte he was going to marry.

"Good evening, Charlotte." Sam had greeted her parents, asking if he might spend some time alone with their daughter. Though he had seen the two older Langdons exchange glances, they had not asked why he wanted to speak with Charlotte. Instead, they had had merely asked her to join them in the parlor, and then had excused themselves. For propriety's sake, they had left the door ajar, though Sam doubted they were standing near enough to hear his words. That was just as well. A proposal was supposed to be a private affair. It was only the lady's answer that would be made public.

"I've enjoyed our walks and the opportunity to get to know you," Sam told Charlotte. He sat in one of the wing chairs facing her. Though Charlotte did not frown, he saw that she was also not smiling. Her face remained calm, as if she were listening to a speech that held only a modicum of interest for her. Sam tried not to let Charlotte's poker face discourage him. Though some might call it a bad sign, Sam preferred to think she was unaware of the reason he had come here tonight.

He cleared his throat and started again. "I admire you very much." Sam knew he ought to tell Charlotte that he loved her, but he couldn't lie. Even with everything that was at stake, he could not compromise his principles. He had told Laura that he wouldn't mislead Charlotte, and he would not. The truth was, he *did* admire her.

Again, Charlotte gave no sign that his words were of any particular interest to her. Surely she must have had some idea that he was courting her. That was common knowledge throughout Gold Landing. Forcing himself to keep a smile fixed on his face, Sam slid to his knees and reached for Charlotte's right hand. It was larger than Laura's, and though it was as soft as hers, it held none of the warmth that Laura's did, nor did it send any sparks shooting through his veins.

Stop it! Sam admonished himself. He was here to propose to Charlotte, not to think about Laura Templeton.

Sam stared at Charlotte's hand as he prepared for the next step. Once the words were spoken, they would be irrevocable. There was, of course, no reason to hesitate. He wanted to marry Charlotte. She was the bride he desired.

Sam swallowed deeply. Then, before his resolve faded, he smiled at Charlotte and asked, "Would you do me the honor of becoming my wife?"

Charlotte's eyes widened in what appeared to be surprise. "No," she said firmly as she tugged her hand from his.

No? Sam heard footsteps in the hallway. Lord, he must look like a fool, kneeling in front of the woman who had just refused his offer of marriage. Perhaps she didn't mean it. Perhaps she had been unprepared for his proposal. That must be it. They would discuss the subject like two rational adults, and then she would agree.

Sam rose. Then, realizing that he might be intimidating Charlotte by standing over her, he returned to the wing chair. "I don't understand." And he didn't. Oh, it wasn't as though Charlotte had given him any indication that she was madly in love with him. That simply wasn't Charlotte's way. But she had been polite to him, and he knew that she was a dutiful daughter. If her parents favored his suit—and they did—surely she would agree.

Charlotte stared at the floor, then clasped her hands in her lap. It was almost as if she was afraid that he would want to hold her hand again and sought to prevent that. Sam forced his lips to remain curved in a smile. A grimace of frustration was no way to woo a woman.

"What's wrong?" he asked as gently as he could.

Twin spots of color rose to Charlotte's cheeks as she met his gaze. "I don't love you," she announced in the firmest tone Sam had ever heard her use. Her fingers pressed into her hands so tightly that the tips whitened. "I know my parents like you and would be happy if I married you, but that's not enough." Sam listened, astonished. For months he had wished he could coax Charlotte into a real conversation, one in which she responded in complete sentences. Tonight he had accomplished that goal. How ironic that her first long, coherent discourse was the one to destroy his hopes. For there was little doubt that Charlotte had made her decision.

"I won't marry without love," she told him.

Love. So that was the problem. Ben and William had warned Sam that women put great store in that particular word. "I've heard that love grows as a couple lives together," Sam said. He leaned forward, hoping that his smile looked genuine, not desperate. "I think we have the foundation for a good marriage. We could make love grow."

Charlotte shook her head. "That might work for some people, but I'm not convinced it would for me." There was a new warmth to Charlotte's voice, and Sam sensed that her regret was genuine. "I'm not willing to risk my happiness . . . and yours." Charlotte unclasped her hands and laid one tentatively on Sam's. "I'm sorry, Sam."

"So am I."

As he made his way home, his feet moving mechanically across the snow, Sam's thoughts were turbulent. He hadn't expected Charlotte to refuse him. Despite her persistent coolness toward him, he had thought that she would marry him. So much depended on that! Without Charlotte, Sam knew, it was unlikely he would be able to claim his inheritance. There simply weren't any other eligible women in Gold Landing, and—with only two months remaining—the odds of finding a bride were low. The thought of forfeiting his father's legacy filled Sam with despair. He couldn't let George keep Baranov Shipping. That would be tantamount to telling his father he didn't love him, that he wasn't willing to do the one thing he had asked of his son.

And yet, though the approach of his birthday and the possibility that he would forfeit his father's final gift saddened him, Sam could not ignore the eagerness in his step or the fact that he found himself whistling. It was not all bad that he would not marry Charlotte. This way he would not have to live the rest of his life with a woman he did not love.

Sam reached down, grabbed a fistful of snow, and flung it into the air, grinning. Perhaps losing his inheritance was not the worst thing that could happen to him.

Laura looked at Charlotte. Something was different today. It wasn't just that she had tied a red ribbon in her hair, her explanation being that she was starting to dress for the holidays. No, something else had changed. Laura waited until she and Charlotte had bundled the children into their heavy clothes and sent them home for the day before she approached her assistant.

"You look happy today," she said. "Did something special happen?"

Charlotte nodded, and the smile that lit her face told Laura she had not been mistaken. This afternoon Charlotte, normally shy and retiring Charlotte, sparkled more than the new-fallen snow. Laura had to admit that Charlotte's ebullience had been welcome. Today, for the first time since she had returned to school, she had been able to watch her students without remembering that Matt would never hold a McGuffey's Reader or recite a multiplication table. Laura smiled at Charlotte, thankful that her enthusiasm had been so contagious, but wondering what had wrought the change in her.

"Sam Baranov asked me to marry him," she said.

The pain that stabbed her heart shocked Laura with its intensity, and for a second she was unable to breathe. She grabbed the back of a chair and lowered her eyes, lest Charlotte read the confusion in them. In and out. In and out. Laura forced herself to breathe evenly. It was foolish, reacting this way. She had known that Sam was courting Charlotte and that he needed to marry before February. Of course he would propose to Charlotte. That was part of the process. There was absolutely no reason Laura should feel this bone-wrenching sadness. It wasn't as if Sam would stop being her best friend when he and Charlotte were wed. It wasn't as if she could—or would—marry him herself.

Laura took another deep breath, expelling it slowly. When her heartbeat had returned to a semblance of normality, she asked, "When is the wedding?" Perfect. Her voice sounded almost normal. If there was the slightest quaver, Charlotte could attribute it to excitement. Weren't women always excited about weddings?

Laura busied herself straightening the books on one of the shelves Sam had made. When she turned back to look at Charlotte, she saw that her assistant's smile had broadened, and her blue eyes sparkled with what could only be called joy. "There won't be a wedding."

The muted crackling of the fire was the only sound as Laura stared. No wedding? Suddenly speechless, she raised an eyebrow in what she hoped Charlotte would recognize as a questioning gesture.

"I refused him," Charlotte said, not bothering to hide her pride in what Laura guessed was the first defiant act of her life. "I know my parents weren't happy, but I couldn't marry a man I didn't love." Charlotte grinned at Laura. "I took your advice and followed my heart."

The surge of happiness that swelled through Laura, warming her veins and sending a frisson of excitement to her nerve endings, surprised her almost as much as her previous pain. She shouldn't be happy that Charlotte would not marry Sam. This was terrible news for her dearest friend. The man needed a bride, and he needed one soon. Between the dearth of unmarried females in Gold Landing and winter's advent, which would complicate finding a wife in another town, Sam was in trouble. Big trouble.

Laura sighed. It wasn't as though she had a solution. She didn't. Though she had lain awake, trying to find an answer to his dilemma, she had failed. With Charlotte's refusal, Sam was brideless, and that meant that his prospects of inheriting Baranov Shipping had just sunk faster than one of his father's anchors.

It was terrible. Then why, oh, why could she not quell the happiness that, despite everything, bubbled through her?

The sound of laughter startled Sam, and he looked up from his ledgers. What could be so amusing about a lesson? There was certainly nothing amusing about working on ledgers. The paperwork was the one part of his business that Sam truly hated. When he had those blasted numbers in front of him, not once did he feel the urge to laugh. But in the other room, the sound was repeated, and this time Sam heard Laura join the young boys' mirth.

Though he hadn't expected to, Sam enjoyed the hours he spent in his office while Laura taught her evening classes. At first he had viewed it as a time when he would feel compelled to work on his books. But even when he had finished the paperwork, he had lingered. Laura had told him that he didn't need to stay with them, that she would turn off the lights and close the door when she and the students left, but something—perhaps chivalry, perhaps simple curiosity—had kept him in the office each night that she was there. And each night he had learned something new about the widowed schoolteacher.

Though he could not always distinguish individual words, he could hear her tone, sometimes cajoling, sometimes playful, always patient with the Indian boys. Her approach toward the adult students was different. With them, she invariably asked for their assistance with some aspect of her life. Sam doubted the woman had so many problems, but he couldn't fault the result. The adult students believed that they were teaching her, and that made them more receptive to the lessons she gave them. Laura Templeton was a special woman. Yes, indeed, she was.

When the last of the Athapaskan children left, Laura walked into Sam's office and reached for her coat. Her face bore the sad expression that Sam suspected meant she was dreading going home to a house with only one child. Though she rarely talked about him, Sam sensed that she missed Matt dreadfully and that the strain of being strong for Meg was wearing on her.

"Whatever tonight's lesson was, your pupils seemed to enjoy it," he told her.

Laura managed a short laugh. "They certainly did." She began to fasten her buttons. "Tonight we talked about winter customs, so I told them about Christmas trees." She paused, and those beautiful sea-blue eyes sparkled with remembered mirth. "Oh, Sam, you should have seen their expressions when I told them we put lighted candles on the branches. One of the boys told me that was dangerous. Why would we risk burning down our houses when there was no good reason for it?"

Though as a man who made his livelihood from wood he, more than most, was aware of the danger of fire, he chuckled. "I hadn't thought about it that way."

"Me neither, but that started a discussion of why we might want to light candles." As Laura glanced at the clock hanging on the far wall, Sam realized that he had never seen her wear a watch. Was she one of the few women in Gold Landing who didn't own one? "I wasn't sure how I was going to introduce the idea of symbolism." A wry smile twisted Laura's lips. "Then another of the boys decided that we must be trying to steal the northern lights. He thinks that the candles are designed to attract the lights into our homes."

It was, Sam had to admit, an intriguing theory, almost as intriguing as the thought of how good Laura's lips had felt pressed to his. He cleared his throat, then said, "I didn't know you were teaching philosophy."

"I wasn't." She reached for her bag and slung it over her shoulder. "It would appear that tonight I was the student."

She was comfortable with the thought, and that surprised Sam. Most adults he knew wanted to be the ones in charge. Children—at least in their view—learned from adults, not the other way around. How refreshing to realize that Laura, who was probably one of the best-educated people in Gold

Landing, felt utterly at ease learning from young boys whom most of the town considered outcasts.

A knock on the door interrupted Sam's thoughts. He turned, surprised. Customers never visited the sawmill at night, and when they did come, they did not knock. This was a store; people simply walked inside. "I'll get it." He opened the door to reveal a tall Indian woman. "Spring Flower!" The last time Sam had seen her had been on Thanksgiving night when she had rejected both the dinner and Laura. Though Laura had told him that the woman had visited her after Matt's death, Sam could not imagine why she was here. "Can I help you with something?"

"Teacher here?" The partitions Sam had built when he created Laura's schoolroom kept Spring Flower from seeing into either the office or the classroom.

Before Sam could answer, he heard rapid footsteps on the floor. "Is something wrong, Spring Flower?" The furrows between Laura's eyes told him she was worried by the woman's visit. Sam felt his hands clench into fists, and forced himself to relax as he took a step toward Laura. Though the visit could be perfectly innocent, if the other woman began to berate Laura, he would force her to leave. No one would ever hurt Laura again, not if he could help it.

Spring Flower nodded solemnly. "Want to read. Like Adam." Laura's quick intake of breath told Sam she was as astonished by the statement as he. "You teach me?" the Athapaskan asked.

Sam watched Laura's expression transform from surprise to happiness. Those sweet lips curved in a smile, and her eyes twinkled. "Yes, oh, yes!" When she and Spring Flower had arranged the schedule of their classes and the other woman had left, Laura turned toward Sam. Her face was more vibrant than he had seen it since the day Matt had been stricken. "Ella told me this was the season of miracles," Laura said with a laugh that stopped short of being a giggle of happiness. "I didn't believe her. Now I do. This was a miracle, Sam, a genuine miracle." She twirled around, then reached for his hand. "I can't believe Spring Flower wants to learn to read."

Her hand was warm next to his, her fingers entwined with his in an oddly comforting gesture. He should have been the one supporting her. Instead he felt that she was giving, while he took. Sam looked down at their hands, hers tiny and white and smooth compared to his. He had held other women's hands, and they had never felt like this. This was not the casual touch of a friend, but something else, something Sam chose not to consider too closely.

"Teaching makes you happy, doesn't it?"

Laura's lovely blue eyes sparkled. "Oh, yes. It's so satisfying, watching the change in the students as they learn new things. It's like seeing a door open, a little at a time." She tightened her grip. "I love all the subjects, but reading is extra special. It's what helps open those doors." Laura's gurgle of happiness warmed Sam's heart. "I can't imagine a world without books."

Sam could not imagine a world without Laura.

After he walked her home, Sam found himself too restless to return to his own house. Instead, he turned and walked down Second Street toward the river. It was shift-change time at the mine, and the street was crowded with men. Though he had no desire to ever experience work in the mine, Sam was intrigued by the camaraderie that grew among the men who spent their days deep within the earth.

William had told him that they were frequently closer than brothers, sharing each other's joys and sorrows. As the shifts changed, the two groups would meet in the street, discussing everything from the gold they had found to the latest betting pool. For one thing Sam had learned was that William's men would bet on anything, a fact that had annoyed William on more than one occasion when the wagering had been on William's relationship with Amelia.

Sam wouldn't want to be betting on his chances of marriage. At this point, it appeared that it would take a miracle for him to be united in holy matrimony prior to his birthday, and miracles were in decidedly short supply this year.

Sam greeted a number of the men, noting that although

they looked weary after their stint in the earth, they also looked satisfied, as if they'd mined a good supply of gold today. Discovering the current lode, William had told him, had seemed like a miracle at the time.

William, Amelia, Laura. They all put credence in miracles. Sam did not, although he had to admit that being with Laura was almost enough to make him believe in miracles. Almost. When he had seen her happiness at Spring Flower's request, Sam had been close to believing that miracles did exist. But they didn't. If there was such a thing as a miracle, surely he would have found one. Surely he would be planning his wedding now rather than counting the days until Baranov Shipping belonged to George.

Sam continued past the mine and Gloria's establishment. With the shift change, many of the men headed directly for Gloria's and the comfort her soiled doves could provide. There had been a time when Sam had found his own measure of comfort there, but for the past few months, ever since the boat had brought Gold Landing's new schoolteacher, he had had no desire to spend an evening or even an hour with one of Gloria's girls. At first Sam had told himself that it wouldn't have been proper for a man who was courting the minister's daughter to frequent such an establishment, but he had soon realized that propriety played no part in his decision. He simply didn't want to go there.

Gloria's doves no longer held any appeal for him. Though she had several blue-eyed blondes, none had silvery hair and eyes the color of the sea. Though some were petite, none had the womanly curves that Laura did. Laura! Why was he thinking of her in this context? For Pete's sake, the woman was in double mourning. She wasn't looking for a husband, and he didn't want to marry a widow with a child.

Sam stamped his boots, knocking off some of the snow. He was almost to the river now. The men's voices had disappeared as the new shift descended into the earth while the others drifted toward home or Gloria's. When he reached the bridge, he would turn around and head back. December in

Gold Landing was too cold for a long walk, even when a man wanted to clear his head. Sam's feet moved rhythmically, and gradually the fog that had clouded his thoughts began to dissipate.

What was that? Though it was hard to tell in the darkness, Sam thought he saw a figure running and another one in pursuit. The first was small and moved with the agility of youth; the second was considerably larger and more ponderous, reminding Sam of an angry bear. Still, the larger man seemed to be gaining on the youth just as bears frequently outran and overpowered their prey.

"You ain't gonna get away with it!" Sam frowned as he recognized the man's voice. Jethro Mooney was known for his bad temper and quick fists. Whoever had angered him had made a mistake. "Give it back, you thieving bastard."

The younger figure continued to run. "Didn't take your gold," he shouted over his shoulder. Sam frowned a second time. Silly young pup. Jason Blake seemed to spend half his time in trouble. As for the rest, no one seemed to know what he did with it.

Half a block away, Jethro sprinted, his huge arm sweeping out to grab Jason's coat. "You lying son of a bitch," he shouted as he spun the young man around to face him, "I'll teach you to mess with Jethro Mooney." He swung his fist, landing it squarely on the youth's face.

Sounds carried clearly through the night air, and Sam heard the sickening thud of fist on flesh. For a second he was transported back in time, and it was his face that was being pummeled. Then he began to run. It was not a fair fight. No matter what Jason had done, he didn't deserve Jethro's fury. Sam increased his pace. He had to stop Jethro. The man was a bully, and Sam knew all about bullies and the way they preyed on the weak.

"Knock it off, Jethro," he shouted as he approached the two men.

Jethro's response was to land another punch on Jason's face. Though the younger man tried to fight back, he was no match for the burly miner, and Sam knew that the dark patches on the snow were Jason's blood. "Mind your own business, Baranov," Jethro yelled over his shoulder. "The brat's got it coming."

Though his voice was nothing like George's, the words could have been Sam's stepbrother's. Sam grabbed Jethro's arm. Wrenching it fiercely, he broke Jethro's grip on Jason. "Why don't you pick on someone your own size?"

"Go to hell." Jethro swung at Jason again.

"I'll see you there." Sam dragged Jethro away from the young man. "You want to fight?" he demanded. "Let's see how you do with someone your own size." He fisted his hand and landed a blow on Jethro's face.

It should have been an unfair match, for Jethro was bigger and heavier than Sam. William's miners would have bet on Jethro, but they would have lost their bets for—although Sam did not have size on his side—he was fueled by fury. Though the man who blackened his eye and cut his cheek, the man who tried to break his ribs and puncture a lung, bore Jethro Mooney's body, it was George's face that Sam saw as he planted blow after blow on it. Afterwards, Sam could not have said how long the fight had lasted. All he knew was that nothing had ever felt quite as satisfying as seeing Jethro Mooney tumble to the snow and not rise.

"Thanks, Mr. Baranov." Jason's voice was muffled, and Sam suspected he would discover at least one of his lips was split. By tomorrow morning, the two of them would look like brothers, for his own face had taken a pummeling at Jethro's hands.

"You keep away from him, son." Sam slung his arm around Jason's shoulders and gave him a quick squeeze. "He's a real mean one."

As he and Jason walked back toward town, Sam heard Jethro shout, "You'll pay for this, Baranov. I'll get even with you if it's the last thing I do."

Oddly enough, the threat did not bother Sam.

Chapter Fourteen

"Oh, Jason, what happened to you?" Every Saturday morning, Charlotte found an excuse to leave home. She would tell her mother she had forgotten something in the schoolhouse, that she had promised Mrs. Templeton she would watch Meg for an hour, or that she needed to look for a new ribbon at Mr. Ashton's store. The excuse didn't matter; what did matter was that she had another opportunity to see Jason. Otherwise, the weekend would have been long and lonely. She saw Jason on Sunday mornings when he sat in the back of the church, listening to her father's sermon, but that wasn't the same as being alone with him, talking to him, and holding his hand.

"What happened?" Charlotte repeated her question. Even from a distance, she could see that he was limping. As he came closer, she gasped. Something horrible had happened to Jason's face. It was bruised and swollen, with deep cuts that had turned an angry red. "Oh, Jason!"

Charlotte ran from the shelter of the trees. Grabbing Jason's hand, she led him toward the schoolhouse. Though the building would be almost as cold as outdoors, Mrs. Templeton kept a box of medical supplies for the all-too-common cuts and minor burns that children seemed to incur. Charlotte knew there were bandages and soothing salves, and she hoped Dr. Amelia had left a new bottle of iodine.

Charlotte darted another glance at Jason and frowned. Those cuts needed to be properly cleaned. Why hadn't his mother done something? But Charlotte knew the answer. In all likelihood, Jason hadn't gone home, and even if he had, his mother was normally so preoccupied with the smaller children that she might not have noticed her eldest son's injuries.

"I'm okay," Jason insisted. He planted his feet on the ground and refused to move.

Charlotte quelled his protests with a firm look and a tug on his hand. "You are not all right. For heaven's sake, Jason, you look terrible." He tried to smile, but only succeeded in wincing when his lips moved. "Now, who did this to you?" For Charlotte wouldn't believe that he had fallen down a flight of stairs or slipped on the ice. His face looked the way that nice Mr. Ferguson's had the day after he and Jethro Mooney had had a fight.

Charlotte knew she wasn't supposed to have heard about that fight, since it had taken place at Gloria's establishment, and nice ladies didn't recognize the existence of a house of ill repute. Still, Charlotte had seen Mr. Ferguson, and she had heard the stories. But Jason didn't fight, and she knew he wouldn't have been at Gloria's. Would he?

She opened the door to the schoolhouse, propelled Jason into the closest chair, then reached for the first-aid box, willing her hands to be steady. Poor Jason!

"It was Jethro Mooney."

Charlotte's hand stilled in the midst of pouring iodine onto a piece of cotton. Though it would sting, she needed to disinfect the wounds. "Jethro? What did you do to anger him?" While the man's fury was legendary, Jason had no reason to incur it, unless—like Mr. Ferguson's fight—it had been a dispute over one of Gloria's girls. Surely that wasn't the case. Charlotte dumped more iodine on the cotton as she murmured a silent prayer that Jason hadn't gone to Gloria's.

He winced as she swabbed his cuts. "Near as I can figure it out," he said, "I was walking on the wrong street at the wrong time."

Charlotte took a deep breath. "Where were you?" It couldn't be that he was on Second Street going to Gloria's. It just couldn't. She stared at the books on Mrs. Templeton's desk. The binding on *David Copperfield* was coming loose. She ought to glue it. That was more important than asking Jason where he had gone.

"Out on Second."

Charlotte bit her lip to keep from shrieking. A lady didn't shriek. She really needed to work on those book bindings. "What were you doing there?" she asked when she had her voice under control.

Charlotte hadn't realized that she was scrubbing his skin so diligently until Jason muttered a loud ouch. He pulled away and turned to face her. "I wasn't going to Gloria's, if that's what you think." Charlotte could feel the color rise to her cheeks in mute confession that that was exactly what she had thought. "I wouldn't do that," Jason insisted, his gray eyes reflecting both sincerity and pain that she hadn't trusted him. "I ain't got no money. Besides, I don't wanna kiss any other girl or . . ." He paused, as if trying to find the right word. "I don't wanna do . . ." Another pause. ". . . anything with them."

Charlotte breathed a sigh of relief. Of course Jason hadn't been visiting Gloria's. Of course he didn't want to be with another girl. Especially not one who expected to be paid for her kisses and her . . . anythings.

"I know that." She spread a soothing salve on Jason's cuts. They weren't as deep as she had feared, but there was no doubt that his face would hurt for days. "It's just that everyone knows Jethro's a bully. You'd better stay away from him."

Jason nodded. "He accused me of stealing his gold. Charlotte, I didn't do that." He rose and paced the floor, heedless of her efforts to spread the salve on his face. "It makes me so da—danged mad. Every time someone in this town misplaces something, they blame me. It ain't fair."

It wasn't fair, and that made Charlotte almost as angry as Jason. She knew Jason. She liked Jason. She trusted Jason. Why couldn't the rest of Gold Landing's citizens see beneath the rough exterior to the man she knew was inside him?

"I don't blame you," she said softly.

He stopped his pacing and stared at her. "No, you don't. You're special."

"Did you hear the news?"

Laura smiled. She hadn't yet reached Herb Ashton's store, and she had already heard it four times. When you considered that she had walked only the one block of Second to Main and then less than half a block to the store, Laura realized she might have set one of Gold Landing's records. Everyone who met her seemed intent on sharing the latest gossip with her.

Meg grinned, pleased with the attention as a young matron bent over the wagon and greeted her. The wagon had proven to be a godsend. Not only had Sam crafted it with high sides so that neither the twins nor her purchases would tumble out, but he had also fashioned runners that could be attached in the winter, turning it from wheeled wagon to sled. Though Meg missed her brother and would ask where he was, she clearly reveled in having the wagon to herself and never fussed when Laura took her shopping.

Laura hoisted her daughter into her arms and entered the store. "Did you hear the news?"

Though she nodded, as she selected a piece of flannel to make a sacque for Ella's baby, Laura was treated to yet another rendition of Gold Landing's latest event, the one that featured Sam as hero. Minutes later, she stood in line to pay for her purchases and pick up her copy of the Seattle newspaper.

It was probably foolish. When she had left Seattle, Laura had told herself that she would never return, that she had put that portion of her life behind her. And yet she had ordered a subscription to the city's major newspaper, to be sent to her in Alaska. Though it still hurt to admit it, the paper had been her primary source of information about her parents ever since her marriage.

"Mr. Sam!" Meg giggled with delight as Sam reached down and pulled her into his arms for a quick hug. They were once again outside the store, the back of the wagon now holding not just the paper and the flannel Laura had planned to buy, but also a length of red and green wool plaid. It had been an impulse buy, and Laura was not a woman prone to impulses, but when she saw the bolt of cheery fabric, she had envisioned it as a muffler wound around Sam's neck. Surely it would not be inappropriate for her to give him a Christmas present after all the things he had done for her and Meg. She would tell him it was a small thank-you for the help he'd given her on the children's pageant.

"I suppose you know that you're Gold Landing's most famous citizen this morning." Laura inspected Sam's face. Other than incipient bruises on one cheek and a shallow cut on the other, he appeared to have come out of the fight unscathed. Jethro Mooney, or so she had heard numerous times, had not been so lucky. Jethro, she had been told, had a broken nose and at least one loose tooth. No one knew what shape Jason's face was in, though speculation was rife.

Sam's eyes twinkled. "Famous?" He laughed as he settled Meg back into the wagon. "Notorious is more like it, although I appear to be in good company. The last person who brawled with Jethro was our attorney."

"Abe?" Laura had met Abe Ferguson, and was surprised that the gentlemanly and apparently meek lawyer would have been involved in a fight with a bully. She would have to ask Amelia what had provoked that incident.

Laura and Sam greeted Vera Kane as she entered Herb Ashton's store. Judging from the speculative look Laura had seen on the widow's face, she would soon be spreading tales about their conversation. She and Sam needed to move, to go their separate ways. Laura started to reach for the wagon's handle, then stopped. She wasn't going to let a gossip's wagging tongue stop her from talking to her friend.

"It's odd, Sam," she told him. "I know knights are supposed to rescue damsels in distress, but this is the first time I've heard of one rescuing his rival."

"Rival?" Sam raised one eyebrow as he handed Meg the doll she had tossed out of the wagon. "What do you mean?"

His question surprised Laura, and she thought quickly. It appeared Charlotte hadn't told Sam the reason she wouldn't marry him. Though Laura could invent a story, Sam would see through it. Other than the massive lie she had been living, pretending to be a widow, she had never been good at deception. The only reasonable course was to tell Sam the truth.

Laura lowered her voice, lest a casual passerby overhear her. "It seems that Charlotte has developed a 'special affection' for Jason," she told Sam. "I imagine he's the reason she refused to marry you."

Sam raised both brows. "I wonder why she confided in you and not me. All she said to me was that she didn't love me. She never mentioned Jason."

Laura hoped Sam wasn't annoyed with Charlotte or hurt by her silence. "I asked her the reason," Laura said quickly. "I doubt Charlotte would have told me otherwise." Sam was fingering his mustache, hiding his expression from her. Was he angry? "Don't be insulted, Sam. I don't think she's told her parents either."

"Insulted?" Sam let his hand drop as he chuckled. "Hardly. I'm simply amazed by the workings of the female brain."

"And I by the workings of the male brain." Mrs. Kane left the store, her expression saying more clearly than words that she was surprised to see Laura and Sam still talking. So what? Sam was her friend. "Why did you intervene in Jason's fight?" Laura asked when the widow had crossed the street.

Sam shrugged, his coat rippling over his broad shoulders. Not for the first time, Laura was amazed that such a big man was so gentle . . . except, it appeared, with Jethro Mooney.

"Jethro's a bully, and I never did have a—what did you call it?—a 'special affection' for that species."

Though the air was cold, Sam's humor warmed Laura, and she realized that she would be happy to spend the rest of the day standing here in the middle of town laughing and talking with him.

"I've seen both Jason and Jethro," she said, "and I'd say it was an unfair fight. Jethro's got to be twice Jason's size."

Meg started to fuss. Though her mother might be content to stand and talk, she was not. Sam gathered her into his arms and tossed her into the air. As she giggled happily, he flashed Laura a conspiratorial smile. "I evened the odds a bit."

He put Meg back into the wagon. Taking the handle, he started toward Laura's cabin. "So Charlotte fancies Jason," he said when they had turned onto Second Street.

Laura nodded. "I don't know him, but I doubt Charlotte's parents would approve of him. From what I've heard, he's Gold Landing's bad boy."

Sam slowed his pace so that Laura could walk easily next to him. "Jason always seems to be in the midst of whatever trouble erupts in town," he agreed. "It's not usually serious, mostly mischievous pranks, but it sure does give him a bad reputation."

That was what Laura had surmised. From the day she arrived, whenever she had heard Jason's name, it had been coupled with a problem. It could be that he was what her mother would have called a "bad boy," but if Sam was right and Jason was involved in pranks rather than serious crimes or vandalism, it was possible that there was another reason for Jason's misbehaving. "When pupils act that way," she said slowly, "it's usually because they don't have enough to do."

As Sam stared into the distance, Laura watched furrows develop between his eyes. "You could be right," he said at last. He turned and smiled at her. "You just could be right."

* * *

"So, Nelson, what have you heard from the prodigal son?" George stared at the lawyer. God, how he hated this man! His fancy clothes, polished shoes, and that disapproving look that seemed to be etched on his face made George want nothing more than to plant his fist on the man's nose. It would be so satisfying to watch blood spurt from that snooty proboscis. George almost laughed at the thought of how surprised the attorney would be that he knew such a big word.

"The last communication I had from your stepbrother"—the attorney emphasized the word, clearly not liking George's reference to the prodigal son—"told me to expect him here on his birthday." Though the man appeared to be struggling to keep his lips from curving upward, George saw him start to smirk. He balled his fist. Lord, it would feel good to punch that mouth and watch the smirk disappear. The miserable excuse for a lawyer wouldn't smirk much longer. No, sirree. George would see to that. But first he had to take care of Sam.

George stalked to the door, kicking it for good measure on his way out. So the bastard thought he was going to take a wife. Not likely. George felt a mild interest in the type of woman his despicable little brother would marry. Some meek female, no doubt. One who wouldn't open her mouth, no matter what Sam said or did.

Striding down the street, George frowned. A wife. He supposed he'd have to find one someday. Hilda was getting downright insistent about his carrying on the bloodline. George spat, then laughed when one of the matrons who were leaving the general store recoiled. Too bad he'd missed her skirt. Too bad he couldn't show Hilda just what he thought of her. You'd think he was a horse, the way she told him how important it was to perpetuate the stock. *Pick a pretty woman, George,* she had admonished, *but make sure she's strong enough to bear children.* George would pick whoever he damn well pleased when he damn well pleased.

The fact was, he saw no reason to marry. There were

plenty of women ready to provide him with all the comforts of marriage without the problems. Although he had no clear memories of his own father, George had seen the way Hilda had controlled Nicholas after their marriage. If that was what the state of matrimony was like—and George didn't doubt that Hilda and Nicholas's union was typical—he wanted no part of it. No woman on earth would treat him the way Hilda had Nicholas. No, sirree. He would be the one in control.

He thrust the door open, smiling when it banged against the wall.

"Precious, is that you? Where were you?"

"Yes, Mother," he said, using the name she so hated, "I'm back. I just took a little walk." There was no reason to tell her where he had gone and why. Hilda might not approve of what he was planning to do, but she sure as shoot wouldn't object to the results.

"Is everything all right?"

George fisted his hands in his pockets. "Everything is perfect," he told her. *Or it will be.*

"You know how Mrs. Taylor says this is the season of miracles." Charlotte lifted her head from the costume she was mending, a question in her eyes.

Laura nodded. She had been grateful when Charlotte had suggested that they check over the costumes for the pageant to be sure there were no missing buttons or ripped hems. Charlotte's instincts had proven accurate, for it was obvious that last year several of the children had tried to disrobe without unfastening their garments. Now, at least, there was time to repair the damage, so the two women sat sewing at Laura's kitchen table while Meg played with her doll in the corner.

"It really is a season of miracles, isn't it?" Laura couldn't help smiling as she thought of Spring Flower. Though the woman wasn't as quick as her son, she was so eager to learn that Laura found the private tutoring sessions she had arranged with the Athapaskan woman one of the most enjoyable parts of her day. And to think that only a few months earlier, Spring Flower had believed books were the cause of her son's death! The change truly was a miracle.

Charlotte snipped a piece of thread. "I can't believe it, but Mr. Baranov offered Jason a job at the mill. He wants him to learn everything about the business—how to select wood, how to cut it, everything." Charlotte's face glowed with happiness and something else, something Laura would have called pride. "Then he's going to let him work in the office and learn that."

Charlotte's enthusiasm was so infectious that Laura couldn't help smiling in return. "It is good news." Sam, it appeared, had wasted no time finding a way to occupy Jason's time. He must have approached him the very day that he and Laura had spoken of the problem, and judging from Charlotte's account, he had found the young man capable. Laura couldn't imagine Sam making promises like the ones Charlotte had recounted unless he was certain that Jason had potential.

"Good news?" Charlotte shook her head. "It's wonderful news! A miracle!" It wasn't like Charlotte to be so effusive. Normally she was quiet and undemonstrative, but normally she wasn't talking about Jason and his future. Charlotte lowered her voice. "Maybe now my parents will let him court me."

Laura nodded. This was the reason for Charlotte's bubbling happiness. It *was* wonderful news . . . for Charlotte and Jason. But what about Sam? Where was *his* miracle?

Chapter Fifteen

He had thought he was prepared. After all, he had worked with the boys to build the set. Sam had thought that experience had taught him about children. He was wrong. Five boys in their teens learning new skills were nothing at all like thirty excited children aged six to sixteen getting ready for the annual Christmas pageant. They milled around, seemingly out of control. A little girl shrieked, while two slightly older boys raced in circles, shouting words that Sam found totally incomprehensible. Other children ran from one side of the room to the other, carrying costumes and props and yelling instructions.

He might have believed he was experiencing the Tower of Babel, but it was worse than that. This was Bedlam, pure Bedlam. And through it all, Laura walked calmly, seemingly serene. Sam didn't know how she did it. Sam knew only two things: Laura was incredible, with powers beyond that of normal mortals, and they would never, ever finish this rehearsal for the pageant.

"Children, listen." Laura spoke in normal tones. Sam could

hardly hear her over the din that her students were creating, and yet somehow they all heard her voice. Almost immediately, the room was so quiet that Sam's first thought was that he had suddenly gone deaf. The sound of someone's shoes scraping on the floor told him that he hadn't lost his hearing. All that had happened was that thirty rambunctious children had stopped shouting. How had Laura managed that?

She stood in the middle of the room, her glance moving slowly as she nodded or smiled at each child. Sam wondered what the silent communication was all about. Was she persuading or commanding her students? Not that it mattered. What was important was that the room was blessedly silent.

"Mr. Baranov is here to help us set up," she told them with a quick smile for Sam. Though he had seen her smile so many times, it had never been quite like this—both warm and conspiratorial, as if they shared a secret. "I expect you to obey him," she continued. "Pretend he's me."

There was a second of silence, as if the students were learning a new and difficult subject. Then one of the older boys announced, "You're prettier, Mrs. Templeton."

She certainly was. Though she still wore her widow's black, today she had draped a deep blue shawl over her shoulders. Sam suspected it was part of someone's costume and that she had forgotten she had it, but he couldn't ignore the way the color highlighted her eyes, making them look even more vibrant than usual.

Laura chuckled. "He's a lot stronger," she told her pupil. "Now, let's get the rehearsal started."

Sam knew the students had rehearsed numerous times, and Laura had told him she was fairly confident that the older children knew their lines. The youngest played angels, since those parts involved no speaking. All they had to do was stand in a row and look angelic. While Sam doubted some of the hellions' ability to master the second part of their role, Laura had assured him that the parents did not expect perfection.

Once they started it, the rehearsal took less than an hour.

Though it had its moments of chaos, and there was one time when he thought he saw Laura frown with displeasure, Sam was amazed at how smoothly everything went. Even more amazing was the way he and Laura had worked together. He would look at her and somehow, without either of them saying a word, he would know what she needed done. They worked as a team, and—even more amazing—they worked as if they were a team that had done this many times before.

Amazing. That was the word to describe Laura. There was no one else like her. Sam took a deep breath as he helped the boys move the stable to the back of the church hall, where they would store it until tomorrow evening. Then it would be moved into the church itself for the performance. The men from Shantytown had promised that they would bring the moose tomorrow afternoon. Since Sam and Laura had agreed that it was too dangerous to have the children sit on the animal, the three wise men would pretend that they were leading the large substitute for a camel.

"You did a wonderful job." Once more Laura was speaking to the children. They stared at her, their faces glowing from the praise. "I know your parents will be proud of you tomorrow night." When her right hand touched the corner of the stable and she smiled with apparent pleasure at the building he and the boys had constructed, Sam suspected his expression was as silly as the children's. Laura's praise could do that to a man.

Sam had never met a woman like her. He wasn't sure how it had happened, but he felt more comfortable with her than he did with anyone else—even his poker-playing buddies William and Ben. Sam nodded at the boys who were carrying the manger toward the back of the room. They didn't need his help. In fact, they were probably more comfortable without him.

Sam hadn't realized it was possible to feel comfortable with a woman, and he certainly hadn't expected to enjoy one's company the way he did Laura's. He liked other women. Amelia, Ella, even Charlotte. But Laura was different. She was special. He liked her, and—more than that—he wanted to make her happy. Although he had never felt that way about the others, he worried about Laura, and he found himself searching for ways to make her smile. It wasn't love, of course. The state that the poets liked to extol didn't exist. What Sam felt for Laura wasn't love, but he wouldn't deny that he cared about her.

The parents had taken the younger children home; the older ones were milling around, apparently excited about the performance they had just completed. When they finished sliding the manger into the stable, Sam brushed the dust from his hands. They were done. As if on cue, the lights flickered, then dimmed. For a second, there was pandemonium as everyone tried to reach the door. Then the lights came back on, ending the stampede. Sam's gaze met Laura's, and as they shared a wry smile, he felt as if a light of a different kind had suddenly been illuminated.

Laura. She was the answer to so many questions. Sam swallowed deeply. Why hadn't he thought of it sooner? He wasn't normally so dense. But perhaps he had been unwilling to see what was right in front of him; his own prejudices about widows had blinded him to the possibility of Laura. He could marry *her*. It was the perfect solution. She was his best friend. If he married her, not only would he fulfill the terms of his father's will, but he'd also spend the rest of his life with a woman he liked. Why had he wasted so much time courting Charlotte?

Sam tried not to frown at his own stupidity. If only . . . But there was no point in dwelling on the past. He needed to make sure that he didn't waste the future. He would ask Laura to marry him. It was too soon after Matt's death, of course, and she was still in mourning for her husband. Sam knew that any woman would be reluctant to marry at this time. If everything had been perfect, he would have waited longer. But everything wasn't perfect. Time was running out. He would wait until after the holidays. He would even wait for all twelve days of Christmas to pass. But then . . . then he would ask Laura to be his bride.

Then everything would be perfect.

Seattle. Why on earth had he come back here? He hated the place. All those gray and rainy days. He had been miserable living in that little apartment, walking in the rain, when he ought to have been living in a mansion on top of a hill and riding in a fine carriage or even in one of those fancy horseless wagons.

He should not have come back. There were other cities and other women. And yet, none of the other women had cared for him the way she had. In the early days, she had made him feel important. A man liked that. Besides, none of the other women had had as much money, and money was important. Damned important. That was one lesson he'd learned well.

And so here he was, looking at the harbor and thinking about the woman who'd been his second wife. He needed a drink, just one, and then he'd go see her. She'd be glad to see him. He knew that. But first, one drink.

He turned the corner and stared at the painted placard in front of the tavern. The Green Shamrock. Shamrocks were good luck, weren't they? It was a sign. He was meant to go to that tavern. The shamrock and the whiskey would bring him luck. Today was going to be his lucky day. He was sure of that.

An hour later, he climbed the hill a little less steadily than he might have if that stranger hadn't persuaded him to have just one more. It had seemed like a shame to waste good Irish whiskey, especially when the stranger had offered to pay for it. Besides, there was no reason to rush. Now that she had the brats to care for, she'd be there waiting.

The place was a hovel. Odd. He hadn't remembered it being so bad. Grime coated the bricks, one of the windows was broken, and the stench that poured out of it made him wrinkle his nose. They'd find another place. He wasn't going to live in a pigsty like this. Still, he had to admit, it was better than his last residence. At least there were no bars here. And she'd be here.

But when he rang the front doorbell, no one answered. Where was she? She and the brats ought to be home. Unless the old man had relented and she had moved back with her parents. Wouldn't that be something? All that nice money.

"Lookin' for someone?" a woman's voice called.

He turned and forced his lips into a smile. He'd seen her kind before, ugly as a mule and starved for a man. As the woman leaned out of the window, her dress gaped open. She was as scrawny as a chicken. He tried not to shudder. "My wife," he said. "Reckon you might know where she is?"

"What's her name?" The woman gave him an assessing look, as if trying to recognize him. Either that, or she was trying to decide how much to offer him for a sample of his talents.

When he told her the name, she nodded sagely. "She's gone to Alaska."

Alaska! He felt a surge of anger that his wife wasn't here when he needed her. Damn it all! He'd been counting on a hot meal and a warm bed. Alaska! What kind of fool would go to that land of snow and ice? If there was one place on earth that was worse than Seattle, that was it. They might have a lot of gold in Alaska and gold, mind you, was good, but he wasn't sure it was worth living with all that ice.

"I hear it's a big place," he said as casually as he could. You never could tell when he'd need to know where in Alaska she had gone. If it turned out that she had her parents' money, he reckoned he could put up with the cold for as long as it took to get his share.

"I didn't pay much mind," the neighbor told him. She was leaning so far out the window that he wondered how she kept her balance. "After all, it ain't as if I figure I'd ever go there. Too cold for a woman. But"—she gave him a wink and a smile—"I reckon you miss your wife. Why don't you come on in? I got some whiskey that might help me remember."

And so he found himself sitting at a scarred table, sharing a drink with a woman who kept leering at him. He'd bedded worse-looking females, but only if they had money, and this one plainly did not. Still, she might have the information he needed, and that could lead to money one of these days. Though it took two hours and more kisses and sweet words than he'd expended in months, at last her memory cleared. "The town's called Gold something." She tipped her head to one side in a gesture he guessed she thought was appealing. He thought it made her look like a robin looking for a worm. He sure didn't like being a worm. "Gold Landing," she said, and the smile she gave him told him she had known the name all along.

He rose and walked toward the door. No point in staying here anymore. Today was going to be his lucky day. He knew it. It would only take one poker game, and he'd have enough money to go anywhere he wanted. And that most certainly wouldn't be Gold Landing, Alaska.

Three hours later, he could feel the sweat rolling down his neck. A man wasn't supposed to sweat when he played poker. It told the others that he wasn't holding a flush. Hell, he wasn't holding nothing, but he sure couldn't tell them that. Not when he owed them as much money as he did. That dark-haired man looked like he could be meaner than the prison guards. Nope, he sure didn't want to tangle with him.

" 'Scuse me, gentlemen," he said with a gesture toward the back of the building. "Man's gotta piss."

A minute later, he was running down the alleyway. "Stop, thief!" He could hear the dark-haired man's footsteps. Sweat poured from his face as he fled. He had to get out of here. Fast. Though his heart was pounding so hard he thought it might burst through his chest, he kept running. And then he realized that the footsteps had stopped. The dark-haired man might be a good poker player, but he couldn't run more than a block.

Another man might think it a close call. He knew it was a sign. He wasn't meant to stay in Seattle. No, sirree. He was going to head for other parts. He had told the men at the poker table that he was fixing to go south. If the dark-haired man had as many friends as he claimed, that might not be a good idea. Leastwise, not right away. For the first time, Gold Landing, Alaska, sounded like a good place.

Roy Templeton grinned. This was his lucky day.

The store was as crowded as she had expected, with people looking for the right Christmas gift. Laura had finished her shopping. But she needed popcorn so that she and Meg could string it for the tree. They had already made paper chains and had decked the house with them. The tree was all that was left.

"Good day, Mrs. Templeton." Herb Ashton greeted Laura with his customarily broad smile. "We got another delivery this mornin'," he told her. "Just in time." Laura returned his smile. On one of the less hectic mornings, Herb had told her that dogsleds, which were the primary method for wintertime deliveries, were less reliable than the boats that plied the Tanana during the summer months. Goods did arrive while the river was frozen, but their arrival was not predictable. "Got one of those Seattle papers for you." He reached behind the counter, rummaged through a pile of newspapers, then handed Laura hers.

"Thank you." Laura paid for the popcorn, then added, "Please tell Mrs. Ashton that I'm grateful she volunteered to make her bean casserole for the party. I've heard so much about it that I can't wait to actually taste it."

The shopkeeper beamed. "She's a good cook, the missus is."

Ella had told Laura that the parents frequently remained in the church after the pageant to talk about the performance. When Laura had heard, she had asked Ella why they didn't plan a party afterward so that everyone had an excuse for staying and socializing.

"Who'll plan it?" ever-practical Ella had asked.

"I will." That, of course, had been before Matt's death. But Laura sometimes thought that the myriad details of rehearsing for the pageant and planning the party had helped her through those terrible days. That and Sam's comforting company.

Ella had agreed to keep Meg with her this morning while Laura did final preparations. It had helped, Laura admitted, not having to watch Meg each moment that she was in the store. And as soon as she got home, she sank into her rocking chair, poured herself a cup of tea, and opened the paper. She would read for just a few minutes before she went to Ella's.

It was on the second page, a small article that might not have caught her attention had she been more rushed. As it was, she scanned the headline, then caught her breath as she read the article once, twice, then a third time. It was true. Her eyes had not deceived her. Two inches of newsprint. Surely something that small should not cause her eyes to tear and her heart to race as if she had run up one of Seattle's steepest hills.

The words were matter-of-fact, a brief recounting of a jailbreak at a northern Oregon prison. Two men had escaped; one had been killed. Though the dead man's face had been mutilated, his identity was established as Roy Templeton, formerly of Seattle.

Laura fought the darkness that threatened to overcome her. Roy was dead! She forced herself to take deep breaths in a desperate attempt to block out the image the article had conjured. Roy was dead! Her eyes filled with tears for the man he could have been, the man she had once thought she loved. Laura leaned back in the chair, trying to reconcile the words she had read with the few happy memories she had of Roy. What a waste of a life! But her sorrow was soon swept away by relief.

The nightmare was over. She no longer needed to fear Roy would return and take the children from her. She no longer had to fear that somehow Meg would learn the truth about her father. Roy was dead!

Relief turned to giddy joy as Laura realized that she was no longer married. The shackles of that loveless union were sundered. She was free.

Truly, it was a season of miracles.

Chapter Sixteen

Laura looked around, amazed at how peaceful the church seemed. Half an hour ago, while the stable had been being maneuvered into position, the normal serenity of the sanctuary had been disturbed by grunts and groans and then a shout of pure glee when the star, which had teetered precariously on a pole, slid into place. In a few minutes, once the pupils and their parents began to arrive, the scene would turn into pure pandemonium. Laura was certain of that. But right now, with the newly constructed stable in place and the carefully stuffed moose standing watch next to it, she was struck by the fact that, at least for this moment in time, everything was perfect.

At Sam's request, she had left the church during the setup and had checked the preparations in the hall. Assured that everything there was under control, she had returned. Though the church was quiet, Laura saw that two men were inside the stable, moving something. She recognized Sam's tall form bent in what had to be an uncomfortable position, but wasn't sure which of the boys who had helped build the props was with him.

"What's next?" the younger man asked Sam as he emerged from the stable. Laura tried to hide her surprise when she recognized him as Jason Blake. Though she knew Jason was working for Sam and had, according to Sam, shown both an aptitude and a willingness to work hard, she hadn't realized that Sam had involved him in the pageant.

Sam straightened, grinning slightly as he pressed the small of his back. When his eyes met Laura's, she saw mirth reflected in them. "This is Mrs. Templeton." Sam clapped Jason on the shoulder in a gesture that seemed almost parental. "We need to ask her, because she's in charge tonight."

Laura didn't miss the questioning look that Jason gave her, almost as if he expected her to dismiss him. "I'm glad you came," she told him truthfully. If Jason had aspirations of marrying Charlotte, it was important for her parents to see him doing something constructive rather than engaging in mischievous acts. Laura suspected Sam knew that, and that was why he had enlisted the young man's aid. "It may be calm now, but I know we're going to have chaos in ten minutes," Laura told him. "It will be good to have another man to help control the children."

As she had hoped, Jason's shoulders straightened ever so slightly when she referred to him as a man. The quick smile Sam gave her said he understood and approved of her tactic. Laura felt a glow deep inside her. It felt so good, working with Sam like this. They seemed to understand each other and be able to communicate without words. Laura had never had that kind of friendship before, but then she had never had a friend like Sam before.

"What do you think?"

Laura blinked before she realized Sam was asking about the stable. The three of them discussed whether the moose should be moved to the other side, with Laura insisting that there was no need to change its position, while Jason suggested that the moose's other side was its better one. Laura wasn't sure a moose had any good sides. In her estimation, they were large, homely animals. Still, even though it wasn't a camel, the moose's presence did add a special touch to the overall effect. Sam had been right about that.

He looked at his watch. "They should be here soon." After hearing Ella's tales of anxious parents who had brought their children to the pageant an hour early, Laura had sent all the students home with notes explaining when they should arrive. She had hoped that that, combined with the fact that the pageant was being held earlier than usual this year—a full week before Christmas—would keep everyone enthusiastic but avoid panic.

Laura heard the door open and felt the air stir. Even this far from the entrance, there was no ignoring the force of an Alaskan winter.

"Jason!" Charlotte fairly shrieked his name when she entered the church. "I didn't expect you here!" She raced up the aisle, and Laura suspected that while the color she saw on her assistant's cheeks might have been caused by the wind, it was enhanced by the proximity of a certain young man.

Jason's face had taken on a distinctly rosy hue. "Mr. Baranov asked me to help him." As he explained, Jason gave Sam a look that said he considered the older man a hero. He wasn't wrong, Laura reflected. Many of the things Sam did, including befriending the town's bad boy, were heroic. That was why she wanted so much to be able to help him. Even heroes sometimes needed assistance.

For a long moment Jason and Charlotte stood like two statues, staring at each other, neither one speaking, though they would occasionally open their mouths, then close them without uttering a word. Finally, Laura took pity on them. "I think we need some more straw around the moose. Charlotte, would you and Jason take care of that?"

As the two young people walked toward the back of the church to retrieve another bale of straw, Laura heard Jason say, "Maybe your parents will like me better if they see me here."

Sam gave Laura a conspiratorial smile as they sank onto

the front pew. "Young love," he said. "Amazing, isn't it?" He stroked his mustache in a pensive gesture. "Everything looks so simple to them right now, because their world consists of only the two of them."

Laura couldn't disagree with him, although she doubted either Charlotte or Jason believed their lives to be simple. "I find it touching." And she did. It was reassuring to see Charlotte looking happy after the months when she had seemed so troubled.

Sam leaned back, apparently enjoying the brief respite. "I imagine you felt the same way when you fell in love with your husband."

The chill that crept up Laura's spine owed nothing to December weather. Sam's statement was innocent. He had no reason to know that he was raising unhappy rather than fond memories. "I don't think I ever had stars in my eyes the way Charlotte does," she said.

Laura had heard that women in love glowed with happiness, but—until she had seen Charlotte with Jason—she had thought that was nothing more than poetic hyperbole. Now she knew it was true, just as she knew it was true that she had never loved Roy. "Charlotte says that Jason makes her feel beautiful. I can't remember ever feeling beautiful when I was with Roy." Laura had been flattered by his attention and the sweet words he had whispered to her. But beautiful? Never.

It was still difficult to realize that Roy was dead. Though he had not been part of her life for almost two years, she had continued to think of him at odd moments, and she had lived with the constant reminder that her widowhood was a sham. Now that he was gone, she felt free. Yet it was as if a festering sore had been lanced. Although she felt better, the wound had not yet fully healed.

And then, as the children and their parents arrived, there was no time to think of anything but the pageant. There were a few problems, like the time the child playing Mary almost dropped the baby Jesus onto the floor. It was at that moment that Laura realized why Ella had insisted that she use a doll rather than a live baby, as the students had urged.

Several of the shepherds and one of the wise men forgot their lines and had to be prompted, but no one seemed to mind. In fact, when the pageant ended, Laura heard nothing but praise. As far as the parents were concerned, this was the best pageant Gold Landing had ever seen. The festive spirit continued as they moved to the church hall for the party.

"The wooden sets were a great idea," Ella told Laura. The two women stood in one corner of the room. Laura wasn't certain why Ella had chosen the spot, but she knew that she had longed for a moment of quiet. With the party in full swing and parents eager to relive their children's success, that was a rare commodity. "I would never have thought of making sets," Ella continued.

Laura glanced at the corral of children on the opposite side of the room, looking for her daughter. Though Meg was more solemn than she had been before Matt's illness and death, she was playing with the other children tonight and appeared to be content. Laura suspected that Meg's memory of Matt had already begun to fade and that the time would come when she would no longer think of her brother. While Laura's pain was less intense now, it remained a constant part of her, ready to resurface at any time, and her fear that somehow Meg might be taken from her did not diminish.

"You know some of the boys worked with Sam to build the sets," Laura said to Ella. "To be honest, I don't know who was teaching whom. The boys certainly learned a lot about woodworking, but I think Sam may have learned more about raising children than he expected."

Ella laughed. "Isn't that the way you felt your first year of teaching? I know I did." She fingered the red and green paper chain that the students had draped over the window frame.

Two of the young pupils, their eyelids drooping with sleepiness, pushed their way through the crowds. "Good night, Teacher," they said. Laura gave them each a quick hug, then accepted their parents' thanks.

As the room began to empty, Ella's husband Ben appeared at her side, lines of worry creasing his face. "Should you be standing so long?" he asked his wife.

Ella gave him an indulgent smile and laid a hand on his arm. "I'm not sick, Ben. I'm just having a baby." She glanced down at her abdomen. Not even a well-cut gown could camouflage the swelling. Ella's gaze returned to her husband's face. "You're the doctor in the family; you ought to realize that this is a perfectly normal condition."

When Ben turned to greet one of his patients, muttering something about stubborn females under his breath, Ella turned to Laura. "Was your husband that protective?"

For a second Laura felt as if someone had punched her. Why was everyone asking about Roy tonight? She doubted anyone in Gold Landing had read the Seattle paper, and surely there would be no reason for news of an Oregon prison break to travel so far north.

"No." How could she tell Ella that no one had ever been protective of her? Her parents had insisted that she learn life's lessons, and Roy . . . Roy had taught her some of life's more difficult lessons. While he had been happy when she announced her pregnancy, and had told her how important it was that she take care of herself, his pleasure and his concern for Laura had disappeared the day he realized that her parents were not going to relent. In retrospect, Laura realized that should have been her first signal that Roy did not love her and had, in fact, loved only the prospect of her inheritance. But Laura did not want to talk or even think about Roy. He was gone, and nothing could change the past. The future was what mattered.

Laura looked closely at Ella. She did appear more tired than usual. Was this why Ben wanted her to sit? "Are you starting to get anxious about the birth?"

Ella nodded. "It's less than two months now. At times I can't wait to hold the baby in my arms, but other times I'm just plain scared."

Laura touched her friend's hand. "I remember feeling exactly the same way." Fear and anticipation had been mingled, both exaggerated by the fact that Laura had had no confidante. "I think it's only natural. After all, this is the first time. You don't know what to expect."

Another family came to thank Laura for her role in the pageant. When they left, Ella continued. "You had twins. That's a lot harder than just one." A small smile crossed her face. "I'll never forget the night I helped Ben deliver the Whitaker twins. It was an incredible experience, holding those two tiny babies." Ella's voice choked, and she covered her mouth. "Oh, Laura, how thoughtless of me! I shouldn't be talking about babies when Matt . . ." She broke off, and Laura saw the tears in her eyes. "I miss Matt," Ella said. "My house isn't the same without him."

Nothing was the same. Laura dressed, fed, bathed, and played with one child, not two. And though she had packed Matt's clothing and toys away where they would not be a constant reminder of the boy she would never again hold, memories could not be so easily hidden. "Each day gets a little easier," she admitted. "Sam was right about that. It isn't that the pain is less; it's that I'm learning to deal with it."

It was odd how often she thought of Sam. It wasn't just that they had been working together on the pageant and that that had placed them in each other's company more often than normal. No, it seemed that no matter where she was or what she was doing, her thoughts would return to Sam. She would remember some of the things he had told her, ordinary things like how to polish the rocking chair he had made or how to tell from the position of the clouds whether it was going to snow the next day. She would picture his smile and the endearing way he would finger his mustache when he was thinking. She would remember the way his arms had felt around her, how they had made her feel warm and comforted.

As if her thoughts conjured him, Sam touched her shoulder. "I hate to interrupt you two ladies," he said with a smile that made mockery of his words, "but I need Laura's help with something."

As Ella walked toward her husband, Sam touched the small of Laura's back and directed her toward the alcove where tables and other supplies were normally stored. What could he possibly need from her? Laura gave Sam a questioning look; then as her eyes moved upward to meet his, she noticed a piece of greenery hanging from the doorway.

"What's that?"

Sam grinned. "It's supposed to be mistletoe. Why else do you think I brought you this way? Only you can help me with it."

He wouldn't. Surely he wouldn't. Not here in a public place. But he did. Slowly Sam drew her into his arms and pressed a kiss on her lips. It was gentle, almost chaste, the kind of kiss that would provoke no undue comments from the citizenry. It lasted only seconds, and yet as they broke apart, Laura felt the blood rush to her cheeks. How could it be that her friend Sam's kisses stirred her more than her husband's embrace ever had? Just the touch of Sam's hand on hers made the blood sing in her veins, and when his lips met hers, the singing turned into a thundering choir.

This wasn't the young love that Charlotte and Jason shared. It wasn't love at all, and yet it was special. Though Sam might not make her feel beautiful, when she was in his arms, Laura felt pretty. And that was a feeling she had never experienced as Roy's wife.

When the party ended, Ella and the other women insisted that Laura leave without helping with the cleanup. "You've already done more than your share," they told her. So she gathered her now-sleeping daughter into her arms and carried her home.

With Meg back in her own bed, Laura made a pot of tea and sat in the rocker, trying to make her thoughts flow as easily as the chair rocked. It wasn't as though the idea was a new one. She had considered it dozens of times since she had learned of Sam's plight. Then it had been nothing more than a possibility, a "what if." At the time she had been unable to turn the idea into reality, and that had been almost incredibly frustrating. Now everything had changed. Now the barriers were gone.

Should she? Laura clasped the mug with both hands, as if its warmth would somehow crystallize her thoughts. It was a huge decision, probably the most important one she had ever made. She set the mug on the floor and slid her hands along the arms of the rocker. In truth, there was no decision to be made. She knew what her answer would be. She wanted to help Sam. He was her dearest friend, and he needed help—help that she could give him. For now she had the means to turn his dream into reality.

Laura started to rock. She would do it. Tomorrow. Before she lost her courage.

Sam paced the room. It was ridiculous, being so concerned. But ever since he had received Laura's note saying that she wanted to see him, he could not dismiss his worries. He stared out the window, then turned, strode to the other wall, and stared out the window. Was something wrong with Meg? Was Laura herself ill? Her note was terse, giving him no idea why she wanted to meet him in his office. And so Sam paced, pulling out his pocket watch so often that he realized there was no reason to close it again. He might as well hold it in his hand. Then he would know just how long he had before she would come.

When she arrived, her cheeks were red, her eyes suspiciously bright, almost as if she had been crying. The feeling of dread that had settled in his stomach from the time he had read her note increased. Something must be terribly wrong!

Sam hung Laura's coat on one of the hooks, then watched as she twisted her hands together. He tried not to let his worry show. Laura was visibly nervous, and that alarmed him even more than the note had. Other than the night Matt had died, Laura had always seemed calm and in control.

"Would you like to sit down?" He led her into the room he had turned into a school, thinking she would be more comfortable here than in his office proper. A minute earlier, her face had been ruddy. Now she looked unnaturally pale, as if she was going to faint.

"Yes." She sank so swiftly into the chair he offered that Sam knew his assessment hadn't been far from wrong. Laura was on the verge of collapsing. Though he tried to force his heart to beat slowly, he failed, utterly and completely.

Laura perched on the edge of the chair and twisted her hands again. Then, apparently realizing what she was doing and what it revealed of her emotional state, she folded her hands and placed them in her lap. "Sit down, Sam," she said.

He dragged a chair closer to hers and sat where he could study her face. Those beautiful blue eyes that were normally so clear were now clouded with confusion.

"I thought I knew how to say this, but I've never done it before," she told him in a voice that quavered. "It's turning out to be harder than I thought."

Sam's heart began to ache. Meg. It must be that Meg was dangerously ill. He couldn't imagine anything else that would cause Laura such distress. Sam tried not to frown. That would only make matters worse. But if the worst happened, how was Laura going to survive the loss of her second child? No mother should have to endure that kind of agony.

Sam leaned forward, resting his hands on his knees in an effort to look calm. Perhaps if he pretended nothing was wrong, Laura would begin to relax. "What's wrong?" he asked in as casual a voice as he could manage. Though he wanted to gather Laura into his arms and comfort her, first he had to know what was causing this distress. "How can I help you?"

There was a moment of silence when he feared that she would not answer, that the only sound would be the howling of the wind and the crackle of the stove. Then Laura laughed, a brittle sound, far different from her normal cheery laugh. "I want to help *you*," she said.

She wanted to help him? Sam knew his expression must have reflected his confusion, for Laura continued, speaking rapidly now. "I know how important your inheritance is, and

I want you to have it." The words spilled out, and that terrible pallor was replaced by heightened color in her cheeks.

Sam stared. His inheritance. She had come to talk about his inheritance, not about some horrible fate. Thank God! Everything would be all right. Laura and Meg were safe. Sam felt the band that had tightened around his heart, threatening to crush the life from him, begin to loosen. But why, oh, why was Laura so upset by his inheritance?

Sam saw her fingers whiten as she pressed her hands together. Something was terribly wrong or Laura wouldn't be so tense. What could it be?

"Would you . . . I will . . . er . . ." The stream of words that had flowed so easily a moment before appeared to have dried up. Though Laura kept her eyes focused on the floor, keeping him from reading her expression, she could not disguise the color that flooded her face.

"What is it?" he prompted her. This was agony, not knowing what was causing her such pain.

At length Laura raised her eyes to his, and the uncertainty he saw reflected in them wrenched his heart. Whatever she was going to say, she doubted his reaction. Sam leaned forward and smiled, trying to reassure her.

She swallowed, stared at him, then opened her mouth. Though no words came out, Sam sensed that she was mustering the courage for whatever it was she had to say.

"Sam, I'm willing to marry you so you can claim your father's company," she blurted out. "If you want me, that is."

Once again her voice quavered, and Sam's heart contracted in sympathy. Then the import of her words hit him, fairly knocking the breath from his chest. Laura had just proposed marriage to him! He had planned to ask her when the holidays were over, and somehow—by some miracle—she had anticipated that. Laura, wonderful, courageous Laura, had done something few women would have dared. She had asked a man to marry her.

As Sam watched, tears filled Laura's eyes. "If you don't want to marry me," she said quietly but in a voice that could not disguise her pain, "I understand. We can still be friends."

What an idiot he was! He'd been so surprised by her proposal that he hadn't answered immediately, and that had hurt her. Wonderful, wonderful Laura, the woman who had just handed him his fondest dream, had suffered because of his stupidity.

"Oh, Laura." Sam leaned forward and took both of her hands in his. Slowly unfolding her fingers, he wrapped her hands with his. "Of course I want to marry you. What man wouldn't? Don't ever think otherwise!" He could kick himself for that delay. Those few seconds had shaken her confidence badly, that much was apparent. "I was just surprised. It's so soon after your husband's and Matt's deaths that I hadn't thought you'd consider marriage."

Sam stroked her hands, trying to warm them. Though he guessed she was trying her best to control them, there was no doubt that they were shaking. "Laura, of course I want to marry you. I was going to ask you to be my wife once the holidays were over." She stared at him, and he could see that she didn't believe him. "You took me by surprise, Laura. That's all. I didn't think you'd be ready for marriage so soon."

Thank goodness, her hands were beginning to warm again. They had felt so small and cold inside his grip. Laura's gaze was constant, and Sam was relieved to see that the tears he had feared had disappeared, even though her wariness had not.

"This isn't a normal situation," she told him. Indeed not. He needed a bride, and one had just offered herself to him. That was about as abnormal as Sam could imagine. "Under the circumstances," Laura continued, "I don't think we should worry about propriety. Your happiness is more important to me than observing a year's mourning." There was no doubting her sincerity. It was reflected in her voice and in the concern he saw shining from those lovely blue eyes. A flush crept up her cheeks, and she lowered her eyes. "Besides," she said, "it won't be a real marriage."

Sam blinked. What did she mean, not a real marriage?

That was the only kind that was going to meet the requirements of his father's will and the only kind he wanted. "What kind of a marriage did you have in mind?"

She kept her eyes focused on the floor, and the way her hands twisted within his told Sam she was uncomfortable with whatever it was she was going to say. "I'm proposing what some call a marriage of convenience."

What the hell was that? Sam had a fleeting thought that he should have listened to William and Ben months ago when they had offered to give him advice. They might have warned him about this marriage of convenience, whatever it was. "I'm not familiar with the term," he said as mildly as he could.

Laura met his gaze for a second. Then her cheeks flamed, and she dropped her eyes again. "It means we share a house," she said, "but not . . ." The red in her cheeks deepened. "Not a bed," she blurted out.

"What?" Sam couldn't keep the word from exploding from his mouth. What kind of marriage was that? Who would agree to an arrangement like that?

"We'd still be friends, Sam," Laura said, her voice small and tentative, as if she feared his reaction. "Married friends."

Sam counted to five. He had heard you were supposed to count to ten, but he couldn't make it that far. "I don't understand why you don't want a normal marriage." He sure as hell wanted one. Laura was warm and womanly, and he most definitely wanted her in his bed.

She looked up at him, her eyes solemn. Laura leaned forward slightly, and this time her hands squeezed his, as if she were comforting him. "I know you don't love me." Though her voice was even, Sam sensed the sorrow that the words provoked. "I don't expect love from you, but I can't imagine intimacy without it."

Sam couldn't fault her logic. Laura had been married once, and she'd known love. Of course she'd want it a second time. Sam's stomach knotted at the realization that while Laura had just given him the thing he wanted most, he was unable to give her anything in return. Love. It was a damn shame that was one thing he couldn't offer her.

"I won't lie to you, Laura. I wish I could tell you that I love you, but I'm not sure any such thing exists." Love hadn't been part of his life so far. Only a fool would expect it to appear magically just because this wonderful woman had offered to marry him and wanted assurances. Sam drew Laura's hands to his lips and pressed kisses on her fingertips. "I care for you, Laura, and I promise you this. I'll do everything I can to make sure you never regret marrying me."

The wind howled again. Sam had never noticed what a lonely sound it was. The truth was, he had never thought much about loneliness. After being alone for so long, he had grown accustomed to it. But now, thanks to Laura, he would never be alone again. He would have her and Meg. He would have a family.

Laura's blue eyes glistened, and he hoped she wasn't regretting her impetuous gesture. But when she spoke, her voice was calm. "When shall we marry?" This was the Laura he knew, ever practical.

"Tomorrow?"

A small smile crossed her lips. "I was thinking about next month. Would January sixteenth be all right?"

Any day before February 14th would be fine for him. "I guess I can wait another month," he drawled. Sam rose and drew Laura to her feet. She looked so tiny standing next to him and so infinitely precious. For a second he felt as lightheaded as she had appeared to be when she had come into the office. Was it possible? Were the months of worry truly over and would he be able to claim his father's legacy?

Sam took a deep breath, trying to clear his head. It was more than relief that his inheritance was safe. That was part of it, for there was no denying that he was happier than he'd been since the day he'd learned the terms of his father's will and had begun his search for a bride. But there was more. The thought of being married to Laura, of waking up and seeing her face every morning for the rest of his life, filled him with a deep contentment that had nothing to do with Baranov Shipping. It would be wonderful, having Laura as his bride.

Sam looked down at her, his heart swelling with happiness at the sight of those beautiful blue eyes, the pert nose, and those deliciously soft lips.

He reached for Laura.

She backed away.

"Can't I kiss my bride-to-be?" Sam asked. He wanted to do that and much more.

Laura shook her head. "We're just friends, Sam. Remember?" It was surely his imagination that there was a tinge of disappointment in her voice.

Friends. That ridiculous marriage-of-convenience idea. He'd have to change her mind about that. Starting now. "These friends have kissed before," he reminded her. Though she hesitated, her eyes clouding with confusion, she did not refuse.

"Come here, Laura." He opened his arms and waited for her to walk into them. Something had frightened her, but for the life of him, Sam couldn't imagine what it was. He waited, smiling, until she took a step toward him. Then he enfolded her in his arms.

He held her for a moment, saying nothing, not daring to kiss her until he felt her trembling stop. Only then did he lower his mouth to hers, giving her a gentle kiss. Though the blood began to pound through his veins and he wanted nothing more than to crush her mouth with his, Sam knew he could not do that. Not with Laura. He needed to be gentle, to woo her the way he had tried to woo Charlotte. He would do whatever he had to. He would even ask Ben and William for advice if he had to, for if there was one thing Sam knew, it was that he most definitely did not want a marriage of convenience.

Just friends? Not likely!

* * *

The sound of picks and shovels filled the mine. It was a normal Thursday morning as the men swung their tools, digging the precious metal from deep within the earth. And as was normal, the sound of metal on earth was punctuated with comments from the men near him. Lord, they were a noisy bunch. Almost as bad as a gaggle of geese or a bunch of women. Jethro knew how to make geese or women be silent, but he hadn't figured out a way to shut these mouths.

"Reckon you heard the news," Chet Wing said to no one in particular. "Gold Landing's gonna have another wedding."

Jake Bolton took the gauntlet. "I heard it's gonna be soon too. Good excuse for a party."

Jethro continued to shovel. Weddings were nonsense, and marriage wasn't much better. A man had to be a fool to saddle himself with a wife.

"Reckon it won't be like William's," Chet said, "but still . . ."

"A party's a party, so long as there's good whiskey in the punch," Jake agreed.

Jethro had heard enough. Somehow he had to get them to stop chattering. "Who's gettin' hitched?" he demanded.

Chet stopped shoveling long enough to glare at Jethro. "That new schoolmarm, Mrs. Templeton."

Figured. She was a pretty one. Jethro didn't have much use for widows with another man's brats, but he had to admit the teacher was a looker, and good-looking single women were as scarce as December sun. He wondered who'd managed to land this prize.

"Takes two to get married." Jethro couldn't believe how dumb these miners were. They couldn't even tell a story straight. "Who's the sucker of a groom?"

Jake Bolton dumped a shovelful of ore into the wagon. "Sam Baranov."

Sam Baranov. Damn it all! Jethro swung the shovel as if it were a pick, laughing when it landed against the far wall and two miners jumped a foot. "Sorry," he said with a grin that put lie to his words, "it musta slipped."

Baranov getting married. A red haze blocked Jethro's vision as he pictured the pretty schoolteacher in Sam Baranov's bed. It wasn't fair.

Jethro clenched his fists as he strode across the mine shaft to retrieve his shovel. That bastard had hurt him. Worse than that, he had tried to make him look like a fool. Course he hadn't been able to do that. No man could make Jethro Mooney look like a fool. Still, Sam Baranov had no right to the good things in life, things like a pretty bride.

He had no right at all.

Chapter Seventeen

"We don't need an engagement party." Laura looked up from the popcorn that she was stringing. Though she had bought the corn earlier, today was the first time she had had a chance to prepare it. She had been in the midst of the task when Ella and Amelia knocked on her door, bearing gaily wrapped gifts, their faces wreathed in smiles brighter than the candles that would light the Christmas tree. After they had deposited the gifts in the root cellar, away from Meg's curious eyes, both women had volunteered to help Laura string popcorn. And they had. Until Amelia suggested the party, Laura had thought she was the recipient a normal holiday visit.

"No one needs a party," Ella agreed as she helped herself to another cup of coffee and one of the gingerbread-men cookies Charlotte had brought the day before. "We may not need them, but everyone loves going to a party." Ella placed her hand on her abdomen, smiling as the baby kicked. "Surely you've figured that out."

Amelia's lovely blue eyes sparkled with mirth as she seconded her friend. "William's even worse. It isn't just that he likes going to parties. He actually likes giving them. Think of it this way, Laura: Your engagement is a good excuse for William to have fun."

Laura, who had heard tales of the elaborate party William had staged for his and Amelia's engagement, shook her head as she knotted a thread. Popcorn with a few shiny red cranberries interspersed made a cheerful garland. Meg would enjoy it. So would she. What she would not enjoy was a big celebration.

"I don't want a large party, and I'm sure Sam doesn't either." She could use the holiday season or her mourning as the reason; there was no need to tell Ella and Amelia the truth, that she felt like a fraud. Since this would not be a real marriage, she didn't want all of the trappings that Gold Landing seemed to think one deserved.

Though Amelia nodded as if she agreed, the twinkle in her eyes made Laura wonder just what she and William had planned. "I thought we'd have an open house the afternoon of the twenty-seventh." Amelia eyed the cookies, then shrugging her shoulders, took one. "It won't be fancy, and people will be free to come and go as they please."

Laura started to relax. That wouldn't be too bad. At least Amelia didn't expect people to come for a formal dinner, and there wouldn't be the dancing and fireworks that had marked Amelia's engagement.

"Besides," Ella added, "this way we can invite all the children."

Now Laura did relax. "That will be perfect." It wasn't simply that she thought her students should be part of the celebration. That was important, but even more so, this way Laura could keep watch over Meg. Meg was now doubly precious because she was the sole reminder Laura had of Matt.

"Your engagement is so romantic," Ella said with a sigh as she brushed cookie crumbs from her fingers. "It's all anyone can talk about—how Sam started courting Charlotte but fell in love with you instead." Ella's smile was arch. "At the time, no one guessed that all those visits to the school were to see you, not Charlotte." Laura knew it was too much to hope that the grapevine hadn't embroidered the story, but she hadn't realized how elaborate the tale had become.

"I hope you and Sam will be as happily married as Ben and I are," Ella concluded.

Laura rose and drew the curtains closed. Though she normally liked to see the stars and moon reflected on the snow, tonight Ella's comments, innocent though they were, made her feel exposed, as if her every movement was being scrutinized. How could she answer Ella? She could hardly tell her friends that this was not the love match everyone assumed, that she was marrying Sam so that he would not lose his inheritance, and that they probably wouldn't share a house for very long.

Though she and Sam hadn't discussed it, Laura expected that she would remain in Gold Landing while Sam went to Seward to run the shipping company. They could claim that she needed to finish the school year, since it would be unfair to expect Charlotte to assume full responsibility for the students. Perhaps Laura would even go to Seward for part of the summer, if only to perpetuate the myth of matrimony. But at some point, it would become obvious to the citizens of Gold Landing that this was not a normal marriage.

"What will you wear to the party?" Amelia reached for the coffeepot and refilled her cup.

Laura turned around in surprise. She had brought no party dresses with her to Alaska, for a woman in mourning would wear only black. Besides, the few fancy frocks she had owned were woefully out of style. There had been no need and no money to buy new dresses when she had lived with Roy.

"My black silk," she told the young doctor. It was the dress she wore to church.

Ella wrinkled her nose. "You can't wear black to your engagement party."

If that was true, Laura had a problem. "My other choices are black wool or black poplin." With only four days, there wasn't time to make a new dress, even if Laura had been an accomplished seamstress. With the Christmas holiday celebrations reducing free time even more, her best hope was to add a lace collar and cuffs to the silk.

Amelia swallowed another bite of cookie, then said, "My sapphire gown would look nice on her, wouldn't it, Ella?"

Though Ella nodded, Laura laughed as she tried to picture herself in one of Amelia's dresses. "It would be six inches too long," she pointed out. Amelia was tall and slender, while Laura barely topped five feet.

But Amelia would not listen to her protests. "That's not a problem," she insisted. "My sister is a good seamstress. She can alter it to fit you."

"And I've got some silk flowers that you can wear in your hair," Ella said. Her sweet smile told Laura how much she was enjoying the opportunity to plan a party, especially one that she considered so romantic.

It was with difficulty that Laura kept a smile on her face. She was a fraud, and she hated it. First she had pretended to be a widow. Now she was pretending to be a happy fiancée, and soon she would pretend to be a happy wife. As she bade her friends good night, handing them the brightly colored gifts she had wrapped for them, Laura had to admit that it was not all pretense. She *was* happy at the prospect of living with Sam. For Meg's sake.

It was the best thing for her daughter. Even if it was only for a few months, Sam would give Meg the attention she needed. Having never known her father and having just lost her brother, Meg needed a male influence and some stability in her life. Sam could help provide both. He would be good for Meg.

As for herself, Laura could not deny the fact that she enjoyed Sam's company. The times that they spent together were the sweetest hours of the day. Sam was her best friend, and while their marriage might not be a true one in every sense, it would give her the chance to enjoy his company far more often.

The marriage would be good for Meg and for her. And, of

course, it would give Sam what he wanted and needed: his father's legacy.

Two days later, Laura and Sam walked into the church together, each holding one of Meg's hands. It was the first time they had appeared in public together since their engagement, and Laura was conscious of curious glances and knowing smiles. She didn't care! Today was Christmas, and her heart was filled with such gladness that there was no room for anything else.

She sat at Sam's side, holding Meg on her lap to make more room in the crowded church, while Reverend Langdon told the age-old story of the Nativity. It was a beautiful tale and one that never failed to stir her heart, but today it had new poignancy for Laura, for it reminded her that every birth is a miracle, every life a gift. And some gifts, like Matt, were only to be enjoyed for a short while. Laura looked down at her daughter. *Thank you, God, for sparing her.*

As if he sensed her thoughts, Sam laid his hand on top of Laura's, squeezing it slightly. When her eyes met his, she saw such caring in his that she could feel her heart soar. Truly it was a season of miracles that had brought this kind, generous man into her life to help her through its darkest moments, and that had freed her from her marriage in time to be able to return some of his generosity.

When the service was over and they had received the townspeople's congratulations and holiday greetings, Sam walked back to Laura's cabin with her, carrying Meg in his arms. They had agreed that he would join Laura while Meg opened her gifts, then go together to dinner at the parsonage.

Laura had been surprised by the invitation, and had asked Sam whether he would feel awkward spending the day with Charlotte and her parents. He had insisted he would not, adding, "Charlotte said she didn't mind either." Once again Laura was surprised by his sensitivity. She doubted Roy had ever considered another person's feelings.

When they entered the cabin and Sam put Meg on her feet, she rushed toward the tree.

"Yes, sweetie. It's almost time." Laura removed her daughter's coat, then settled her on the floor a safe distance from the lighted candles.

Though the little girl seemed more interested in the pretty wrappings than the contents of several packages, she giggled happily when she tore the paper off one and saw the wooden dog Sam had carved for her. Though it was simply made, with few of the details that Sam used on his rocking chairs, he had captured the alert expression and eager posture of a husky. Laura smiled when she saw that Sam had put wheels on the dog's feet and attached a leash around its neck so that Meg could pull the animal behind her. This was one toy that would not be abandoned by New Year's.

Meg stared at the dog, tipping her head to one side as if she were considering something. "Nugget," she announced.

Laura looked at Sam and raised an eyebrow, surprised that her daughter remembered the name of William's lead dog.

Sam grinned. "Little Miss Meg remembers everything about those sled dogs, doesn't she?"

Just as Laura remembered so much about that day, the way Sam had brought joy into her children's lives, the wonderful feeling that somehow, some way they had all belonged together. So much had changed. They were only three now, and Laura's heart had an empty spot that would never be filled. But one thing had not changed: the happiness that Sam brought.

Laura smiled at the tall man who seemed so at ease in her home. It was Christmas, and by some miracle, he was here with her.

While Meg rolled her toy around the room, apparently oblivious to the adults, Laura handed Sam the package she had wrapped for him. It was silly to be so nervous, worrying about his reaction to the gift. Nothing horrible would happen if he didn't like it.

"Merry Christmas, Sam," she said in a voice that quavered ever so slightly. Though she hoped her face did not betray her anxiety, Laura watched carefully as Sam opened the box.

Would he notice that her hems weren't as perfect as Charlotte's or Ella's? Would he like the plaid or think it too bright? Would he even want a muffler?

There was a moment of near-silence as Sam looked at the gift, when the only sound was the wheels of Meg's toy on the planked floor. Then Sam took the length of soft wool from the box and grinned. "This is perfect," he said. His lips curved in a smile, and the expression in his eyes was warm. Unless he was acting, Sam liked the gift.

Laura felt the tension that had knotted her shoulders begin to ease. She smiled back at Sam. Then, to her surprise, he rose and drew her to her feet. Lopping one end of the muffler around his neck, he put the other around hers and used it as a lasso to draw her close to him. "Perfect," he repeated as he lowered his mouth to hers.

This was not like the kiss they had shared under the mistletoe, or even the one he had given her the day she had proposed to him. Both of those kisses had been flavored with restraint, as if he were afraid of shocking her. Today Laura sensed that Sam was putting his whole heart into his embrace. And what a difference that made!

His lips were sweet and tender, caressing hers and sending shivers of delight through her body. When his tongue traced the outline of her mouth, it triggered waves of warmth that rose from her fingertips and spread along her arms. And when Sam deepened the kiss, Laura could have sworn that she heard music. It was only her imagination, of course. There was no music in her cabin. But the lilting melody that rang in her mind was more haunting than anything she had ever heard.

"Mama." Meg's plaintive cry brought Laura back to reality.

With a rueful smile, Sam released Laura and swung Meg into his arms. "I think Nugget is lonely," he said when he had marched around the room several times with Meg perched on his shoulders, pretending that she was the angel on top of the tree.

Once the little girl was settled back on the floor, Sam

pulled a small box from his pocket. His smile was tentative as he handed it to Laura, and she realized that he was as unsure of her reaction to his gift as she had been about hers. "I noticed that you didn't have one," he said. "So I hope you'll wear this."

Though the box was unwrapped, Sam had tied a ribbon around it. Laura smiled at the crooked bow, wishing she didn't have to undo the evidence that he had wrapped this himself rather than asking Charlotte or one of the other women to help him. That made the gift doubly precious to her. Slowly, savoring the moment, she untied the bow and removed the lid.

"Oh, Sam!" He was right. It was something she needed. Laura looked at the gold ladies' watch that lay inside the box. It would be so much easier to time classes now that she once again had a watch. That alone made the gift special, but as Laura pulled the case from the box, she realized that Sam's gift was priceless. He had not bought it at Herb Ashton's store. The scratches on the cover told Laura this was old, a family heirloom.

With hands that were once more unsteady, she touched the knob on the top, releasing the front. Inside the cover was a picture of a couple. Laura's eyes misted as she realized what Sam had given her. Though the picture was faded, Sam's resemblance to the man made Laura certain that this was his father. The smiling woman with the pretty face could only be his mother. Sam had given her one of his few remembrances—if not his only one—of his mother.

"Oh, Sam! It's beautiful."

"If you'd rather have a new one," he said in a voice that was uncharacteristically gruff, "I'll buy one for you. This watch was Papa's wedding gift to my mother. He gave it to me the day George locked me in the coffin. He said it would help keep me safe." Sam swallowed deeply. "Papa had a matching one that was my mother's gift to him. He promised that it would be mine when he died." Sam frowned. "Somehow it disappeared. I always figured Hilda had sold it."

Laura's heart ached for the boy who had lost so much the day his father had died. She couldn't change what had happened to him, much as she wanted to. All she could do was try to make the future happier.

"It's beautiful," Laura said as she pinned the watch to her bodice. "Thank you, Sam. There's nothing that could have made me happier than this." She touched the gold case, awed by the fact that Sam had given her something so precious. Though she had told him theirs would be a marriage of convenience, he was treating her like a real wife.

Laura rose on her toes and pressed her lips to his. For a second, Sam did not respond. Then, with a muffled groan, he wrapped his arms around her and pulled her into his embrace. His mouth was firm and insistent, urging her to part her lips so that he could savor her sweetness. And when she did, his hands moved down her back, molding her ever closer to him. The kiss was endless, or perhaps it lasted only a second. Laura could not have said. All she knew was that she had never felt so wonderful.

"Merry Christmas, sweetheart," Sam said when at length they drew apart.

Laura's eyes widened. He didn't mean anything special by the endearment. She was certain of that. The sweet word was part of the holiday magic like the trees and wreathes and candles. And yet, just for a moment, it felt so good to be someone's sweetheart. If only the magic could last!

"If I weren't already married to the most wonderful woman in Alaska, I'd be downright jealous of you for snatching away this beautiful lady."

Laura's eyes widened at both William's extravagant words and the room in which she found herself. Although she had been in Amelia and William's parlor on several occasions, it had never looked like this. There had never been garlands and dried flowers bent into the shape of hearts. There had never been huge silver trays laden with cookies and small cakes. There had never been an enormous crystal punch bowl filled with a beverage that smelled as delicious as it looked. If this was William's idea of a simple party, Laura could hardly imagine what an elaborate one would be.

Sam put his arm around Laura's waist and drew her closer. "Make sure you remember it's me that she's marrying, old man," he said playfully.

Though the party had just begun, the room was already close to full. This time, unlike the social events that had taken place in the church hall, there was no separate section for children. Instead, they remained with their parents. Laura felt a pang of sympathy for them. How boring it must be for them to listen to adult conversation. As soon as she could, she would separate a few from their parents by asking them to sing one of the songs they had practiced at school. Maybe once they were in a group, the adults would let others join them.

Ben Taylor, who had been standing a few feet away from Laura and Sam, pushed his spectacles back on his nose. "It does my heart good to hear someone else called 'old man,' " he told William. His eyes sparkled as he turned to Laura. "May I extend my felicitations, madam?" he asked. With a formal bow, he reached for her hand and pressed a kiss on it.

"Why, Ben!" Laura wasn't sure whether that was surprise or outrage she heard in Ella's voice. "You never kissed *my* hand."

The doctor flashed Laura an impish grin, then turned to his wife. "Let me correct that oversight." He reached for Ella's right hand. Bending low, he pressed a kiss on the back of her hand. Then he turned it over and kissed the palm. Laura heard Ella gasp. But Ben was not finished. His mouth moved upward, pressing kisses on her wrist, then pushing up her sleeve so that he had access to her arm.

"Ben!" Ella's face flamed as she jerked her hand away from her husband.

"Yes, Ben." Sam repeated Ella's words, his voice filled with mock outrage. "There are children present."

And indeed two were approaching, their parents close behind them.

"Are you still gonna be our teacher?" the boy asked Laura, his expression so solemn that she could not guess his thoughts.

"Yes, Jeremy," she said, punctuating her answer with a touch to his shoulder.

His sister grinned. "Told you so! Told you you don't know nothin'."

Laura exchanged a smile with Jeremy's mother. Siblings were so predictable.

A smile lit Jeremy's face. "Good," he announced as he elbowed his sister in the ribs. "We like you."

Sam bent to whisper in Laura's ear. "Me too."

The food was delicious, the children's singing delightfully off-key, the adults' congratulations heartfelt. It had been, Laura realized as she and Sam walked back to her cabin, one of the most enjoyable afternoons of her life. The reason wasn't hard to find: Sam. He had changed her life in so many ways, bringing her newfound happiness and companionship and friendship. But the changes had not stopped there. Their engagement had completed the process that had begun the day she had disembarked from the boat. Laura now felt as if she were a member of the town. She belonged here and, oh, how good that felt!

"Charlotte, come in here, please." Her father poked his head through the doorway to the parlor where she had been sitting, staring sightlessly at a book while her mind whirled, trying to guess what was happening in Father's study.

Charlotte rose on shaky legs. This was worse, far worse than the first time she had taught a class for Mrs. Templeton. Then she had been scared. Now she was petrified. Perhaps that was why her legs refused to move. Perhaps that was why her heart was pounding so furiously. Jason had been with her father for only ten minutes. Or was it ten hours? Charlotte couldn't say. All she knew was that the time had gone so slowly that she had feared the interview would never end. And all the while, she had found it difficult to swallow, difficult even to breathe. Oh, what would Father say?

As she entered the small room where her father prepared his sermons and counseled parishioners, Jason rose from one of the two chairs in front of the desk. His face was deathly pale, and Charlotte could see the way his pulse pounded. She knew why he had come. But what had Father told him?

"Sit down, my dear." Father gestured toward the other visitor's chair, then took his seat behind the desk. He steepled his hands and gave Charlotte a long look that made her knees weaken even more. *Please*, she prayed silently, *say yes*. For a moment her father said nothing. Then he inclined his head toward Jason. "This young man has asked for your hand in marriage."

Charlotte nodded. She already knew that. She and Jason had agreed that he would ask permission to marry her. Now that he was working, neither one of them wanted to continue their clandestine meetings. They loved each other and wanted all of Gold Landing to know it. Most of all, they wanted her parents to agree to their marriage.

Charlotte studied her father's face. He looked so stern, and Jason was so pale, that she was certain Father had refused to consider Jason's suit. What would they do? She couldn't live without Jason. She just couldn't.

"You know your mother and I only want your happiness." Father was speaking as solemnly as he did when he preached what Charlotte called his fire-and-brimstone sermons. "It's sometimes difficult for us to realize that you're old enough to marry," he continued. That was part of the problem. They wanted her to remain their child, when she wanted to begin her life as an adult.

"I'm not a child any longer," she said as calmly as she could. *Please, just tell me what you've told Jason*, she pleaded silently.

Her father's smile was tinged with sadness. "I know that," he admitted, "and I also know that I was wrong to give Sam

Baranov permission to court you without asking if you were interested in him." Charlotte stared at her father. Did this mean that he hadn't made up his mind about Jason? "I won't make that mistake again." Hope began to surge deep within Charlotte. Maybe Father hadn't refused Jason. Maybe they still had a chance at happiness.

Her father leaned across the desk, as if trying to lessen the distance between them. "Do you want Jason to court you?"

The hope that had begun to grow blossomed into joy. Surely Father hadn't said no if he was asking that question. "Yes, oh, yes!" She smiled at Jason, and watched the color begin to return to his face.

Her father leaned back in his chair. "I see," he said at last. "You think you're in love."

From the corner of her eye, Charlotte saw Jason straighten his shoulders. "Sir, I don't think I'm in love. I know I love your daughter." Charlotte's heart pounded with pride and happiness. Though he spoke quietly, there was no disguising the confidence of Jason's words.

"And I love Jason." It felt so good to say the words aloud. She had hated having to sneak around to be with Jason. Charlotte turned toward him, and when her eyes met his, she hoped he could see the love shining in hers.

There was another long silence while her father looked from her to Jason and back again, as if he were trying to see deep inside their hearts. If he could look into hers, Charlotte was certain he would see nothing other than pure love. And Jason, she was sure with every fiber of her being, felt the same way.

"You believe you're in love, and perhaps you are." Charlotte turned her gaze to her father. Was he going to give them a sermon? "True love does not fade or die," he said firmly. He looked at Charlotte, then turned his attention to Jason. "If you still want to marry my daughter in a year, I will give you my blessing."

"A year!" The words burst forth from Charlotte's mouth. "That's so long!"

Her father nodded. "It may seem that way now, Charlotte. You probably think I'm being harsh, when the truth is, your mother and I want to be sure you'll be happy." When Charlotte blinked in confusion, he added, "You can, of course, marry without my consent before then, but I hope you will not."

"A year. Oh, Father!" How could they wait so long?

"It'll be all right, Charlotte." Jason spoke so softly she doubted her father overheard his words. Then he said in a normal voice, "A year will give me time to build us a house."

For the first time since she had entered the room, her father smiled. "That's right, son."

Son! Charlotte stared in astonishment. Her father had called Jason "son." It was one short word, a single syllable, and yet Charlotte knew that to Jason it meant much more. After years of being condemned and blamed for mischief not of his making, he was finally on the road to acceptance. Her father was showing his approval, making Jason feel that he would one day be part of the family.

Charlotte smiled. Somehow they would survive the year. And then . . .

George hated the cold. He hated the darkness. He hated everything about Alaskan winters. If he had his way, he would be on a ship, heading for warmer climates. He had heard there were some tropical islands where the sun always shone and the women were even warmer than the sun. Now, that was where he ought to be, not trudging through the snow on the way to see that useless lawyer. Once again, the man had summoned him, and George doubted it was to impart good tidings. That damned attorney seemed to specialize in bad news.

"All right, Nelson. Why did you want to see me?" George demanded as he walked into the man's office, slamming the door behind him for effect. Let the lawyer realize who was in charge here.

Nelson rose from behind his desk and peered over his spectacles. "I received a communication from your stepbrother."

George plopped into one of the chairs and thrust his boots in front of him. Hilda would tell him that a gentleman did not slouch, and that a gentleman would have scraped his boots before entering a building. George didn't give a hoot for what Hilda would say. He was sending this miserable lawyer a message.

"Another letter, I presume." Nelson wasn't the only one who knew highfalutin words.

"In point of fact, no." The man's eyes were as cold as an iron anchor. "I received a telegram. Your stepbrother informed me that he is engaged to marry a woman named Laura Templeton on the sixteenth of January." Nelson removed his spectacles, polished them carefully, then said in a voice that made no effort to hide his gloating, "Samuel will be here for his birthday."

George stared at the man for a second while the words registered. Templeton. January 16th. Birthday. A deep rage filled him, and he jumped to his feet, flinging the chair back against the wall.

The attorney was wrong. George swung his cane from side to side as he strode down the street, daring anyone to come too close. Sam was not going to marry Laura Templeton or any woman. Sam was not going to come to Seward on his birthday. Sam was never going to inherit Baranov Shipping. No, sirree.

Chapter Eighteen

The days passed quickly. Laura thought her life had been full before. Between normal classes and her special evening tutoring sessions, there had been few idle moments. But now that she was planning a wedding, she wondered if she would ever find a moment to just sit and think or read. Though both she and Sam had said they wanted a simple wedding and would be content to have Reverend Langdon perform the ceremony in his study, Ella and Amelia had refused to consider the idea, telling Laura that the town would be disappointed if she and Sam deprived them of another excuse to celebrate. The engagement party, they informed her, was not enough. The people of Gold Landing wanted a wedding. And so Laura found herself planning menus with Charlotte and discussing wedding gowns with Amelia's sister, who was once again altering one of Amelia's older dresses.

Everyone was acting as if this were a real wedding. And, in many respects, it was. Her life and Meg's would change once Laura married Sam. For one thing, they would move into Sam's house. Though part of Laura balked at the move, knowing it would not be a permanent one, the other part of her welcomed the idea of a new home, one that had no sad memories clinging to it.

Laura looked around the schoolhouse, trying not to frown at the number of children who were fidgeting. It was, she had discovered, even more difficult to keep her students' attention focused on lessons now they knew that "Teacher," as the younger pupils called her, was to marry the man who had helped make the pageant such a success. Sam and the stuffed moose were the children's new heroes. It was, Sam had told Laura, a lesson in humility, to be valued no more highly than a dead animal.

"I like Mr. Sam," Laura overheard one of the seven-year-olds tell his friend. "He's almost as nice as Teacher." Laura bit the inside of her lip to keep from smiling. Would Sam consider this a step above the moose?

The other little boy looked pensive. "I reckon we'll have to call her Mrs. Sam, won't we?"

Mrs. Sam. It had a nice ring. Though Laura tried not to smile, she saw from the amused expression on Charlotte's face that she had overheard the children.

"I'm so happy for you, Mrs. Sam," Charlotte said that afternoon as they cleaned the schoolroom. She dipped a rag into the bucket of water and began to wash the blackboard. "My mother always told me that God has a plan, and things happen for a reason. If I ever doubted that, this would be my proof." Charlotte turned to face Laura. "Just think. If Sam hadn't come here courting me, he might not have gotten to know you. Oh, Mrs. Templeton." Charlotte's eyes shone with emotion. "I'm so happy about the way everything has worked out. Sam wasn't the right man for me, but you two were meant for each other."

Though Laura wasn't sure anyone was meant for her, she could not deny that she was happy at the prospect of being married to Sam Baranov, even if it was to be only a temporary marriage. Mrs. Langdon was right. There was a plan, and that plan had placed Laura in a position to help Sam.

Every time she thought about his face when he had first spoken of his inheritance, and then the joy she had seen when he had realized he would be able to fulfill the terms of his father's will, a bubble of happiness floated through Laura. It was wonderful that she, Laura Templeton, the woman even her parents had not loved, was able to help her friend.

Laura straightened the first row of desks, smiling at the physical evidence of her pupils' fidgeting. Their moods, like hers, seemed affected by the long winter nights. Though Laura told them that the days were already growing longer, and had made a game of guessing when they would start feeling the sun's warmth through the window, they remained as anxious as she for spring's advent.

As Laura moved to the second row, she touched the watch that Sam had given her. Since Christmas morning, the only time she had been without it had been while she slept. Otherwise, she kept the gold timepiece pinned to her bodice. And if she consulted it more often than absolutely necessary, no one was rude enough to comment on it. Sam's gift had become her talisman, the proof that she had a friend.

Laura heard the soft sound of Charlotte's rag moving over the blackboard. Though Charlotte had always been a willing helper, the change since her father had agreed to Jason's courtship had been dramatic. "I'm glad your parents approved of Jason," Laura told Charlotte. The enthusiasm Laura had once seen only when Charlotte taught now extended to all aspects of her life. Even washing blackboards. She smiled almost constantly, and Laura had caught her humming under her breath. Not only had the young woman blossomed, but—like some of the flowers Laura had seen in a botanical garden—the ordinary bud had turned into a truly beautiful blossom.

"Some days I can't believe it's true that in a year I'll be a bride," Charlotte said as she finished cleaning the board. "My mother was right. Things do work out."

Laura handed Charlotte a towel to dry her hands. Only a foolhardy person would go outside in the Alaskan winter with hands that were even slightly damp. "What about teaching?" Laura asked. Though she didn't want to quench Charlotte's happiness, she had been surprised that the young woman no longer spoke of getting her teaching certificate.

A small frown crossed Charlotte's face. "I still dream about a school of my own," she admitted, "but I don't want to leave Jason. He's more important than anything in my life." Her blue eyes were earnest as she added, "I just wish I didn't have to choose." She spread the towel over the back of a chair to dry, then reached for her schoolbag, her enthusiasm momentarily diminished.

Laura wasn't surprised by Charlotte's reaction. She knew how much the young woman enjoyed teaching, yet she couldn't blame her for wanting to stay with the man who loved her so dearly. Hadn't Laura herself once given up dreams to be with a man who had whispered words of love? "It's possible you wouldn't have to choose," Laura said slowly. She had written several letters, trying to find a solution to Charlotte's problem. The latest response had come only yesterday. "You might be able to take correspondence courses and get your certification that way."

"Really?" The smile that lit Charlotte's eyes was all the answer Laura needed. "That would be wonderful."

"My normal school said they would consider a correspondence course for you," Laura explained. "They've never done it before, but they're willing to try. It won't be easy for you, though."

Charlotte shook her head, dismissing Laura's warning. "I can do it. I'm not afraid of hard work, and you know I love teaching."

Laura laid the last of her books in her cloth bag, closing the flap carefully so that no snow would make its way inside. "You'll be a good teacher," she told Charlotte. "The children trust and respect you. That's the first step."

"Oh, Mrs. Templeton, thank you, thank you, thank you." Charlotte wrapped her muffler around her lower face and slung her bag over her shoulder. "I'm so happy!" She executed a small pirouette, then fairly flew out of the schoolhouse, leaving Laura to follow at a more sedate pace.

"Good afternoon, darlin'." Sam strode rapidly down the road to join Laura. Since the day they'd become engaged, he had met her every afternoon, walking with her to Ella's to pick up Meg. It was the one quiet moment of Laura's day, and she had quickly grown to cherish the few minutes she spent with Sam.

Normally they would talk about ordinary topics—her students' latest antics, the chairs he was making. Normally he would say, "Good afternoon, Laura." Never before had he called her "darling." Of course he meant nothing by it. It must have just slipped out. Laura hoped that her face wasn't as flushed as it felt. She didn't want to embarrass Sam by letting him see her reaction to his greetings. "Darling." How good that sounded. The warmth of the endearment dispelled the wind that threatened to penetrate even the heavy layers of clothing she wore.

"Hello, Sam." If her voice sounded a little choked, surely he would understand that it was the wind chasing her breath away. Just as the wind was reddening her cheeks.

Sam stood directly in front of her now, unmoving. He raised an eyebrow. "Don't you think your husband-to-be deserves a warmer welcome than that?"

Laura felt the blood rush to her already flushed face, for the expression she saw in Sam's eyes warmed her as much as a coal stove.

"What did you have in mind?" she asked, trying to pretend that this was the way he always acted, that this was a normal conversation.

She heard him chuckle as he closed the gap between them. "This," he said, and lowered his mouth to hers.

Perhaps it was foolish to be standing outside exposing skin to the cold air when the wind howled around them. Perhaps the townspeople would brand them as crazy people. Laura didn't care. For the moment, nothing mattered except the touch of Sam's lips on hers. Cold was forgotten, and the wind became nothing more than a minor annoyance that drew her closer to Sam and the sweet warmth that only he was able to send rushing through her veins. This was Sam, her dearest friend, the man who would soon be her husband. How she loved being with him!

When they broke apart, Laura felt as if the only source of warmth in the universe had been taken from her. She stared at him for a moment, watching the moonlight that danced through the tree branches light his face. Sam smiled, and when she shivered, he slipped his arm around her. "Let's get you indoors," he said softly.

Though they were ordinary words, the look on Sam's face was anything but ordinary. Why had she never noticed the tiny creases that formed at the corners of his eyes when he smiled? How could she have missed the way his eyebrows knit when he studied her? Laura shivered again, not from cold but from the realization that nothing about this afternoon seemed ordinary. She and Sam had walked the same road dozens of times. They had said the same words. Nothing was changed, and yet to Laura it felt as if everything was different.

It was only when they reached Ella's house that normalcy returned. The kitchen was as neat as ever, despite the fact that Ella was in the midst of making bread. With an apologetic glance at her floury hands, Ella nodded a greeting.

"Mr. Sam!" Meg dropped her toys and scampered across the floor, her arms outstretched. Though she had once been wary of Sam, Meg had lost her shyness.

"Hi, honey!" He swung her into his arms, whirling her around in what had become a daily routine.

Laura drew a deep breath of relief that everything seemed normal here. Perhaps it was a phase of the moon that had made Sam murmur endearments and kiss her. As he gave Meg a noisy kiss, Laura nodded. He had meant nothing special by it. After all, he called Meg "honey" and kissed her.

Happy that she had found a logical explanation, Laura wrinkled her nose at Sam as he put her daughter back on the floor. "She's more excited to see you than me." Meg suffered her mother's hug, then raced back to the corner and cradled Nugget in her arms.

"Don't be jealous," Sam advised. "Meg's merely transferred her love for that wooden dog to me."

As she watched her daughter croon to the toy, Laura shrugged. "She won't go anywhere without it. I swear, she'd put it in her bed if I let her sleep with it."

Ella looked up from the bread she was kneading. "Is that why she tries to sneak it into the bed when she takes her nap? I wondered."

"Ah, yes, I'm a cruel mother." Laura laughed. "I'm afraid she'll bruise herself if she rolls over on it during the night."

The tantalizing aroma of rising yeast filled the room. Sam sniffed appreciatively. "What if you made a padded sleeping pouch for the dog?"

Laura shook her head in mock dismay, then glanced down at her watch. "Oh, Sam! Stop indulging my daughter. She can be parted from her dog for a few hours." Just as Laura could put the watch on the bureau while she slept. She reached for Meg. "Come on, sweetie. Time to go home."

"No!" Laura woke with a start, her body trembling with fear. Something was terribly wrong. Meg! Something had happened to Meg! Heedless of the cold, Laura ran to the other bedroom. *Please be all right,* she prayed silently as she approached her daughter. With a heart that was pounding so hard that it threatened to burst through her chest, Laura bent over the bed. Thank God! Meg lay under the heavy blankets, her breathing deep and even. She was safe.

Though the cold from the floor began to penetrate the thick socks that she wore to bed, Laura stood for a long moment watching her baby. Meg was fine. There was no reason that Laura should feel that she had lost something important and that nothing would ever be the same unless she found it. Everything was here. The fear was irrational.

Unless . . . Laura's hand flew to her breast. It was gone! She had lost Sam's watch!

For a second Laura stood paralyzed. Then she returned to her room and turned up the light. Reality returned. She had been asleep. Of course she wasn't wearing the watch. She always removed it from her shirtwaist and placed it on the bureau. If she looked, she would find it there, right where it should be. Yes, it was there. Laura cradled the timepiece in her hand, taking comfort from its familiar weight.

She hadn't lost it. She wouldn't lose Sam.

Laura stopped, stunned. Where had that thought come from? Now shaking from cold and something even worse, Laura climbed back into bed. Wrapping an extra quilt around her shoulders, she sat propped against the headboard, the watch still clutched in her right hand. Why was she worried about losing Sam? It was true; she didn't want to lose him. In the short time that she had been in Alaska, he had become a very important part of her life. But surely that wasn't enough to cause this blind panic. For that was the only way Laura could describe how she had felt. This wasn't an ordinary fear. Oh, no. Though it might seem irrational, it had progressed beyond fear to pure terror.

Why? Why was the thought of losing her friend so painful?

Laura gripped the watch so tightly that the hinge dug into her palm.

Her friend. Perhaps that was the reason. Perhaps she had been wrong. Perhaps what she felt for Sam wasn't simply friendship.

She closed her eyes, remembering the day Charlotte had described her feelings for Jason. Charlotte had been speaking of love. Though Laura knew about love in theory, other than the love she had for her children, she'd had no practical experience. Until today. Today she recognized the truth in Charlotte's words. Sam was her friend, and she cared deeply for him. But there was more. She loved him.

How had it happened?

Laura stared at the gold watch, opening its cover as if the

portraits of Sam's parents somehow held an answer. But though she saw two smiling faces, there were no hints as to why or how they had fallen in love.

Were the poets right? Was love like a thunderbolt, striking the unwary? Or was it what Sam's father had described, a rainbow at midnight, growing in the aftermath of a storm, a soft, beautiful reminder that miracles could happen, that sorrow could be transformed into joy? Laura wasn't sure. All she knew was that she hadn't intended to fall in love with Sam. But somehow she had. And now that she had, nothing would ever be the same. Her whole life would be divided into two parts: before she loved Sam, and after.

The shivers that wracked Laura's body had nothing to do with the cold room. It was emotion, pure and simple, that caused her to tremble. She loved Sam and because she did, she wanted a real marriage. She wanted Sam's kisses and his embrace. She wanted to make love and babies. She wanted every part of a true marriage. Laura shivered again. Just as there was nothing false about the way she felt for him, she wanted nothing false about their life together.

God help her, but she loved Sam Baranov with all her heart. Laura pressed the watch to her lips, wishing it were Sam himself and not his gift that she was holding so close. She loved Sam, and she wanted to spend the rest of her life showing him how much she cared. Loving Sam would make ordinary events special. It would lessen pain and multiply joy. It would be the most wonderful thing on earth. If only Sam loved her!

He did not. Laura knew that, just as she knew how deeply she loved him. Sam hadn't tried to lie to her. He had been honest when he had told her that he didn't believe love existed. He liked her. He was grateful to her. He even lusted after her. But love? No, Sam did not love her. And that was the problem. That was the reason Laura could not tell him of her own love.

She couldn't burden Sam that way. It was bad enough that he felt beholden to her because she was helping him claim his legacy. If he knew she loved him, he would feel an even greater obligation to her. Sam was an honorable man. Faced with the knowledge of her love, he might believe that he should stay married to her. Laura couldn't let him do that. She couldn't shackle him that way.

Love existed. She knew that. Sam might not believe in love today, but he would when he met the right woman. Laura wanted him to be free to find that woman. Of course she did. Love was the most wonderful thing in the world. She loved Sam, and because she did, she wanted him to know that wonder.

The question was, how would she bear it when he left?

He was halfway there. George dismounted from the dogsled, shaking his head to dislodge some of the snow. When he had asked for directions to Gold Landing, no one had bothered to tell him just how long it would take to get there or just how miserable the trip would be. Of course, he couldn't ask too many people in Seward. He had told most of them, Hilda included, that he was going to Anchorage to meet with a potential investor. It wouldn't do to let anyone guess where he was really going or what he intended to do once he got there. No, sirree. When Sam Baranov was found mysteriously dead in his bed, no one was going to connect it with George. It would be an unfortunate accident, that was all.

George smirked as he climbed back onto the runners and cracked the whip. He had made his plans, mighty fine plans. All George's plans were fine plans. Now all he had to do was get to that godforsaken place called Gold Landing.

Leave it to Sam to live in the middle of the frozen wilderness. Only fools and Indians lived there. George managed a short laugh at the thought that Sam wouldn't be living there or anywhere much longer. No, sirree. Not much longer at all.

George shouted as the dogs headed into the trees, chasing a rabbit. Damn fool dogs! They were almost as dumb as Sam. If the man had had any brains, he wouldn't have tried to steal the company from George. Look where that foolishness was going to get him: dead before his birthday.

"Back, you miserable curs!" George jerked on the brake. He wished there was another way. It wasn't that he minded the thought of killing Sam. Not at all. The man had it coming. George should have gotten rid of him when he was a boy. He would have too, if old Nicholas hadn't figured out about the coffin.

The way George saw it, Sam's death was years overdue. He wouldn't regret it one bit. It was just that it would be cleaner if George was in Seward when the tragic event occurred. That way no one would ever be able to connect him to it. That damned attorney wasn't too smart, but George didn't want him to start asking questions.

It would be better if he could hire someone to kill Sam. The problem was, George didn't know anyone he could trust enough to do the job the right way. That was why he and these flea-bitten dogs were crossing some of the most desolate land George had ever seen.

Just a few more days on this miserable dogsled, and then he'd be in Gold Landing. George grinned at the thought. *Sam, old boy, your days are numbered.* In the meantime, George would get himself a hot dinner and a warm bed in the next roadhouse.

The roadhouse was more crowded than he'd expected. Apparently other men were crazy enough to travel across Alaska's interior in the winter, although for the life of him he couldn't figure out why anyone would do it voluntarily. Still, George had to admit that a little company might not be so bad. It was damned boring having nothing but the dogs to talk to all day.

While he was eating his fill of stew and biscuits, he looked around the room. Four men were playing cards in one corner, and if he wasn't mistaken, one of them was about to fold. Might as well join them. He could use a little entertainment, and taking money from fools was good entertainment.

"Mind if I join you gentlemen?" he asked.

An hour later, his initial judgment was confirmed. These men were fools. Either that, or they'd never played poker before. He had had to make some deliberately bad moves to keep from ending the game within the first ten minutes. Normally, he would have done that for the pure pleasure of bankrupting them. But something about the blond man opposite him made George keep the game going. He wanted to study the man.

Blondie was a lousy poker player, the worst of the lot. And yet there was something about him that intrigued George. He looked mean as if he had seen the rougher side of life and knew how to deal with it. This was one man George had no desire to meet in a dark corner.

Maybe he was the answer.

It was not Roy's lucky day. The men were cheats, all of them. At first, he'd thought it was just bad luck that he kept losing. Now he knew better. He had watched them carefully, and he could see what they were doing. They were cheating. That was why they kept winning and why his stack of chips was almost gone. It wasn't that he was losing his skill. Hell, no! Alaskan men were cheaters.

Look at the one on the other side of the table. He kept staring at Roy, almost as if he was looking through him. He wasn't. Even a fool knew he was trying to see what cards Roy held so that he could place his bets.

One more hand. If he lost it, he'd know it was a sign and he'd turn around. Forget Gold Landing and his plans for a warm reunion with his wife. No matter what waited for him back in the States, it had to be better than this. At least there, they didn't all cheat.

"My hand, I believe." The steely-eyed man swept the chips onto his pile.

Roy rose. That was the sign. He sure as hell wasn't going to play another game tonight. Not even if he had any more money, which he did not.

"Hey, blondie." The steely eyed man caught Roy's wrist as

he started to leave. "Let me buy you a drink."

Roy considered. He sure could use a drink, especially a free one, and no matter what, he wasn't going to leave until the morning after he'd already paid for a bed.

"Sure."

When the other two men left, Steely Eyes ordered double whiskeys. Good whiskey too. The man might be a cheat, but he knew his liquor. They drank in silence; then Steely Eyes ordered another round. "I got a proposition for you," he said when the drinks arrived. "I got a little problem, and I need a clever man to help me solve it."

Roy began to preen. Steely Eyes wasn't so dumb after all. He recognized a real man when he saw him. "I reckon I could be your man, depending . . ." The way Roy figured it, Steely Eyes was going to pay him to solve this problem. Roy was no fool. He knew better than to look too interested.

Steely Eyes leaned across the table and lowered his voice. Roy liked that. It meant this was a big problem, not the little one the man had claimed. The bigger the problem, the more gold he would pay to have it solved.

"Seems this man swindled me out of some money," Steely Eyes said. Roy leaned back, considering. If Steely Eyes had lost so much money, he might not have enough to pay him. In that case, he'd have to find another problem-solver. Roy sure as winter snow wasn't going to do no favors for free. "Not only that," Steely Eyes continued, "but he ran off with my wife, and I heard he's fixing to marry her."

Roy's eyes widened, and he licked his lips as he took a large swallow of whiskey. This was serious. There could be real money involved here.

"That would be big . . . big . . ."

"Bigamy," Steely Eyes said.

"Right."

"I can't let him get away with that," Steely Eyes told Roy. "I need him stopped, if you know what I mean."

Roy leaned forward. This was getting interesting. Mighty interesting. "Permanently?"

"Exactly." Steely Eyes nodded.

Roy almost rubbed his hands together. He could feel it. This meant lots of money. "I don't know. I ain't never done no permanent stopping." It was a lie, but Steely Eyes had no way of knowing that. Besides, a man couldn't appear too eager.

Steely Eyes nodded as if he understood Roy's dilemma. "I'd make it worth your while." He lowered his voice again and mentioned a sum that took Roy's breath away.

"Where's the bastard?" No way was Roy going to let that amount of money get away. No way.

Steely Eyes leaned back in his chair. "A town called Gold Landing."

Roy nearly fell off his chair. Gold Landing! It was a sign. *She* was there. He'd collect the money, and then his dear, sweet wife would welcome him with open arms.

He had been wrong before. This was his lucky day. Yes, indeed.

Chapter Nineteen

Only two days! Sam whistled as he headed for William's mine office. Two days until the wedding! The excitement that rushed through his veins had nothing to do with the frigid temperatures or the snow that had blanketed the town again last night. It had nothing to do with the fact that he and William had agreed to meet for a quick game of cribbage, the loser to buy drinks for the winner. It had everything to do with the woman who in just in two days would become Mrs. Samuel Baranov, Sam's bride.

Sam exhaled, watching his breath turn to white frost. He had never expected to feel this way. Oh, he had always assumed that one day he would take a bride, but he had not expected to be so happy about it. It wasn't as if Laura was the woman he had dreamt of all his life, for until a few months ago Sam had never dreamt of a wife. He had had nebulous thoughts of her, of course, but he had never formed a clear picture of the woman who would one day share his life. Now the picture was as clear as the icicles that hung from the eaves. His bride was a petite blonde with the most beautiful blue eyes he had ever seen.

Sam's boots crunched on the snow, and the weak winter sun was bright enough that he squinted. When had it happened? When had he changed from considering marriage a duty, something he would do to save the company from George, to believing it to be the best thing that could happen to him? Though Sam could not pinpoint the moment, he knew that it had occurred after Charlotte had refused him. Until that point, wedlock had held little appeal beyond insuring his legacy.

Sam hadn't disliked Charlotte. He would never have contemplated marrying her if he had, but he had never felt about her the way he did about Laura. Even when he had believed she would become his bride, he had gone days without thinking about Charlotte, while Laura was never far from his thoughts. And dreams . . . had any man had such disturbing dreams? He would waken, filled with the deepest of longings, convinced that there was only one way to ease those longings. Soon. Soon he would be with the woman who would quench those longings and then ignite a new set.

"What's that gleam I see in your eye?" William demanded as Sam tossed his coat onto one of the hooks and turned to face him. William had positioned the cribbage board on his desk and sat in one of the visitors' chairs, clearly waiting for Sam to join him.

Gleam in his eye? He hadn't realized it was so obvious. Damn it all! There were some things he didn't want to discuss with anyone, even William. Sam reached for the coffeepot and poured himself a cup. "Want one?" he asked.

William shook his head. "Avoiding my question, are you?"

Sam settled into the chair and took a long drink of the steaming liquid before he answered. "Nope. Just trying to figure out what you're talking about." With some luck, his story would sound plausible. "If you see a gleam, it must be satisfaction that you agreed to my plan."

William's short burst of laughter told Sam he hadn't bought the tale. "A likely story. The prospect of a puppy for Meg wouldn't make you look like that." William had agreed that when his bitch had her litter, Sam could choose one for Meg. After seeing the little girl's excitement over her wooden dog, Sam knew that she would be thrilled by a live pet, and though Laura had groused about spoiled children, she had concurred with Sam's suggestion.

"I don't know what to tell you, William, other than that you don't know how much that child loves dogs. If she knew she was getting a puppy, she wouldn't sleep for a month." Just as Sam hadn't slept—at least not well—ever since he'd realized that he was getting a wife. Not just any wife, but Laura.

William rolled the dice, then gave Sam an assessing look. "I may not know much about children," he admitted, "but I do know how a man feels when he loves a woman and can't wait to get her into his bed."

And that, of course, was why there was a gleam in Sam's eye. "I can't deny that I'm looking forward to that aspect of marriage," he agreed. Why pretend otherwise? Though William knew why Sam needed to marry, only a blind man would fail to realize that marriage to Laura would bring other very pleasant benefits.

Sam's blood began to race at the mere thought of Laura in his bed. For despite what she had said initially, Sam did not doubt that they would share a bed. After the way Laura had responded to his kisses, he couldn't believe that she would continue to insist on a marriage of convenience.

Even though he could not offer the pretty words and the declaration of undying love that she wanted, Laura was no young virgin, afraid of a man. She had been married before; she knew the pleasure a man and woman could share. Sam knew that she found him attractive, and he most definitely found her attractive. It was only natural that they would have a marriage in every sense of the word. "My bride-to-be is a beautiful woman," he told William.

"And you're a red-blooded man. Believe me, Sam, I understand."

Sam wasn't certain William did. After all, Sam's reasons

for marrying Amelia were far different from Sam's. "It sure isn't turning out the way I thought it would," Sam said.

William waited while Sam rolled the dice and moved his peg. "So your business arrangement turned to love. That's not bad, is it?" His tone told Sam William had never believed the marriage would be a cold-blooded arrangement. It wasn't. Sam would admit that. But why did everyone place so much importance on that fantasy called love?

He took another swallow of coffee. "I've told you before: I'm not convinced love exists."

William plunked the dice onto the desk. "What kind of nonsense are you talking?" His face mirrored the incredulity that Sam heard in his voice.

"It's not nonsense. Love is a myth the poets have created. It's an excuse people use to justify marriage, when the reality is that they marry for lust or money."

Leaning so far back in his chair that Sam feared he would tip over, William laughed. "Sam, my friend, you are wrong—dead wrong. I know you started looking for a bride because of your father's will, and any fool can see that you lust for Laura. But there's more to it than that." Abruptly William sat up and pointed a finger at Sam. "What on earth do you call what you feel for Laura?"

That was easy. "Friendship. What else?"

William laughed.

Only two days! Laura hummed under her breath as she hurried to Ella's house. Two days until the wedding, and she was literally counting the hours. In forty-six hours and thirty-seven minutes she would be Sam's wife. It was astonishing just how excited she was over that prospect. She, sensible Laura Templeton, was almost giddy with happiness. If someone had predicted that she would feel this way, she would have scoffed. But she could not deny that she was almost delirious with joy that she was marrying Sam.

"You look happy." The softness of Ella's tone told Laura that Meg was still napping.

"I am," Laura admitted. Why deny it? Everyone expected a prospective bride to be happy. What no one needed to know was why she was so happy and why that happiness was unexpected. "Everyone in Gold Landing has been so good to me—especially you and Amelia." Laura's eyes filled with the tears that seemed dangerously close to the surface these days. Unlike the tears she had shed when Matt died, these were tears of happiness.

Ella shrugged, as if dismissing Laura's words. "That's what friends are for."

She was wrong. Friends did many things, but they didn't necessarily help others in all the ways Ella and Amelia had. "You've gone beyond friendship," Laura insisted. "Look at Amelia giving me her gowns and you volunteering to take Meg."

At the sound of Meg stirring in the other room, Ella rose. "Ben and I enjoy her. You know that—and it's not just that she's giving us good practice for the day our own child arrives." Ella patted her well-rounded stomach. "Even if we didn't love Meg the way we do, we'd want to keep her for a day or two. Ben and I believe every newly married couple deserves time alone."

Laura couldn't disagree. Normally every set of newlyweds needed time to become a couple, time to spend together without the distractions of a young child, time to spend learning each other's bodies as well as their own. But Laura and Sam were not going to be normal newlyweds.

As she walked home, Meg's tiny hand clasped tightly in hers, Laura's thoughts were muddled. She wanted to be Sam's wife. Oh, how she did! She had lost count of the number of times she had wakened in the middle of the night, longing for the comfort of his arms around her, aching for his embrace. And Sam wanted her. She had no doubt of that. The warmth of his kisses, the strength of his embrace told her that he craved her touch.

The question was, could she give herself to Sam, surrender to the magic she was sure she would find making love to him, when she knew that he didn't love her? When she had shared a bed and given her body to Roy, she had believed that he loved her and that she had been in love with him. Though his kisses had never stirred her the way Sam's did, she had still had the illusion of love. This was different.

The sound of seven barking dogs interrupted Laura's reverie. "No, Meg," she said, pulling her daughter closer when she started to run toward the dogsled. "You can't play with those dogs."

"Want Nugget!" Meg cried. She tugged on Laura's hand, trying to break free. The yipping grew louder, and Meg's cries increased in volume. "Nugget!" she insisted.

"Here he is." Laura reached into the small bag that contained Meg's extra clothes and toys and handed her the carved wooden dog.

Meg shook her head wildly. "No! Want real dog!" She flung the toy aside.

Laura sighed. Her normally sweet-tempered daughter was on the verge of crying. The sled raced down Main Street, the dogs yipping, the musher shouting his commands. Meg wailed. From the corner of her eye, Laura saw a man enter Herb Ashton's store. Though his clothes proclaimed him a newcomer to Alaska, something about him seemed familiar. Perhaps she had met him at church the day the townspeople had congratulated her and Sam on their engagement.

"Want own dog!" Meg shrieked. With her free hand, she began to pound on Laura's legs. "Want own dog!"

All thoughts of the stranger fled as Laura knelt next to her daughter. It was not like Meg to have a tantrum, but there was no doubt that one was brewing. "You can't have a dog, sweetie. Not now." Though Sam had mentioned the possibility of getting a puppy for Meg, he had warned Laura that the litters wouldn't be born until spring. Meg only shrieked louder and continued pounding her fist against Laura.

Dismayed, Laura swept her crying daughter into her arms. She had to distract her. Once they were home, Laura set Meg to playing with her blocks, and gradually her tears subsided. When her daughter's sobs turned into nothing more than a few hiccups, Laura began to prepare supper. Fortunately, tonight's meal was one of Meg's favorites: vegetable soup and sourdough bread.

Laura was slicing bread when someone knocked on the door. That was odd. She hadn't expected any visitors tonight. Perhaps it was one of the women with a basket of canned goods. The townspeople had been generous in their gifts of food. Though Sam claimed it was normal Alaskan hospitality, Laura suspected word of her limited culinary skills had spread, and her neighbors wanted to ensure that Sam did not starve. She laid down the knife and walked to the door, an amused smile on her face.

The smile vanished, and for a long moment Laura could do nothing more than stare. "Roy!" she gasped.

It couldn't be! Her eyes were playing tricks on her, making her think that the man who stood on the front stoop was her husband.

It couldn't be. Roy was dead. But that smug smile was so familiar, and those blue eyes that now regarded her with such cynicism were the ones she had seen opposite her at the dinner table so many nights.

Laura stared, willing the vision to disappear. But as the man stood there, smirking at her obvious astonishment, Laura realized that somehow, some way her husband was still alive. The shock hit her with a force as strong as a physical blow, and she reeled backward, clutching the door frame to keep from falling. As her legs turned to jelly and her knees began to buckle, she felt the world go black. No! She would not faint. Forcing herself to take a deep breath and to exhale slowly, she stared at Roy.

"They said you were dead," she whispered. The simple act of speaking drained her remaining energy. Who would have thought that five words would deplete her stores so greatly? But it wasn't the words themselves; it was the fact that this man she had come so far to escape had somehow, against all odds, found her.

Roy's grin widened. "They're gonna have to try harder than that to kill me," he said, the satisfaction evident in his voice. If she had had any doubts, the familiar cadence and the unspeakable arrogance she heard swept them away. Roy was alive. Even worse, he was here in her home.

Laura tightened her grip on the door frame. She was vaguely aware of cold air rushing into the room, and she could feel the grain of the wood imprinted on her fingertips. In the distance the church bells chimed. It was an ordinary day in Gold Landing. It was only here that the unthinkable was happening.

"I read it in the paper." Laura was still trying to understand how the mistake had been made. "They said you were killed escaping from prison."

Roy laughed again and pushed his way past Laura. "You can't believe everything you read. I'm a whole lot smarter than those guards." She moved to block him from going further into the room. He closed the door behind himself and glanced around. Laura hated the assessing look she saw in his eyes. This was her home, not a place that Roy could turn into personal profit.

"Get out!" she hissed, wishing she still had the knife in her hand. Though she had never hurt another human being, never before had she felt so defenseless. "Get out!" She balled her fists as if to strike him.

Before Roy could react, a small voice called, "Mama!" Meg raced toward the door and grabbed Laura's legs, her eyes demanding to know who this stranger was.

"The brat's growing up." When Roy reached for the child, Laura moved again, putting her body between them. "She's gonna be a beauty like her ma some day." He licked his lips in a parody of lust.

Laura laid her hand on Meg's head. "Take Nugget," she said, "and go into your room."

"Don't wanna." Meg's lips turned downward, and she prepared to cry.

"Go. Now." Laura would not let her remain, not when this

monster stood in the same room. Meg stared at her mother for a long moment, patently startled by the harshness in Laura's tone. Then, as if she sensed the seriousness of the situation, she scampered into her bedroom, closing the door firmly behind her.

"Still used to getting your own way, I see." Roy sneered and took another step into the room, tracking snow onto the floor. He pulled off his cap, then looked around, as if he were searching for something. Laura kept her position, standing between Roy and Meg's room. If she was lucky, Roy would tell her why he had come and then leave.

"Where's the boy?" he demanded at last.

The boy! A shaft of pain stabbed Laura at the realization that Matt's father didn't refer to him by name or as his son. To Roy he was only "the boy."

"Matt," she said, stressing his name, "died of pneumonia two months ago." She blinked her eyes, trying to hold back the tears that thoughts of Matt always brought to the surface.

Roy shrugged. "Good riddance."

For a second Laura stood speechless. She had known that Roy didn't love either her or the children, but she had never realized that he would be deliberately cruel to a child. "How can you say that?" she demanded. "You were his father."

Roy shrugged again, as if denying his paternity. The face she had once found handsome twisted into a sneer. "There was only one reason to have those brats, and it didn't work. Your parents wouldn't loosen the purse strings, even when I presented them with grandchildren."

Though Roy was saying nothing more than she had surmised, hearing him speak the words filled Laura with rage. "You monster!" The man had no human emotions other than greed. Laura wondered how she could ever have thought that she loved him. And how, oh, how had she ever thought Sam was like this pathetic example of a man? "Get out of here!"

Roy stood his ground. "Not so fast," he drawled. "Not till I get what I came for."

"And what's that?" Laura could not imagine why he had

come to Alaska, since it appeared that the only thing he valued was money. Surely he had learned that she and her parents had not reconciled and that there was no hope of his gaining their fortune.

Laura stared at the man who had once been the most important part of her life. How could she have been so easily fooled? Other than the fact that they were both male, there were no similarities between Roy and Sam. Roy was a taker; Sam was not. Sam gave and gave and gave, while Roy had never given anything unless he expected something better in return.

"Why are you here?" she demanded.

To Laura's surprise, Roy seemed to hesitate. "For you," he said at last. When she raised a skeptical eyebrow, he continued. "I want some of those comforts only a wife can provide." The leer that accompanied his words told Laura exactly what he wanted.

Bile rose in her throat. "Not on your life." Though they might be legally married, she would never again let him touch her.

As if he knew the reason for her distress and was amused by it, Roy grinned. "Haven't you learned yet that I'm like a cat? I have more than one life."

Laura shivered. What a frightening thought. "You should have died in that prison break." It might be a sin to wish someone else harm, but Laura couldn't help herself. This man did not deserve to live.

"No, sweet wife of mine, I shouldn't have died. I'm too smart for that." Roy preened. "I was smart enough to pick me the right partner," he bragged. "He looked a little like me. Not as handsome, of course." Laura stared at the man she had once believed loved her. Why had she been so blind that she couldn't see that Roy could love no one but himself?

"He was my backup man," Roy explained. "Literally. I kept him between me and the guards. That way, when they shot, they killed him. Then, it was easy. I quickly switched our identifying shirts, messed up his face a bit, and when the guards found the body, no one knew that it wasn't Roy Templeton who died. Like I told you, Laura, honey, you married one smart man."

Laura felt the blood drain from her face at the realization that Roy had killed the man as surely as if he had pulled the trigger. "Get out!" She couldn't bear to look at him or hear his voice an instant longer. He was a liar, a thief, a murderer, and—oh, dear God—her husband. Laura gripped the back of a chair as the full impact hit her. "Get out!"

Roy feigned sadness. "Is that any way to treat your long-lost husband?"

Her husband! She took a deep breath, trying to quell her fears. "You just told me that Roy Templeton was dead. That means that you're *not* my husband, so get out of here."

He stared at her for a moment, then shrugged and walked toward the door. When he was gone, Laura dragged a chair and propped it under the knob. Then she sank onto Sam's rocking chair, cradling her head in her hands.

Damn Roy! Damn the man to Hell! It was bad enough that he had tricked her into marrying him. She could forgive that, for the marriage—painful though it had been—had given her Matt and Meg. But she could not forgive this. Coming to Gold Landing had destroyed Sam's hope for his inheritance.

Why, oh, why hadn't Roy died?

Sam frowned as he read the note Laura had left on his desk. "I must talk to you. It's urgent." The words were enough to start his pulse pounding, but what worried Sam even more than the message itself was the sight of Laura's scribbles. He had seen her normally neat penmanship enough times to know that something must be seriously amiss if she could not form precise letters.

He grabbed his parka and headed toward Laura's house. Bending his head as he walked into the wind, he could feel the adrenaline continue to pulse through his veins as he worried about Laura. The last time she had asked to meet him had been the day she proposed marriage. Today, he was certain, was not such a happy occasion.

"What's wrong?" he asked as she opened the door. If he had had any doubts about the gravity of the situation, they were erased by the sight of Laura's face. Pale and drawn with deep furrows between her eyes, she was the picture of a frantic woman.

"Oh, Sam!" Laura took his hand and drew him into the cabin. "He's here." There was such pain in her voice that Sam wanted nothing more than to gather her into his arms and comfort her.

"Who's here?" he asked as gently as he could. What he wanted was to find the man who had caused her such distress and make certain he never again bothered Laura.

As she looked up at him, Sam saw tears hovering on the edge of Laura's eyelids. Though she was not a tall woman, Sam had never thought of her as fragile, but today it seemed as if the slightest noise would cause her to shatter. He pulled her close, stroking her hair, wishing there was something he could say or do to stop her trembling. Never before, not even the day Matt had died, had he seen Laura so distraught. Those beautiful blue eyes that reminded him of the ocean on a sunny day were clouded with anguish, and her lips quivered.

"Who's here?" he repeated.

Laura's eyes met his, and this time the tears began to fall. "Roy," she sobbed. "My husband."

A gust of wind rattled the panes, and he could hear blood pounding in his ears. He must have misunderstood her. But the pain on Laura's face told him he had not. Sam's hand stilled as he tried to absorb her words. "It's not possible. Your husband is dead."

Shaking her head, Laura said, "That's what I thought." She wrapped her arms around Sam's waist and laid her head against his chest as if she needed to draw strength from him. But as Laura's tale unfolded, it was Sam who sought strength. Never before, not even when he had endured George's malicious tricks, had he felt such rage. It would take a superhuman effort not to kill the man who had caused Laura so much pain.

"No wonder you were so skittish about marriage at first," he said when she explained why Roy had married her and why he had left. After life with her first husband, it was a small miracle that she had ever considered taking another man into her her home. And now, to have the bastard return and threaten her bid for happiness . . . Though Sam had never considered himself a violent man, he began to imagine Roy Templeton dying a slow, painful death.

"I hope you can understand why I pretended to be a widow." As Laura's eyes reflected her uncertainty, Sam felt his anger grow. While Laura had appeared to be confident and self-assured, underneath the fragile shell, she was soft and vulnerable, thanks to her useless parents and the cur she had married. The poor woman! From what Sam could gather, no one had ever given her the approval she needed . . . and deserved.

"Of course I understand." Did she think he would condemn her for her attempt at self-preservation? Sam began to stroke her back in long gentle motions that were designed to tell her how much he cared for her. "Being a widow meant fewer explanations and more freedom." And, as she had told him, it helped shield her children from the ugly truth about their father.

"Oh, Sam." As Laura reached up and touched his cheek, he caught a whiff of the sweet scent of flowers and spices that was so much a part of her. Her hand was soft against his skin, reminding him of the fundamental differences between them. Laura's lips quivered. "When I saw the article about Roy's death, I was happy. It's probably a sin, but I couldn't help it. All I could think about was that now I was free to help you." The tears began to flow again. Laura tried vainly to brush them away. "What can we do now?"

There was only one answer. "I'll force Roy to leave Gold Landing. He can't stay with you." Just the thought of this man who had hurt Laura living with her, touching her, once again sharing her bed, made Sam so furious that he could barely speak. Roy Templeton had to leave town. Immediately. If he stayed, Sam wasn't sure how long he could go without taking matters into his own hands.

A small smile crossed Laura's face. "It's not me I'm worried about. It's you. What will you do now?"

For a second Sam didn't know what Laura meant. Then he shook his head. "Don't worry about me."

The wind whistled again, reminding Sam that although Laura was gazing at him with eyes as warm as the summer sun, an Alaskan winter reigned outside.

"Of course I worry about you," she said firmly. "It's only a month until your birthday, and you need a bride."

Sam couldn't help it. He smiled. She was wonderful, this tiny woman who stood so close to him. Here she was, facing a brute of a man who could destroy the life she had worked so hard to establish for herself and her daughter, and her only thought was for him. That knowledge made Sam feel as proud as the most powerful monarch at the same time that it filled him with humility. Truly, he didn't deserve a woman like Laura.

"You're more important than my inheritance."

A month ago, he might have said the words merely to comfort her. Today, as he heard himself pronouncing them, Sam realized that they were true. He cared about his inheritance, and he would regret losing it. But nothing—nothing on earth—mattered more than keeping the woman he loved safe.

Loved. Sam blinked, astonished by the thought. He loved Laura. He blinked again and swallowed deeply. Of course he loved her. What a fool he had been not to realize it sooner. It wasn't friendship he felt for her; it was something stronger, more powerful, more wonderful.

Sam drew Laura closer, trying to still the trembling in his arms. He wasn't sure how or when it had happened. All he knew was that the poets hadn't lied. Love was everything they had claimed and more. It was the most beautiful, most frightening thing on earth. And somehow he, Sam Baranov, had found it.

Chapter Twenty

"Come here, Precious!" The strident voice carried through the wall that separated what she called her morning room from his office.

George winced and put down the newspaper. There was no doubt that his mother was angry. The question was, why? She had been in a cheerful mood at breakfast, even taking second helpings of eggs and bacon. Since then she had ventured to the store, presumably to purchase a new hat. Surely the failure to find a hat that flattered her wasn't enough to cause her to vent her anger on him.

"Right away, Hilda." Though he normally responded to "Precious" by calling her "Mother," there was no point in annoying her further. George straightened his clothes and plastered a smile on his face.

"Wipe that smile off your face and tell me what's happening." She stood with her back to the window, her shoulders held as rigid as a general's. It had been a long time since George had seen his mother this angry. Something had obviously upset her, but he had no idea what it could be.

Though she had a volatile temper that she frequently inflicted on the servants, other than the day the lawyer had told her the terms of Nicholas's will, George could not remember her lashing out at him.

"What do you mean?" He had no need to feign ignorance. George truly did not know why she was angry. What he did know was that he ought not to smile at her, and he most definitely would not address her as "Mother." "What's amiss?"

His mother took a step toward him, pointing her index finger in a gesture that announced his culpability. "I saw that attorney today." Her voice seethed with barely controlled fury. "He told me Sam would be here to collect his inheritance." Hilda took another step forward. Though the rug muffled the sound of her shoes, George could hear her angry gasps of breath. "You said he wouldn't be a problem."

Sam. Of course. Everything bad that had ever happened in this household had been caused by that miserable excuse for a stepbrother. Nicholas's darling. The heir.

"Sam will not be a problem," George said smoothly. "You don't need to worry about him."

But Hilda was not so easily placated. She strode forward until she was only inches from George. Placing her finger squarely on his chest, she said, "After everything I've done for you, the way I've protected you, the sacrifices I've made for you . . ." George tried not to wince at the speech that he had heard so often that he could practically recite it. Hilda continued her tirade, ending, "You can't let the money slip through your fingers now."

George nodded. He knew that Hilda's concern was for herself, not him. She liked living in the Baranov mansion, buying expensive clothes, and being waited on by a large staff of servants. If Sam were to claim his inheritance, Hilda would lose her comfortable life.

"I'm not going to let Sam take it, Hilda. I didn't want to worry you with the details, but everything is under control." Perhaps he should have told her about the gambler who was going to end the problems with Sam once and for all. At the time, George had thought it better not to confide in anyone, not even his mother. Now he wasn't sure that had been the wisest course. If she had known what he had planned, she would not have spoken to the attorney, and this scene would never have occurred.

"I can promise you you'll never have to see Sam again." George turned toward the small cabinet that held Hilda's supply of spirits. "Now, let me pour you a glass of sherry."

"Are you sure about Sam?" she demanded.

"Completely." To emphasize his conviction, George nodded, then reached for a crystal glass.

"Put that sherry away," his mother commanded. "I want whiskey. A big glass."

"I told you, I don't want you in my home."

The man ignored her, pushing his way past her into the cabin. "Don't you mean 'our' home?" Roy demanded.

Laura wasn't certain whether the cold that permeated the room came from the door he had left ajar or the man himself. All she knew was that her face warmed with anger. "No, I do not mean that." She closed the door firmly, then moved past Roy to stand between him and Meg. "This house is mine. Mine and Meg's, not yours." Though her daughter had looked up from the castle she was constructing of wooden blocks, she had made no move to join Laura.

"The way I figure it," Roy drawled, punctuating his words with a smirk, "anything you have is mine. That's why a man marries—to get his wife's money."

Laura stared at him. He was loathsome, slimier than the slugs that had infested her mother's garden. She couldn't bear to have him in her home a moment longer, poisoning the very air with his evil thoughts. "Get out of here, Roy, and don't come back." When Roy did not move, she took another step toward him. "Get out!" He remained motionless, his expression taunting her. Laura could stand it no more. She reached out and shoved him toward the door.

Roy stared at her for a moment, then spun around and

started walking. When he reached the door, he turned and glared at her. "You'd better watch out, dear wife, or I just might take something you value." His gaze moved slowly around the cabin, as if inventorying the contents. "Yes," he said in a tone that sent shivers down her spine, "you'd better watch out." As he looked at the back of the room, he smiled. It was an expression of pure malice, yet even that did not prepare Laura for his next words. "I might take the brat."

The blood drained from Laura's head so quickly that she felt dizzy. "You wouldn't. You never wanted her."

Roy shrugged. "Maybe I've changed." And before Laura could say anything more, he strode outside, slamming the door behind him.

He hadn't changed. She was sure of that. If he wanted Meg, it was only to use her.

"Oh, Jason, I've missed you." Charlotte extended both of her hands to him as he entered the parsonage parlor. It was so wonderful, being able to see Jason here rather than having to sneak into the forest to meet him.

"I wanted to come last night," he explained, his gray eyes sparkling with enthusiasm, "but Mr. Baranov needed me to work late. He's letting me help with his ledgers. Oh, Charlotte, it's exciting."

Charlotte smiled. "Mrs. Templeton said he was pleased with your progress." As Jason flushed with pleasure, Charlotte smiled again. She had always known Jason wasn't a bad boy. Now all of Gold Landing was aware of it, for Sam Baranov wouldn't have a troublemaker working in his sawmill.

Jason sat next to her on the settee and held her hand in his. "Mr. Baranov paid me extra cuz I worked late."

"That's nice."

"It sure is, specially for a man who's saving for something important."

Charlotte looked at Jason in surprise. "What would that be?"

"A surprise." And though she teased him, he would say no more.

"It sure is a shame about Mr. Baranov and Mrs. Templeton, isn't it?" Jason asked a few minutes later. "All anybody can talk about is the way her husband showed up not dead after all."

Charlotte's heart sank the way it did every time she thought about the wedding that wouldn't take place. "That husband of hers makes my skin creep," she told Jason. "I can't imagine why she married him."

Charlotte remembered the story Laura had told her of the way she had met Roy, how he had saved her from the carriage. Had something happened to addle her brains that day? Mrs. Templeton was a smart lady. She should have seen that even though Roy had a handsome face, his eyes were cold and cruel. He was not a good man. He was not like Jason.

Laura's teeth chattered and her legs were trembling as she left Abe Ferguson's office. She wrapped her arms around her waist, trying to quell the shaking that owed nothing to the cold wind. Though it was only a block from the attorney's home to hers, she wasn't certain that her limbs would carry her that distance.

"What did he say?" The speed with which Sam emerged from the hotel made Laura wonder if he had been waiting for her. He had known she was going to talk to Abe this afternoon as soon as school was dismissed, and had offered to accompany her, but Laura had refused. Surely she could meet with the lawyer alone. In retrospect, Laura had realized she should have accepted Sam's offer. The appointment itself hadn't been difficult. She had remained calm while Abe had explained her options. It was only when she walked outside, and the impact of his words hit her with more force than the brutal cold, that Laura had begun to tremble.

Sam took her arm, his brown eyes searching her face. Without saying anything more, he steered her across the street and into the hotel. "You need to sit down," he said, guiding her toward one of the horsehair chairs that stood in a corner of the lobby. When the desk clerk approached, Sam shook his head. "Mrs. Templeton just needs to rest."

Sam tugged off her gloves and helped her unbutton her coat. It was, Laura thought, similar to the way she undressed Meg on days when the child was particularly tired. When she was seated, Sam pulled another chair close to hers and sat facing her. "Now, tell me what Abe said." Sam took both of her hands in his, his warmth beginning to dissipate the cold that had settled in her bones.

"Oh, Sam!" Laura hated to even voice the words she had heard. They hadn't truly come as a surprise, but hearing Abe utter them and seeing the concern on his face had disturbed her more than she would have believed possible. "Abe says that as long as we're married, Roy has rights."

A shadow crossed Sam's face. "What kind of rights?"

There was no easy way to say this. "All kinds. The house . . . Meg . . . me."

Sam's eyes widened, and Laura saw pure anger shining from them. "No!" He squeezed her hands so tightly that she winced.

The front door opened, letting in two guests and a blast of cold air. Laura shivered. "Just because Roy has legal rights doesn't mean I'm going to allow him to—to use Abe's word—exercise them," she said. It didn't matter what the law claimed. There was no way Laura was going to let Roy Templeton into her house or her life again, and he most definitely was not going to touch Meg.

"We'll stop him," Sam announced. Though he kept his voice low so that the other guests would not overhear their conversation, he made no effort to disguise his determination.

"Abe says there's only one way."

As if he hadn't heard her, Sam continued "I'll persuade him the way I did Jethro Mooney." Sam looked down at his hands and grinned, as if picturing his fists connecting with

Roy's face. "When I get done with him, Roy won't want to be within a hundred miles of Gold Landing."

The ferocity of his claim made Laura smile. "I always suspected you were born in the wrong century. You should have been a knight in the Middle Ages."

"Then I could have challenged Roy to a joust."

"And I would have scandalized everyone by giving you my favor to wear." Laura's smile faded. "Oh, Sam, it's not a laughing matter. Abe told me I needed to file for a divorce." It was, he had explained, her only option. And then he had told her how long the process would take.

"Does the idea of a divorce make you unhappy?" Sam asked. His face was sober, and Laura thought she detected a hint of vulnerability in his eyes. Surely he didn't think she wanted to remain married to Roy.

"Only for Meg's sake," she said quickly. "One of the reasons I brought the twins to Alaska was so that they would never have to know that their father was in prison. I didn't want them to grow up with that stigma. Now everyone in Gold Landing will know the truth, and Meg will have to endure not just that shame but the added burden of divorced parents."

Sam drew Laura's hands to his face and pressed a kiss on her knuckles, ignoring the curious looks that the other guests gave him. "It's not your fault or Meg's that Roy is a thief."

Laura sighed. "Not everyone's as tolerant as you, Sam. I've seen too much of guilt by association to think otherwise." Laura knew that she could weather the scandal. If the townspeople believed she was unfit to teach their children, she would move to another town. But, oh, how she hated the thought that her daughter would be punished for a crime she had not committed and that she would grow up being known as the child of a thief.

The other couple rose and headed for the dining room.

"I don't see that you have any choice," Sam said slowly. "You need to divorce Roy to protect yourself and Meg."

"I know that. That's why I asked Abe to start preparing

the papers." Laura pulled her hands from Sam's and clasped them tightly, hoping to stop the trembling that had returned when she thought of how long Abe had said it would take. "Oh, Sam, I wish the divorce could happen fast enough to save your inheritance."

One way or another, even without the divorce, she would protect Meg. But there was nothing she could do to help Sam. Abe had been blunt in his assessment. There wouldn't be enough time for papers to be filed and the divorce ruling to take effect before Sam's birthday. And that, even more than the threat to herself and Meg, was the reason Laura's heart was filled with despair.

She had failed Sam.

It wasn't just his lucky day, Roy mused as he pushed open the door to the saloon. It was his lucky year. Yes, indeed.

"Gimme a whiskey," he ordered, settling onto one of the bar stools. The bartender complied, although the look he gave Roy made it clear that he wasn't happy to have him as a patron. Damn fool Alaskans! They were the coldest bastards Roy had ever met. Not that it mattered. He'd do what he had to do, and then he'd head for warmer spots. No one would be able to stop him then.

Roy took a long drink, then plunked the glass back onto the bar. One good thing you could say about Alaskans. They had mighty fine whiskey. Roy figured they needed it to survive the endless winters. He shuddered, thinking of the frozen wilderness he had crossed to get here. Cold and dark. It was a mystery to him why anyone would want to live in a place where the sun barely shone, but it didn't matter. No, sirree. The sun might not be shining on Alaska, but Lady Luck sure was shining on Roy.

He downed the last of the whiskey and ordered another. It was plain as could be that he was having a run of good luck. How else could you explain the fact that old Steely Eyes had paid him to go to the very town where he had been headed anyway? If that wasn't luck, Roy didn't know what it was. But it just got better.

Old Steely Eyes had lied. He had told Roy that the man he was supposed to kill wanted to marry his wife, when the truth was, it was Roy's wife, not the wife of Steely Eyes, that Sam Baranov wanted to marry. Roy hadn't figured out why Steely Eyes had lied about the wife, but it didn't matter. Killing was killing. Once it was over and he went back to Seward to collect the rest of his payment, Roy knew Steely Eyes wouldn't want his lie exposed. No, sirree. And there was only one way of making sure that Roy didn't talk. He rubbed his hands together, thinking about the extra money he was going to get.

Yes, indeed, Fate had been kind to him. By the time he was done with Sam Baranov, Roy was going to be a rich man. A very rich man. Because it wasn't just Steely Eyes who was gonna pay him. Roy's own sweet wife wanted to marry Sam Baranov, and was fixing to get a divorce so that she could do just that.

Roy chuckled. When the bartender gave him a questioning look, Roy glared at him. Fool! Didn't he know that he was serving someone who just might become the richest man in all of Alaska? Laura didn't have much money. Roy knew that. But it sure looked like the sawmill owner had more than his share. If he was so all-fired anxious to marry Laura, it stood to reason that Sam Baranov would be willing to pay Roy to hasten that joyous event.

A man had rights, and Roy knew his. He had rights to Laura and the brat. But if Sam was sniffing around the bitch, chances were he would be willing to make a generous payment so that Roy wouldn't contest the divorce.

It was perfect. Absolutely perfect. A three-step plan. He would collect the money from Sam Baranov. That was the first step. As soon as he had that money, he would take care of business for Steely Eyes and "stop" Sam. Step two. And then, dear sweet Laura would be so heartbroken over Sam's death that she would need to turn to a man. Who better than her lawfully wedded husband? In step three, they would leave this godforsaken frozen wilderness and go where the sun shone all the time.

Yes, indeed, this was Roy's lucky year.

Chapter Twenty-one

Laura clasped her hands together. Bless Ella for agreeing that she and Sam could meet in her parlor. Ever since Roy had come to Gold Landing, Laura had forbidden Sam to come to her house, lest their being together without a chaperone give Roy a reason to contest the divorce. If it were summer, she and Sam could have met outdoors without anyone looking askance, but Alaskan winters were hardly conducive to long conversations, and today she simply had to talk to Sam.

Laura twisted her hands, then forced them to remain still. Oh, how she wished she didn't have to have this conversation. For a few days, she had believed there would be a happy ending for her and Sam. Now she knew how elusive happiness was, and her only hope was that she would somehow help Sam find it. As for herself . . .

She stared at the man she loved so dearly. He stood only inches from her, his sheer size seeming to fill Ella's parlor as completely as thoughts of him filled her life. She loved him. She wanted him to be happy. And yet . . .

Laura swallowed. Why was it that her heart felt as if it

were in her throat and that her voice would come out as a croak? It shouldn't be so difficult to pronounce the words. They were, after all, both important and inevitable.

"What is it, Laura? Your message sounded urgent." Sam's forehead furrowed, and those brown eyes that normally sparkled with happiness radiated concern. Placing one hand on the small of Laura's back, he propelled her to one of the chairs that flanked the stove and took the other.

She swallowed again, not wanting to voice her thoughts. "It is urgent," she agreed. There were only a few weeks left. She stared at Sam for a moment. He leaned forward in the chair. Though his hands rested on his knees, Laura saw that his fingers were tense. *Oh, Sam!* Laura closed her eyes for a second, gathering strength. When she opened them, she forced herself to meet Sam's gaze.

"You need to find someone else to marry." It was sensible. Of course it was. It wasn't just sensible; it was Sam's only choice. Though Laura knew that, her heart ached at the thought of Sam with another woman. Thank goodness he and his new wife would move to Seward. At least then she wouldn't have to see them and wonder whether they were happy.

Sam's eyebrows rose in surprise, and she saw an expression of incredulity cross his face. "Are you saying that you don't want to marry me?"

The grandfather clock in the hall began to chime, and the sound of pans clattering told Laura Ella had begun her supper preparations. None of that seemed real. All that was real was the man who sat so near to her today, the man who would soon be lost to her forever.

Blinking fiercely so that the tears that had welled in her eyes would not fall, Laura shook her head. Of course she wanted to marry Sam. Though the marriage they had planned might have been a business arrangement for him, for Laura it had become much more. But now it would never be.

"I'm not free to marry you," she said slowly. "You know

that, Sam, just as you know that you can't lose your inheritance."

When Sam reached forward and laid his hand on hers, she realized that she had been wringing them. Her hands stilled under his touch, and she could feel his warmth begin to permeate her fingers, then start to work its way up her arm. "I talked to Abe again," Laura said. "He told me that if I could convince Roy to cooperate, we might be able to get the divorce decree before your birthday." The thought had filled Laura with elation until she had faced the realization that she was pinning her hopes and Sam's future on a man who had never performed an unselfish act in his life. That was when she had known that Sam needed to find another bride.

He stroked the back of her hand. Though his fingers were calloused and rough from work, Laura was sure that even the finest of silks and velvets would not feel so good. This was Sam, the man she loved.

"I don't want to marry anyone else," Sam said firmly. He kept his gaze fixed on hers, his expression as serious as she had ever seen it. "I only want to marry you."

Laura caught her breath. Sam wanted to marry *her!* She swallowed, trying to quell the twin tremors of delight and dread that swept through her. Though her heart rejoiced at the fierceness of his words, Laura knew she could not let Sam make a mistake that would haunt them both for the rest of their lives.

"We can't count on the divorce coming in time. Oh, Sam, I'm so afraid it will be too late and George will keep the company."

Sam pried her fingers apart. Clasping her right hand in his, he drew it to his lips and pressed a soft kiss on her fingertips. "The company doesn't matter." He paused, his eyes searching her face as if trying to see whether she believed him. "You're more important to me than money."

Laura felt the blood drain from her face. It was a wonderful thought. What woman wouldn't want to think that she was the most important part of a man's life? Laura blinked as she tried to clear her head. How she wished she could believe it was true! Unfortunately, she knew better. Though Sam might think he cared for her more than his inheritance, the time would come when he would regret their marriage and the loss of his father's company. Laura knew that as surely as she knew the sun would rise tomorrow.

Willing her voice to be steady, she said, "Baranov Shipping is more than money. It's your last tie to your father." Laura touched the watch that Sam's father had given his mother. She would return it to Sam so that he could present it to his bride. "Sam, almost from the first time I met you, you told me how important it is that you return to Seward to continue the family business."

The sounds of Ella's humming and the rhythmic noise of vegetables being chopped drifted into the parlor. Though Laura could not yet smell the food, Ella had told her she was making vegetable soup. Would Sam's new wife spend hours preparing meals the way Ella did?

Sam shook his head, and for a second Laura thought he had read her thoughts. Then he said, "The company isn't important anymore. I've lived in Gold Landing for a long time. I have a good life here, and I'm proud of the sawmill. There's no reason for me to give it up."

"But Sam . . . Your father's legacy . . ."

Sam shook his head again. "I won't lie to you, Laura. I wish I had something tangible of my father's. That was one of the reasons inheriting the company was so important. It's like his watch—I just wanted to own something that had been his." Sam put his hand on Laura's chin, forcing her to meet his gaze. "Those are important, but I don't want them if it means losing you."

"But Sam . . ."

He jumped to his feet and tugged her to hers, then put his hands on her shoulders. "Hell, Laura," he said, his eyes flashing with what appeared to be anger, "you're forcing me to say something I wasn't ready to." His lips thinned, and she saw the indecision on his face. Whatever Sam was about to say, he wasn't happy about it. Laura knew her own face must reflect her bewilderment.

Sam released her shoulders and took both of her hands in his. For a long moment he did nothing more than stare at her. When he spoke, his voice was surprisingly gentle. "This isn't the time or place I would have chosen, but you need to understand. Laura, the reason Baranov Shipping doesn't matter anymore is that I love you more than I could ever care about a company."

Not even in her dreams had she imagined Sam saying that. For a second Laura was too shocked to speak. Sam loved her? She shook her head slowly. Though it was a wonderful thought, it couldn't be true. Sam only imagined he loved her. "Oh, Sam, you didn't have to say that. I didn't mean to force you into saying something you didn't mean."

Quickly, before she could lose courage, she added, "I know you don't love me." Even though she knew it was true, she had never before said the words aloud. It was surprising how much it hurt to pronounce them. Still, there was no choice. If Sam was going to be happy, they had to be honest with each other.

Sam dropped her hands and ran one of his through his hair in a gesture of pure exasperation. "Confound it, woman. For a smart lady, you're sure slow to understand." He reached forward and cupped her cheek, his tender gesture at odds with his angry words. "The reason I wasn't ready to tell you I love you isn't that I don't mean it. It's because you're still married." His fingers moved down her cheek, touching her chin, then brushing her lips. Though it was the lightest of touches, it sent shivers of pleasure coursing through Laura. And yet, delightful though it was, the physical pleasure paled compared to the joy Sam's words wrought. He loved her! He did!

"You can call me old-fashioned," Sam said, continuing to trace a path along the curves of her face. "I try to keep the commandments but, sweetheart, you're making it damned difficult. It's bad enough that I covet another man's wife."

When Laura's eyes widened in surprise, Sam smiled. "Did you ever doubt that I covet you? That was the first of the commandments to go. I don't want to add adultery to my list of sins."

Adultery. It was unthinkable. "But Sam . . ."

He raised his other hand, laying one on each side of her face, his brown eyes solemn as he spoke. "Do you have any idea how difficult it's been to keep my hands off you? I dream about you every night and wake up aching for you." His smile was wry. "The days are just as bad. All I can think about is getting you into my bed, holding that beautiful body of yours close to mine, tasting every inch of you."

Laura could feel herself blushing. She thought she was the only one who had those dreams. "We agreed to a marriage of convenience," she said, grasping at the last straw of sanity.

Sam shook his head. He rubbed his thumb over her lower lip. Laura trembled. Why was it that his lightest touch could turn her legs to jelly?

"You agreed to those ridiculous terms," he reminded her. "I had every intention of making it a real marriage—in every sense. If it weren't for what little sense of honor I have left, I'd lock the door and show you just how much I want you." His eyes dropped to the floor, as if assessing the rug's comfort.

Laura's heart sank. Sam didn't love her. Not really. He had been honest when he told her he wasn't sure he would recognize love, and so it was no wonder that he had made this mistake. Lust. That was what Sam felt. It was, Laura supposed, flattering to be lusted after or, to use Sam's old-fashioned word, coveted. But lust and love were two very different emotions, and there was only one she craved.

"We can't," she said.

Sam flashed her another wry smile. "Believe me, sweetheart, I know that. Ella may be married, but she's still the biggest prude in Gold Landing. We can't scandalize her. C'mon." Sam turned toward the door. "We'd better get out of here before I forget my good intentions."

When they walked into Ella's kitchen, they found her

peering into a cabinet. "Perfect timing," she said as she straightened and rubbed the small of her back. Ella gestured toward the stove, where soup simmered in a large kettle. "I need another turnip. Sam, would you mind getting it for me from the root cellar?" Ella looked down at her stomach. "I told Ben he would have to enlarge the cellar before we have our next child, because I have trouble fitting."

Laura had seen Ella's root cellar. It was small and dark, constructed more like a tunnel than a cave. The one time Laura had been in it, she had found it difficult to breathe and had almost forgotten to bring out the potatoes Ella needed. "I'll go," she said quietly. Ella's root cellar was almost as bad as a coffin, clearly no place for Sam.

Ella frowned as she looked at Laura's skirt. "It's dirty," she said. "Sam can get the turnip."

If she hadn't been looking at him, Laura might have missed the momentary stiffening of Sam's face. Though she doubted he would refuse Ella's request, for Sam was every inch a gentleman, Laura knew how much he hated dark confined spaces. "I'll go," she repeated. "Sam needs to get back to his office."

The grateful look Sam gave her told Laura he knew what she had done and why. He might not love her, but they were friends. Good friends. And friends did what they could to help each other.

The cold air felt good. At least it helped cool his face. Maybe it would even cool his thoughts. Sam strode down First Street, sparing only a glance at his house, then headed left on River. Although it had been a useful ploy, a good way to keep him from what would surely have been an unpleasant experience in the cellar, Laura was wrong. Sam's needs had nothing to do with his office. There was no reason he had to return to the sawmill, and he had no desire to go home. His needs and desires were simpler. And more complex.

He couldn't go home. At home there would be nothing to distract him from thoughts of Laura and the way her skin had felt beneath his fingers. It got harder each day, trying to keep his hands from touching her. He could think of little besides unpinning that silvery blond hair, removing her clothes, and feasting on her beauty. But he couldn't. Not yet. And knowing that that bastard of a husband was still lurking around Gold Landing only fueled Sam's anger . . . and his desire. How he wanted Laura: in his home, in his bed, in his life! But until Abe Ferguson worked his magic and got the divorce decree, Sam would have to, as the Good Book said, "burn."

Sam strode past his office. Being there was almost worse than being at home, for only a thin wall separated his office from the area Laura used as her classroom. When he sat at his desk, staring at ledgers, he would picture her laughing with her students, then coming into the office after class to share anecdotes with him.

He kept walking. "Want some coffee?" William asked as Sam entered the mine office.

Sam shook his head. William couldn't give him what he wanted. No one could. As Sam shed his outerwear, William chuckled. "Looks like you need something stronger than coffee." He pulled a bottle from his bottom drawer and poured them each a healthy serving.

Sam settled in a chair and took a long swallow. Whiskey didn't solve any problems, but sometimes it helped dull the pain. He stretched his legs out and tried to relax.

"I thought Amelia and I kept the Gold Landing gossips busy." William leaned back in his chair, the picture of an indolent man. It was, Sam knew, a pose. Those half-closed eyelids hid a shrewd gaze that missed very little. There had been times when Sam had rued his friend's perception. Today, though, he craved his companionship. William, more than anyone else in Gold Landing, could appreciate Sam's predicament, for William's own marriage had been postponed once, leaving the town speculating that he would never win Amelia's hand.

"You and Laura have us beaten, hands down." William

opened his eyes long enough to reach for his glass.

Sam took another swallow before he replied. "It's sure as winter snow not by choice." He looked around the office. That pile of books in the corner needed a set of shelves. Maybe he'd work on that tonight. Honest labor was even better than whiskey at dulling pain.

Propping his boots on the desk, William leaned back in his chair. "What's Roy's story? I thought Laura was a widow."

"She did too." Sam explained about the prison break and Roy's alleged death, deliberately neglecting to tell William that Laura had come to Gold Landing under false pretenses. There was no reason anyone in town—even his best friend—had to know that. A gentleman protected a lady's reputation, especially when the gentleman had every intention of marrying that lady.

William dropped his indolent pose. "With Laura unable to marry you, what are you going to do about your inheritance?" Sam heard genuine concern in his friend's voice. That was one of the reasons he had come. William was a true friend.

"I reckon I'm gonna lose it." Sam noted with pride that his voice was as calm as if he were discussing the weather. The thought still hurt, but not as much as the prospect of the alternatives. "Laura's divorce won't be final until after my birthday."

The wind howled, and the smell of drying wool filled the room. It was a normal winter afternoon in Gold Landing. It was only Sam's life that was so far from normal.

William refilled Sam's glass, then splashed more whiskey into his own. "You don't have to lose the shipping company," he said. "It's not much of a secret that Vera Kane would be mighty happy to marry you."

Sam plunked his glass onto the desk, not caring that the liquid sprayed onto the wood. Friendship had its boundaries, and William had ventured beyond them. "Vera Kane would marry anything that wore pants." He glared at William, daring him to dispute the facts. "As for me, I have no intention of marrying anyone other than Laura."

For a second William was silent. Then he chuckled. "It hit you too, didn't it?" Though he smiled, his eyes were filled with understanding and compassion.

"What do you mean?" Sam was pretty sure he knew what William meant, but a man didn't want to make a fool of himself, admitting to the wrong thing.

"Love."

Sam nodded. There was no point in denying it any longer. "It's like that Dickens fellow says, the best and worst of times."

William pushed the bottle toward Sam. "I reckon you need a bit of consolation."

They were toasting the vagaries of love when the door opened. "Oh," Alex Fielding said when he saw Sam, "I guess I'm interrupting."

William lowered his feet to the floor and stood. "What's wrong?" he asked his cousin. Since Alex had been injured in an accident and could no longer mine, William had given him a position as shift foreman.

"It's Jethro Mooney." Alex didn't bother to hide his disgust. "He started another fight."

Sam clenched his own fists as he thought of the miner who seemed to take great pleasure from fighting with smaller men.

"Did he hurt anyone this time?" William asked. The way he looked at Alex told Sam he was checking to see whether Jethro had inflicted his rage on Alex.

Alex nodded. "Knocked out a couple of Chet Wing's front teeth."

"That's it." William moved from behind the desk and flexed his muscles, as if he were considering some biblical retribution for Jethro's fighting. "I warned him the last time this happened that I wasn't gonna tolerate any more brawling in the mine. Damn it all. They're supposed to working down there."

Sam drained his glass. Thank God he'd reached Jethro before he had turned Jason's face into a bloody pulp. Though

Jethro glared at Sam every time he saw him, he had never ventured toward Jason since that night. "Jethro likes to pick on weaker men," said Sam.

"I can't stop that," William admitted, "but I can stop it from happening in my mine." He turned to Alex. "Tell Jethro I want to see him."

Sam grabbed his coat. "I think I'd better get out of here." There was no point in waving a red flag in front of an already enraged bull.

They were bastards, all of them. Jethro Mooney swung his ax as he strode toward the mine office. Bastards, starting with that pipsqueak Chet Wing and ending with Mr. High-and-Mighty William Gunning. Bastards. They thought they were so good, but he showed them. Once the others saw the way he had rearranged Chet's face, they'd know better than to mess around with Jethro Mooney. A shirker. The damn fool called him a shirker. Jethro showed him, just like he'd show William.

Jethro swung his ax again, laughing when it chewed a piece out of the side of the sawmill office. He'd take a piece out of that bastard Sam Baranov the next time he saw him. He still owed him for the time he spoiled his fun with that little runt Jason Blake. Yes, indeed, Jethro was gonna make sure Sam paid for that. But first he had to settle things with that big fool who owned the mine.

The man was standing there, his feet planted on the floor, his head held high just as if he thought he was the king of Gold Landing. The other men might believe that. They might say that William Gunning was the best mine owner in all of Alaska. Jethro knew better.

"I reckon you know why I asked you to come here." Though William kept his hands at his sides, something about his stance told Jethro he was angry. Hell, *he* was angry too.

"Sure. I reckon you heard about how Chet Wing attacked me." Jethro touched his nose. The little bastard had gotten in a good punch or two. Pure luck, of course. Chet Wing couldn't fight to save his life. Jethro had proven that.

"That's not the way I heard the story." William took a step closer.

"A man's got a right to defend himself." That was all it was. Self-defense. He'd had to hit him. No one was going to get away with calling Jethro Mooney names.

William took another step, and this time Jethro moved back a pace. Only a fool would pick a fight with William Gunning. The man was too big. You had to catch him unawares, hit him from behind. "No one has the right to fight in my mine," the big bastard said. "I told you that the last time. I also told you what would happen if you started another fight."

Damn it all! He was treating Jethro like a child. He wasn't a child. No, sirree. He was a man. A big man. A powerful man.

"It was Chet's fault."

William shook his head. "I don't think so. I've got plenty of witnesses who said you threw the first punch." William shook his head again, and this time his lip curled with disgust. "You know the consequences." He reached for an envelope on the desk. "Take your pay," he said, handing the coins to Jethro. "But don't you ever set foot in my mine again. You're fired."

Fired! How the hell was he supposed to pay for the girls at Gloria's if he was fired?

"You can't do that!"

William shrugged. "I just did. Now, get out of here."

Fired! Jethro spat. "You'll be sorry for this, you bastard." He slammed the door behind him, then picked up the ax. He'd be sorry. They'd all be sorry. He swung the ax as he strode down the street.

A man was coming toward him, whistling as if he didn't have a care in the world. Baranov! It was that bastard Sam Baranov. He was the cause of this. Jethro knew it.

"It's your fault. You're gonna pay."

Jethro raised his ax.

* * *

Today was the day. Roy Templeton grinned as he buttoned his coat. How he hated Alaska and its endless cold! A man wasn't meant to live in a place like that. A man was meant to be warm. A man was meant to have a woman taking care of him. A man was meant to have lots of money. Soon Roy would have all those things: a warm home, a willing woman, and more money than he could ever spend. Yes, sirree. Today was the day.

He gritted his teeth as the wind blew through his coat. Temporary. That's all it was. In just a few minutes, he would have had his little talk with Sam Baranov, and Sam would have sealed their agreement in the best of ways: with some nice gold coins. Roy had it all planned. He was going to pay a visit to Sam and explain a few things to him. Like the fact that he, Roy Templeton, was a kindly man who understood another man's needs. Like the fact that he would be willing—happy, in fact—to help smooth the way for the divorce. Like the fact that he knew Sam would be so grateful over the prospect of getting Laura into his bed that he would be willing to do some smoothing of his own. Smoothing of a monetary nature.

Roy almost laughed as he turned onto River, heading for the sawmill. It was so easy. In less than a week, it would all be done, and he'd be rich as Croesus. He figured Sam wouldn't have all the money in the office. Only a fool would keep that much just sitting around. But he'd have enough to give Roy the down payment today. Then, tomorrow or the day after, he'd get the rest. And then Roy would take the next step.

He'd make that man in Seward grateful by permanently stopping Sam Baranov. He would get lots of money from that. And then there would be nothing keeping him and Laura from that tropical paradise he'd heard about. Roy could already picture the warm sun and the many ways Laura would show her gratitude. Today was gonna be his lucky day.

As Roy approached the mill, his grin widened. Yes, indeed,

this was his lucky day. There was Sam, coming down the street. He looked happy. Good. A happy man was a grateful man. And a grateful man was a generous man. Roy doubled the amount he was going to suggest for the smoothing.

"Sam!" he called.

But Sam didn't hear him. He continued walking and whistling.

A man emerged from the mine office. Judging from the way he was swinging that ax, he was not a happy man. Roy didn't care. All that mattered was Sam.

The man raised his ax.

No! It was too soon! Sam couldn't die. Not yet!

"Stop!" Roy shouted the word as he lunged at the man.

In the distance, someone screamed.

"Laura!" There was no mistaking the voice, but never before had she heard that tone. Laura flung the door open, her heart pounding with fear. What could have made Sam sound so frantic?

He stood there, his face ashen, blood staining his coat and gloves. As the blood drained from her own face, Laura felt the world begin to go black. She grabbed the door knob, willing herself to remain upright. She would be unable to help Sam if she fainted.

"Oh, my God!" There was so much blood. "What happened?" At least he was alive. Thank God he was alive! Laura reached a hand toward Sam. "Who hurt you?"

Brushing her hand aside, Sam entered the house. "I'm okay, but I think we'd better both sit down."

He didn't look okay. He looked so pale that Laura wondered if he would suddenly keel over. "Sam, what's wrong? You're scaring me." She sank onto the horsehair couch and tugged Sam's hand, urging him to sit next to her. Her eyes scanned his face. There was no blood there. But why, oh why was there so much on his clothing? "What's wrong?"

Sam stared at her for a long moment, as if trying to decide what to say, and his eyes were filled with pain as he took both of her hands between his. "It's Roy," he said softly.

"Roy?" Of course. Trouble seemed to follow Roy wherever he went. "What did he do?"

"He saved my life." The wonderment she heard in Sam's voice told Laura he was still shocked by whatever Roy had done. She looked at Sam, trying to understand. The words made sense, but not when they were applied to Roy. Roy didn't save lives. He took them.

"Best as I can figure it," Sam continued, "William fired Jethro Mooney for fighting in the mine. Jethro must have thought I was somehow responsible, because when he saw me walking down the street, he swung his ax at me."

Laura shuddered, picturing a bully like Jethro wielding an ax. She tugged one of her hands loose and stroked Sam's cheek. Thank God he was alive. She wasn't sure how she would have borne it if something had happened to Sam.

He shook his head, as if in disbelief. "I never even saw Roy. All I heard was someone shouting 'Stop!' and the next thing I knew, Roy was between Jethro and me." He looked down at his coat. "Jethro's ax hit him."

Though the smell of blood turned Laura's stomach, she breathed a small sigh of relief that it wasn't Sam's blood staining his clothing. "How badly is Roy hurt?"

Sam shifted his feet on the floor and swallowed. Capturing Laura's hand again, he met her gaze and once more she saw pain reflected in his eyes. "He's dead," Sam said at last.

The room began to whirl. Dead! Roy was dead! "I can't believe it." Laura's voice was harsh with emotion. It had been easy to believe the newspaper account of Roy's death in a prison break. That seemed like the Roy she knew. But somehow, Sam's tale that her husband had been killed in Gold Landing did not ring true. Any minute now, Roy would pound on the door and demand to know what Laura and Sam were doing together.

Sam nodded slowly. "It's true. Roy died saving my life." That same incredulous tone that she had heard before colored his words.

Laura swallowed, trying to accept what Sam was saying. It was true. Roy was gone. He would never again frighten her. He would never again threaten Meg. As the full realization of "never" hit her with the force of a physical blow, tears began to stream down Laura's face. "I don't know why I'm crying," she said, brushing the tears aside with an impatient gesture. "I wanted him dead."

Sam cupped her cheek and turned her to face him. "No, you didn't," he said softly. "You wanted him out of your life. That's different." When Laura started to protest, Sam said, "I know you, Laura. You wouldn't truly wish for anyone's death."

His words unleashed another torrent of tears. With her arms wrapped around Sam as if he were the sole stable force in her life, Laura cried for the man she had once thought she loved, for the man who had fathered her children, for the man who had wasted his life. And then, as the tears subsided, Laura realized that Roy hadn't wasted his life. Not all of it.

"He was a hero," she said, her voice as astonished as Sam's had been. "No matter what he did before this, Roy died a hero." A small smile crossed Laura's face. "I can tell Meg that. She'll have a reason to be proud of her father."

Chapter Twenty-two

Charlotte didn't mean to eavesdrop. Her mother had taught her that polite people did not listen to conversations that were not intended for them. But what was she to do when the women's voices carried into the kitchen? If she closed the door, surely the Ladies' Benevolent Society would realize that she had been able to overhear their discussion, and surely that would be embarrassing for them.

It hadn't mattered when they were talking about Jethro Mooney and speculating on what the judge in Fairbanks was going to do with him. Everyone in Gold Landing was saying the same thing. But now the ladies were discussing Mrs. Templeton and Mr. Baranov. They might not like knowing that Charlotte was listening. Surely it was better to continue arranging sandwiches on the tray and interrupt only when she was finished.

"I'm so happy there's going to be a wedding after all." Susan Whitaker's sweet voice was unmistakable. Charlotte smiled. Susan had always been nice to her, and ever since her twins had been born, she had been especially pleasant to everyone in town, even Jason. That made Susan one of Charlotte's favorite people.

Charlotte spread jam on the fine white bread she had made this morning, then cut the sandwich into four triangles. Thank goodness the bread had risen properly. She had worried about it the whole time it had been in the proofing bowl. Her mother liked everything to be perfect when the Society met at the parsonage, and today's meeting was especially important. Today was the day the ladies would finish the quilt they were making for Mrs. Templeton and Mr. Baranov.

"You just want an excuse to cry," Ella chided Susan. Charlotte smiled again. She couldn't imagine the former schoolteacher crying, no matter what the occasion.

Karen Fielding laughed. "It's all right to cry at weddings," she announced. "Almost everyone did at mine."

When the teakettle began to hiss, Charlotte switched off the burner and filled the teapot. The coffee was almost ready, and by the time the tea steeped, she would have the sandwiches finished.

"I hate to pour vinegar on your pudding." Charlotte frowned at Vera Kane's voice. Despite her words, it didn't sound as though she regretted whatever she was going to say. "It all seems a bit hasty to me. Why, Mr. Templeton just died. Surely his wife owes him the decency of a full year's mourning." There was such a self-righteous tone to Mrs. Kane's voice that Charlotte's frown deepened. If her mother were in the room with the ladies instead of having been delayed at a sick parishioner's side, she would have changed the subject.

"Laura already mourned him," Susan Whitaker pointed out. Charlotte heard a metallic clank. Someone must have dropped a pair of scissors. "It's not her fault that he wasn't really dead," Susan continued. "She thought he was, and she mourned him right proper like." Charlotte nodded, remembering how difficult it had been to convince Mrs. Templeton to attend the ice cream social.

But Vera Kane wasn't satisfied. "Still, it seems to me a

schoolteacher ought to set an example. Don't you agree, Ella?"

"I most certainly do," said Ella. Charlotte bit back a surprised cry. When she had worked as Mrs. Taylor's assistant, she had heard her complain more than once that she and Vera Kane would never agree. "Laura has indeed set an example," Ella continued. "She's putting aside her own sorrow to help another human being."

"What do you mean?" Karen Fielding asked.

The tray was ready. All she needed was the pitcher of cream. On her way to the icebox, Charlotte looked into the parlor. Though the four women had their heads bent over their sewing, only Ella's needle appeared to be moving. The other women were waiting for her response.

"Sam's father left him an inheritance," she explained, "but he'll receive it only if he's married by next Tuesday. That's his twenty-fifth birthday."

So that was why the wedding was so rushed. Charlotte had heard the townspeople speculating. The women started to murmur.

Charlotte gripped the pitcher handle tightly, lest it slip from her hand. An inheritance. Was that why Sam had courted *her*? He had needed a bride, and she was convenient. Charlotte's face reddened at the thought that he had wanted to marry her for such mercenary reasons. Sam had never claimed he loved her. But still. Charlotte placed the pitcher on the tray and started toward the parlor. Imagine having to spend the rest of your life with a man who didn't love you!

She stopped in the doorway as a new fear assailed her. Would Mrs. Templeton be happy in that kind of marriage? She obviously knew why Sam wanted to marry her, and yet she had seemed happy with him, at least until that creepy husband of hers had appeared. Maybe this was the kind of marriage she wanted. Charlotte hoped so.

"A likely story." Once more Vera Kane interjected a sour note into the conversation.

"Oh, hush, Vera." As Charlotte carried the tray into the

parlor, she saw Ella lean forward and shake her finger at Mrs. Kane. "You're just sorry Sam didn't ask you to marry him."

Charlotte couldn't help it. She laughed.

The sun was shining, and Laura couldn't stop smiling. For the past two days, the fiercest blizzard she had experienced since coming to Gold Landing had buffeted the town, blowing drifts of snow so high that there was no question of going outdoors. Somehow, Sam had forced his way through the blinding snow each day, coming to her cabin long enough to ensure that she had enough food and wood and to reassure her that they would indeed be wed.

"The snow will stop," he had told her.

And it had. When she wakened this morning, the sky had been clear, and now that the sun had risen, the snow sparkled under its brilliance.

"You look beautiful," Ella said as she buttoned the back of Laura's gown. She and Amelia had insisted on helping Laura prepare for the wedding, though she had assured them she was perfectly capable of dressing herself. "Brides are supposed to be pampered," Ella had told her.

Laura smoothed the folds of lavender silk. Once again Amelia's sister had done a wonderful job of altering a gown for her. No one would know that the shimmering silk with its rows of soft ruffles had been designed for a much taller woman. "If I look beautiful, it's because I'm happy," said Laura.

Laura glanced at her reflection in the cheval glass. It was true. Her face looked different today, softer and prettier. Though she would never be tall and thin like Amelia, today she felt beautiful. Thanks to Sam. "I'm not happy that Roy died," she told her friends, "but I am glad that I can help Sam. I was so worried about him."

Meg, apparently tired of playing with her wooden dog, scampered into Laura's bedroom. "Pretty!" she declared.

The three women laughed.

"So are you, sweetheart," Laura said as she bent down to hug her daughter.

When she rose, Amelia smiled. "Let me pin your hat on." She settled the concoction of velvet and feathers on Laura's head. "Remember when I did this for you, Ella?"

Ella nodded and touched her stomach. "Look where it got me."

"Right where you wanted to be," Amelia agreed.

Laura felt a bubble of happiness rise within her. She was so fortunate to have these two women as friends. "It's your turn next," she said to Amelia.

To her surprise, Amelia didn't respond immediately. Instead, she and Ella exchanged glances. Then she said, "Few things would make me happier. Now, tell me," she said, in an obvious attempt to change the subject, "are you happy that you're marrying Sam or only that you're able to help him?"

Ella shook her head in mock dismay. "Don't be silly, Amelia. You only have to look at Laura to know she's head over heels in love with him."

It was true.

By the time Laura arrived at the church, it was filled. She stood in the back, a little awed by the number of people who crowded into the pews. When she and Sam had agreed on their second wedding date, she had suggested a small ceremony in the minister's study, but Sam had demurred, agreeing with Ella's statement that the town wanted another reason to celebrate. "Besides, I want a real wedding," he had told Laura. "I want to watch you walk down the aisle." And so, here she was, walking down the aisle on William's arm, smiling so much her face hurt. This was the stuff of fairy tales, the bride approaching the man she loved, preparing to take vows that would bind them together. If only . . .

Laura's smile faltered as she realized that the fairy tale would come true only if the groom loved the bride. But he didn't. Sam might say he loved her. He might even believe it, but Laura knew otherwise. What Sam felt was lust. Lust and friendship. That would have to be enough.

Laura looked around the church at all the people who had come to witness her wedding. These were the same people who had been so supportive of her when Matt died, the ones who had made her proud to be an Alaskan. She wouldn't disappoint them. Just for today she would pretend that everything was perfect, that Sam loved her.

As she walked past the pew where Meg sat with Ella and Amelia, Laura reached out to touch her daughter's head. Meg had pouted all morning over the fact that she could not bring her wooden dog to church with her. Now that she was here, she appeared curious over her mother's procession down the aisle. When she looked as if she wanted to join Laura, Amelia pulled her onto her lap and wrapped an arm around her.

"Dearly beloved." Reverend Langdon's voice echoed throughout the church.

If only she were beloved! Laura looked up at Sam. Today it wasn't difficult to pretend that she was loved, not with the smile she saw on his face. It was filled with warmth and friendship and something else, something Laura couldn't identify. All she knew was that this was Sam, the man she loved more than she had ever dreamed possible.

He looked more handsome than ever in his stiff shirt and formal coat. The fine wool of his coat emphasized his broad shoulders, while the starched shirt highlighted his dark hair and eyes. Sam smiled again. Another man might seem ill at ease, but he looked as if he were born to wear formal clothes.

"Do you take this man?"

Laura's gaze met Sam's, and she asked him the question silently. *Are you sure?* He nodded almost imperceptibly.

"I do."

Sam's smile widened, and the gleam in his eye filled Laura with warmth. Sam, the man she loved, was happy. In two days they would set out for Seward, and then he would have what he had wanted for so long: his father's legacy. No wonder Sam was happy. Laura's smile broadened. How good it felt to know that she was partly responsible for that happiness!

"I now pronounce you man and wife."

"At last." Surely it was her imagination that Sam murmured the words, just as surely it was her imagination that his eyes sparkled with what appeared to be moisture.

All thoughts fled as Sam lowered his lips to hers. His mouth was warm and sweet, his kiss suitably chaste for the church. But Laura knew there had never before been such a perfect moment. She was Sam's wife!

An hour later, as Sam held her in his arms for a waltz, his lips quirked in a wry smile. "Gold Landing will never forget our wedding," he prophesied.

Laura raised one eyebrow. The church hall was filled with people who appeared to be enjoying the music and refreshments. "Because it was almost postponed by the blizzard or because of everything that led up to it?" Either one would make it a memorable event.

Sam shook his head as he drew her closer. The warmth of his hand radiated through the thin silk of her gown, and she inhaled the scents of citrus and sawdust that were his alone. He bent his head and whispered in her ear. "When people talk about our wedding, they're going to say that Sam Baranov has the most beautiful bride in all of Alaska."

Another couple jostled them, then apologized profusely. Though the man had stepped on her foot, Laura couldn't stop smiling. Today was her wedding day!

"Don't you know," she asked Sam with a wry smile, "that all brides are supposed to be beautiful? It's part of the tradition."

Sam tightened his grip. "Just how would I know that? I've never had a bride before, and I sure don't plan to have another one." Though his words were joking, something in his expression warmed Laura, telling her that—at least for the moment—he was pleased with their marriage.

"Everyone's so happy today." She gestured toward the other side of the floor, where Charlotte was dancing with Jason. "Who would have believed the change in them? It's almost a miracle."

Sam shook his head. "The miracle is that you're my bride."

Charlotte had never been happier. Weddings were always wonderful, and this one had been even nicer than usual. It wasn't just that Mrs. Templeton and Mr. Baranov had looked so happy. Charlotte was glad for that. But what had made the ceremony extra special was that all the while, she had been thinking that in less than a year, she would be the one walking down the aisle toward Jason. Oh, what a glorious day that would be!

Today wasn't so bad either. Jason had agreed to come to the wedding, and here she was, dancing with him. Almost everyone in Gold Landing was here, and they could all see her with Jason. The thought filled Charlotte with pride.

"I'm so glad you came." Charlotte knew he had been apprehensive, afraid some of the people would shun him. It was only because she had asked him to come that he had agreed.

"I wanted to be with you," he admitted. Though he managed to smile at her, he seemed ill at ease. It shouldn't be that he was nervous about his dancing. After all the times they had practiced in the forest, he was an accomplished partner.

"Is something wrong?" Charlotte asked. "No one has been mean to you, have they?" One of the reasons she had stayed so close to Jason was that she didn't want anyone to have the chance to say something unpleasant. At least that was a good excuse. The simple fact was, Charlotte liked being close to Jason.

It was wonderful that they no longer had to hide their meetings. It was wonderful that they could now dance in public. Charlotte didn't mind that people bumped them. Though their dances in the forest had been special, she liked the fact that she and Jason were now an acknowledged couple.

He shrugged. "I can't get used to this collar," he said with a downward glance at the offending garment. "Mr. Baranov said I had to wear it."

Charlotte smiled. No wonder he was uncomfortable. That stiff collar did appear painful.

"You look handsome." And he did. Of course, he was handsome whether he wore a formal collar or his normal chambray shirt. The new suit was nice, but Charlotte also liked his work clothes.

To Charlotte's surprise, Jason blushed. "You think so?"

"Oh, yes!" He gripped her hand and blushed again.

"May I have this dance?" Charlotte looked up, surprised to hear her father's voice and see him tap Jason on the shoulder. For a moment she had been only vaguely aware of the other guests.

As the blood drained from Jason's face, Charlotte realized that he still found her father intimidating. Though she tried to give Jason reassuring smile, she knew it would take a while before he felt comfortable with Father.

"Of course, sir." Jason gave Charlotte a little smile, then scurried to the edge of the room as Charlotte moved into her father's arms.

"He's a nice young man," her father said as he whirled her to the music.

Her father liked Jason! Truly, this was the most perfect day.

Hours later, when the reception had ended and she had returned home, her mother called to her. "Charlotte, Jason's here to see you."

Jason! Charlotte ran from her room, hastily smoothing her hair. Why had he come? Tonight was not their night to meet.

"You can sit in the parlor," her mother said. "Just leave the door open."

To Charlotte's surprise, Jason was still wearing the shirt and collar that had caused him so much discomfort at the wedding, and he looked even more nervous than he had at the reception.

"Is something wrong?" she asked when they had taken seats in the two chairs that flanked the stove. One of her mother's new rules was that they not sit on the settee.

Jason blushed, then shook his head. "No . . . er . . . would you . . . ?"

A lump formed in Charlotte's throat. Something was terribly wrong to make him stammer like that. Since he had been working in the sawmill, Jason had become much more confident. He walked with his head held high and his shoulders squared in an imitation of Mr. Baranov, and he normally spoke with assurance.

"What is it, Jason? You're making me nervous." Charlotte couldn't imagine what was causing Jason to act this way. It wasn't simply his stiff collar; she knew that. Whatever it was, he'd been worrying about it all day. "Please, Jason," she implored him. "Tell me."

His color heightened as he thrust his hand into his pocket. Pulling out a small package, he extended it toward her. "Would you wear this?" he asked, his voice so hesitant that Charlotte wanted to put her arms around Jason and reassure him that everything would be fine.

She stared at the tiny box, not daring to think what might be inside it. There was only one thing that came in a box that size. It couldn't be that, could it? It was too soon.

"Please." It was Jason's turn to implore her. "Open it."

And she did.

"Oh, Jason! It's beautiful." Inside the box was a simple gold ring with a blue stone. The stone was tiny, little more than a chip, but Charlotte knew she had never seen anything so magnificent.

"I saw it in Mr. Ashton's store," Jason explained. "The blue stone reminded me of your eyes."

Tears filled those blue eyes as Charlotte realized that Jason must have saved every cent Sam Baranov paid him to buy her gift. "It's the most beautiful thing I've ever seen." She ran a finger over the stone, still not believing Jason had bought it for her. "Here," she said, handing him the box and extending her left hand. "Put it on me. Please, Jason."

He slid it on her finger, then leaned forward to press a soft kiss on her lips. "I love you," he whispered.

Everything was perfect.

It was the first time she had ever been in Sam's house. Oh, she had seen it from the outside, and he had described the interior, but Sam's descriptions did not do the house justice. Though it was very simple, the combination of the large windows that Sam loved and his meticulously crafted woodwork made it different from any of the other homes in Gold Landing that Laura had visited. It was at the same time rustic and refined, simple and stylish.

Sam led her through the front door, showing her the parlor with its horsehair sofa and chairs, the kitchen that boasted not one but two of his rocking chairs, and the small room that would be Meg's. She looked around, trying to concentrate on her surroundings, trying not to think about the tall man who stood next to her, his arm draped casually around her shoulders. Sam was her lawfully wedded husband, and in a few minutes she would be his wife in every sense of the word.

Laura took a deep breath, trying to quell the shivers of excitement that raced through her. She loved Sam—oh, how she loved him!—and because she did, she wanted theirs to be a true marriage.

"What do you think?"

What she thought was that she couldn't wait to touch him, to be held in his arms, to know the wonder of his embrace. But Sam was talking about the bed that he had made for her daughter.

"I doubt Meg will sleep a wink here," Laura said, running her hand over the line of dogs that he had carved in the headboard. "She'll want to play with them."

Sam smiled. "I figured it wouldn't hurt to keep Meg occupied while we're otherwise engaged." The twinkle in his eyes and the smile he gave Laura left no doubt about the activity he had in mind.

She blushed. Never before had a man been so honest in his desire for her. Never before had she wanted a man the way she did him. But never before had there been a man like Sam. Taking her hand in his, he opened the last door. "This is our room." Something in his voice made Laura catch her breath. There was the slightest hesitation, almost as if he was as nervous as she was.

To hide her own confusion, Laura looked around. It was not a huge room. Although large enough to accommodate the oversized bed and a bureau, there was not even enough space for a chair. The furniture was not elaborate, and the only color came from the patchwork quilt the women of Gold Landing had made for them. It was a simple room, and yet somehow it seemed to welcome Laura. It was, she reflected, like Sam, open and honest.

Sam drew her into the room and closed the door behind them. When he turned to face her, the smile she saw on his face made Laura's heart skip a beat. "This is a dream come true," he said softly.

Laura nodded. The whole day had been a dream for her. Though at first she had thought she would pretend, there was nothing false about her happiness or her love for Sam. "I'm so glad I can help you," she told him.

He shook his head and laid his finger on her lips. "This isn't about the company, Laura. You're the dream—having you here in my house, having you as my bride."

His words were perfect, everything she had wanted to hear the man she loved say. They filled her heart with so much happiness that she thought it might burst. "I never dreamt I could be so happy," she told him. "This has been the most wonderful day of my life."

Sam chuckled. "You act like it's over. Sweetheart, this is only the beginning." He feathered a kiss on her lips. "I know you said you wanted a marriage of convenience, but . . ."

Sam's voice trailed off, and Laura saw a flicker of doubt cross his face. "I won't ask you to do anything you don't want, but . . ." Again he stopped, apparently trying to find the right words. "Oh, hell! Laura, I'm so crazy wanting you that I can't think of a delicate way to say it." He laid his hands on her shoulders and smiled down at her. "Will you let us have a real marriage?"

Laura stood on her toes and pressed a kiss on his lips. "That's what I want too."

For a second he stared at her, as if he couldn't believe what he'd heard. Then he wrapped his arms around her and lowered his lips to hers. Though he had kissed her before, never before had Laura tasted such unbridled hunger. Sam's lips devoured her mouth the way a starving man might consume a loaf of bread. She returned kiss for kiss, taste for taste. It was the headiest of sensations, knowing she could inspire such passion, knowing that he felt the way she did.

"Let me undress you." Sam's voice was harsh with desire when he wrenched his lips from hers.

Laura shook her head as she tried to catch her breath. "Only if I can undress you too," she said softly.

Her reply startled him, as she knew it would. She could see the surprise in his eyes and the appraising look he gave her. Then he chuckled. "I suppose that's only fair, but I want to start."

Sam reached for her and slowly drew the pins from her hair. When it hung free, he ran his fingers through the long locks. "Your hair is so beautiful," he said. "It reminds me of moonlight." He continued to run his fingers through her hair, caressing her scalp and sending shivers throughout her body. His touch was gentle now, far different from his ravenous kiss, but no less exciting. The soft caresses ignited new fires that rushed to join the conflagration he had already unleashed.

"I used to sleep with the curtains open." His voice was soft and dreamy and almost unbearably erotic. This was Sam, the man she loved, murmuring words of love. "When I'd see a moonbeam on my pillow, I wanted it to be your head there, so close to me."

His hand cupped her cheek, and he pressed another kiss on her lips. "It's your turn."

Though her hands were trembling, Laura reached up and touched the lapels of his coat, then eased it off his shoulders. Sam's warmth and the scent that was his alone clung to it, and for a second she buried her face in the coat, savoring Sam's surprised chuckle. His chuckle turned to a gasp as she ran her hands over his shoulders, trying to memorize the muscles that had fascinated her for so long. "I would dream about your arms enfolding me," she said softly, "and how wonderful it would feel to wake up in the circle of your arms."

Sam's quick intake of breath told Laura that her words had startled him as much as her insistence that she would undress him. "Darling, that's one dream I can make come true," he drawled. "But you're gonna have to wait a while, because I want some of my dreams to come true *before* we sleep."

While his fingers had moved slowly before, he quickened his pace as he unbuttoned her dress and let it tumble to the floor, then slid his hands over her shoulders and down her arms. "Your skin is so beautiful," he murmured, pressing kisses where his fingers had been.

Though the room was cool, the warmth of Sam's touch fed the flames of desire. If only she could show him how wonderful this felt. If only she could return some of the joy he was giving her. Laura removed Sam's shirt and echoed his actions, first caressing, then kissing his arms. "No more beautiful than yours."

"Sweetheart, that's the first time anyone's called me beautiful," he said with a short laugh.

"It won't be the last," she promised. Though Sam might not realize it, he was the most beautiful creature she had ever seen.

Kneeling, he removed Laura's shoes and stockings. "Your feet are tiny and perfect, like the rest of you."

Laura motioned to him to sit on the edge of the bed. When she had tugged off his boots and socks, she touched his feet. "Your feet are big and perfect, like the rest of you."

Laughing, Sam pulled her into his arms. "Oh, my darling, what did I do to deserve you? You're the only woman on earth who knows that making love should be fun."

She shook her head, reveling in the sensation of her hair drifting over her shoulders onto Sam's arms, enjoying the look of wonder in his eyes at the soft caress. "It's you who make it fun," she said.

Though he had moved slowly, almost languorously, now Sam hastened to remove her remaining garments and shucked his own. When she stood naked in front of him, he took a step backward and stared at her, his gaze moving from the top of her head down to her feet. It was only a look, and yet Laura felt as though she were being stroked.

"You look like an angel," he murmured.

Laura chuckled. "I assure you, Sam, my thoughts are *not* angelic." Deliberately, she moistened her lips, watching the way Sam's eyes followed her tongue.

"Let's see if your thoughts are the same as mine." He swept her into his arms and carried her to the bed, laying her on the cool sheets as if she was the most precious thing he had ever held.

His hands moved slowly, caressing each inch of her body, while hers followed an exploration of their own, learning the hard planes of his. He touched; she touched; he kissed; she kissed; he tasted; she tasted. Nothing in Laura's life had prepared her for this. Nothing had ever felt so wonderful. Nothing had ever felt so right.

Outside, the wind blew and snow swirled, obscuring the moon. Inside, each caress, each touch of Sam's fingers ignited new flames of desire. And just when Laura knew she could bear no more, that she would be consumed by the flames, Sam's body molded itself to hers, and the flames became a single, incredibly pure light that shone with all the colors of the rainbow.

When at length the fire subsided, Laura knew that for the first time in her life, she was complete.

Chapter Twenty-three

Someone was pounding on the door. Laura opened her eyes, momentarily bemused by the unfamiliar surroundings. Her bedroom had flowered wallpaper, not white paint, and her mattress was softer than this. Where was she? She blinked at the brightness. Why was the sun streaming through the window? She never slept late enough for the winter sun to have risen. Meg ensured that. As Laura turned ever so slightly, she saw Sam lying next to her, and she smiled. It hadn't been a dream. Those magical hours that she had spent in his arms had happened. Sam was her husband.

The pounding continued. "Sam." Laura laid her palm on his cheek. "Someone's at the door." Her head still slightly muddled by sleep and sweet memories, she wondered what business could be so important that anyone would disturb Sam at home on the morning after his wedding.

"This better not be Ben and William's idea of a shivaree," her husband muttered.

But as the pounding was replaced by a woman's voice calling her name, dread swept through Laura. Charlotte would not be here unless it was an emergency. "Something's wrong!"

Laura leapt from the bed and thrust her arms into a wrapper while Sam pulled on his trousers. "Oh, Sam!" Laura tried to quiet the horrible fear that assailed her. She wouldn't voice it aloud—that would give it too much credence—but she could not escape the terrifying thought that something had happened to her daughter. It had been that way ever since Matt had died. Though Amelia had tried to reassure her, telling her that Meg had a strong constitution, a mother's fears were not so easily eradicated.

Her heart pounding furiously, Laura raced to the front door. Though Sam was right behind her, she couldn't wait even another second. As she flung the door open, Laura saw Charlotte standing there, tears streaming down her face. Laura gasped at the pain that filled her heart. Something was terribly wrong.

"Oh, Mrs. Templeton." When Sam put his arm around Laura's waist, Charlotte bit her lip. "I'm sorry. I forgot you're Mrs. Baranov now." She began to sob again. "I didn't mean to. It's just that Mrs. Taylor started having pains, and Dr. Amelia thought the baby was coming, and so they asked me to take her, and . . ."

Meg! The remaining blood drained from Laura's face as she listened to Charlotte's babbling. "What's wrong with Meg?" she demanded. Something terrible had happened. Laura knew it. Normally calm Charlotte wouldn't be acting this way if it was some small mishap. As Sam tightened his grip on Laura's waist, she leaned back, seeking strength from him.

"I don't know how it happened." Charlotte blew her nose noisily. "I only took my eyes off her for a minute. Oh, I feel so awful."

Laura felt her legs begin to buckle. Why was Charlotte torturing her? Why wouldn't she tell her what had happened to Meg? The morning that had dawned so bright and beautiful had turned into Laura's worst nightmare. She couldn't—

she simply could not—lose her only child. As she started to tremble, Sam led her to the settee. He was big and strong, and Laura clung to him as if he were her lifeline.

"Sit down, Charlotte," Sam said calmly. "Tell us what happened."

For answer, Charlotte buried her face in her hands and continued to sob.

"Charlotte, we need to know." This time Sam's voice was stern.

Charlotte raised her tearstained face. "It was such a pretty morning," she said. "Meg wanted to go outside, so I put her in the sled, and then . . ." A new wave of tears ensued.

Laura gasped. Though she tried not to picture the end of Charlotte's sentence, her mind conjured the image of Meg lying injured . . . or worse.

"Where is my daughter?" Sam demanded. Laura stared at him, as shocked by his reference to Meg as his daughter as she was by the ferocity of his voice. He moved his arm so that it circled her shoulders and drew her closer. Laura laid her head on his chest, once more trying to draw from his strength. As horrible as this moment was, she knew it would be a hundred times worse without Sam.

Charlotte's face was blotchy from weeping. "Jason came," she said, dropping her eyes as a flush colored her cheeks. "We only talked for a minute. That's all. Then when I looked at the sled, Meg was gone."

Laura heard Sam's exasperated sigh and felt him tense, as if he were trying to keep himself from throttling Charlotte. Laura laid a hand on Sam's forearm and shook her head. Charlotte's tale made no sense. "Meg is a timid little girl," Laura said. "She wouldn't just wander away."

Her baby couldn't be lost outside in the cold. Charlotte began to tremble, although whether from fear or the cold room, Laura wasn't certain. All she knew was that her own shaking increased at the thought that Meg was somewhere outdoors.

"Let's go, Sam." They had to do something. They couldn't just sit here.

He shook his head slightly. "We need to know where she might be; otherwise we'll be looking in the wrong places." Though it made sense, the inactivity was almost as bad as the fear that clawed at Laura.

"Do you suppose she was looking for you, Laura?" Sam asked.

It was a possibility. Meg might have been worried by her mother's absence. Charlotte had told her that Meg had searched the parsonage for Laura when she had stayed there during Matt's illness. "Where did you look?" Laura asked Charlotte.

"All around." Charlotte gestured expansively. "I saw no sign of her."

When Laura shuddered, Sam squeezed her shoulders. "What about footprints?" he asked. His voice had gentled, as if he realized the futility of being angry with Charlotte. Whatever she had done, it had not been deliberate.

The young woman shook her head. "The road is packed, and the wind is blowing pretty hard. Footprints don't last long." As if to confirm Charlotte's words, a gust rattled the windowpanes. "Besides," she added, "a dog team went by. Their tracks tore up the snow."

A dog team. Of course. Laura nodded. "That's what happened. Meg followed the dogs. She tries to do it every time one drives by."

Dogs were the one thing that would have convinced timid Meg to leave the safety of the sled. But where had she gone? A small child had no chance of catching a team of huskies. Wherever she had gone, Charlotte should have been able to see her.

"Come, Laura." Sam rose and drew Laura to her feet. "We'll find her." His voice was firm and reassuring, and for a moment Laura believed him. Together they dressed hurriedly.

"Show us exactly where you were," Sam directed Charlotte

as they left his house. Though the wind was so strong that it knocked her backward and the sun made her eyes water, Laura tried to remind herself to remain calm. *Take deep breaths*, she urged herself at the same time that she tried to keep the hand that hugged Sam's arm from clutching too tightly. It would be all right. He had told her that, and somehow—some way—she had to believe it. They would find Meg safe and sound. The alternative was unthinkable.

Charlotte led the way to River Street. "We were right here," she said, pointing to the area across the street from the mine office. "I stopped for just a minute."

Laura scanned the street, looking for a small figure dressed in a navy-blue parka. With her dark coat, Meg should be easy to find against the white snow. But there was no sign of her daughter.

"Meg!" Laura cried, trying to keep her tears from falling. "Meg!" Her baby had to be here.

Sam pulled her close to him, pressing her head against his chest. "It'll be all right," he said firmly. "We'll find her." Then he turned to Charlotte. "Why don't you go back to Laura's house." Though he phrased it as a suggestion, Laura heard the steel in his voice and knew that this was a command. "If Meg goes home, she will need a familiar face."

"She can't have disappeared." Laura said the words aloud to convince herself. She and Sam had begun to walk rapidly down the street, looking behind each of the buildings. It was possible that Meg had fallen while she chased the dogs and could not get up. But the area behind the mine office was empty, and though the blizzard had covered the pile of logs near the sawmill, the smooth white surface left no doubt that Meg had not climbed on them. The only prints visible were those of the dog team and the sled.

"We'll find her." Sam's voice continued to be firm, as if he had no doubts. Laura was not so sure. Doubts assailed her with each step she took. It was so cold outside. Seasoned Alaskans well versed in survival skills died in weather like this. How could little Meg survive for more than a few hours?

"Sam, I can't lose my last baby." That was the thought that terrified her. First Matt, now Meg. Dear God, it couldn't happen. She would give anything, even her own life, to keep her daughter safe.

"You won't lose her. If we have to, we'll organize a search party."

A search party. Of course. If a dozen people were covering the area, they would surely find one little girl. "Let's do it."

Laura looked up at Sam, but he was staring at the tracks. Although they had been moving in a straight line, for some reason, the team had veered sharply to the left, heading toward a bend in the river. Sam frowned and fingered his mustache.

"What's wrong?" The panic that was never far away settled in Laura's throat. Something horrible had to be wrong if Sam, who had been steadfastly optimistic, was frowning.

"Maybe nothing." But Sam's frown deepened as he and Laura followed the tracks. "William told me there are some abandoned mine shafts in that area," he said, his reluctance to pronounce the words obvious.

Laura shuddered as the implication hit her. "Meg might have fallen into one." Dear God, her baby might be lying inside a mine shaft, injured . . . or worse. The world spun and began to turn black. Laura gripped Sam's arm, willing herself to remain upright.

"It's a possibility." She felt him shudder, and knew he was reliving being locked in a coffin. Sam had told her that he didn't have to be confined. Even thoughts of small dark spaces evoked those horrible memories.

Laura slid her arm around his waist and hugged him. "It's not a coffin, Sam. There's light and a way out." But Sam's expression remained bleak. "Meg will be safe." For the first time since Charlotte had pounded on their front door, Laura found herself in the position of offering rather than accepting comfort.

"You're right." Though Sam nodded, Laura saw that his face was still unnaturally pale. "Let's find her!"

They moved more slowly now, searching the ground for the slightest indentation, since Sam had told Laura that the snow would have obscured all but the largest openings. Progress was painfully slow, for the wind had blown the snow into hills and valleys, and they had to investigate each one.

"Is that a hole?" Laura pointed to a small depression on the left. With the sun glaring off the bright snow, it was difficult to see anything. She had heard tales of travelers becoming lost in the snow and blinded by its light, but this was the first time she had realized how easily that could occur. Was that what had happened to Meg? Had she become disoriented following the dogs and stumbled into a hole?

Sam squinted as he looked where Laura had pointed. "It could be a shaft," he agreed, grabbing Laura's hand. They ran across the snow. It no longer mattered that they might slip and fall. All that mattered was finding Meg. If only this was not an illusion. If only it was the place where she was hidden.

It was a hole. Now if only Meg was in it.

Laura knelt. Though she placed her head into the opening, she could see nothing. The darkness appeared impenetrable.

"Meg!" she shouted. "Where are you?"

A faint cry echoed from deep within the earth. "Mama!"

For a second Laura's heart stopped. When it resumed its beating, she thought it would break through her chest. "Sam! She's in there!"

Her daughter was alive! "I'm here, sweetie," she called. Thank God, Meg was alive! Laura began to crawl into the abandoned mine shaft.

"Hurt, Mama. Leg hurt." Meg's voice was weak, and the pain she heard in her daughter's voice wrenched Laura's heart.

"Mama's coming," she said. Though at one time the mine shaft had been tall enough for men to walk through it, the ceiling had collapsed, and now there was barely enough room for Laura to crawl. Boulders that had once formed the roof blocked more than half of the passageway, leaving only enough space for a child or a small adult.

"I'll come with you." Laura heard Sam's voice behind her. She swiveled her head. "No, Sam. You stay here. There's only room for one of us." And Sam, with his fear of dark enclosed spaces, should not be that one.

"You'll need a torch," he told her. "Wait here, and I'll get it."

It was one of the most difficult things Laura had ever done, remaining at the entrance of the mine shaft when she knew that her daughter was lying injured somewhere in the ground. But Laura waited, for she recognized the validity of Sam's words. Without illumination, she would be unable to see Meg and help her.

"I'm coming, Meg," she called. "Mama will be there soon." While she waited for Sam, Laura began to tell Meg a story, a long involved tale of a brave little girl who waited for her mother. And all the while she talked, Laura wondered why her normally timid child had gone so far into the mine shaft and how she had hurt her leg.

Though it seemed like hours, Laura knew it was only minutes until Sam returned with the torch. "Be careful," he admonished as he handed it to her. "The shaft may be slippery." Laura nodded. Though it felt warmer here, away from the wind's battering, the floor was icy in spots.

Why had Meg come here? Laura doubted she would ever know. It wasn't important. What was important was getting her daughter out of the mine. As Laura crawled through the dark tunnel, she continued telling Meg the story. "Mama's coming," she repeated, incorporating the refrain into the tale. And somehow, though her heart was pounding fiercely and she could hardly breathe, her voice sounded soothing. Whatever she did, she must not frighten Meg. The poor child had already endured too much pain and fear.

At one point, the tunnel widened. Here the ceiling had not collapsed. Laura rose and stretched her back. Though she wanted to see and touch her daughter, she needed to be able to move freely, and crawling, at times sliding on her stomach, had taken its toll on her strength.

"I'm almost there," she told Meg when the shaft narrowed again. Her daughter's voice was louder now. She must be close. Laura held the torch in front of her, trying to see Meg. Where was she? Why couldn't Laura see her? She ought to be there. Even in the dark tunnel, Laura ought to be able to see Meg's face. It should be visible, even if her dark coat blended with the walls. Unless, of course, Meg had fallen facedown. Still, her voice didn't sound as if she was facing the floor. Where was she?

Laura crawled another few feet, her eyes searching for her daughter. Where was she? As she played the light in front of her, Laura gasped. *No! Dear God, no!* For less than a yard away was a gaping hole in the floor. Not only had the beams supporting the ceiling collapsed, but here the ground had given way. Meg had fallen into a crevasse.

"And the little girl went into the cellar." Laura continued the tale, trying not to shudder. Her heart was pounding so hard that she could barely hear her own voice over it. "Is that where you are, Meg? Did you climb into the cellar?"

Laura inched forward, moving cautiously, lest more of the ground disintegrate. She was almost there.

"Fell." Meg confirmed Laura's fears.

Behind her she heard a shuffling sound. *Please, dear God, don't let any more of the ceiling collapse!* She slid toward the hole. Another foot. That was all she needed. When she reached the edge, Laura shone the torch down and stifled a moan. There, lying six or seven feet below her, was her daughter. "I'm here, sweetie. Mama's here."

Propping the torch near the opening, Laura stretched out on the ground and extended her arm into the hole. "Can you touch me?" she asked Meg. Her daughter lay on her side, her right leg bent in an unnatural angle. Laura doubted Meg could stand, but perhaps she could kneel. "Raise your arm toward me." Perhaps that would be enough. Perhaps she could reach her.

Meg complied, but when her fingers fell short of touching Laura's, she whimpered. "Too far, Mama." And it was.

Inwardly cursing her short stature, Laura tried to keep her voice calm as she considered how to rescue her daughter. She couldn't climb into the hole and boost Meg out, because she herself would have no way of getting out again, and with her broken leg, Meg would be unable to crawl to safety.

Laura closed her eyes and prayed as she searched for other solutions. She could find only one. Though it meant asking him to face his nightmare, she would have to beg for Sam's help. "Meg, honey, it'll just be a little longer," she said. "You be a brave little girl, and Mama will be back soon. We'll get you out of here."

Laying the torch near the edge of the hole so that Meg would have some illumination, Laura turned. Though she hated to leave her daughter lying helpless in that dark mine shaft, she had no choice. As she twisted her body around and prepared to leave the tunnel, Laura's eyes widened in surprise. Just a few yards behind her in the wide area was Sam.

"Sam!" she cried. "Oh, Sam!" Somehow he had known she would need him, and he had come through that horrible, dark, cramped tunnel to help her. Meg's savior had arrived. In the faint light, Laura saw that his face was pale with beads of perspiration on his forehead that could not have been caused by the cold air. She swallowed deeply at the realization of how great an effort Sam had made for her.

When she started to speak, he shook his head. "If you come here," he said, gesturing to the wide spot, "I think we can change places." His voice was calm, betraying none of the strain he must be feeling. "Do you think I can reach her?" Sam spoke softly so that Meg would not hear him.

Laura nodded. "I miss by about six inches." And Sam was a foot taller than she was: "I think she has a broken leg," Laura whispered when she stood next to him.

He laid his hand on Laura's cheek in a wordless gesture of comfort. It was a simple touch, nothing that should have triggered tears, and yet it did. "I'll get her out, Laura. I promise. Trust me."

As the tears streamed down her cheeks, Laura nodded. "I do." There was no one in the world she trusted the way she did Sam. She raised her voice and called to Meg, "Meg, honey, Mr. Sam is going to help you. When he gets there, you hold onto his hand as tightly as you can. Okay?"

"Okay." Meg's voice was clear.

Sam lowered himself to the ground. Because he barely fit through the tunnel, it took him longer to crawl to Meg than it had Laura, but still he continued, inching his way as carefully as Laura had. When he reached the hole, Laura saw him extend his arm into it. "I see you, Meg," he said firmly, but with a playful tone to his voice. "Do you see me?"

"Uh-huh."

"Good. Now, here's what I want you to do. Hold up both of your hands. I'm going to pull you up. Okay?"

"Okay."

Laura forced herself to breathe evenly. In just a moment or two, Sam would have Meg out of the hole. But, oh, how he must hate it. The section of the mine shaft where he was lying was almost as small as a coffin. He could barely move, and though he had the torch, it was still a horrible place to be. Yet he had come—without being asked—through the dark, lonely tunnel to help her and Meg.

As Laura brushed the tears from her cheeks, she realized that they were tears of wonder and joy. What Sam had done was not an act of friendship. It was not motivated by lust. Only one thing could have gotten Sam into the mine shaft: love.

Laura shook her head, trying to clear her thoughts. How could she ever have doubted Sam's love? Only a man who truly loved her would have confronted his worst fears to help her daughter.

"That's a good girl," she heard Sam saying, a smile in his voice. "Now, hang on tight." Laura heard the slight motion as Sam leaned forward, stretching into the crevasse. "Upsie-daisie." Meg squeaked, then whimpered, and Laura heard Sam mutter something under his breath. It was only a second or two, but it felt like hours before she heard him say, "See, now, it wasn't hard, was it?"

And still Laura could not see her daughter, for Sam's body blocked her view. In the light of the torch, she could see him moving, struggling out of his coat, but she could not guess what he was doing. Laura brushed the last of the tears from her face and forced a smile onto it. No matter how she worried about Meg, she couldn't let her daughter see her fear.

What was Sam doing?

"We're gonna use my coat like a sled," he told Meg. "I'll be the dog. What do you think about that?"

Of course. Sam had realized that the tunnel was too small for either one of them to carry Meg, and the child could not crawl with her injured leg. He had to devise another way to get her out.

Meg giggled. The sound was so normal, so reassuring, that Laura almost laughed herself. Her daughter was going to be all right, thanks to Sam. Whatever was wrong with her leg, Amelia would heal it. But, oh, how Laura wished she could see Meg and hold her in her arms.

"Meg, honey, I'm here," she said.

Her daughter giggled. "You gonna be a dog, Mama?"

"No, sweetheart, we'll let Mr. Sam do that."

Sam reached behind himself and pulled out the torch. "Laura, if you go ahead of us and hold the light, Miss Meg and I will be out of here in a minute."

Laura nodded. It was awkward, holding the torch behind her as she crawled out of the tunnel, and it seemed to take forever. It had to be her imagination that the tunnel seemed narrower and longer than before and that the remaining timbers creaked as if they were on the verge of breaking. At last she could see daylight. Laura moved more quickly now, anxious to have both Sam and Meg out of that dark space.

When Sam emerged, dragging Meg behind him, Laura blinked back her tears. "Oh, honey!" she cried as she swept her daughter into her arms. Meg was safe. Thank God, she was safe.

"Too tight!" Meg protested. She blinked at the bright sunlight, then held her arms out to Sam, who was buttoning his coat. "Mr. Sam!" she cried.

He flashed Laura an apologetic look and made no effort to reach for Meg. Laura shook her head as she transferred her daughter into his arms. It was right that Sam should be the one who carried Meg. He was the one who had rescued her.

"Let's get her to Amelia," he said.

Laura wrapped her arms around Sam's waist and hugged him. "I love you, Sam Baranov."

His grin outshone the sun. "And I love you, Laura Baranov."

"I know." No matter what happened, she would never again doubt that this wonderful, wonderful man who by some stroke of fate was her husband loved her.

Had there ever been such a glorious day?

Chapter Twenty-four

"I think I'm more nervous than you."

Sam looked at his bride standing by the window of their hotel room. Although she had remained calm on the journey from Gold Landing to Seward, combining her teaching and mothering skills to keep Meg entertained and contented despite the immobility that the child's broken leg enforced, now Laura plaited her skirt between her fingers in an apprehensive gesture Sam had never before seen. A lock had tumbled from her hairdo and bounced on her shoulders, and those lovely blue eyes were clouded with anxiety.

Sam reached for his wife's hand and found it cold, further proof of her distress. Sam felt a knot lodge in his throat at the realization that this woman loved him so much that she worried more about his legacy than he did himself. "It's almost over, Laura. Just a few more hours."

He slipped his arm around her shoulders and drew her close to him. She was his own private miracle. How else could you explain the fact that in the two weeks that they had been married, she had brought him more happiness than he'd known in the rest of his twenty-five years?

"I love you, Mrs. Baranov," he said, savoring the sound of the name.

Though her lips trembled, she smiled up at him. "Not as much as I love you." It was a game they played, each trying to outdo the other with expressions of love. And Sam, who had played few games as a child, found this almost as pleasant as the games he and Laura played in bed.

He looked at the bed and grinned at Laura. "Tonight," he said.

Her laugh was shaky. "You're just trying to keep me from thinking about your meeting."

"Did I succeed?"

She shook her head. "I don't understand why you're not nervous."

Sam wasn't sure he understood either. There was no doubt that Laura was right. He was not apprehensive. For years he had been hurt and angry that his father had disinherited him. Then, when he had learned the terms of the will, the anger had disappeared, and he had been happy and anxious. Now Sam was oddly calm, even though he knew that in the next hour he would face the man who had made his childhood so hellish. But at the end of the meeting, his parents' home and the shipping company would be his. Perhaps that was why he was calm, knowing that the wait was almost over.

"I want to go with you."

Sam shook his head. "This is something I have to do alone." That was true. What was also true was that he did not want Laura to face George's venom. Sam doubted that age had changed his stepbrother from a vicious bully into a kindly man, and he did not want his wife exposed to any more evil. She had faced enough of that in her first marriage.

"I'll worry less if I know you and Meg are here." Though not as luxurious as the home his father had built, the hotel was clean and safe. He and Laura had checked in as soon as they had arrived in Seward, and Sam had sent a message to the attorney, asking to meet him the same day. He might not be nervous, but he wanted everything settled quickly.

"Here. Let me." Laura reached up and straightened his cravat. Sam couldn't help smiling at the wifely gesture and the pleasure she seemed to derive from it. "Meg and I will be waiting," she said with a fond glance at her daughter.

Sam looked at the little girl, who played so contentedly in the corner of the hotel room, and wondered if any child, even one of his own blood, could be more dear to him. Meg was special, not because she was Laura's daughter, but because she was herself, an enchanting little girl whose smile tugged on his heartstrings. Ever since he had pulled Meg from the tunnel, she had tried to follow Sam around the house, moving awkwardly because of her cast, occasionally beating her fists on the plaster in sheer frustration that she could no longer run. "Upsie-daisie," the phrase he had used when he had lifted her out of the hole, had become her favorite refrain.

Sam reached for his coat and muffler. Laura still didn't understand about that day. She treated him as if he were some sort of hero, just because he had crawled through that tunnel to rescue her daughter. The truth was, Sam didn't understand what had happened either. Ever since the day George had nailed him in that coffin, the mere thought of small, dark spaces had sent shivers of fear through him. But when he had realized that Meg was in the mine shaft, that she needed him, all that Sam had been able to think about was reaching Laura's daughter. He had been aware of the way the tunnel walls scraped against his shoulders, he had been aware of the darkness as he had followed behind Laura, but not once had he felt the shortness of breath or the overwhelming dread that had always accompanied thoughts of confined spaces. All that had mattered was Meg.

Sam finished buttoning his coat and wound the muffler around his neck. Though it was noticeably warmer in Seward than Gold Landing, it was hardly summery outside.

Laura smiled as she handed him his hat, reminding Sam

of how she had laughed when she had seen the way Meg followed Sam. Laura insisted that he had become her daughter's knight in shining armor because he had saved a very small damsel in distress. Though Sam found Meg's devotion touching, he also knew that he owed her a huge debt. Of course, he would never have wished for Meg to be trapped in the mine shaft, but there was no denying that at least one good thing had come from that experience. The act of going into the tunnel to rescue Meg had freed Sam from his fears. He had faced dark confined spaces and emerged victorious. Dealing with George could be no more difficult.

"I want to help you," Laura said.

Sam drew her hand to his lips and pressed a kiss on each finger. She was so sweet, this wife of his! "You are helping," he told her. "Just knowing that you and Meg will be here when I come back is the help I need."

He pressed a final kiss on her lips, then strode from the hotel. Perhaps he was being superstitious, but Sam avoided the streets that would have taken him past his father's house or the shipyard. He didn't want to see them again until they belonged to him . . . and Laura. When everything was settled, he would take Laura and Meg to see the home that would be theirs.

Sam frowned as the image of his simple white-frame house in Gold Landing flashed before him. It was foolish to regret leaving that. After all, his parents' home was far grander. He would sell the Gold Landing house along with the sawmill. That was what he and Laura had agreed on.

Fifteen minutes later Sam walked into his father's attorney's office. "Good day, Mr. Nelson," he said, extending his hand to the lawyer. "I'm Sam Baranov."

Nelson was a middle-aged man with gray sprinkled through his brown hair and a face that Sam imagined could be forbidding. Right now that face wore a wide grin. "I'd have known you anywhere," the lawyer said. "You're the spitting image of your father. Come in, my boy."

Though the office was larger than Abe Ferguson's, Sam

smiled when he realized how much alike the two attorneys' offices were. It wasn't only that they had the same books on their shelves; their furniture was arranged the same way, even to the potted palm in one corner.

"Does George know I'm here?" Sam asked. Everything about Nelson inspired confidence in Sam. Though the lawyer must have been quite young when his father hired him, Sam understood the choice. When today's business was concluded, perhaps the attorney would join Sam and Laura for dinner. Sam guessed it would not take much encouragement for Mr. Nelson to share his memories of Sam's father, and that would be pleasant. But first they had to settle the will.

Nelson nodded. "George sounded surprised. I don't understand why. I've notified him each time I received a telegram from you." The lawyer picked up a thin pile of papers from his desk, leafed through them, and frowned. "I hope you're not disappoin—"

Before he could finish the sentence, the door was flung open.

"It is you, you bastard." The stepbrother he had not seen in almost fifteen years glared at Sam. George's face was an older version of the one Sam remembered. His jowls had thickened a bit and faint lines etched the corners of his mouth, but there was no mistaking that angry expression. "I didn't believe Nelson when he said you were coming." George's voice, several decibels louder than necessary, was filled with hostility, and he stood with his feet apart in a pugilist's stance. Though the man bore no physical resemblance to Jethro Mooney, the clenched fists, jutting jaw, and narrowed eyes marked them as members of the same species: bully.

For a moment Sam said nothing, merely stared at George, studying him from the top of his now-wind-tousled head to his snow-covered boots. The almost unnatural calm that had descended on Sam when he arrived in Seward continued, and for the first time he was able to view George objectively.

His stepbrother was not an omnipotent monster; he was only a man.

George took a step forward, swinging his fists, and glared at Sam. In response Sam raised an eyebrow. As a child, he would have cowered before George's anger, knowing that George would reinforce it with his fists. Today Sam watched, almost amused by the juvenile behavior. "I won't say it's good to see you, George." His voice was as neutral as if he were meeting a stranger.

His movements unhurried, Sam sank into one of the two chairs in front of the desk and gestured toward the attorney to take his own seat. If George preferred to stand, let him. He would gain no advantage by towering over Sam.

George smacked one fist into his palm. Though the sound reverberated in the room, and Sam knew George wished it were his face that he was hitting, neither Sam nor Mr. Nelson reacted. Only the slightest tightening of the lawyer's lips told Sam he was fighting not to smile at George's futile attempts at intimidation.

George glared down at Sam, his anger almost palpable. "You were supposed to be dead!" George spat the words, his voice filled with fury and what sounded like frustration.

As the memory of Jethro Mooney's attack flashed before him, Sam wondered if George had heard about that and had wished Jethro had been successful. Of course he hadn't. There was no reason for that kind of news to make its way to Seward and George. George was merely indulging in wishful thinking. He wanted Sam dead so that the estate would be his.

"Unfortunately for you, George, I'm not dead." Sam spoke calmly, knowing that would only irritate George more. As a child George had had the advantages of age and size; now he had none.

"Not yet!" Sam's stepbrother clenched his fist and took a step toward him.

"Gentlemen." Mr. Nelson rose and gave George an admonishing look. "If we could get to the business at hand. Sit down," he directed George. To Sam's surprise, his stepbrother took the chair next to him. "Now," Nelson said, "according to the terms of Nicholas Baranov's last will and testament, his son Samuel will inherit the entire estate—it consists primarily of the family residence and the shipping company—so long as he is married by his twenty-fifth birthday."

"Hurry up," George muttered. "We know that."

Nelson shot a quelling look at George, then pulled a piece of paper from the pile on his desk. "Sam has shown me his marriage license. I am satisfied that he has fulfilled the terms of the will."

The estate was his. Oddly, the thought did not bring the rush of pleasure Sam had expected. Perhaps that would come when George was gone and Sam was back with Laura.

George clenched his fists, then kicked the desk. "Where's the wife? I don't see no wife."

Though the attorney gave him another disapproving look, he said nothing.

Sam leaned back in his chair, watching his stepbrother. He was a bully like Jethro Mooney, and just like Jethro, a stronger man could easily cow him. Though George obviously didn't like the attorney, he recognized his power and responded to it.

Nelson picked up a document and appeared to peruse it. Sam almost smiled. He was certain that the attorney knew every pertinent clause of the will verbatim. He was delaying only to annoy George. Sam's esteem for the lawyer grew. Yes, indeed, his father had chosen well.

"In point of fact," the attorney said at last, "if Mrs. Baranov died or they divorced, Sam would still inherit the estate. The will says only that he must be married on the day of his birthday."

George jumped to his feet and pounded on the desk. "It ain't fair! You were supposed to be dead!" When he reached for a brass paperweight, the attorney placed it on the credenza behind him.

"That refrain is becoming a little tedious," Sam said. He

watched the veins on George's forehead bulge with rage. "I'm here. I'm clearly not dead. Now I suggest that we let Mr. Nelson proceed."

"The estate is yours, Sam," the attorney said. He picked up the second set of papers, the one he had been consulting when George had stormed into the room. "Unfortunately..." He paused, frowning at the papers. When he raised his head and met Sam's gaze, Sam saw pain reflected in Mr. Nelson's eyes. Whatever was on the papers disturbed him. "Sam, there's no easy way to say this." He spoke slowly, his reluctance to voice the words obvious. Nelson shot a baleful look at George, then turned back to Sam. "I've investigated the condition of your father's estate, and I must say that I was shocked."

"What do you mean?" It was odd. Though they were discussing his inheritance, the legacy that had once been the most important part of his life, he felt as if he was a bystander watching a scene in a play unfold.

The attorney frowned. "It appears that your stepmother has heavily mortgaged the house. The bank is ready to foreclose on it."

Sam turned to George. "Is that true?"

His veins bulged again, telling Sam what he wanted to know. "It wasn't my doing." George's voice took on a whining tone. "Hilda likes pretty things."

"How much?"

The attorney's response made Sam raise an eyebrow. Hilda must like a great many pretty things. Sam thought quickly. If he paid off the loans, he would be left with little to invest in the company. Perhaps it would be better to let the creditors take the house. He could build another one for Laura. She might even prefer that, because the new house would give them a fresh start.

"There's still the company," Sam said.

Mr. Nelson looked uncomfortable. "Perhaps," he said. "It appears that your stepbrother has mismanaged it." The accusing look that he shot George had him cowering in his chair. "Deliveries have been so unreliable that the few remaining customers are looking for another shipping company."

The rage that filled Sam was white hot, and he gripped the chair arms to keep from striking George. How could the man have been so stupid? How could he sully the proud name of Baranov? Still gripping the chair, Sam turned to George, and this time his voice seethed with anger. "You destroyed my father's company. You ruined everything he worked for. You had no right. No right at all!"

As if he was afraid that Sam would hit him, George held his hands before his face. "It's not my fault."

Sam shook his head. "It never is, is it?" He looked at the man who had been his childhood nemesis and felt no fear, no hatred, only disgust that one human being could be so worthless. "You're a pathetic excuse for a man."

George cringed as if Sam had struck him.

Mr. Nelson folded his hands and leaned forward. "Sam, I want to advise you that you can sue Mrs. Baranov—your father's wife, that is—for mismanagement. Even though she allowed George to run the company, under the terms of your father's will, she's responsible. You appear to have a clear case of malfeasance."

From the corner of his eye, Sam saw George blanch, as if he was imagining Hilda's rage. Hilda, Sam knew, was as much a bully as George. But Hilda and George were not his problem. His father's legacy was. Sam took a deep breath, trying to marshal his thoughts. His anger had faded, replaced by an almost overwhelming sadness. The house didn't matter; it could be replaced. But the company was different. Years of incompetence could not be easily undone.

Sam shook his head. "I won't sue. It wouldn't get the money back, and it wouldn't restore the company's reputation." The damage, Sam knew, was irreparable. He was silent for a moment, thinking. For so many years he had lived with the dream of running his father's company, never truly believing that it would be possible. Then, for six months, the dream had been within reach. And now . . . Sam looked at the attorney, surprised by how easy the decision was.

"George can keep the company," he said.

"I knew it!" George gloated. "You're not man enough to run it yourself."

"Shut your mouth, George, before I change my mind." Sam did not deign to look at his stepbrother.

On the other side of the desk, Mr. Nelson gasped. "Are you sure?"

Sam nodded. The relief that he had felt when he had pronounced the words told him the decision was the right one. "Draw up the papers and I'll sign them." He leaned back in his chair, extending his legs, apparently the picture of a man at ease. But though he spoke to the attorney, Sam watched George, waiting for his reaction to his next words. "There is one stipulation," he said slowly. "Both George and Hilda will need to change their name. Neither one of them can be called a Baranov." As George's face reddened, Sam continued. "I won't have my father's name sullied any longer. It goes without saying that the company will cease to be called Baranov Shipping."

George gasped. "But . . . but . . ." George sputtered as he realized the implications of Sam's decree. Though he and Hilda had damaged the company's reputation, it still bore the proud name of Baranov, and that alone might help win new customers. Without the name, they had nothing.

Sam stared at the man he had once feared. "Consider it your chance to start over," he advised George. "Whatever happens, this time it *will* be your fault. Now, I advise you to get out of here before I reconsider."

If the situation hadn't been so serious, Sam would have been amused by the way George scurried from the attorney's office.

"I think we both need this," Mr. Nelson said as he poured a generous serving of whiskey into two tumblers. "Now, my boy, are you sure you don't want to reconsider your decision?"

Sam shook his head. "No. Even though this isn't what I

thought would happen, perhaps it's for the best. I have a wife and a child and a life in Gold Landing. They're my future. This was my past."

The attorney nodded. "You sound like your father. He believed in a man making his own life." Mr. Nelson leaned forward, his eyes thoughtful. "Although he never said it in so many words, I think that's why your father didn't give you the company immediately on his death. He wanted you to have time to decide what you wanted from life."

Sam was silent for a moment, thinking of the house that had filled his father with such pride and the ships whose reliability had been legendary. Both were lost. "There's one thing of my father's that I would have liked, but I imagine George has already sold it."

"And what is that?"

"His watch."

The attorney shook his head, and Sam felt a moment of sadness at the realization that this too was lost to him. Then Mr. Nelson said, "George and Hilda didn't sell the watch. They couldn't, because they didn't have it." He rose and spun the dial on a small safe. When the door swung open, he pulled out an envelope. "When your father was ill and knew that the end was near, he gave the watch to me, asking that I keep it for you. He wanted it to be your twenty-fifth birthday gift." The lawyer handed Sam the envelope. "Happy birthday, Sam."

With hands that were suddenly unsteady, Sam slid the heavy gold timepiece from the envelope. It was just as he remembered, the mate to the one he had given Laura. Though it was larger and heavier, the shape and design were identical.

The sun, which had been hiding behind a cloud, emerged, filling the room with such brightness that Sam blinked. He turned the watch to look at the initials carved in the case, then flipped it open. The sun glinted on the bright metal. As his eyes moved from his parents' photograph to the watch itself, the blood drained from Sam's face. This was what Papa meant!

"Are you all right, Sam?"

He gave the attorney a reassuring smile. "I've never been better."

"Are you sure, Sam?" Laura's beautiful blue-green eyes were filled with concern as she listened to his account of the meeting with George. He had raced back to the hotel, anxious to tell her of his decision, anxious to begin the next part of his life. Since Meg was napping in the next room, they sat on the bench at the foot of their bed and spoke softly. "You've wanted the company for so long," Laura continued. "I hate to think that you've given up a dream."

Sam heard the worry in her voice, and knew it was a reflection of her love for him. How lucky he was to have this wonderful, generous, loving woman in his life!

"I haven't given up a dream," he told her. "I've found one."

She stared at him, confusion clouding those lovely eyes. "But what . . . ?"

Sam laid one finger on her lips. "For years I wanted the company. At first I told myself it was my birthright, but gradually I realized that I saw it as proof that my father loved me. I don't need that proof any longer. I know Papa loved me, and now I know why he wrote the will the way he did."

Laura's eyes widened, and Sam could see that she did not understand. "Mr. Nelson told me why he thinks Papa made me wait until I was twenty-five." Sam repeated the attorney's hypothesis. "That makes sense, but it doesn't explain why my father insisted I be married."

Sam pulled the watch from his pocket and handed it to Laura.

"Your father's watch." She handled it almost reverently, then touched the one she wore.

"That's what showed me the answer," he said. "A scientist would tell me there was a logical explanation for what happened." Sam shook his head. "I don't care about logical explanations. I know what I saw and what it meant." He touched the watch. "When I opened it, I saw a rainbow." Laura's eyes widened with the same wonder he had felt in the attorney's office. "It may have been an optical illusion, nothing more than a glint of sun on the glass. I don't believe that, though. I know that the rainbow was real and that it was a sign from my father."

Sam wrapped his arms around Laura. "When I saw that rainbow, I remembered my father talking about my mother and calling her his midnight rainbow. Oh, Laura, sweetheart, don't you see? When Papa wrote the will, he wasn't worried about my running the company. He wanted me to marry. He wanted me to know the love he and my mother had shared. That's why he put that clause into the will—to convince me to find a bride."

Sam rose and drew the woman who had filled his heart with love, who had banished his darkest fears and brought light into his life, into his arms. As he lowered his lips to hers, he said, "Laura, you're the legacy Papa wanted for me. You're my rainbow at midnight."

AUTHOR'S NOTE

Dear Reader,

A writer's inspiration comes from many sources. When I finished writing *Midnight Sun,* I hadn't planned to return to Gold Landing for a few years. I was in the midst of plotting *North Star,* with its Buffalo setting, and had plans for a second medieval romance. But when I started receiving fan letters telling me how much you enjoyed the people of Gold Landing and that you wanted another Alaskan book, I realized it was time for another trip north.

At first the story was going to be the tale of a mail-order bride. I had started scribbling notes about the characters and the plot when one night I woke up thinking, "Sam Baranov needs a bride, too." *Rainbows at Midnight* was born. Although I couldn't argue with the fact that Sam did need a wife, I didn't appreciate being wakened in the middle of the night. That's why Sam had so many problems finding the right bride. I had to get even with him for disturbing my sleep.

What's next? A chance encounter with a carousel horse in southern New York State started me thinking about merry-go-rounds, the people who rode them and those who carved the horses. Before I knew it, I had not one but three books planned.

Carousel of Dreams, the first of the carousel trilogy, will be available from Leisure Books in August 2002. I hope you'll mark your calendars and join me in the small town of Hidden Falls, NY, where the building of a carousel uncovers secrets that should have remained as hidden as the falls, and where three siblings discover love when they least expect it.

Emma Craig,
Leigh Greenwood,
Amanda Harte,
Linda O. Johnston

Christmas is coming, and the streets are alive with the sounds of the season: "Silver Bells" and sleigh rides, jingle bells and carolers. Choruses of "Here Comes Santa Claus" float over the snow-covered landscape, bringing the joy of the holiday to revelers as they deck the halls and string the lights "Up on the Rooftop." And when the songs of the season touch four charmed couples, melody turns to romance and harmony turns to passion. For these "Merry Gentlemen" and their lovely ladies will learn that with the love they have found, not even a spring thaw will cool their desire or destroy their winter wonderland.

___52339-6 $5.99 US/$6.99 CAN

Dorchester Publishing Co., Inc.
P.O. Box 6640
Wayne, PA 19087-8640

Please add $1.75 for shipping and handling for the first book and $.50 for each book thereafter. NY, NYC, and PA residents, please add appropriate sales tax. No cash, stamps, or C.O.D.s. All orders shipped within 6 weeks via postal service book rate.
Canadian orders require $2.00 extra postage and must be paid in U.S. dollars through a U.S. banking facility.

Name____
Address____
City___________________________State_______Zip__________
I have enclosed $__________ in payment for the checked book(s).
Payment <u>must</u> accompany all orders. ❑ Please send a free catalog.
CHECK OUT OUR WEBSITE! www.dorchesterpub.com

Susan Plunkett

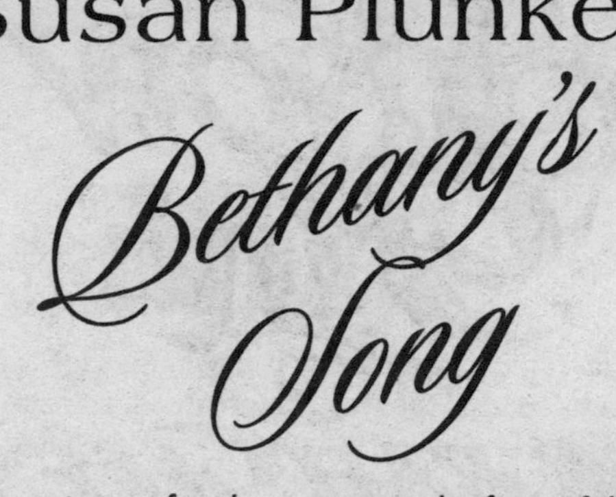

For Bethany James, freedom comes in the form of the River of Time, sweeping her away from her old life to 1895. But on awakening in Juneau, Alaska, Bethany discovers a whole new batch of problems. For one thing, she has been separated from her sisters—the only ones with whom she shares perfect harmony. And the widowed mine-owner who finds her—Matthew Gray—is hardly someone with whom she expects to connect. Yet struggling to survive, drawing on every skill she possesses, the violet-eyed beauty finds herself growing into a stronger person. She is learning to trust, learning to love. And in helping Matt do the same, Bethany realizes the laments of the past are only too soon made the sweet strains of happiness.

___52463-5 $5.50 US/$6.50 CAN